Montagu Cyril Bickersteth

A Sketch of the Life and Episcopate of the Right Reverend Robert

Bickersteth

D.D., Bishop of Ripon, 1857-1884

Montagu Cyril Bickersteth

A Sketch of the Life and Episcopate of the Right Reverend Robert Bickersteth
D.D., Bishop of Ripon, 1857-1884

ISBN/EAN: 9783337009847

Printed in Europe, USA, Canada, Australia, Japan

Cover: Foto ©Raphael Reischuk / pixelio.de

More available books at **www.hansebooks.com**

LIFE OF ROBERT BICKERSTETH

BISHOP OF RIPON

A SKETCH

OF THE LIFE AND EPISCOPATE OF

THE RIGHT REVEREND

ROBERT BICKERSTETH, D.D.

BISHOP OF RIPON, 1857—1884

BY HIS SON

MONTAGU CYRIL BICKERSTETH, M.A.

VICAR OF ST. PAUL'S, PUDSEY, LEEDS

WITH A PREFACE BY HIS COUSIN

EDWARD HENRY BICKERSTETH, D.D.

LORD BISHOP OF EXETER

New York
E. P. DUTTON AND COMPANY
PUBLISHERS AND IMPORTERS
31, WEST TWENTY-THIRD STREET
MDCCCLXXXVII

PREFACE

THIS volume will be treasured by many, as recording for them the deliberate judgments of no common man on some of the great religious and social problems of our time. These judgments are not always expressed in his sayings or writings, though not seldom the reader will be able to glean them from extracts of letters, or speeches, or Charges in the following pages. But even when not so expressed, the mind of the workman is transparent in his work. He was a working Bishop in a working age; and what he did, as sketched in this biography, tells what he thought. It has been so with many of the truest sons of this nineteenth century. They have had but little leisure for writing learned treatises. They have wrought the twelve hours of the solid day. But their actions, prompt, decisive, masterful, in perplexed circumstances have proved an intimate acquaintance with the great issues at stake. Such a labourer was Robert Bickersteth.

And this makes me regret the less that an interval of nearly three years has elapsed since his death, before these memorials have been given to the Church. When a Cathedral stands in the centre of a crowded city, you may be very near it, and yet see little or nothing of its grandeur ; a row of ordinary houses may obscure or hide it altogether ; but if you pass beyond the city walls and gain a distant point of view, you see at once how easily that Minster in its magnificent structure and proportions dwarfs all the inferior buildings around it, and is the centre to which all the thoroughfares and streets converge. And the work of many servants of Christ is not fully known even by the men of their own generation, until the lapse of time reveals its symmetry and completeness. This memoir will at least afford a vantage ground from which to contemplate the life now before us.

All patient observers must acknowledge the simplicity and godly sincerity of his course. His character was indeed without a fold. As an undergraduate at Cambridge, as a curate at Sapcote and Reading, as Vicar of St. John's Clapham, as Rector of St. Giles-in-the-Fields, as Canon of Salisbury, as Bishop of one of the most arduous dioceses in England—whether as pastor and evangelist, or as a standard-bearer in the front ranks of Evangelical Churchmen ; whether in the sacred circle of his own home, as son, and brother, and husband, and father, and friend, or on the public platform and in the House of Lords, as an unflinching witness for the truth and denouncer of compromise,—one motive animated Robert Bickersteth, and all who knew him will confess the motive was, The love of Christ constraineth us not to live unto ourselves, but unto Him Who died for us.

It was this which gave him such influence with men

of all parties in the Church and State. It was not only his genial courtesy to all, nor his singular felicity of utterance, nor his indefatigable labours in journeying and preaching and correspondence, nor his administrative power, invaluable as these talents were, but it was his unwavering adherence to the Scriptural principles of our Reformed Church, and his downright honesty in avowing them, which made men feel they could trust him through and through. They rallied round one who was staunch and true to the Church of their fathers. I have been told by members of the Upper House of Convocation, that his clear incisive sentences in the united meetings of Bishops at Lambeth were looked for with an interest, and listened to with a respect not inferior to that accorded to the eloquent words of the late Bishop Wilberforce of Winchester. Even where others conscientiously and resolutely differed from him (and I confess on the subject of marriage with a deceased wife's sister, I strongly hold the very opposite view to that he strongly advocated) no one could doubt the sincerity of his convictions, nor the simplicity of his aim.

Unwearying industry, and an apparently inexhaustible cheerfulness characterised him. I remember him once saying to me, "You cannot think what those words have been to me in the throng and pressure of work—'Do your best, and leave the rest.'"

He did his best, grudging no toil, never asking, "Is it so nominated in the bond?" seeking only the Master's approval, and counting not his life dear unto himself, that he might finish his course with joy, and the ministry which he had received of the Lord Jesus, to testify the Gospel of the grace of God. And having done his best, he could afford to leave the rest confidingly and gladly in a Heavenly Father's hand. Duties were his; events were God's; and thus the joy of the Lord was his strength. It never seemed to cross his mind, Will this display my knowledge, my judgment, my tact? but only, Is this for the glory of God and for the promotion of the Redeemer's kingdom? And so, amid the innumerable claims of his busy life, he ever seemed to live like one who said—

> "All is, if I have grace to use it so,
> As ever in my great Taskmaster's eye,"

and realized the double benediction which rested on Abraham of old, "I will bless thee, and thou shalt be a blessing." Surely it was of such single-hearted labourers, Charles Kingsley sang—

> "Be good, and let who will be clever:
> Do noble things, not dream them, all day long;
> And so make life, death, and that vast for-ever,
> One grand sweet song."

I have deeply felt the responsibility of reading the proof sheets of this memoir as they passed through the press, for it has brought me into such close contact with one whose walk with God and consecration to duty must, I think, be very humbling to all who are seeking to be imitators of those who by faith and patience inherit the promises. God grant us all to follow him as he followed Christ.

This life needs no preface. It speaks for itself. But I cannot close these few words without saying how much I am persuaded the Church is indebted to his son, who, aided by other members of his family circle, has so patiently and skilfully grouped together these life-etchings of his beloved and honoured father. The biographer is hidden throughout ; for his only object has been to present his father to us just as he was, a noble type of personal piety, of Evangelical Churchmanship, and of whole-hearted devotion in every office of the ministry to the Great Shepherd and Bishop of souls.

E. H. EXON.

THE PALACE, EXETER,
January 7, 1887.

ILLUSTRATIONS

CONTENTS

CHAPTER I.

EARLY FAMILY HISTORY.

CHAPTER II.

BOYHOOD AT ACTON.

CHAPTER III.

YOUTH AND EARLY MANHOOD.

CHAPTER IV.

ST. GILES'S, 1851-1857.

CHAPTER V.

SALISBURY, 1854-1856.

CHAPTER VI.

DIOCESE OF RIPON, 1857.

CHAPTER VII.

DIOCESAN WORK: PREACHING.

CHAPTER VIII.

HOME LIFE AT RIPON.

CHAPTER I.

PROFESSOR DRUMMOND reminds us, in his most interesting chapter on environment in "Natural Law
in the Spiritual World," that it is of the essence of
a good biography to point out, in the earlier chapters,
how the subject has been influenced by his parents
and remote ancestors, no less than by the religious and
political atmosphere of the times in which he lived.

This is especially true when we try to sketch
the portrait of one who may be regarded as a typical
representative of a great religious movement.

Bishop Bickersteth was always known as an
Evangelical bishop, and, though no one was more
anxious than he to be the bishop of his whole
diocese rather than the bishop of a party, his consistent public action, no less than his training and his
avowed sympathies, leave us in no doubt as to the
party within the Church to which he was uniformly
attached.

B

Happily now the old party lines are less strongly marked. Nevertheless, a very large body of the clergy are still reckoned as Evangelicals, and not a few High Churchmen are ready to admit that they owe at least as much to the Evangelical traditions as to the great Oxford Movement itself.

It is this which gives a permanent interest to the life of one who was connected by birth with the pioneers of the Evangelical Movement, and who, through the course of a long ministerial life, never wavered in his attachment to the same great truths; while he learned to love and work in harmony with men of widely different views, so long as they loved the same Lord in sincerity and truth.

This must be the excuse, if one is needed, for a son, who desires to do honour to his father's memory, and to sketch his life as best he can for the sake of many who loved him, as well as for the wider circle who may profit by reading the record of a good man's life.

I call this book a sketch, for there is material for nothing more. My father's life was not eventful; and his correspondence consisted almost entirely of short business letters. Many of those which have been preserved are admirable illustrations of clear judgment and lucid expression, while some of them, written to his family and near relatives, are the index to a character of the deepest piety and the tenderest affection; but they do not in themselves present a complete picture of his mind, like the letters of Bishop Thirlwall, or take us behind the scenes of Church politics, as many letters of fascinating interest preserved in the life of Bishop Wilberforce.

All I can attempt to do is to show something of the "environment," and let a busy life speak for itself.

To follow the hint of Professor Drummond to which I have already alluded, I must take my readers to the little country town of Kirkby Lonsdale, in Westmoreland. At the close of the last century there lived in that place a surgeon, named Henry Bickersteth. The family name was often spelt Bickerstaffe, and their earlier origin is to be traced to the manor of that name near Ormskirk, in Lancashire.[1] Henry Bickersteth, the surgeon, married a lady named Elisabeth Batty. She was, according to the testimony of all who knew her, a woman of strong individuality and high character, and an account of her is given in the life of her distinguished son, Edward Bickersteth of Watton.

Henry Bickersteth was the author of a little book entitled, " Medical Hints for the Use of Clergymen," which we notice with interest, because it is the first trace of the steps by which so many of the family have been led from the cure of the body to the cure of souls.

The surgeon's family was a large one. The eldest son, James by name, was lost at sea in early

---

[1] The Bickersteths, or Bickerstaffes, were seated at Bickerstaffe as early as the twelfth century. In the reign of Edward II. the office of Sheriff of Lancashire was held more than once by a member of the family, and Dugdale's " Monasticon " testifies to numerous benefactions which religious houses in the county received at the hands of one or other of the same name. The manor passed, by the marriage of an heiress, to an ancestor of the present Earl of Derby, but a branch of the family continued to reside in the neighbourhood, until James Bickersteth, or Bickerstaffe, the father of the above-named Henry, left his native county to settle in Westmoreland, rather before the middle of the last century.

youth; but his four brothers, born in Kirkby Lonsdale, each earned more or less distinction in Church or State.

Henry, the third son, was, like the rest, intended by his father for the medical profession, and went to London in his sixteenth year, to walk the hospitals with his uncle, Dr. Batty, who was practising there. He seems never to have cared for his father's profession, and went to Caius College, Cambridge. His University career was one of great distinction, and he took his degree as senior wrangler in 1808.

In those days, at any rate, senior wranglers made themselves a name in after life, and Henry Bickersteth became equally distinguished at the Bar. His chief public work was devoted to the reform of legal procedure, and he showed a remarkable absence of ambition in refusing the Great Seal when it was pressed upon him by Lord John Russell, in 1850.

He had, however, been raised to the peerage as Baron Langdale, many years before; and held the office of Master of the Rolls from 1836 till his death, in 1851.

It will probably be interesting to my readers to be reminded that Lord Langdale, as Master of the Rolls, drew up the judgment of the final court of appeal in the celebrated Gorham case. Whether right or wrong, that judgment was the means of preventing a schism which threatened to tear asunder the Church of England; for it is notorious that a large section of the Evangelical clergy would have considered their position in the Church untenable, if the contention of the Bishop of Exeter had been maintained. As it is, the baptismal controversy has well-nigh ceased, and the great majority of the clergy accept the language of the Prayer-book ; though they are not agreed in the exact sense of the word "regenerate."

Of this judgment, Dean Stanley said, in the course of an essay on the connection of Church and State—

"There is perhaps no decision of any council or Holy Office equal in moderation and insight to that of the Gorham judgment, unless it be that which so greatly resembles it, in its inclusion of two opposite principles—the decision of the first Council of Jerusalem " (Essay, p. 284).

Of Edward Bickersteth, the fourth son, there is less need to speak, for those who read this book are likely to be familiar with the outline of his life, and as a great leader of the Evangelical party, and a zealous supporter of the Church Missionary Society, his name is in all the Churches. He was for many years Rector of Watton, Herts.

His influence and position were almost unique ; his spiritual force was intense, and the active energy of his character brought him into contact with many of the most zealous clergy throughout the country,[1] while he was disposed warmly to co-operate with those whom he regarded as Evangelical ministers outside the Anglican Church. In this direction he was more tolerant or more lax than his brother

---

[1] In the Life of Lord Shaftesbury, by Mr. Edwin Hodder, there are several allusions to the intimate relations existing between the Evangelical leader and the great philanthropist. The latter wrote in his journal, February 17th, 1850, "Lord, he whom Thou lovest is sick. Is this too much to say of Bickersteth? I trow not. This dearly beloved friend and fellow-servant is grievously ill ; and prayers, we bless God, are daily made for him throughout the Church. How little can we afford to lose such a champion for the truth !"

John, who occupied a position of comparative obscurity as Vicar of Acton, in Suffolk, and afterwards Rector of Sapcote, in Leicestershire.

Edward Bickersteth left behind him one son, who, after thirty years of laborious work as Vicar of Christ Church, Hampstead, was appointed to the deanery of Gloucester in 1885, and on the very day of his installation was offered the bishopric of Exeter.

Robert Bickersteth, the youngest of the Kirkby Lonsdale family, was the only one who remained in his father's profession, and became a surgeon at Liverpool. He was distinguished in religious and philanthropic work, no less than in his medical profession.

John Bickersteth, my grandfather, was the second son; and his sons were, Henry, who, in the course of a long residence as a medical man at the Cape of Good Hope, earned the gratitude of churchmen by his devotion to the interests of the Church of England in that colony; Edward, now Dean of Lichfield, who was for many years Archdeacon of Buckinghamshire, Vicar of Aylesbury, and Prolocutor of the Lower House of the Convocation of Canterbury; and the subject of this sketch, Robert, Bishop of Ripon.

If the Vicar of Acton occupied a position of comparative obscurity, yet his work was of a very remarkable character; and it will not be without interest to some readers to dwell for a space on the uneventful life of a country clergyman in the first half of the present century.

Several modern biographies, and especially Mr.

Mozley's Reminiscences, give a graphic picture of the time when the Oxford Tracts were first launched upon the world, and startled the slumber of many a quiet parsonage with the perplexing rush of ideas at once new and old.

But it would be a great mistake to suppose that till the Tractarian Movement, there was nothing to break the deep sleep in which the Church had lain all through the Georgian era. The burning love of souls and the fiery energy of the Methodist Revival found an echo within the Church, and there were those who combined the fervour and piety of the Wesleys with a spirit of sober loyalty to Church order, the lack of which had turned a powerful auxiliary of the Church into a sect separate from her. These were the men who formed the Bible . Society, who supported Missions to the Jews, and, with Wilberforce and Clarkson, stormed against the slave-trade till the conscience of the nation was aroused to roll away that terrible reproach to England and Christendom.

Such a man was John Bickersteth, of Acton. Like his younger brother, he had left Kirkby Lonsdale for a clerkship in the Post Office, but, not content with any calling lower than what he deemed the highest, took Holy Orders.

The Rev. John Bickersteth was a young man when he went to Acton in 1812, and his ministry there lasted till 1837.

What the life at Acton was like, we are able to picture vividly enough from a few letters which have been preserved, and from the recollections of some of those who lived at the vicarage as pupils of Mr. Bickersteth, or candidates for Holy Orders who spent a year or two with him to gain an insight into parochial work.

At Cambridge John Bickersteth had made the acquaintance of the Rev. C. Simeon, whose great influence over the younger members of the University made itself felt long before his name became a household word throughout the Church. The following letter, which was preserved by the Rev. Canon Carus amongst Mr. Simeon's correspondence, shows how strong an admiration and respect the writer had for the great Cambridge leader :—

Dear Sir,—Believe me, though I have had so little opportunity of manifesting it, I have not ceased to retain a lively gratitude towards you for all your undeserved kindnesses to me during my residence in the University, and an affectionate interest in your spiritual and temporal prosperity. May the great Head of the Church long continue your valuable labours for the good of His people! I think you will pardon the freedom of my writing to you upon the subject of one dear to *you*, and dear also to me ; on different accounts, and yet not wholly dissimilar. You, dear sir, were, I believe, under God, Mr. Martyn's spiritual father : I am not sure whether, under God, I am not the same Mr. Martyn's spiritual son : I am sure that his preaching, which most providentially I had the happiness of hearing, just before he left England, at St. John's Chapel, was the means, by God's grace, of strengthening if not establishing impressions still, alas! too feebly operative in a heart not yet sufficiently made captive in every thought to the obedience of Jesus Christ. Under these circumstances, though I never had any personal knowledge of Mr. Martyn, nor could have, as he left England almost immediately after I first saw and heard him, yet, feeling a lively regret for the loss which the Church sustains in him, and desiring to contribute my mite towards the promotion of an object near his heart, I, in common with a London friend, who wishes to remain unknown, but was alike a partaker of the benefit of his public labours, beg to enclose two guineas (one from each of us), which we doubt not you will be at the trouble of appropriating to the right channel. I am afraid amidst your numerous avocations it would be too much to hope for the happiness of seeing you at our humble vicarage. Permit me, however, to add that we should consider such a sight of you so great a happiness that we will hope you would not neglect a favourable opportunity of gratifying us in this particular. In the mean time I am sure we shall have your prayers, which I hope, together with our own, and those of other Christian friends, God will continue to bless for the good of the little but dear flock which God my Saviour has put into my hands. I feel that I am unworthy of being His under-shepherd ; but if He guides, directs, and blesses, then I am safe. Mrs. Bickersteth has lately presented me with a dear babe. She would feel herself honoured by an introduction to your acquaintance, which she both is prepared and knows how to value.

I am, dear sir,

Your sincerely obliged and grateful,

JOHN BICKERSTETH.

Acton Vicarage, near Sudbury,
June 2, 1813.

The infant to whom reference is made in the letter was Edward, the present Dean of Lichfield ; but on a subsequent occasion Mr. Simeon visited Acton, and it was thought a matter of great rejoicing in the family that he consented to act as sponsor to Robert, the future Bishop of Ripon.

The Rev. John Bickersteth had married Miss Henrietta Lang, who seems to have been admirably fitted for the position of a clergyman's wife. After her death in 1830, her widowed husband published a little memoir, which shows her to have been a very remarkable woman, and one who could not fail to have a most powerful influence upon her children.   Before her marriage she had passed through a change in her religious convictions, which led her to give herself almost entirely to good works amongst the poor in the little village of Natland, near Kirkby Lonsdale.

At Casterton Hall, where she was a frequent guest, she made the acquaintance of her future husband, who had just commenced his work at Acton.

How deeply she was impressed with the responsibility of becoming a clergyman's wife is shown in a letter written to a friend before her marriage. She writes :—

I humbly trust I did not presume to listen to the proposal till I had begged the blessing and guidance of my Heavenly Master. And though it appears to be His will hitherto to sanction the step I am about to take, yet it is a duty still to pray for a negative to any plan which will not promote my spiritual progress. By the assisting grace of God, it is my wish unreservedly to surrender all I have and am to His service and glory; and I can earnestly pray that I may be kept from anything that would interrupt such a surrender. I am in some measure sensible of my present temptation. Oh, implore of Him Who hears and answers prayer, that all His gifts may be sanctified ; that the streams of mercy may never draw me from the Fountain ; and that, through all created comfort, the steady eye of faith may be fixed on the Creator. Acton is a retired corner of the vineyard : pray for its minister that he may be endued with strength from on high equal to his day ; and especially pray for her who must so soon share his labours. Oh, that my heart may be carefully impressed with a sense of the responsibility attached to such a situation, and also with a still deeper sense of God's distinguishing mercy and my own unworthiness !

Mrs. John Bickersteth was fitted to share in her husband's work—not only because of her deeply devotional mind and the simple love of Christ, which forms the strongest bond of union even between those who have learned their faith in different schools, but she, like her husband, had imbibed an almost identical form of Evangelical piety, long before their acquaintance commenced.

It may be that some who read these pages will be puzzled to know exactly what is meant by the constantly recurring phrases that belong to the early period of the Evangelical Movement.

Religious phrases are so apt to mislead, and so soon lose their value, if they become the watchwords of a party instead of the natural utterances of those who feel them, that a word of caution is needed to explain their use.

If good people talked and wrote to-day in the language in which their grandfathers expressed themselves seventy or eighty years ago, the world would not be very far wrong in bidding them beware of cant ; but in those days it was natural enough for them to talk as they felt, and there is no question that in such a home as the vicarage at Acton, the inmates felt as strongly as they spoke of the great need of an entire separation between Christ's people and the world.

It was a very different thing fifty years later, when the Evangelical party had become powerful and wealthy; and it was high time for Charles Kingsley to warn us that the religious world might be at least as worldly, as full of envy, hatred, and malice, and all uncharitableness, as the other world which it professed to shun.

But the few clergy who called themselves Evangelicals at the beginning of the century were certainly not taking the popular course.

Their clerical neighbours were not in a position to rebuke them for neglected duties and defective loyalty to the Church, for there was hardly one of the old High Church party who made any attempt to carry out the Prayer-book scheme with the diligence that is now happily so common. And the laity—squires, farmers, and labourers alike—had been so long familiar with an easy compromise between the claims of this world and the next, that a clergyman who boldly rebuked vice, and spoke of Sin and Hell as great realities, could hardly escape some measure of unpopularity and opposition.

In trying to show what the home life at Acton was like, I make no apology for borrowing largely from the memoir of Mrs. Bickersteth, to which allusion has already been made. Her husband says of her—

In her ardent thirst for spiritual knowledge, and in that devotional spirit with which she was so eminently blessed, will be found the mainspring which guided and regulated the movements of her active and industrious life. What delight she took in, and how unremitting was her study of, the Word of God! Besides chapters and portions daily read, morning and evening, with her husband, children, and servants, and in the constant routine of the family worship; besides what she read occasionally in her visits amongst the poor, and statedly twice in the week when she assembled around her, in her own house, those of her own sex who chose to attend,—every day, and twice, at least, in the day for herself, and solely upon her own account, she was an accurate, diligent, and prayerful Bible student.

Then follows a list of devotional books which were in constant use. Amongst them were "Jenks' Prayers," "Thomas à Kempis," Adam's "Private Thoughts," Bishop Taylor's "Holy Living and Holy Dying," with the devotional expositions of her brother-in-law, and Bridges on Psalm cxix.

"In her," says her husband, "the flame of devotion, like the fire upon the altar, never went out ; it pervaded and sanctified all she attempted, said, or did. Even in her little account books, which were most methodically arranged, and kept with scrupulous exactness, may be discovered traces of the same devotional spirit. In that for the opening current year was transcribed, by her own hand, within the cover, Agur's beautiful prayer, 'Give me neither poverty nor riches,' etc. (Prov. xxx. 8, 9), and, just beneath it, the important Apostolic aphorism, 'Godliness with contentment is great gain.' "

Next in the memoir come two forms of self-examination, and some " Rules of Daily Use," which were constantly employed. It may interest the reader to see them, and they are noticeable for this reason : It is often supposed that the tendency of "Evangelical principles " was rather to make light of Manuals of Devotion and strict habits in the religious life. It has been the fashion to contrast the strict rules of life, the minute self-examination, and the rigorous insistence on such matters as fasting and the sterner side of religious discipline, with a supposed laxity in those who are called Evangelical.

Certainly there is no ground for this comparison in the glimpse of a spiritual life which this memoir gives.

The forms of self-examination could only have been drawn up by one who had a very definite view of the meaning of holiness, and who was prepared to seek it by a life of strict self-discipline.

An attentive reader will notice that they differ from most modern forms, because they are based on holiness, rather than on sin. That is to say, the soul is taught to inquire and accuse itself, rather for the neglect of grace given and privileges bestowed, than for the faults which may have been committed.

But others will, perhaps, like to see these forms for the same reason which makes them precious to the writer. The memoir of his mother was the only book, except the Bible, which my father constantly used in his own devotions, and the little book from which this copy is taken is soiled, and its pages almost worn through with constant use.

SELF-EXAMINATION.—No. 1.

1. Did I awake as with God this morning, and rise with a grateful sense of His goodness? How were the secret devotions of the morning performed? Did I offer my solemn praises, and renew the dedication of myself to God with becoming attention and suitable affections?

2. Did I lay my scheme for the business of the day wisely and well? How did I read the Scripture, and any other devotional book, or practical one? Did it do my *heart* good, or was it mere amusement? How have the other stated devotions of the day been performed, whether secret, family, or public?

3. Have I pursued the common business of the day with diligence and spirituality of mind, doing everything in season, and with all convenient dispatch, as unto the Lord? What time have I lost this day in the morning, or at noon-day, or in the evening? and what occasioned this loss? With what temper, and under what regulations have the recreations of this day been pursued?

4. Have I seen the hand of God in my mercies, in my health, cheerfulness, food, journeys, clothing, books, preservation, success in my avocations, kindness of friends, conversation, etc.?

5. Have I seen the hand of God in afflictions? and, very particularly, in *little* things which had a tendency to vex and disquiet me? And, with regard to this interposition, have I received my comforts thankfully, and my afflictions submissively? How have I guarded against the temptations of the day, particularly against this, or that, temptation, which I foresaw in the morning?

6. Have I maintained an humble dependence on divine influences? Have I lived by faith on the Son of God, and regarded Jesus Christ as my Teacher and Governor, my Atonement and Intercessor, my Example and Guardian, my Strength and Forerunner? Have I been looking forward this day, to death, and judgment, and eternity, and considered myself as a probationer for Heaven, and, through grace, an expectant of it?

7. Have I governed my thoughts well, especially in my intervals of solitude?

8. How was my subject of thought chosen for to-day, and how has it been regarded? Have I governed my discourse wisely and piously in such and such company? Did I say nothing passionate, mischievous, slanderous, imprudent, or impertinent?

9. Has my heart been full of love to God this day? and to all mankind? and have I sought, and found, and improved opportunities of doing and getting good? With what attention have I read the Scriptures this day? How was self-examination performed the last night? and how

have I profited this day by any remarks I then made on former negligences and mistakes?

SELF-EXAMINATION.—No. 2.

1. Do I walk by faith in an unseen world, Saviour, Eternity?

2. Do I love God, trying always to please, and fearing to offend Him? Desiring to draw near to, and longing to enjoy Him?

3. What end do I propose to myself in my pursuits, endeavours, and studies? Is it the glory of God (1 Cor. x. 31)?

4. How are the Scriptures heard and read? Do I desire and pray for spiritual knowledge?

5. Of what sort are my prayers? Do I watch, strive, and pray against distractions and wanderings in prayer, against coldness, deadness, dulness, formality, etc.? or do my tempers, words, and actions contradict my prayers?

6. Do I daily call myself to account for my daily sins, humbling myself before God with a broken and a contrite heart, seeking, through Jesus, pardon and peace, and not allowing myself in any known sin?

7. Do I love the Lord Jesus Christ in sincerity?

8. How is my heart kept? Have I found out my besetting sin, and placed the curb on that in particular? Do I aim at heart purity, and freedom from inward, secret sins?

9. Do I eat and drink to the glory of God, and practise daily self-denial in governing and restraining my appetites and passions?

10. Do I keep an eye to the standard, "Love God with all thy heart," and "Love thy neighbour as thyself"?

11. Am I hasty or rash in judging any? Do I despise or slight any on account of natural defects or infirmities? Do I abstain from uncharitable and unkind looks, thoughts, words? Am I quick to see, willing to own, and anxious to undo, as far as may be, what has been done amiss?

12. Do I pray for, and desire the spiritual good of all

doing what in me lies to promote it by my consistent example and patient, persevering endeavours? Do I earnestly desire the spread of the Gospel, and the success of its ministers? And do I cherish the sanctifying influences of the Holy Spirit for my own growth and fruitfulness in grace?

RULES OF DAILY USE.

1. Begin with God. Never neglect to make prayer *first*. Should anything unforeseen occur to shorten, yet upon no account, and for no pretence, omit the duty. Though short, be devout, earnest, serious. Be this your motto, " Begin with God " (Ps. v. 3).

2. Expect trials, and to have your own will often thwarted. Seek strength for the day of trial, and grace for the duty of that day (Deut. xxxiii. 25).

3. Watch occasions of good, to improve, and of evil, to shun them (Rom. xii. 9).

4. Make the best of that which looks ill, and let not the sins of others provoke you to sin.

5. Be not weary of well-doing (Gal. vi. 9), nor cease from striving against sin (Heb. xii. 4).

Enough has been quoted to show the character of the mother whose influence left such a permanent impression upon my father's whole after-life, and the little volume with its evident traces of incessant use, is a sufficient record for those who loved him of that inner life which is hid with Christ in God.

But I cannot forbear to add an extract from the blank leaf of his mother's Testament, which has a special interest after seventy years, when one feels that its prayer has been fulfilled.

The extract is dated August 24, 1816, and that is the day on which Robert, the fourth son of John

and Henrietta Bickersteth, was born.   It is written
in pencil in the mother's hand:—

Again I have received richly the support and mercy of
my Lord.   O bind my heart and future life to Thee and
to Thy service for ever!   Sanctify this Thy new and
precious gift to us; teach us, that we may be enabled
through Thy grace to train our child in the way wherein
it ought to go.   O adopt it, blessed Jesus, into Thy family
on earth; and may it be partaker of eternal glory hereafter!
Amen.

And the father adds when, fifteen years afterwards, the mother has passed away—

May this striking recognition of a mother's gratitude,
and memorial of affectionate interest in, and thoughts for
his welfare in the season of his own unconscious infancy,
be imprinted on the youthful breast of him who is most
concerned, as with an iron pen and an indelible mark! and
may the solemn charge, "Be faithful unto death,"[1] also
appended to this document by the same hand, be as a
talisman to guard him from the sins of unfaithfulness, that
none such may cleave unto him, and as his never-to-be
obliterated watchword in every hour of trial or peril!

---

[1] In 1857 my father adopted the words "Esto Fidelis" as his motto, in
place of "Frappe Fort," which had been borne by his family.

CHAPTER II.

BOYHOOD AT ACTON.

The parish of Acton—Pupils at the vicarage—Dean Alford, Bishop
Pelham, etc.—Recollections of the latter—A model parish—Large
numbers of communicants—Strict churchmanship of the older
Evangelicals—Robert Bickersteth as a boy—His early talent for
surgery—Portrait of a true parish priest—Evangelical, but not
Low Church.

THE village of Acton stands in a purely agricultural
district of Suffolk, about three miles from Sudbury.
The old church is mentioned in Domesday Book,
and part of the present structure dates from the
eleventh century. It is now sorely in need of
the repairs which have just been commenced by the
present vicar, the Rev. Arundel Leaky, and there
is good hope that the restoration will be completed
in such a way as to preserve several interesting relics.

There is in the church a fine brass of one Roger
de Brues, a crusader, which is said to be one of the
oldest and best in England. However, the antiqui-
ties with which we are concerned date no further
back than 1812, when the Rev. John Bickersteth
was appointed to the living by Lady Howe.

The parish contains several outlying hamlets,
and there is but one gentleman's house, called
Acton Place; so the vicarage, which was unfortu-

nately placed nearly half a mile distant from the church, was necessarily the centre of charitable and medical relief, no less than of directly spiritual influence.

What the home life was like at Acton, appears from a Journal which my father kept in his thirteenth year, and from the recollections of some of the pupils who lived beneath his father's roof.

His parents enjoyed eighteen years of unbroken happiness in their married life. One child died in infancy, but on the mother's death in 1830, four sons and three daughters survived. At the time of his mother's death, Robert was fourteen years old, but as he was evidently much older than his years, it is not surprising that his mother's influence should have left so deep an impression. In after-years he remembered a conversation which he had with her only a week before her death, in which she said, " I should die happily if I knew that you were to be a clergyman."

It is evident from the Journal that his thoughts had been already turned in this direction. Each day there is the record of large portions of the Bible read, and there are elaborate notes of his father's sermons, of which the texts were noted each week. Besides this, he was already his father's constant companion in pastoral visitation, so he was initiated at only thirteen years of age into all the fascinating interests of the life of an active parish priest. But there is nothing morbid or unlike the healthy instincts of a light-hearted boy. Side by side with the sick visiting and the catechising of his class in the Sunday school, are the records of bathing in the Stour, rides on his pony, fishing, sliding, and all sorts of country pleasures which he shared with his brothers and his father's pupils.[1]

Amongst the pupils who were from time to time inmates of his father's house, were Lord Thomas Hay, Francis and John, two sons of Lord Grey (the Lord Grey of the first Reform Bill), Henry Alford, afterwards Dean of Canterbury, Bishop Pelham of Norwich, and Lawrence Ottley, who married Miss Elisabeth Bickersteth. The latter succeeded his father-in-law as Vicar of Acton, became Rector of Richmond, Yorkshire, and Canon Residentiary of Ripon. The Rev. John Bickersteth was an old-fashioned classical scholar, and thus his children, who never went to a public school, shared with his pupils the opportunity of gaining a good education.

But the great feature of the home at Acton was the prominent place given to religious duties, and the incessant effort of the vicar to frame and fashion the family life according to the doctrine of Christ, and to make both himself and his, as much as in him lay, wholesome examples of the flock of Christ.

For a further sketch of Acton, I am indebted to Bishop Pelham of Norwich, who allowed me to take down the reminiscences that occurred to him after an interval of fifty years.

Bishop Pelham has a vivid recollection of the two years he spent at Acton Vicarage, from November, 1832, to October, 1834. He had just taken his degree, and was recommended to spend the interval

[1] There is a brief entry in Dean Alford's Life which refers to one of their bathing expeditions :—" Saved Robert's life while bathing in the Stour."

before receiving Holy Orders in getting some insight into parochial work.

Amongst other clergymen to whom his father applied, was the Rev. John Bickersteth. At that time my grandfather had given up taking pupils, and was reluctant to begin again. However, Mr. Pelham was invited to spend two or three days at Acton, and on the first night of his visit he was so much struck by the piety and simplicity of the household, and by the kindness of his reception, that he registered a vow, that if God would allow him to go to Acton, he should esteem it among his greatest blessings. The vicar's scruples were overcome, and Mr. Pelham was for two years an inmate of the vicarage. Mr. Bickersteth allowed Mr. Pelham the use of his library, and constantly took him on his daily round of pastoral visitation, and to the three cottage lectures which were held weekly in the outlying hamlets of the parish.

Mr. Pelham esteemed this as a very valuable opportunity, and still looks back upon Acton as a wonderful parish.

He remembers several points in illustration of this. First, there was the average attendance of ninety at the monthly Communion, out of a parish of six hundred, and this in spite of the fact that the farmers were at first, at any rate, hostile or indifferent to the teaching of the vicar, and, with the exception of the family at Acton Place, the communicants were all of the labouring class. One proof of the hold which religion had upon the hearts of the parishioners was, that it was quite the exception when a household had not morning and evening family prayer. A card of prayers used to hang up in each cottage, and in his pastoral visits the vicar would notice whether it had been duly used on the previous morning or evening.

Mr. Bickersteth's teaching was very accurate and thorough. Each Sunday in Lent, and on the first Sunday in the month throughout the year, there was public catechising in church, and on these occasions the church, always full, was crowded with the parents and others, anxious to hear their children's answers. Each child was thoroughly grounded in the Church Catechism, which formed the basis of all his teaching ; and, in addition to this, there were three little Catechisms compiled by Mr. Bickersteth on Baptism, Confirmation, and Holy Communion, which all the Acton children were made to learn by heart. Mr. Bickersteth always insisted on the children giving the exact words of the answers for the sake of the older people, and when the correct answer was given, he had great skill in eliciting the children's knowledge of the sense. Of my grandfather's accurate teaching and strict churchmanship there is more to say by-and-bye, but I continue Bishop Pelham's recollections as they come.

At that time Edward was at Cambridge, so Robert, then a boy of sixteen, was Mr. Pelham's usual companion. He remembers his eager interest and enthusiasm in all kinds of subjects, and especially his early love of surgery. Though he was only sixteen, Master Robert was often sent for as the village doctor, and many of the poor people preferred him to any other practitioner. He had a sympathetic power and skill which were quite remarkable. An instance of this occurred in the case of an old man named J—— E——. He had been ailing for some time, and was constantly visited by the family at the vicarage. One evening Robert came home and told his father that he believed E—— was suffering from an acute disease requiring an immediate operation.

His father, who had some knowledge of surgery, went to the cottage at once, and sent for the surgeon at Long Melford, a man of great ability and repute. The doctor came, but did not admit the gravity of the case, and, promising to send some medicine, went home.

About midnight, J—— E—— was worse, and again sent for Master Robert, who persisted in his former opinion. He obtained leave from his father, and set off in the pony carriage to fetch the doctor. He came, was much surprised at the development of the malady, and was forced to exclaim, " The boy is right !" Robert was sent off at once to Sudbury for another surgeon, and the operation was performed ; but both surgeons were very much impressed by the skilful diagnosis of the boy. It seems he had acquired all the information on medical subjects within his reach from encyclo-pædias, etc.

In connection with the services in Acton Church, the Bishop remembers how in the Communion service, in the midst of the deep solemnity which always prevailed, Mr. Bickersteth, who had a beautiful tenor voice, would begin very softly to sing the words " Therefore with angels," and the *Sanctus* was taken up by the whole congregation. This was a long while before the era of choral Celebrations.

Mr. Bickersteth was very scrupulous about the church, and would never suffer a speck of dust to be seen in the building. On Wednesday afternoon it was Robert's duty to see that the lamps had been made bright, and that everything was in good order for the weekly lecture, and he was usually the organist.

It was this training which made him in after-life so exceedingly particular that there should be nothing slovenly or untidy in the House of God.

I am also indebted to Bishop Pelham for an amusing illustration of the feelings of reverence and affection with which the parishioners of Acton regarded their vicar. The time came for his removal from Acton, after a ministry of twenty-five years among them, and there was a dispute amongst the farmers as to which should have the honour of conveying his furniture and books into Leicestershire. Somewhat to his annoyance, all refused to let him hire, and at last it was arranged that two farmers should supply the necessary waggons and horses to convey his effects to Sapcote, free of charge.

Mr. Pelham spent a Sunday in Acton soon after Mr. Bickersteth had left. It so happened that he was delayed by sickness on the road to London, and, being in the neighbourhood of Acton, was compelled by the people, ill as he was, to come over and preach. He was led to give out the same text that Mr. Bickersteth had chosen for his farewell sermon, and no sooner had he uttered it, than he found he had touched a chord which strangely moved the congregation.

As he went about the parish afterwards, even the roughest lads and the least religious people welcomed him warmly as " one of Mr. Bickersteth's gentlemen," and so a link with the happy past.

Bishop Pelham tells a touching story of a visit which he paid on that occasion to an old woman, who, though a very pious person, often suffered from great depression. He was surprised to find her quite happy, while nearly every one else in the parish seemed cast down by the recent separation. He inquired the reason of the contrast, and she replied, " Well, sir, you see when I had been to the Table and to sermon, and came back happy in my mind, I used sometimes to think my religion was all Mr. Bicker-steth ; and now he is gone, I know it is all Christ." The scaffold was removed, but the edifice remained.

These are happy recollections which are likely enough to find a parallel in the simple annals of many another country parish, but they may possibly interest some of those who loved my father, and help them to see how the early training influenced his whole after-life.

Surely there is a reminiscence of Acton days and a half-unconscious portrait of his father in this passage from his Charge to the clergy of the diocese of Ripon, delivered in 1873 :—

The influence which a clergyman may exert for good is beyond the power of utterance. . . . Let him be a man of intellectual culture and refinement, fitted by taste and habit and previous education for the work of the ministry ; let him be possessed of those higher qualifications which no mere human training can impart; let him be an able minister of the New Testament, a man of faith, a man of prayer, full of the Holy Ghost, under the all-constraining influence of the love of Christ, and one who yearns for the souls for whom Christ shed His Blood; let him exemplify in life and conversation the Gospel which he has been set apart to proclaim ; and let it be evident to every beholder that he is a man whose settled purpose it is to live to the glory of God, and to commend to others the religion which has brought peace and comfort to his own soul ; let him be diligent in the discharge of the varied duties of his sacred calling, a faithful dispenser of the Word of God and of His Holy Sacraments, a watcher for souls as one that must give account, a true pastor to whom his parishioners may at all times turn for advice, instruction, or sympathy, as their several needs require ; and lives there, I ask, a man from whom a more blessed, a more hallowed, or a more potent influence for good may be expected to emanate than such a parochial clergyman? You have but to imagine the whole country subdivided into such parishes and blessed with such clergymen, and who would then dare lift up his hand against the National Church?

This is probably the place to draw a distinction which was ever present to my father's mind, and which he doubtless owed to the example of his father. He gloried in the title of Evangelical, but he always repudiated the charge of being a Low Churchman. And certainly no one can attentively read these notices of Acton or some of the later letters of my grandfather without seeing that his Evangelical principles were quite consistent with genuine loyalty to the Church.

The Church Catechism was thoroughly taught. The whole Liturgy was constantly explained in the course of sermons and lectures, and, to notice a trivial but significant detail, salt fish always appeared upon the table on Fridays and Fast-days throughout the year.

With regard to daily service, the Dean of Lichfield remembers that at one time his father felt it right to obey the rubric, and read the morning prayers in Acton Church. He did not long continue the practice, because the church was at a very inconvenient distance from the vicarage, and, indeed, from the bulk of the parishioners; but it was his habit to welcome all who would come to family prayers in his own house.

On the question of Dissent, or rather, of union with others outside the Church, my grandfather was a stricter churchman than his brother Edward of Watton. The latter took a prominent part in connection with the Evangelical Alliance, but my grandfather, though full of charity to all who loved our Lord Jesus Christ in sincerity and truth, felt it inconsistent to join in public worship with those who caused needless division in the Body of Christ.

This difference between them comes out in a letter written by Edward Bickersteth to his brother John, dated October 31, 1810 :—

To Christians of all other classes (excepting Socinians, Arians, and Pelagians), who love the Lord with sincerity, I would give the right hand of fellowship, however they may differ in non-essentials; nor should I, after mature consideration, hesitate to go to their assemblies. *I know you differ from me here,* . . . I am not, therefore, anxious to be exonerated from the charge of Methodism, nor to prove my principles by the Church of England.

It is only right to notice that the letter was

written before either of the brothers had been ordained, but it seems to indicate a certain difference in standpoint which both of them maintained in after-days.

In 1837 my grandfather was offered the living of Sapcote, in Leicestershire. This was not altogether a happy change from Acton, but, since his wife's death, Acton could never be the same as in the earlier days, when he had seen his children growing up around him, and his parish gradually transformed under the influence of the Gospel which he preached.

There were sundry changes made in the manner of conducting service at Sapcote which gave some offence to the Chapel party.

In a letter written to my father in 1838 my grandfather says—

We are all alive at Sapcote, and as we have begun catechising in the church, I suppose we shall soon be imitated in this also by the chapel. Alas! I really believe some of those who now cry out, " The Chapel in danger ! " would have been much better pleased had what they call " the Gospil " never come to the church.

In another letter to my father there is a graphic description of the opening of a new organ, and the introduction of choral service, with the *Te Deum* sung after the evening service :—

When the organ came, which old Mrs. W. designated a " load of summut," the cry of the Wesleyans was, " Here comes Mr. B.'s Dagon."

Another letter to my father speaks still more strongly. It is dated February 7, 1839, and, after some family news, he says—

The spirit of division is rampant. Ranters first, I suspect, were encouraged by the Methodists, to whom *now* they are beginning to be troublesome : a result which might have been anticipated, if the " Chapellists " had not, in their shortsightedness, forgotten that this mode of warfare against the Church would probably act with double force against themselves. On Sunday afternoon, from Hosea vi., I preached with the view to an improvement of the present opportunities, and spoke of the parish, 1st, as torn with religious divisions, 2nd, as smitten both with sin and sickness. Under the first head I started the question whether religious divisions might not be shown to be the fruitful source, on one side, of infidelity and atheism, on the other, of profligacy and profaneness.

This was tolerably plain speaking for a representative of the party who are sometimes supposed by their amiable weakness to have encouraged the sin of schism.

There will be more to say of Sapcote later on, when my father commenced his ministry as curate there. A few years have been anticipated to complete the picture of my grandfather. Some of the old folks at Acton still remember him. One told the writer she " minded Mr. Bickersteth. He was very strict about the Catechism." Another remembered the first sermon that led her to think seriously of her soul ; and she can never forget many texts imprinted upon her memory by his singularly impressive manner of preaching. Many of his special sermons were published, and he occasionally visited neighbouring parishes on behalf of the Church Missionary Society ; but he was, as a rule, singularly retiring, and was content to live amongst his own people.

The same devoted spirit which was shown at
Acton distinguished him at Sapcote, and letters
written from thence to his children mention different
people with the same affectionate individual interest,
which shows how closely the heart of the pastor was
bound up with the joys and sorrows of the people
committed to his care.

One more quotation from a letter addressed to
my father while an undergraduate at Cambridge,
is an amusing illustration of the writer's theological
sentiments. He speaks of having been to preach in
a neighbouring church, and says of the incumbent—

God can work by any instrument, but I do not think
that —— seems at all likely to draw around him any of the
mass of no-church-goers at T——. Mr. P. is mighty easy
and low in his churchmanship notions, although a holy,
good man. His plan does not seem to prosper. He says
of his people—" They respect, but they do not mind me ; "
but surely a people will mind the man whom they truly
respect.

It may be interesting to add an extract from a
letter to my father, in 1835, in which my grandfather explains his somewhat neutral position in
politics :—

To-day is our county election. We have a sort of
opposition, and no opposition ; we have Rushbrook, and
Logan, a religious man and a temperate Reformist, and
Hales, of whom I know nothing, except that he is claimed
by the Radicals. Though quite unpledged, I shall probably
give one vote to Logan and one to Wilson. Logan called
and behaved very courteously, but I consider a vote like
that I am going to give rather imperfect as a specimen of
my own feeling, and all but neutralizing, as it respects

those it may seem to benefit; still, it seems to be better than not voting at all.

At this time the sympathies of the Evangelical clergy were mainly with the party of reform, chiefly because they had been allied with Wilberforce, Clarkson, and the so-called Clapham sect, on the question of slavery; and my grandfather had an additional reason for being in the main a Liberal from his intercourse with his brother Henry (afterwards Lord Langdale), with whom, at one time, he used to spend his annual summer holiday. However, it is not surprising that a country clergyman should hesitate to vote for a candidate of whom he knew nothing, but that he was claimed by the Radicals.

In the general upheaval of political parties that followed the first Reform Bill, there was a good deal of wild talk about the disestablishment of the Church, and the Radical in question may have been committed to some such scheme.

If it be true, as a very eminent authority is reported to have said, that the disestablishment of the Church looked more remote in 1885 than it did in 1835, the change in public opinion, and the firmer grasp which the Church has obtained upon the hearts of the people, is largely due to the faithful efforts to promote their religious and social interests, of which the work of the Rev. John Bickersteth at Acton is a conspicuous example.

CHAPTER III.

AT the time of his mother's death my father had evidently begun to think of being a clergyman, and it was not strange that all his father's sons should have shared, for a time at least, the same intention; but it was not yet the settled purpose of his life, and for a time he was attracted by the offer of a career in the Royal Navy. His father's friend, Lord John Hay, entered his name at the Admiralty, and promised him a midshipman's berth. However, there was a delay of two years before Lord John got a ship, and by that time my father's naval ardour had cooled.

Meanwhile he had followed up his taste for

D

surgery, and in 1833 he went to Norwich as a
pupil to Mr. Crosse, one of the surgeons of the
Norwich Infirmary.   His stay at Norwich was cut
short by a trifling accident which brought him home
to Acton, and in the following year he went to
London.   There he lodged in the house of Dr.
Whiting, in Rodney Buildings, New Kent Road—
one of the lecturers at the Webb Street Medical
School.   He entered as a student at St. Thomas's
Hospital, which then stood in Tooley Street, opposite to Guy's.

Bishop Pelham was then a curate in London,
and the friendship which had begun at Acton was
steadily maintained.   The student confided in the
clergyman the difficulties which beset a young man
who was beginning to walk the hospitals.   Coming
fresh from the religious atmosphere of Acton, he
found himself in a world very different from that to
which he had been accustomed.   The rough jokes and
the vulgar materialism of the dissecting-room were
doubtless a sore trial, but he was well able to hold
his own, and no doubt his faith was strengthened
by the opposition against which he had to fight.

In 1836 he passed his classical examination at
the Apothecaries' Hall, and subsequently went to
Paris to attend the hospitals there, before applying
for the licence of the College of Surgeons.   A few
letters from Paris, to his father and sisters, seem to
show that his life was a lonely one.   He speaks of
his little chamber in the Hôtel Corneille being
"like that of the prophet Elisha in the house of the
Shunamite," and in these days his spare time was
spent in the composition of sermons, which marks

how the leading motive of his life was becoming more and more apparent.

My father was elected in after-years a governor of Guy's Hospital, and retained the office to the end of his life.

From the time of his first leaving home, he had always been a regular teacher in the Sunday School connected with Mr. Hawtrey's church in Southwark, and it was during his residence in London that a change, or rather, a deepening, of his religious convictions took place. At that time no preacher in London exercised a wider influence than Henry Melville. Camden Chapel, Camden Town, was always densely crowded, and the charm of his sermons, evident enough to those who are only able to read them, was enhanced by an exquisite delivery, and the strange fascination of the crowd which hung upon his lips. My father was generally amongst his hearers each Sunday night, and in after-days he could never speak of Melville without emotion. He writes in a Journal with which he relieved the weariness of the last months, while he was waiting for the end—

I can never be sufficiently thankful for the privilege of hearing that wonderful man. The marvellousness of his eloquence was to me something entirely new. I had never heard anything to compare with it. And now, after a lapse of forty years, the impressions made upon me by his unrivalled power as a preacher remain as vividly fixed in my recollection as if they were only of yesterday.

His sisters recollect how, in holiday visits to Sapcote, my father would repeat whole passages of Melville's sermons, which he had committed to memory.   And the same remained stored up for after-years, when sometimes they would be repeated to his children in the course of a ride through the woody lanes round our beautiful home at Ripon.

The influence of Melville upon my father was of a double character.   It was his ministry, under God, which, co-operating with other providential circumstances, led him to forsake the medical profession for the ministry of the Gospel of Christ ; and his manner of preaching doubtless had its effect upon my father's style.   Of other external circumstances which led to his decision to take Holy Orders, there is no need to speak.

For a long time there was a conflict in his mind whether to give up the profession in which he had every prospect of success ; and he seems to have shrunk from throwing upon his father the additional burden of maintaining another son at Cambridge, when the whole cost of his medical training would be thrown away.   However, he confided his desire of ordination to his uncle, Edward Bickersteth of Watton, in the course of a Sunday morning walk through St. James's Park, and the latter urged him to acquaint his father with his wish.

It was late in life for so important a change. His classical attainments had been growing less during the last four years, and his early mathematical training had been scanty enough.

However, unwearied industry, and the concentrated purpose of one who had at last found his work, and meant to do it, enabled him to pass

through Cambridge with greater distinction than
might have been expected from his training. He
entered at Queen's College in October, 1837, and
used to recall in after-years the fact that he came
into residence on St. Luke's Day. The coincidence
marked the providence by which he, too, was called
to be an evangelist and physician of the soul.

Of his career at Cambridge there is little to
say. In his second year he obtained a scholarship
at Queen's.

He entered the University later than other men,
and with his mind already made up on points
which are, to most young men, a source of perplexing speculation at the outset of college life.
This, perhaps, accounts for the fact that he mixed
little in the ordinary pursuits of undergraduates,
and was less affected than others by the secondary
influences of University life.

The venerable Master of Queen's, Dr. Phillips,
who had been his tutor, wrote after my father's death
to testify to the recollection, after forty-seven years,
of his high example, and the feeling of respect with
which he himself used to regard his pupil. As a
teacher in the Jesus Lane Sunday school, he retained
the habit which had been formed at Acton and maintained in London. There was nothing in his undergraduate life to which he looked back with greater
pleasure than the opportunity of hearing Melville as
select preacher in two successive years, and it was
at Cambridge that he first had the opportunity of
meeting in private the great teacher to whose public
ministry he owed so much.

My father's private tutor was Mr. P. Mason, and

the latter was grievously disappointed at the degree which his pupil obtained.

Coming, as he did, to the University after four or five years spent in the preparation for another profession, it was not likely that my father would do justice to his natural ability ; but Mr. Mason had given him every hope of being a wrangler. When the list came out, and my father appeared amongst the junior optimes, it was explained by the fact that he had followed too literally his tutor's advice, and had neglected parts of the work on which the examiners were determined to insist. And yet it is impossible to regret it. My father used often to trace the Hand of God in thus stopping the career which might have been his had he obtained a higher degree, and, in consequence, a Fellowship at his College. My father took his degree in January, 1841, and was ordained Deacon by the Bishop of Peterborough in Peterborough Cathedral, in the following March.

His father gave him a title to the curacy of Sapcote, where the former had been for the past four years.

The time of ordination can hardly fail to be the most solemn period in a man's life, and yet the arrangements at Peterborough, as everywhere else until recent days, were not of a kind to deepen the natural feelings of solemnity appropriate to such a time. The candidates were all lodged at the principal hotel, and dined together each evening, at an hour which might have been utilised as a precious opportunity of prayer and meditation. The examination itself was purely formal, and there was no address or devotional help given to the candidates.

My father remembered this in after-days, and was very particular at Ripon, where it was impossible to lodge all the candidates at the Palace, to arrange that they should obtain quiet lodgings, while he was anxious to make the most of the golden opportunity for deepening the spiritual life of those who were entering on their sacred profession.

The curacy of Sapcote was an admirable preparation for future work, and in the Journal to which I have already alluded my father wrote—

I had ample time for reading. As a rule, I read in my father's library every morning from nine till one, spent the afternoon in visiting the poor, and got some time for reading every evening besides. It was seldom that I had to preach more than once on Sunday, and this allowed of my giving full time to the preparation of sermons. It was then, and for several years afterwards, my habit to write out every sermon, word for word, and spend an amount of care on the style and composition which was invaluable to me in after-years, and other places of ministerial labour.

These sermons preached at Sapcote bear evident traces of most careful study. The original text of the New Testament and the Septuagint seem to have been always consulted.

From a bundle of the sermons I cannot forbear to quote the concluding paragraph of the first he ever preached, sounding as it does so emphatically the keynote of his ministry. The text is 1 Cor. ii. 2 : "I determined not to know anything among you, save Jesus Christ, and Him crucified." Showing how every doctrine necessary to salvation centred round the Cross, he concluded with one of those intensely earnest personal appeals which were the chief characteristic of all his sermons :—

I glory in the privilege of being permitted to proclaim the glad tidings of redemption—that there is not one of you for whom Christ's Blood has not been shed, not one who has not salvation within his reach. I care not what may have been your sins in time past. They may be like mountains, but there is strength in Christ to cast them into the depths of the sea ; and He is just as willing as He is able. " Him that cometh to Me I will in no wise cast out." Then yield yourselves, body and soul, to the touch of your Redeemer. But come like men resolved to be saved ; like men who feel that unless on the Rock they must finally sink in a deluge of wrath.

You will readily believe it is not without much anxiety that I enter this day on the duties of the ministerial office. It is an office from which I can only be released by death ; an office on which may be dependent the interests of hundreds, nay, of thousands ; their interests not for time alone, but for eternity. Each soul that comes within the reach of the sound of my voice may hereafter be a witness either for or against me. This I know, that nothing can prevent their being written against me, but the determination on my part to preach nothing but Christ and Him crucified. How, then, can I forbear on this, the first morning of my ministry, to entreat your prayers that, whether called to labour for a brief or an extended period, it may be my lot at the last, in summing up my ministry, to say of it, I determined, and through God's grace have kept the determination, to know nothing but Jesus and Him crucified ?

A cousin, Mrs. Wheeler, wrote last year, only a few hours before she died, some reminiscences of my father as curate of Sapcote :—

I very frequently visited Sapcote. My cousin Robert had recently been ordained to his father's curacy ; the people were already growing attached to him, he showed such sympathy in their troubles. One Sunday my uncle asked, " Why did you preach about the lion and the bear this morning ? " " Because they took a lamb out of the flock, and I wanted to say something that might comfort poor Mrs. ——, who has so lately lost a little lamb out of her flock." It was beautiful to see the loving, trustful terms on which father and son were.

About this time he was invited to preach by his uncle at Watton, " And," says a family letter, " considering what the Watton Sundays are, we all think this no small honour for so recently ordained a curate."

A pretty story is preserved of a little cousin Janey, only child of his uncle Henry, who, when only eight years old, and a visitor at Sapcote, used to say, " I do like Cousin Robert's sermons ; they always make me want to be good." Can any preacher have a higher tribute paid to him than that ?

In 1841 my father paid a visit to his old friend Mr. Hawtrey, who had charge of St. Mary's, Guernsey, and occasionally preached in that and other churches in the Channel Islands, where he first addressed an educated congregation. In the following year he took charge of the parish of Wooler in Northumberland for six or seven weeks, for his friend, Mr. John Grey ; but, with these exceptions, the curacy of Sapcote was a very quiet time, in which my father was laying up a store of material which stood him in good stead in busier days to come. My father often quoted the advantages he received by this time for study, in advising young men to seek their first curacies in parishes where they could have some leisure for personal improvement.

And the moderate work of a country parish helped to form the habit of close pastoral oversight and house to house visitation, which, when once formed, sets the ideal of the ministry, even when overgrown populations render its realisation almost impossible.

Leaving Sapcote in 1843, my father accepted the curacy of St. Giles, Reading, under the Rev. T. C. Grainger. The two years spent at Reading were very happy ones. A kindly vicar, whose holy example and powerful preaching he always gratefully remembered, and the active work of a large parish, were important elements in his training; while he gradually obtained an insight into the larger questions which were perplexing the Church. Writing on December 10, 1844, to his brother Edward, the present Dean of Lichfield, my father says—

What a fearful state our poor Church is in! I am anxious to see what the Exeter diocese clergy do. I should be greatly puzzled whether or no to obey the bishop. His letter seems very cleverly written, but his decisions appear to me to go upon entirely false assumptions, and certainly they are in the direction of Tractarianism.

The same letter has another item of curious interest—

I have been asked to look out for clergymen for some of the new districts in Yorkshire, under Peel's Act. The salary is £130 till a church is built; it will then be £150, with a house. It is a relative of the Bishop of Ripon's who asked me, and if you know of any one, I should be glad to get his name put before the bishop.

From Reading my father went to Clapham, to a

curacy at the parish church, under Dr. Dealtry, to whom he had been recommended by the Rev. Charles Bradley, father of the present Dean of Westminster.

He entered on his duties at Clapham in 1845, and about the same time, without any solicitation on his part, he was elected to the Limborough Lectureship, at Christ Church, Spitalfields, and the chaplaincy of the Weavers' Company. His power as a preacher had already attracted considerable attention; and his name, well known through the wide reputation of his uncles, soon brought offers of preferment; but he remained at the parish church until Dr. Dealtry offered him, at the close of 1845, the incumbency of St. John's, Clapham Rise.

This appointment was a very important one to my father, for not only did it place him in a position of great influence, where his preaching soon attracted a large congregation, but it enabled him to contemplate a step which secured the singular happiness of his whole domestic life. He wrote in the dark days to which I have already alluded, when he was so much dependent on the loving tenderness of the best of all possible nurses—

To that period I look back with the deepest thankfulness to Almighty God, as a turning-point in my life, the commencement of a career of unmingled happiness and prosperity, and the occasion of never ceasing praise to God for His mercy, in having guided me to the choice of one so incomparably qualified to promote my happiness in every possible way.

My father entered upon his new duties on St. Matthew's Day, 1845, and he writes—

From that day until the close of my ministry in St. John's, goodness and mercy seemed to follow me without interruption.

In the beginning of 1846 he resigned the preachership at the Magdalene, which he had held for some months, and devoted his whole time and energy to St. John's.

Some two years before this my father had first made the acquaintance of his future wife, Miss Elisabeth Garde, the third daughter of Mr. Joseph Garde, of Cork. Her parents had died many years before, and she was then staying with her brother, the Rev. Richard Garde, in whose church, at Harold, in Bedfordshire, my father and mother were married by my grandfather, on the 21st of July, 1846; and, after a brief wedding tour, my father brought his bride home to Clapham.

St. John's Church soon became filled with a very large congregation, devotedly attached to their new Incumbent. The Rev. Clement Cobb, who served under my father as curate at St. John's, and was afterwards one of his chaplains, has kindly written a sketch of his ministry at Clapham, to which this narrative is largely indebted.

The parishioners of St. John's consisted chiefly of business men, who resided at Clapham, and were engaged daily in the city.

My father made it a rule to devote his evenings to the wealthier members of his flock, but he certainly did not mingle with them in merely social intercourse. It was clearly understood at St. John's, that when Mr. Bickersteth was a guest at some social gathering, the conversation would turn on matters uppermost in the hearts of Christian people, and the evening would be closed with family prayer. In this way many fast friendships were formed, and a powerful influence for good was brought to bear upon the families and friends of those attending the church.

But the public ministries of the pulpit were the means of exercising a wider influence.

At this time, at any rate, my father's sermons on Sunday were always written, and bear the marks of laborious preparation of both style and matter. Though there was nothing in the least artificial in his diction, yet the exquisite modulation of his voice, which contributed so largely to cast a spell over his hearers, was not acquired without careful cultivation. On Sunday mornings the sermons were comparatively free from any appeal to the emotions, and were addressed rather to the head than the heart ; but the evening sermons, which attracted a wider class, were models of popular oratory.

Mr. Cobb, speaking of the crowds which were attracted to St. John's, says—

The plain and unecclesiastical church had its best ornament in the eighteen hundred people who filled every seat that was constructed, or could be extemporised, and hung on the preacher's lips with breathless attention. I never saw anything like it, excepting when I have heard Melville, the then prince of sacred orators, preach a special sermon.

Though by no means his only power, there is no doubt that preaching was Mr. Bickersteth's great power. There was no complaint of long sermons, though he usually preached for fifty minutes. His sermons on Sunday were written throughout. They would frequently commence with a clear *resumé* of the Scriptural narrative with which the text was connected, which enlisted the interest of all, and was most instructive to those who had read their Bible without careful thought. On this would be founded the argument, usually divided into several periods.

Every one was attentive to the forcible closing up of each of these; after which the silence caused by pent-up feeling was relaxed in a momentary outburst of coughs, movements of position, etc.

It is certainly true that the chief attraction at St. John's was the pulpit, and there was nothing in the externals of the church or its services to account for its popularity. The old black gown was the preaching vestment, and a surpliced choir was unheard of; but the service was by no means carelessly rendered. A volume of sound showed that the responses were heartily given, and the fervour of the worshippers was evidence that the preaching really stirred their hearts, as it delighted their ears. Then, as always, my father had the greatest dislike to any negligent ways in the House of God. His own reverence was instinctive and contagious, and no service for which he was responsible could fail to be rendered decently and in order.

The immense number of communicants compelled my father to be one of the first to introduce the early Celebrations of Holy Communion, which have been at once the effect and the cause of much revival of spiritual life.

The elaborate preparation of his sermons, and the growing calls of public duty beyond the limits of his parish, did not mean that the ordinary parochial duties were neglected. The schools were a first claim upon his attention; and the whole parish was mapped out and regularly visited by himself and his curates, as well as by an organised staff of district visitors; while every kind of parochial charity was largely supported by the wealthy laity who were drawn to the church.

One feature at St. John's, which he reproduced in St. Giles's, and which was always very near my father's heart, was a special service for the poor, which he held every Monday night. It was the rule that people should come in their working clothes, and each Monday night the schoolroom was filled with an audience, chiefly of laundresses, to whom he would preach in homely language the Gospel which "the common people" hear as gladly now as when they flocked round the Master Himself in Galilee. My father used sometimes to tell us how people invaded this service for whom it was not intended, and well-to-do parishioners used to try to sit unnoticed amongst their poorer neighbours.

The one subject uppermost in the preaching at St. John's was the everlasting Gospel of our Lord and Saviour Jesus Christ. Then, and throughout his life, my father used to say, that no sermon was worthy of the name which did not contain the message of the Gospel, urging the sinner to be reconciled with God; and he himself never forgot that he spoke as the ambassador of the King of kings, bearing the tidings of pardon to all who knew their need of forgiveness and of peace. Yet this never meant a ceaseless repetition, nor that identical sermons were formed on different texts. The sermons were full of scriptural exegesis, and

were often masterly expositions of great doctrines
of the Trinity, the Incarnation, or the Person and
work of the Holy Spirit. Sometimes, at Clapham,
my father was controversial, and he was by no
means backward to avow an uncompromising hostility to what he thought the deadly errors of the
Roman Church. On the occasion of the Papal
aggression he delivered a series of lectures on the
characteristics of Romanism, which were listened
to with eager interest by very large congregations.
To my father's mind the Papacy was the gigantic
lie which attempts to stand between the soul and
Christ. He thought the whole system dishonouring
to our Blessed Lord as the one Mediator between
God and man. He dreaded what he thought
showed a growing tendency in our own Church
towards similar doctrines, and he was by no means
displeased to be known as a champion of those who
were opposed to the Tractarian Movement. He
had an intense desire to bring each soul into contact with Christ; and though he did not insist on
a sudden, sensible conversion, he taught that a
conscious turning from sin to God was the crisis
of the religious life, and the only true foundation of
future peace and progress. He was very jealous
for the true relation between the processes of justification and sanctification, and felt how great an injury
is done to souls, by trying to build up a holy life
when the right foundation has never been laid in
the surrender of the heart and will to God.

In later days my father fully believed that this
Evangelical doctrine was faithfully taught by many
High Churchmen, and if he was once convinced

that the aim of a ministry was to exalt Jesus only, he had no heart to quarrel with other beliefs and practices widely different from his own.

His strong anti-Roman views led my father to embrace with all his heart the work of the Society for promoting the Irish Church Missions to Roman Catholics.

From his close connection with this work, it may be interesting to give a brief account of the origin of the society, which was founded by a very zealous and able clergyman, the Rev. Alexander Dallas, in the year 1847.

Of course there had previously been efforts to influence Roman Catholics, but up to this date the Irish Church, as such, had not made any effort to grapple with the difficulty of Romanism.

The clergy had been content to minister to their scanty flock, consisting of what the Nationalists call the English garrison and their few dependents. It was a humiliating position for a national religious establishment, which claimed to be the representative of the same Catholic Church as St. Patrick. They had sunk so low as to surrender the past to the Romanists ; and, careless of the fact that Romanism itself had, in many districts, only a slender influence on the morals and civilisation of the people, the Established Church made no adequate effort to preach the Gospel to the poor. Of course their position was one of peculiar difficulty ; and my father clearly stated its extent in the House of Lords, in the course of a speech in which he strongly opposed the disestablishment of the Irish Church. The speech will be found at length in

E

a later chapter of this book, so I will not quote it here.

If my father and his friends had been able, thirty years ago, to fire the Irish clergy with their own evangelistic spirit, the state of Ireland might have been very different to-day. We should have seen a fusion of hostile interests in the love of a common Redeemer, and the Irish Church, instead of meeting with the treatment its apathy had done much to justify, might still have been the cherished heritage of a people at once Catholic and reformed.

The story of the Irish Church Missions, as told by Mr. Dallas, is one of thrilling interest, and some of my father's happiest days were those he spent in company with his honoured friend in visiting the mission stations, and preaching the Gospel of Christ where the utmost spiritual destitution prevailed.

It is only fair to notice, in treating the religious question in Ireland, that the Romanists have been blamed for a state of things which they were powerless to prevent.

In the thinly-populated districts of Connemara, where the people had lapsed into a state of uncivilised barbarism, many were attached to the Roman Church only in name; but it is a strange characteristic of the Roman system, that it retains some sort of hold over the affections of people who are practically untouched by its moral and spiritual teaching. Without charging the Roman clergy with wilfully keeping their nominal adherents in ignorance and superstition, it is no exaggeration to say that they left vast tracts of country untaught.

Surely this left the more responsibility upon the ordained ministers of Christ, who were settled in each parish as teachers of a pure Catholic and reformed faith. These were the men whom Mr. Dallas and my father tried to stimulate to a sense of compassion for the outcast and degraded people amongst whom they lived.

In the course of a lecture delivered in London to the Young Men's Christian Association, at Exeter Hall, in 1852, my father gives a graphic description of the Irish Church Mission work. After showing the method of attack, which was to promote inquiry and bring every doctrine to the touchstone of Holy Scripture, he goes on—

I come, thirdly, to the results, the visible and appreciable results, which have followed from the labours of the society in Ireland. . . . Within four years of the commencement of the work, an impression has been made which has far exceeded the most sanguine expectations of the founders of the Association, aroused the attention of the empire, and wrung from the Romish hierarchy the unwilling admission that their power in Ireland is fast approaching destruction. The reformation, which commenced in Galway, at Castle Kirk, quickly gained ground in various parts in and around that place. Spite of every opposition on the part of Romish priests and those who were influenced by them, the preaching of the missionaries was attended by crowds of eager listeners; the agents found ready access to the cabins of the Romanists, the school-houses became overcrowded by children and adults, thirsting for instruction out of God's Word. A place called Oughterard was soon adopted as a second missionary station; agents of the society were planted there, opposition was kindled; but it issued in the advancement of the truth. . . . Conversions rapidly succeeded each other. The spell of the priest was broken, and the desire for spiritual freedom, then kindled for the first time for ages, was developed in the irresistible determination to shake off the bondage of Romanism.

From thence the reformation proceeded right and left. Clifden, an important town about thirty miles west of Castle Kirk, soon became a rallying place for an extensive district all around. January, 1848, witnessed the first operations of the missionaries in that quarter. In an almost incredibly short space of time 250 children were under regular weekly instruction in the mission schools. The light which had dawned upon Clifden radiated to other villages on every side, till, ere long, the ray fell upon Sellerna, Cleggan, Salruc, Barratrough, Ballyconre, Ballynaboy, Duholla, and Derrygimla.

All Connemara caught the glorious illumination. In each of these places mission schools were established, Protestant services were held ; slaves of Popery, being instructed in the truth of the Gospel, rejoiced to shake off their bondage and embrace the liberty wherewith Christ makes His people free. Within one year from the commencement of the work 401 converts came forward to receive at the hands of the Bishop of Tuam the rite of Confirmation : to a man have these converts remained staunch to the profession which they then made, and forty-six have died rejoicing in Christ Jesus. In September last the Bishop of Tuam again held a tour of Confirmations in the same district, when 712 converts publicly avowed their renunciation of Popery, and their adhesion to the Protestant faith. In one union of parishes in West Galway, where in 1840 there were not more than 500 Protestants, there are now between 5000 and 6000 converts.

In the same district there are 3500 children in daily attendance at the mission schools. The erection of ten new churches for the accommodation of as many congregations has become imperatively needful. . . . So decisive has been the progress of the work, we are able to affirm that a tract of country extending about fifty miles in length from Galway to Omey, and thirty miles in breadth

from Salruc to Inverin, which five years ago was essentially
Popish and ecclesiastically desert, has now become cha-
racteristically convert and Protestant, dotted with churches
and schoolrooms, with a flock gathered by pastors of the
United Church.

Nor is this great work of reformation confined to Galway. It is gradually advancing throughout various other
extensive tracts of country. The flame which was kindled
amid the rocky passes of Connemara soon extended to the
town of Galway; from thence it has reached Limerick,
Belfast, Carlow, Kilkenny, Drogheda, Enniscorthy, and
Wicklow; and it is even now lighting up at this moment
some of the murkiest alleys in Dublin itself. Two thousand
Romanists in that city are visited weekly by the agents of
the Irish Church Mission Society. The lanes and courts
of the metropolis are penetrated by these indefatigable
pioneers of the Gospel. Every Tuesday evening there
meets a class of inquiring Romanists, in a large schoolroom
attached to St. Michan's Church, for the express purpose of
comparing the doctrines of God's Word with the dogmas
of the Church of Rome.

These are no coloured representations. These are no
exaggerated statements. I speak of what I have seen; I
am giving you the facts which I have verified from my own
observation. I have wandered through the desert wilds of
Connemara, I have preached to the poor wretched peasantry there the truths of the everlasting Gospel, and I
have watched with delighted amazement the devouring
eagerness with which they drank in the tidings of the
blessed story of peace. I have seen the hearty and spirit-
catching enthusiasm with which they welcomed the appearance amongst them of the English missionary. I have
heard the young and old, men, women, and children, wake
the mountain echoes with their "Cead mille fealthe!" for
the messengers who came from afar to disenthral them,
by the sword of the Spirit, from the chains which Rome had
forged and fastened. I have examined the children in the
crowded school-houses, where hundreds and hundreds are

packed into the narrowest compass, and never did I witness quicker intelligence, readier apprehension, or a more intimate acquaintance with the facts and the precepts, the promises and the distinguishing doctrines of the Gospel. I have been present at the inquiry classes in Dublin when the avenues of approach were blocked up by the crowds, eager to gain admission to the overthronged room in which the fortress of Romanism in that city is being undermined by the diligent search into the doctrines of God's Word.

It does not come within the scope of this sketch to inquire how far the Irish Church Missions have fulfilled the promise of their opening years. The disestablishment and disendowment of the Irish Church, which have crippled its resources, have in some degree altered the responsibility of that Church towards the Romanists; but still the work of the Irish Church Mission goes forward, not without signs of encouragement; and the friends of the society were cheered by the appointment of Lord Plunket to the archbishopric of Dublin, as one who has always had warm sympathy with its view of the wider obligation of the Irish Church.

I have quoted this passage from my father's speech for two reasons: first, because no one can understand his life and ministry aright without knowing the warm interest he took in this work, and how it reacted on his view of contemporary Church questions at home; and again, because the closing portion is a sample of my father's power as a platform speaker.

During his ministry at Clapham and St. Giles's, much of his spare time was devoted to the deputation of the society in many of the large towns in

England; and it was in this capacity that he first made the acquaintance of some of the Ripon clergy at a meeting held in Bradford in 1856.

No sketch of my father's work at Clapham would be complete without a notice of an institution in which he took the deepest interest. The British Orphan Asylum, which now stands opposite the Great Western Station at Slough, was then located on Clapham Rise, and my father acted as honorary chaplain to it. He used to conduct a service there each Saturday night, giving an address to the children. And in after-days he had frequently the comfort of hearing how gratefully his words of counsel were remembered by those who were thus brought under his influence.

He was never weary of advocating the claims of the Orphanage in London pulpits; and his power of pleading earnestly for charitable purposes, which was so useful in his episcopal work, was discovered and developed in connection with this and similar societies, whose practical philanthropy was so near his heart.

To complete this chapter, perhaps the best idea of what the affection of the Clapham people for my father was, is given in the following letter, written to my mother, when he had the happiness of revisiting St. John's in 1858. He was staying in London, and writes from the House of Lords :—

I had a pleasant day yesterday. In the morning I preached for Burgess, at Chelsea. He is always very kind, and seemed pleased at my preaching for him. There was a very large congregation, several M.P.'s, and, amongst others, the solicitor-general, etc. I preached a written

sermon on the Rainbow, and then made an extempore
appeal for the Charity. Burgess seemed grateful, and said
the case had never been so clearly stated to the congregation before. I came home afterwards, had luncheon, and
remained in my room all the afternoon ; dined between five
and six, and at six I went to Clapham. Somehow I had
not expected a great crowd there, but when I got to
Kennington I soon suspected what it would be. The
people were pouring along the roads in crowds, and, in its
most crowded days of yore, I never saw poor St. John's
fuller. Every seat full ; the aisles, double columns of
people all the way up, and people standing up the middle
aisle. It was a work of time and difficulty to get up the
aisle, and you may imagine what a crushing the lawn
sleeves got ! All my old friends seemed to be there ;
even my old churchwarden Hill was in his old place. . . .
It seemed to me like a dream, so like what it was in
times past. The B.'s were there, Mr. B. in his father's old
place, and all the E.'s. I was very glad I had not a written
sermon. I preached from St. John xiv. 6. They were very
attentive. I think the sermon was nearly fifty minutes,
and we closed with " All hail the power of Jesus' name."
Mr. Beddome came into the vestry afterwards, very affectionate, and much moved by the whole scene. Perhaps
it would not be well to occur often, but it made me feel
what a golden opportunity God gave me in those years of
my life when I was in that sphere. Oh that I had done
more for His glory ! I looked to the old corner where my
heart's treasure used to sit. F. sat in our pew. One could
almost fancy it was old times, and that we had been going
afterwards to our wee house in Bedford Place. . . . I had
a nice note from poor old Miss B., regretting that she
cannot get out to church, and enclosing 10s. for the collection ;—this, by the way, amounted to £37 18s., which
they thought very good for the evening. To-night I have
to preach at Spitalfields, at eight. Indeed, I almost wish
I had a service every night. It seems nearly the only way
in which I can be doing any good in London.

CHAPTER IV.

ST. GILES'S, 1851-1857.

Rector of St. Giles's—Organisation of an overgrown parish—Secular
and sanitary work—Strong views on the connection between the
physical condition of the people and spiritual work—The possibilities of vast improvement—What the Church has done for
London—A sudden diminution of income and providential supply
of temporal wants—Offer of canonry at Salisbury and other preferment—Lay work and district visitors—A controversial class for
inquiring Romanists.

DURING the time of his residence at Clapham my
father received the offer of several other livings,
and amongst them was a very important post in the
diocese of Ripon, the rectory of Richmond. This
was in the gift of his uncle, Lord Langdale, who at
that time was one of the commissioners who held
the Great Seal. The fair country town which stands
so grandly on the banks of the Swale, with its grim
Castle and fine old parish church, was certainly an
attractive spot; but my father had no mind to
exchange his busy life at Clapham, with its manifold
opportunities of external usefulness in London, for
a post of comparative ease. Not long afterwards,
however, he was offered by Lord Truro, who had
succeeded to the vacant Woolsack, the important
rectory of St. Giles-in-the-Fields.

Thirty years ago the duties of the Rector of St. Giles's were formidable enough. The population was about forty thousand, and round about the church there lay a dense mass of pauperism and crime, like a festering sore in the heart of London. It was more like a little missionary diocese than the care of a single parish priest.

The existing spiritual agency for grappling with this great task was wholly inadequate.

One rector, one curate, one Scripture-reader, had been the representatives of the Church's efforts to evangelise and shepherd a flock which needed an immense amount of loving labour if they were to be kept, in any sense, within the fold of Christ.

But this was not all for which the rector of the great town-parish was held responsible; for his energy and strength were taxed by an amount of work which really formed no part of clerical duty. The government of the whole district was in the hands of a select Vestry, of which the rector was *ex-officio* chairman, who, if he was to do his duty, must spend hours of valuable time in considering questions of lighting, paving, and draining a tract of London quite sufficient to form an independent municipality.

It was no wonder my father shrank from such a task; and it was not without a very serious wrench that he left a work so full of happiness, and a congregation so generous and sympathetic, as that of St. John's.

He recalls in his diary a touching scene on the day when he announced to the congregation that he was about to leave them. After the morning service, in response to his invitation, thirteen or fourteen of the leading parishioners met him in the vestry. He told them of his decision. They uttered no reproach, and all felt he was right to accept the post ; but one gentleman expressed the feeling of them all, when he asked my father to unite with them in prayer, that God would send them a faithful minister to fill his place.

The kindness of the people of St. John's was unfailing ; and not content with giving the usual testimonials of their affectionate regret when my father left them, they agreed to provide him with funds to further his work at St. Giles's.

If the years spent at Clapham had drawn out my father's capacity as a preacher, the rectory of St. Giles's afforded scope for talents of a different, and perhaps a higher order. He was by no means content with the comparatively easy task of filling his church, for in London an able preacher is sure of a large congregation ; but he set himself resolutely to face the gigantic problem of how to reach the masses under his care, who were not in the least likely to come to church until the Church had shown its capacity for serving them, and relieving to some extent the hard lot of their daily lives.

And my father began his work in no narrow spirit. Theologically he had little sympathy with the Broad Church party, but he was in substantial practical agreement with those who recognised that the Church had a wider mission than merely to save souls in the world to come.

He gladly availed himself of the right, as chairman of the Vestry, to make himself acquainted with the secular matters that were entrusted to that body. The remarkable business talents he displayed, and his singular grasp of detail, were cultivated and developed by this experience. In later days Yorkshire laymen were often surprised at the aptitude their Bishop showed for deciding problems, with which they not unjustly considered the clergy are generally incompetent to deal; and the secret was the training he had received in the patient discharge of his duty in the Vestry of St. Giles's. In the course of a lecture which he delivered to the Leeds Philosophical Society in 1860, my father showed the robust and practical view he took of the obligations of the Church, and the clergyman's duty towards the squalor and misery of the dense populations and overcrowded dwellings of great towns. He says—

For several years it was my lot, as a parochial clergyman, to live in one of the densely populated metropolitan parishes. The population was little short of forty thousand. A large proportion consisted of the poorest classes. Within the limits of that parish it might have been easy at any time to meet with every type and form of social, moral, and physical degradation. Various practical measures had been adopted with a view to counteract the manifold evils which existed in every direction. Thus we had churches, clergymen, schools, ragged schools, district visitors, Scripture-readers, and city missionaries all in active operation. Other remedial efforts had also been tried, and happily not altogether in vain. The provisions of the Common Lodging Houses Act and the Nuisance Removal Act were, so far as practicable, enforced. Baths and wash-houses were also erected, from which great good resulted; and yet, in spite of all these efforts, it was too painfully evident that there still remained a dense mass of the population unreached and unbenefited—a multitude of our fellow-parishioners, fellow-immortals, upon whom all attempts for their social or moral amelioration were apparently so much wasted energy.

It was their physical condition, as to the wretched dwellings in which they lived, which paralysed the action of the clergyman, the schoolmaster, the Scripture-reader, and the city missionary. Till this was remedied I could see little prospect of permanent benefit. We must cease to do evil, that we may learn to do well. Mind and matter are closely connected ; and the moral constitution, like the mental, may be elevated and depressed according to the material influences to which it is constantly exposed.

He goes on to urge the importance of studying the actual condition of the masses in the provincial towns, no less than in London. Now that the housing of the poor and the condition of the people is the question of the hour, no excuse is needed for these rather lengthy extracts ; which are given in the hope that they may quicken the zeal of clergy and laity alike in the discharge of a very important part of their duty.

In describing the class of persons with whom he had to deal, my father says—

The district is composed mainly of those who reside in narrow alleys, courts, and lanes, closely packed together in houses ill-ventilated, with no adequate provision for the access of air or light—two of the most important requisites for the preservation of health, — badly drained, with no adequate supply of water, no arrangements for securing domestic privacy, or that separation of the sexes which a regard to the first principles of morality demands ; a class amongst whom you meet with persons who seem utterly devoid of all moral sense ; in whom conscience is seared ; who live in defiance alike of religious control or obligation ; to whom all days are alike ; in whose creed theft is no crime, immorality no disgrace, intemperance no reproach ; who know nothing of self-control or self-respect ; who see nothing degrading in falsehood, and whose standard of superiority is dexterity in crime ; persons who never use the Name of God but to blaspheme ; who are as ignorant of Christianity as if their lot had been amongst the unevangelised heathen ; who regard the distinctions of society as simply a combination of the rich to oppress the poor ; whose only regard to the law is inspired by some lingering dread of its penalties, and of whom, as regards their moral condition, the description which an inspired Apostle gave of the Gentile population is strictly accurate—" They have no hope, and are without God in the world."

All this may appear exaggerated ; but I venture to affirm it will appear so to none who will be at the pains to investigate for themselves.

Of course it is not intended that all these features of moral debasement are presented alike in every member of the class to which the description applies; but of its general accuracy, I scarcely believe that any one who is qualified by experience to give an opinion will for a moment doubt.

In the course of the same paper there follow statistics to show the overcrowded condition of the Metropolis at large, which are no longer interesting, as, in spite of much recent improvement, there are facts equally distressing still before our minds ; but some figures with regard to the parish of St. Giles's show the nature of the work my father undertook.

" In one street," he says, " there were thirteen houses in a row, containing a population of 1300, or an average of one hundred to each house. In another lane in the same parish, there were thirty-two houses, containing in all 190 rooms. Till the provisions of the Common Lodging Houses Act were enforced, the number of persons inhabiting those thirty-two houses was 1710. The average number

living and sleeping in each room was *nine*, but in many of
the rooms the number was nearly twice as great. In a
Return which was printed by order of the House of Com-
mons in 1851, it is stated by Mr. Grainger, that he found
in a certain street as many as eighteen or twenty persons
living in one room. There is a place in the parish of St.
Giles-in-the-Fields called Short's Gardens. A man hired
a house in that quarter, for which he was to pay £1 a
week. He immediately sub-let one of the rooms for 12*s.*
to one set of lodgers, who used it by day, and to another
set of lodgers for 12*s.* a week, who used it by night, thus
realising by the sub-letting of one room more than he paid
for the whole house."

There follows a forcible statement of the direct
connection between this state of things and the
prevalence of epidemic disease ; for my father's mind
used often to revert to its early medical bias ; and
while he was labouring to be a true physician of the
soul, he never forgot that it is of the essence of
Christlike work to labour for the "redemption of
the body."

He gives an instance, drawn from his own
observation, of the fearful contagion of vice :—

The father of the family, up to the time of his death,
was a practical thief ; the eldest daughter lived on the
wages of infamy ; the eldest son was a convict under
sentence of transportation for fourteen years. The second
brother was also a convict under sentence of transportation.
The third brother, who, at the time of which I speak, was
only nineteen years of age, had been a thief for five years,
and in prison eight times. Imagine the cost of such a
family to the country. It is said that every prisoner costs,
while in prison, at the rate of from £40 to £50 a year.
The Pentonville prison alone costs £100,000 a year. At
a reformatory institution which I occasionally visited in

London, there were at one time one hundred inmates. The amount of money which had been stolen by these men, as proved by evidence, was not less than £76,400. The aggregate number of years spent in prison had been one hundred and eighty; and the expense incurred through their imprisonment was computed at £4500. Thus the crime of these one hundred men had cost the public and the country at the lowest estimate £80,900.

Now, if there were only a faint probability that the physical condition of the people could have anything to do with the several points to which I have alluded—public health or sickness, the crime of intemperance, or the immorality of the community—it would be a case demanding investigation; but when it is morally certain that the health of the whole population is endangered, that crime of every sort, drunkenness, and immorality, are fostered by this cause, surely it is a matter which ought to engage the attention of the wise and good, of politicians, philosophers, magistrates, ministers of religion, of all who have a heart to feel or any influence to exert.

These fearful pictures of misery and crime would be enough to drive one mad, were it not for the practical results which can be shown to have attended the efforts made to combine sanitary and social improvements with the all-powerful instrument of the Gospel of Christ.

My father insists in conclusion—

It is no unreal or unattainable result to which we may look forward—the converting the dwellings of the millions into dwellings where morality and peace and contentment and godliness may abide.

I have seen, in courts that were once the receptacle of all that was materially abominable and morally vile, this amazing transformation; a transformation, moreover, effected at a comparatively small cost, and that outlay actually remunerative.

Thank God, there is to-day a widespread zeal for the cause of God and the poor, in London and other large towns, that has never been surpassed, and the bitter cry of outcast London has reached the hearts of many who were long careless of the needs of those less fortunate than themselves; but in days of new-born enthusiasm it is well to recollect that there has been for many years a steady, and on the whole successful, effort put forward by the Church. If the Gospel of Christ has not expelled the glaring sins of our great cities, at least the salt has been thrown in which has hindered London from perishing in one mass of corruption. And the record of all honest effort, whether of a Lowder at St. Peter's, London Docks, or of work like that of St. Giles's and many another London church, is as full of hope as it is full of inspiration.

Before attempting to give some account of the parochial work at St. Giles's, and of the organisation my father was enabled to set on foot, we must refer to an incident which greatly affected my father's future career. It is best told in his own words :—

About the year 1854 what at the first appeared a calamity befell me. An Act of Parliament had been passed by the Government for putting an end to intramural interments, and under the provisions of the act the cemetery belonging to St. Giles's, from which the greater part of the rectorial income was derived, was closed. No compensation whatever was provided, and the income of the rectory was suddenly diminished from at least £1400 to about £400 a year, a sum upon which it was impossible to maintain the position. I wish here to record the goodness of God more especially displayed in answer to prayer. Within a few weeks of its becoming generally known what a loss I had

F

sustained, I received from Mr. Courthope (a gentleman with whom I had not the least personal acquaintance) the offer of the living of Brenchley, in Kent. It was a valuable living in a beautiful part of the country, near to Tunbridge Wells. Mr. Courthope made the offer in a most generous way, expressing his readiness to do anything towards enlarging the house if I wished it.

There was much about the proposal which appeared at first sight to make it my duty to accept the appointment. On the other hand, the vast population of St. Giles's and the fact that the blessing of God was apparently resting on my ministry, made me most unwilling to leave. Accordingly, I thanked Mr. Courthope gratefully for his offer, and requested a fortnight's time for consideration. In the mean time my beloved wife and myself made it a matter of constant daily prayer that it would please God to show us His Will in the matter.

In the course of a few days a leading publisher in London called upon me, to ask if I would undertake the nominal editorship of a biographical series which he was about to bring out, and which he wished to connect with the name of some well-known clergyman. The salary he offered was £300 a year, certainly for five years and possibly for much longer. I could not but regard this as an indication of Providence that my wants would be graciously provided for; but still it did not plainly follow that I was to go into the country, although, under one point of view, it might be thought that a country living would afford more leisure for literary employment. We still continued our prayer that God would show us what to do, and strange to relate, the same week a gentleman called upon me from the committee of the Foundling Hospital, to offer me the Sunday afternoon Lectureship of that Institution.

The income arising from the two offers thus mentioned would have enabled me to retain my position in St. Giles's, although at the risk of being somewhat overworked. My mind was made up at once, and within an hour of my receiving the offer of the Foundling I wrote to Mr.

Courthope, declining the offer of Brenchley, and announced to him my intention of remaining in St. Giles's.

This being decided, my first impulse was to go and see my dear friend, Mr. Montagu Villiers (afterwards Bishop of Carlisle), who had taken a warm interest in the whole matter. He expressed his unqualified gratification with the decision at which I had arrived. My interview with him lasted only a few minutes, and I returned to my house in Gower Street. In the brief interval since I left I found that Sir Culling Eardley had called, and left a message to the effect that he was leaving town, but wished to see me before doing so. His carriage was at the door to convey me down to Adam Street, Adelphi, where he had gone. I immediately went thither, and my surprise and thankfulness may be imagined, when he told me that his object in wishing to see me was to convey a message from the Lord Chancellor (then Lord Cranworth) that the Government had determined to appoint me to a canonry in Salisbury, then vacant by the appointment of Dr. Hamilton to the bishopric of that city. There was a degree of uncertainty whether the appointment was vested in the Prime Minister (then Lord Aberdeen) or the Lord Chancellor; but in either case the canonry was to be mine. Such was the unexpected relief which, in the Providence of God, set my mind free from all anxiety with regard to my stay at St. Giles's.

I declined the Preachership at the Foundling, and resolved to devote all my energies to the work in St. Giles's and the duties connected with my new office in Salisbury.

The canonry at Salisbury set my father free from pecuniary anxiety, and enabled him to devote his undivided attention to the cure of St. Giles's. The details of the work are full of interest, but are not very different from the system of parochial work now happily general; it should, however, be borne in mind that the best specimens of parish work to-day are seen in parishes where the population is, at most, not greater than 10,000 or 12,000.

My father carried with him to St. Giles's the ideal of being in a real sense the shepherd and overseer of the 37,000 souls committed to his care. The Evangelical tradition which he had learned at Acton was to bring the parish priest, if possible, into direct contact with each family. At St. Giles's, then, he did not set himself to evangelise a small fraction of the whole, but at once set on foot a complete system of house to house visitation.

The number of clergy working in the parish towards the close of my father's incumbency was seven. The whole parish was mapped out into districts, and a staff of no less than eleven Scripture-readers and city missionaries were paid exclusively for spiritual work amongst the poor and destitute classes. Each reader was personally responsible to the rector, and was summoned to meet him every fortnight in the vestry. As often as possible the rector would accompany the readers into the worst parts of the parish, and so become familiar with every class of his parishioners. In the course of his annual report in 1856, he justifies this method to those of his parishioners who were doubtful of the value of such lay ministrations. He says—

At the first, I believe, there was a misgiving as to its probable results. Some thought that the employment of lay agents to read the Scriptures to the poor and to visit from house to house, might insensibly have the effect of weakening their attachment to the Church. Five years' experience of the working of the agency in the parish ought to have scattered their objections to the winds. So far from weakening their attachment to the Church, this agency has kindled an attachment where it never existed before, and only confirmed it when it did ; it has given practical evidence to the poor of the sympathy which is felt for their spiritual wants, on the part of those who love the Lord Jesus Christ. In very many cases it has led the careless and the unconverted to inquire and seek after the things which belong to their peace. The visits of these agents are purely of a spiritual character ; they go to the poor in no other capacity and on no other errand than as messengers of the Gospel. There is nothing to make their visits attractive but the simple fact that they are for a spiritual object, to read the Word of God, and point out the way of salvation through faith in Jesus. And yet it would be impossible to find a body of men whose visits are more welcome or whose labours are more successful.

It has been my privilege repeatedly to go with them (though not so often by far as I could have wished), and I have witnessed the cheerfulness with which they are welcomed, even in some places where, a few years ago, when their work was less understood or appreciated, they would have met with insult or repulse. Of all agencies for the spiritual good of the parish, there is not any which exceeds in value that of the Scripture-reader and city missionary. But for the employment of this agency it would be utterly impossible to bring the dense masses of our poor under systematic visitation ; as it is there is no portion of the parish (I allude, of course, to those parts of the parish which are inhabited by the poorer classes) which is not included within some district assigned to one or another of our lay agents.

It was of the essence of this scheme that the ministrations of Scripture-readers should be of a purely spiritual character, while the alms of the Church for the relief of temporal distress were administered through a separate organisation. A number of ladies devoted almost their whole time, and worked with the same devotion as the members of Sisterhoods and Deaconess institutions who now form so important a part of the Church's ministry. In later days my father was deeply sensible of the value to the Church of those who, for the love of Christ, would sacrifice family ties and live wholly amongst the poor.   Jealously as he watched the obvious danger of our Anglican Sisterhoods in their threatened approach to the Roman model, he had the heartiest appreciation for the devout spirit and consecrated lives of some whom he knew as Sisters of Charity.[1]   But his own feeling was, I think, far more in favour of the system which sends a lady fresh from the purifying influence of a Christian home, to carry with her into the poor man's cottage the idea of the home life at Nazareth, or the family at Bethany, where Jesus lodged with Martha, and Mary, and Lazarus.

This thought is expressed in words which drew their inspiration from the singular gladness of his own home life, and form part of the address on the physical condition of the people which has been largely quoted above :—

Let the poor learn that there is a sympathy felt for them amongst the classes which, in social rank, are above them.   Encourage, by all means, neatness, order, and cleanliness in the cottages of the poor.   Let all, as far as they have the ability, strive to make the dwellings of the poor really habitable ; worthy, in every sense, of that musical word, "home."   What a thousand hallowing associations belong to that one word !   Which of us has not felt

---

[1] My father willingly accepted the office of Visitor to the Sisterhood established at Horbury, in his own diocese.

its endearing, ennobling, purifying influence? Alas! that in this Christian land there should be so many tens of thousands to whom that word *home* brings no recollection of parental love; no sweet remembrance of happy hours spent under one roof, sheltering fond and united hearts, happy in each other's love; no sanctifying memories of solemn seasons, when, morning by morning and evening hy evening, the family group gathered round the family altar in supplication and praise to the God and Father of us all.

Of the various parochial works an authentic record remains in the annual statements which were circulated by the rector each year. A map of the district, showing how each part was allotted to one of the Scripture-readers or members of the district visiting society, is evidence of the care with which the whole was superintended; and the subscription lists show how heartily the congregation attending the church supported the various works for the amelioration of the condition of their poorer neighbours.

It appears from the report for 1856 that the district visiting society had in the previous year expended £513, most of which was distributed in kind, and money was only given directly in some urgent cases. Over and above this, upwards of £110 was spent on a maternity charity managed by Mrs. Bickersteth, and at the same time £250 was raised by voluntary subscriptions for the National Schools. Nor did these charities begin and end at home. My father was an enthusiastic supporter of the Ragged Schools so justly connected with the great name of Lord Shaftesbury, and for this object, in the year 1855, a sum of £702 was remitted by the congregation of St. Giles's.

In the last year of his stay in London the contributions towards the Church Missionary Society had reached £76, and to the Irish Church Missions £123.

The offertories in church were always exceedingly liberal, and £60, £70, or £80 were often raised by what in those days was termed a Charity Sermon. Amongst the great variety of classes and institutions to which allusion is made in the annual report, appears one which forms an unusual feature. Each Tuesday night a controversial class for inquiring Romanists was held in the vestry. In 1855 the rector was able to report—

The controversial class for Romanists continues to be well attended. Many cases of conversion have occurred in the course of the past year, in which there is reason to believe there has been not only a turning from the errors and superstitions of Romanism, but also a real turning of the heart to God.

Many people are inclined to think that a clergyman in charge of a vast town population is entitled to wipe off all responsibility for a large section of his parishioners, if he can comfort himself with the assurance that they are sufficiently cared for by the Roman priesthood; but if it be the business of a clergyman to reclaim those who are wandering from the Church in the direction of Protestant Dissent, it must be no less a duty to do what in him lies to recover those who, though nominally adherents of the Bishop of Rome, are often the most degraded and the most spiritually destitute of the souls committed to his care.

A candid critic of the parochial system at St.

Giles's is drawn to the conclusion that the " Contro-versial Class for Romanists " is evidence, not so much of the rector's Protestant bias, as of his effort to leave no section of his parishioners beyond the reach of the Gospel he was commissioned to offer to all alike.

Behind this varied organisation there lay a depth of spiritual work of which it is difficult to speak. Neither crowded congregations nor numbers of communicants thronging the Holy Table are a trustworthy indication of the life of God energising Christian hearts. No one shrank more than the Rector of St. Giles's from the thought that any out-ward sign could adequately describe the operation of the Holy Spirit, Who worketh where He will. From year to year he could tell of an ever-increasing body of communicants, and the church had con-stantly to be expanded to receive the congregations eager to hear sermons whose principal charm lay in the simplicity and earnestness of the way in which the preacher sought to exalt the saving Name of Jesus.

In a farewell Address my father gives a table showing the acts of Communion of the five preceding years, as follows :—

1852	1853	1854	1855	1856
2885	3387	3670	4128	4289

One gets nearer to the subtle charm of a real spiritual influence, when one reads the recollec-tions of those who date strong and undying convictions from words spoken in St. Giles's thirty years ago.

One who first began to work in the district visiting society in 1856, and still carries on in a little mission chapel in Short's Gardens—a work of self-denying charity which God has greatly blessed—wrote shortly after my father entered into rest—

Well do I remember in the autumn of 1851, when the Rev. J. Endell Tyler, Rector of St. Giles's for twenty-five years, died (after having been laid aside for two years from active work), the anxiety and excitement felt throughout the parish as to whom his successor would be. When we heard the living had been offered to, and accepted by the Rev. Robert Bickersteth, of St. John's, Clapham, the name prepared us to welcome and honour him; and when he appeared and preached his first sermon all our favourable expectations were confirmed. He commenced his ministry on New Year's Day, 1852, and his first sermon on Ps. xxxvii. 5 is still graven on our memories. The holy expression of his face, with his genial manner and never varying kindness, soon won the affection and confidence of his parishioners. Of course he found the parish (after being so long without a head) somewhat out of order, but he soon reorganised it; and during the five short, happy years of his ministry in St. Giles's he was "instant in season and out of season," and did more than most would have accomplished in ten years.

One of his first appeals was for district visitors, and very soon he had eight ladies hard at work; he also obtained a staff of Scripture-readers, in addition to the city missionaries at work in the parish. One of these, Mr. Huston, carried on his work for at least twenty-five years, and was looked up to and respected as a father by the poor in St. Giles's. He only retired when his health completely gave way. Now he also "rests from his labours, but his works do follow him."

Mr. Bickersteth put the Sunday and day schools on a new footing. He always opened the Sunday school himself, and soon gathered a large staff of able, willing teachers, who still look back with pleasure to the monthly meetings for preparation. The fine old church ere long was crowded with attentive listeners; his preaching was so simple, earnest, and loving. In every sermon the whole scheme of the Gospel was unfolded and pressed home to the hearts and consciences of the hearers. On Whitsundays he preached an annual sermon to young men, and on those evenings there was scarcely standing room in the church; the pulpit stairs were full, many standing outside the doors and half-way down the gallery stairs. His Bible class for ladies, held in his own house once a fortnight, was greatly valued and regularly attended. We have notes of all, and frequently, when teaching others, refer to, and are helped by them. On Monday evening the minister of Christ Church, Endell Street, Mr. Swaine, placed his church at his disposal for a special service for the poor, who most thoroughly appreciated their privilege. Hundreds thronged in, and truly "to the poor the Gospel was preached," with very blessed results to many. He also had meetings of the "Labourers' Friendly Society," to try and improve the dwellings of the poor.

During the five years he was in St. Giles's he relighted the church, rearranged the pews, greatly increasing the accommodation, and almost rebuilt the organ at a considerable cost; the funds came in quickly and cheerfully, no debt incurred. When the canonry of Salisbury was accepted by him all his parishioners were heartily pleased; but when the announcement suddenly came that he was appointed to the bishopric of Ripon, and St. Giles's was to lose the rector so greatly beloved, it was an effort to be able to rejoice; and the next few weeks were very sad and trying to those about to be parted from one to whom they owed so much. His farewell sermon was on S. Jude 24, 25.

One of the last of his evening sermons, which made a great impression on us, was on the text, "Blessed are they that are called to the marriage supper of the Lamb ; " and many of those who listened to it are now with him in the presence of the Lamb, and know what that blessedness is. Our dear Bishop of Ripon did not forget his friends in St. Giles's, but was ever ready to help them. When I began a "Mother's Meeting" in 1866, and wrote to him on the subject, with his wonted generosity and kindness he at once promised an annual subscription, which was continued to the last ; and on one occasion he came to the mission room and gave a beautiful address to eighty mothers, who gave a hearty welcome to their former loved Rector whom they gratefully remembered. During the London Mission in 1874 he occupied his old pulpit on two Sunday mornings, besides giving addresses in the afternoons to the children in the school.

Almost the last time I had the pleasure and privilege of speaking to him was at Tunbridge Wells, in June, 1879. I had gone there with my dear sister, then in the first stage of her last illness. To my great joy and surprise, the day after our arrival I met our dear Bishop, who had come on a visit to some friends for a few days. He welcomed me with his usual hearty kindness, came the next day and paid us a long visit, and then proposed coming on Sunday after-noon to read the service for my sister. She was deeply touched with such thoughtful kindness, and looked eagerly forward to the promised treat ; and though it was a cold, wet afternoon, and he was then in failing health, he ap-peared at the appointed time ; and a very happy, blessed hour we spent together, the lesson being 1 S. Peter i. As he read it we recalled the happy hours spent at the Bible classes more than twenty years before, when he explained the meaning of each verse. My dear sister often referred with gratitude and pleasure to that Sunday afternoon during her long and suffering illness.

There are few left in St. Giles's who knew him ; but there are *many* who will be his "joy and crown of rejoicing in the day of our Lord's appearing" to "count up His jewels."

I must add that God in His great goodness sent to St. Giles's one[1] who carried on all that he had begun, and continued to build on the foundation he had laid. "One soweth and another reapeth, that both he that soweth and he that reapeth may rejoice together."

C. G. H.

[1] My father's successor at St. Giles's was the Rev. A. W. Thorold, now Lord Bishop of Rochester.

CHAPTER V.

Residence at Salisbury—Intercourse with Bishop Hamilton—Strict attention to cathedral duties — Correspondence with Bishop Hamilton—Bible Society, etc.—Narrative of the way in which my father received the offer of Ripon—Palmerstonian bishops —Bishop Ryan's summary of Providential preparation for the episcopate.

THERE is a twofold interest about my father's residence at Salisbury ; for not only was an intimate acquaintance with the working of the cathedral system a part of the Providential preparation for the episcopate, but it brought him into close contact, perhaps for the first time, with a very able and very attractive representative of the High Church party.

The canonry had made it possible for him to remain in St. Giles's in spite of diminished income, and a sojourn for three months in that beautiful country sent him back refreshed in mind and body for his arduous work in London.

Happily, now there is a growing feeling that it is time to revert to the old ideal of the cathedral system, in which the canons are engaged exclusively in diocesan work ; but the income of a canonry was well spent when it enabled a man without large private means to hold elsewhere a post of great importance, which otherwise he would have been obliged to resign.

My father's conception of the duties of a canon during his term of residence was very strict, and nothing was deemed a sufficient excuse for absence from the daily services. Even when his father lay very ill at Sapcote, it was a great surprise to the family that the Canon of Salisbury could tear himself away from his cathedral engagements. When in residence, my father used to preach every Sunday afternoon in the cathedral, and he was always ready to preach in the surrounding churches on Sunday nights.

In the cathedral services he found a source of keen enjoyment, and though his experience had lain rather amongst those whose ideal of worship is a hearty service and congregational hymnody, he could thoroughly appreciate the same devotional rendering of the Liturgy which had charmed George Herbert after his walks across the Plain from Bemerton.

My father's intercourse with the saintly Bishop Hamilton demands more than a passing word. Attached by training and inclination to widely different schools of thought, both Bishop and Canon were united by the highest of all bonds, in devotion to their common Lord ; and if it was an edifying sight to notice the Bishop's gladdened expression, and hear his ungrudging words of pleasure as his people flocked in unexampled numbers to hear the new canon's simple pleadings for Christ, it is no less touching to observe the ready deference which the latter was well content to pay to his Father in God.

There is an interesting correspondence between my father and Bishop Hamilton, which illustrates the submission to episcopal authority of the one, and the true Christian courtesy of the other. Then, as always, my father was a warm advocate of the Bible Society and the Irish Church Missions to Roman Catholics. In the eyes of not a few churchmen these societies had fallen into disrepute, because their advocates seemed to disparage Church order, and their operations had unhappily engendered strife. Bishop Hamilton had expressed a strong opinion on the unwisdom of some of their methods ; hence this letter :—

The Close, July 23, 1855.

Dear Lord Bishop,—Will you pardon me for troubling you with one line relative to the conversation which I had with you this morning ? I am most anxious to refrain from anything which might be painful to you, or have even the appearance of a want of deference to your wishes.

After the strong opinion which your Lordship has expressed, relative to the Irish Church Missions, I can take no part in any public meeting for that Society in this place.

But the point upon which I desire to be clear is this : I understand that the annual meetings for the Bible and Church Pastoral Aid Societies are to take place in Salisbury in the course of the ensuing month. Under ordinary circumstances I should attend those meetings as a matter of course, as I did last year. But it would be a great relief to my mind to be assured that you will not consider me as acting contrary to your wishes in doing so ; for if this is your feeling, I shall endeavour to believe that

the cause of Christ will be better promoted by my re-
fraining from taking any part in these meetings.

Believe me to remain, dear Lord Bishop,

Very faithfully yours,

R. BICKERSTETH.

The Bishop replied—

Palace, Sarum, July 24, 1855.

Dear Canon Bickersteth,—I have just received your
considerate and Christian letter. I am, believe me, fully
aware of the difficulties of the whole question ; and as
the bishops are not agreed together, we can hardly expect
the clergy to act differently.

That it is an enormous evil that meetings should be
held for circulating God's most blessed Book, and for providing destitute parishes with the means of grace, and that
yet principles should be involved in these works which separate the clergy and laity from their bishops, and from one
another, I cannot doubt. But perhaps the things said at
such meetings, not only by our lay brethren, but constantly
by the clergy, are still more mischievous.

But pray do not let anything I said to you in free conversation be an unfair shackle to you, for I am not prepared
to lay down any definite rule about these matters.

I will certainly do what I can to prevent intrusion into
the parishes of clergy who disapprove of particular societies,
but I see not my way further. Pray, I must repeat it, be
assured I shall be always ready to enter upon any question
with you in a most friendly spirit.

Yours very truly,

W. K. SARUM.

Another letter, two years later, after my father
removed from Salisbury, shows how their mutual
regard ripened into a relation of warm personal
affection. Bishop Hamilton had occasion to write
upon a matter of business, and ended—

G

I am writing this note at my old desk.[1]   It recalls to my mind much duty and much happiness in former days, and will, I trust, not only be a memorial of our relations to one another here, which have been full of pleasure, and not, I trust, without profit to me, but will constantly remind me to do for you, as, I trust, you will be able sometimes to do for me, and assist me with your prayers.

With affectionate remembrances to Mrs. Bickersteth, and with all hearty good wishes,

I remain, my dear Bishop,

Your sincerely and affectionately,

W. K. SARUM.

March 21, 1857.

The three months' residence at Salisbury in the glorious summer weather was always a very happy time.   The roomy house, in which my father was able to entertain a number of relatives and friends, stood, like the Deanery and other ecclesiastical residences, in the beautiful Close, in a garden which stretched down to the river.   His immediate predecessor in the tenure of both house and canonry had been Bishop Hamilton himself, and it would be difficult to say whether the constant visits of the Bishop and his family to their old house gave more pleasure to them or to its new occupants.

By a curious coincidence, this one house was the temporary residence of three bishops in succession; for my father, who succeeded Bishop Hamilton, was in turn followed by Canon Waldegrave, who, after holding the canonry for three years, the same period as each of his immediate predecessors, was appointed to the See of Carlisle.   My father had much friendly

---

[1] This desk was a piece of furniture which had stood in the house occupied by Bishop Hamilton and my father in succession, as Canons of Salisbury.

intercourse with Mr. Waldegrave during his residence at Salisbury; and he thus had for near
neighbours in the Northern Province two bishops
with whom he had been closely associated in London
and Salisbury work, Bishop Villiers and Bishop
Waldegrave.

My father busied himself in Salisbury affairs;
took an active interest in the Training College, and
preached frequently for neighbouring clergy; but
still it was a time of comparative rest, and the diary
he kept mentions pleasant drives and evenings spent
in playing "with the chicks," an occupation very
delightful to him and to them, for which there was
no leisure in London.

One great trouble overshadowed the second year
of his residence at Salisbury—the death of his father,
who had paid him a visit at Salisbury, and greatly
rejoiced in his son's growing usefulness and ministerial success.

But in September, 1855, the latter was called to
his rest, after a few weeks' illness. He had been
tenderly nursed by his children and by my mother,
whom he always regarded as his own daughter, and
my father was able to be with him at the last.

He notes in his diary on September 2—

This day, at 3.45 in the morning, my beloved father
passed away! Oh that it may be henceforth my constant
aim, in dependence on the grace of the Holy Spirit, to follow
him as he followed Christ. Wrote a number of letters this
morning; walked a little in the garden. Very, very sad.
May God bless and comfort us, and sanctify this grievous
trial.

The intensity of his family affection was one of

the most marked features in my dear father's character; and the complete sympathy in all their work between his father and himself, made the bereavement a far heavier trial than it is to most men to lose a parent who has fulfilled the allotted span of life.

Before passing from Salisbury it should be noticed that my father was elected Proctor for the Chapter in the Convocation of Canterbury (of which his brother Edward, then Archdeacon of Bucks and Vicar of Aylesbury, shortly afterwards became the Prolocutor), and that he held the office of Treasurer of the Cathedral.

It was at Salisbury also that my father made the acquaintance of another who became very highly distinguished on the Episcopal Bench. The Rev. James Fraser wrote to him in 1870 to announce his nomination to the See of Manchester; and after saying, with characteristic modesty, how he shrank from the office, adds—

I believe a bishop elect has the privilege of choosing the bishops who will present him at his consecration. The Bishop of Chester (Dr. Jacobson), who is an old Oxford friend, has promised to act as one, and I thought I should like to ask you, on the strength of the acquaintance we formed at Salisbury, and out of the respect I have for your character, to be the other. Will you grant me this favour?

It is best to tell in his own words the story of my father's appointment to the bishopric of Ripon, of which he received the offer on November 27, 1856. He wrote—

I was hardly aware of the fact that the See was vacant, so little attention did I pay at that time to such ecclesiastical events. It was brought to my knowledge in a singular way. For some time past I had been Honorary Secretary of the Society for Irish Church Missions to Roman Catholics, and had taken a warm interest in that society. Certain difficulties in the working of the Bradford Associations led the committee to ask me to go down to Bradford to preach for the society, and to attend the annual meeting. I was received in Bradford with great hospitality by Mr. Hollings, and a large number of clergy met me at his house in the evening. Almost before anything else was said, they asked me if I could tell them who was to be their new bishop. I could tell them nothing. It was their question which first brought to my knowledge the fact that the Ripon diocese was vacant, and that Bradford was one of its principal towns. I preached the same evening in St. Andrew's Church for the Irish Church Missions, and spoke at the meeting on the following day. I then returned to London; and two or three days later, while sitting alone with my wife, a messenger arrived, bearing a letter from Lord Palmerston, in which he stated that he was authorised by the Queen to offer me the See of Ripon.

The private journal for that evening notes: " Committed myself in prayer with B. to God. Oh, how unworthy am I ! "

My father called on Lord Palmerston the following morning and accepted the offer.

An apocryphal story was for a time current in certain quarters where my father's appointment was viewed with disfavour, that Lord Palmerston, who was advised in the distribution of his ecclesiastical patronage by Lord Shaftesbury, made some confusion between his uncle and himself; but for this there was absolutely no foundation, for the Rector of St. Giles's and Canon of Salisbury had a personality quite sufficiently distinct to be known even

to one so little versed in ecclesiastical affairs as Lord
Palmerston; and the Rev. Edward Bickersteth, of
Watton, had died six years before.

At that time there had been a quick succession
of changes on the Episcopal Bench, and Lord
Palmerston had appointed a considerable number
of so-called Evangelical bishops. The group of
Palmerstonian bishops included, however, men
differing as widely as Samuel Waldegrave of Carlisle, and Archibald Campbell Tait; and those who
are most opposed to the party principles of the
Evangelical bishops, will generally admit that Lord
Palmerston was well advised in appointing men
who were chiefly eminent as parish priests.

The days of " Greek Play Bishops " were over,
and the times demanded something more than a
dignified prelate with a large store of theological
learning, but removed equally from the clergy and
the people.

Happily there are still upon the Bench men
who represent the highest culture and the soundest
learning, whose solid theological work is the glory
of the English Church, and the bulwark of the Faith
in conflict with unbelief all over Christendom; but
the credit is due to Lord Palmerston of having
sought to appoint the practical, working bishops,
who have been so singularly successful in infusing
into the clergy their own energy and spiritual force;
and it is the work of men like these which has
restored the office of a bishop to so high a place in
popular esteem.

A clergyman, who was at Cambridge at the
time, writes that the episcopal appointments of Lord

Palmerston in 1856–57 caused great excitement in the University :—

The idea of Evangelical principles having authority in the Church seemed, to the profound theologians who thronged the college halls, the height of absurdity. The appointment of Mr. Bickersteth was the occasion of a manifestation of great bitterness and wrath. When it was known that the new Bishop of Ripon was to be the University preacher in that year (1857), much curiosity was roused. It is only just to say that a vast amount of the dislike of Evangelicals then shown, arose from sheer ignorance, and from creating ideals of men and opinions which had very limited, if any, existence.

The undergraduates who favoured the new appointments had a hard time of it; and were subjected to unceasing ridicule and ironical comment.

I shall not easily forget the total change in the situation brought by the Bishop's first University sermon. It was on Advent Sunday. St. Mary's was crowded in every part. The personal appearance of the Bishop, and his remarkably dignified manner, did not fail from the first to produce a favourable impression. He preached from Rev. i. 7 : " Behold, He cometh with clouds ; and every eye shall see Him," etc. The sermon was listened to with riveted attention ; so different from an ordinary University sermon ! It was a thrilling and eloquent statement of the certainty and nature of Christ's second coming, and of the rapid completion of the world's story. Towards the close he vividly depicted the different states and conditions in which men would be found at that Advent, and the joy or consternation which must ensue. Evidently a profound impression was made on all present. In the hall of my own college that evening the difference was marked. A reverential tone prevailed ; and from that day I *never* heard anything in Cambridge but praise of the Bishop of Ripon, and hearty appreciation of his after-words in the University church.

To leave St. Giles's was a serious wrench, for the work was one in which my father was associated with many valued personal friends; and the ties between the pastor and his flock were of the same affectionate character as those which had rendered the separation from St. John's so painful only five years before.

There were, of course, many outward tokens of regard; but no personal gift was more valued than the portrait of my mother, by George Richmond, which was given by the members of the Bible class.

In Yorkshire my father was welcomed with the utmost kindness by Archbishop Musgrave, and his first visits to Ripon were made from Bishopthorpe, and from Richmond Rectory, the home of his brother-in-law, the Rev. Lawrence Ottley.

This brings to a close the sketch of my father's life, up to the time of his consecration; and I must leave for a new chapter a review of the diocese at the time when my father was consecrated second Bishop of Ripon, in the parish church of Bishop-thorpe, on January 18, 1857.

But here should be noticed a point which was well drawn out by Bishop Ryan, in a sermon preached in Ripon Cathedral, on the Sunday following my father's death. He showed how remarkable was the Providential preparation by which my father was trained for the duties of a bishop. The influence of his father's saintly character in the quiet home at Acton; the successive curacies of Sapcote, Reading, and Clapham; the varieties of parish work afforded by the widely different cures of St. John's, Clapham, and St. Giles's-in-the-Fields,—all contri-

buted their part to the sum of his pastoral efficiency ; while his skill in organising work as secretary of a great religious society, and an insight into
the cathedral system gained by his residence at
Salisbury, enabled him to enter on the duties of his
new sphere with a wide experience, and a heart
well qualified to sympathise with the clergy in the
varied necessities of parishes so different as the
busy manufacturing towns in the West Riding, and
the little villages sleeping peacefully in Craven and
the northern dales.

CHAPTER VI.

Diocese of Ripon—Wilfrid and the distant past—Reconstitution of the See in 1836—Bishop Longley and his work—Rapid progress and great needs—Dr. Hook's work at Leeds—His estimate of religious life in Yorkshire—Relations between High Churchmen and an Evangelical Bishop—Rev. C. Clayton—Letters from Dr. Hook and Bishop Barry.

THE diocese of Ripon, when my father was con-secrated, on January 18, 1857, was one of the most important cures within the English Church. If there were some of wider area and two or three of denser population, there was no diocese within the United Kingdom which, both in area and popu-lation, exceeded that of Ripon. The Minster church, though it had long been shorn of its episcopal dignity, had traditions stretching into the distant past; and the diocesan history, whenever it is written, must begin not with Bishop Longley, but with Wilfrid and the line of Saxon bishops who made Ripon a centre from which mission priests went forth to evangelize the Yorkshire dales one thousand years ago.

For the present we are only concerned with the state of the diocese within the memory of living men ; but it would be a graceless act to tell the story of my father's work at Ripon without speaking of the great debt which the diocese owes to Bishop Longley, who spent in it the best years of his life before he was called in quick succession to the greater Sees of Durham, York, and Canterbury. Unhappily, no life of Bishop Longley has yet been written, though it would be of real interest, both for his own sake, and for the insight it would give into the marvellous growth of Church feeling during the last half-century.

My father's first Charge, delivered in 1858, gives a striking picture of the condition of the diocese on his appointment, and contains an eulogy of his predecessor which I feel sure he would wish preserved. He says—

The name of Bishop Longley will never cease to be remembered in this diocese with grateful affection. I believe it may truly be said that this affection was entertained for him amongst all classes, as well for his office as for his work's sake.

As the first bishop of the diocese, it fell to his lot to do more for the organisation of the work of the Church within its limits than will probably ever devolve again to his successors in office. How admirably, with what unwearied diligence, with what a combination of zeal and kindness, and with what patiently sustained effort he discharged the duties of his office, for the long period during which he presided over the diocese, many of you, my reverend brethren, well know, and many an enduring evidence will testify for years to come.

You will bear with me, if I embrace the present opportunity briefly to remind you of some of those more prominent works of piety and usefulness, which your late Bishop was instrumental to inaugurate. The benefits

resulting from them are felt in every part of the diocese ;
and I trust that even a slight recapitulation of them may
strengthen our perception of the responsibilities which lie
before us, and give increased vigour to the determination,
by God's grace, to act up to the measure of our high obligations.

It will not be necessary for me to dwell upon what more
immediately relates to the constitution of the See ; such as
the territorial boundaries of the diocese, and other matters
of a similar nature ; although it would not be difficult to
show in regard to these, how largely the whole diocese
is indebted to the forethought and judgment of its first
bishop.   Passing by these topics, I shall simply refer to
what has been attempted in furtherance of the work of the
Church within the limits of the diocese since the comparatively recent revival of the ancient See of Ripon.   The
present diocese was reconstituted in the year 1836.   It was
an eventful period in the history of our Church.   Public
attention was beginning to be awakened to the fearful
amount of spiritual destitution which prevailed in many
parts of the country.   The appalling fact had been recently
brought to light, that upwards of three millions of our
home population were in a state of comparative spiritual
destitution.   Successive years had witnessed the almost miraculous increase of the population.   It was computed that
this increase had been going on at the annual rate of above
300,000 souls ; yet little or no corresponding effort had been
made to render the spiritual provision within our Church
commensurate with the continually augmenting spiritual
necessity.   In the second Report of the Commissioners, who
were appointed in 1835 to consider the state of the Established Church in England and Wales, it is put on record :—
" The growth of the population has been so rapid as to
outrun the means possessed by the Establishment of meeting its spiritual wants; and the result has been that a
vast proportion of the people are left destitute of the
opportunities of public worship and Christian instruction,
even when every allowance is made for the exertions of

those religious bodies which are not in connection with the Established Church."

I am not aware of the relative proportion in which the destitution prevailed in this particular diocese, as compared with other parts of the kingdom. At the same time, bearing in mind that the evil itself had arisen in great measure from the attraction of large masses to certain districts, where the facility for manufacture or for commerce called for the employment of a vast amount of labour ; and recollecting also that, with only one or two exceptions, all the great manufacturing towns of Yorkshire are included within the diocese of Ripon, it is a reasonable inference that this diocese must have had its full share of the spiritual necessity which was then proved to exist in the country at large.

Hence it arose that one of the most pressing wants which were immediately forced upon the notice of my predecessor in office was, the necessity for a large extension of Church accommodation.

To meet this want, within two years of his appointment to the See, Bishop Longley founded the Diocesan Society for the Increase of Church Accommodation. In addition to promoting the erection and enlargement of churches, it was proposed, by means of this society, to aid the endowment of churches, and the erection of parsonage-houses, with a view to secure, as far as possible, to each separate benefice the advantage of a resident incumbent.

The results which have followed afford ground for thankfulness and encouragement.

The society has been the direct instrument to accomplish much, and it has also served indirectly to awaken a lively zeal for the building of churches, of which the fruits are apparent in every part of the diocese.

It is just twenty years since the society was first established. In the course of that period of time, it has made the following grants :—

For the erection of eighty-six new churches, a sum total of £29,965.

For increased accommodation in twenty-six churches, a sum total of £4,836.

For converting into churches two buildings which previously existed, £500.

For the provision or the augmentation of endowments in fifty-one different parishes, a sum total of £10,970.

For the erection of parsonage-houses in 107 separate parishes, a sum total of £21,700.

The general summary of the society's operations shows that a total amount of £67,971 has been raised and expended for the objects already specified. And through its means the church accommodation of the diocese has been augmented to the extent of 50,744 sittings for adults, and 13,345 sittings for scholars, in Sunday schools.

But the foregoing statistics do not nearly represent the whole of what has been done for the increase of church accommodation in the diocese during the episcopate of your late Diocesan.

In the year 1836, when the present See was formed, there were in the whole diocese 307 churches, 297 incumbents, 76 curates, and 170 parsonage-houses.

At the close of the year 1856, when, in the Providence of God, I was called to my present office, I found in the diocese 432 churches, 419 incumbents, 146 curates, and 301 parsonage-houses. Consequently there had been during . my predecessor's term of office an increase within the diocese of 125 churches, 122 incumbents, 70 curates, and 131 parsonage-houses.

Such facts, my reverend brethren, speak for themselves. They call for thankful acknowledgment. They tell aloud of generous, self-denying effort put forth for the glory of God and the welfare of His Church—nor put forth in vain, but signally owned and recompensed with the Divine blessing.

There is another great work, with the commencement of which the name of Bishop Longley is inseparably connected. I allude to the Ripon Diocesan Board of Education.

This institution was founded in the year 1841. The design, as originally set forth, was to promote and extend popular education, according to the principles of the Established Church. It was proposed, by aid of grants, to assist in the erection of schools ; to provide stipends for masters ; to facilitate the training of young persons for the office of teachers ; to afford pensions in certain cases for masters and mistresses ; to grant rewards for scholars, and to provide for the periodical inspection of schools.

The funds which have been hitherto placed at the disposal of the Board, have been insufficient to accomplish more than three of the proposed objects : at the same time the society has done much towards the promotion of education. The educational wants of the diocese have been ascertained and made known. To a large extent those wants have been supplied ; and it is due, in a great measure, to the existence of the Diocesan Board of Education, that, with the exception of only twelve churches, every church and district in the diocese has one or more schools connected with it. And in almost all of those exceptional cases, the children are instructed in Church schools which are situated in adjoining parishes and districts.

Amongst other measures which have contributed to the efficiency of the Church within the diocese, I may enumerate the subdivision of the whole diocese into rural deaneries, the appointment of a rural dean to each of these deaneries, and the increased number of parishes in which the rite of Confirmation is periodically administered. The former of these arrangements is calculated to promote in various ways the well-being of the diocese, especially by bringing the clergy into more frequent intercourse with each other, and, through the rural dean, with their bishop : and it is owing to the latter arrangement with regard to Confirmation, that this important service has come to be better understood, more highly valued, and more numerously frequented.

The foregoing remarks will serve to indicate how much cause for thankfulness we have upon the review of the

labours of your late Diocesan.   May the time never come
when the work which God permitted him to accomplish
in this diocese shall cease to be held in grateful and
affectionate remembrance !

These words describe twenty years of continuous
progress; and yet it was evident that the Church in
Yorkshire still came immeasurably short of fulfilling
her responsibility to the great masses of population
with which she had to deal.

One year after the consecration of Bishop Longley, Walter Farquhar Hook was instituted to the
vicarage of Leeds; and the record of his work is
the history of a magnificent struggle, which ended in
restoring the Church to something like her true
position, in one town at least, and forming a noble
ideal for the parish priest of a vast commercial
community.

This is not the place to give a detailed account
of the marvellous growth of Church work in Leeds,
under Dr. Hook, for those who are interested in
the history of the Church in the West Riding, are
familiar with the volumes in which the Rev. W.
R. W. Stephens has told the story of his life.   But
outsiders may easily suppose that the changes in
Leeds are unique.

Certainly Yorkshire churchmen cheerfully acknowledge the supremacy of Leeds Parish Church,
and he would be a bold man who denied to the
great vicar the title of the " prince of parish priests ; "
but there are results no less striking in other West
Riding towns.

Bradford has its group of more than twenty
churches within the borough to mark the progress

of the Church during the last thirty or forty years. There are living men who remember when there were three churches only for the whole borough of Bradford, and when the system of parish work, as we know it to-day, was so little understood that the visitation of the sick throughout the whole town was divided by an amicable arrangement between the vicar and two or three non-conforming ministers. There is not a word to say against courtesy and brotherly love between those who are trying to serve in different ways the same Lord and Master ; but Church people would be not a little astonished to-day, if a clergyman refused to visit his own congregation on the ground that the services of a Nonconformist minister were at their disposal.

Dr. Hook, after a short experience of Leeds, pronounced that " Methodism was the established religion of the West Riding ;" and it was a long time before Church principles took its place.

We feel sure that Dr. Hook would be as little likely as my father to use these words in any sense offensive to the Methodists. It was so obvious to a thoughtful man that the Methodist societies had kept alive the flame of religious zeal during the days of torpor in the Church, that to speak of Methodism as the established religion was to admit a fact very creditable to the Wesleyans, if it cast a not unmerited reproof upon the apathy of the clergy in days gone by. Yet it would be a great mistake to suppose that there was no feeling for the Church, or no real religion in the hearts of the people who were living without the means of grace.

Many a Yorkshire clergyman has marvelled at

H

the ready response which has been made by his parishioners where the Church has been shown to them in its true light. Unexpected changes reveal a deep-rooted attachment to the parish churches in which their children were christened, and around whose venerable walls their fathers sleep. Let the people recognise that the Gospel is preached with the same freedom and fulness in the Church, and with the same simple earnestness that makes so attractive the ministrations of the pious local preachers, and the Methodists develop very quickly into the most zealous adherents of the Church.

It is the evidence of a gradual awakening to such facts as these that gives the real interest to the statistics of the new churches and schools, which sprang up in the Ripon diocese with such startling rapidity.

Those who attribute this marvellous extension to the impulse of the Oxford Movement, and in Leeds, at any rate, to the influence of Dr. Hook, may be inclined to say that they have not been in the habit of thinking that Bishop Bickersteth was working on the same lines. Certainly he was at times, like Dr. Hook himself, a staunch opponent of the Romanising element in the Tractarian party; but none who knew him will question his sympathy for all that was at once Evangelical and Catholic.

It was not unnatural that those who knew my father's reputation as a controversialist, and a zealous advocate of societies supported by one party in the Church, should have felt some misgivings when he first went to Ripon as to what might be his relations with the High Church clergy of his diocese.

Of his own convictions an unmistakable sign was given in the choice of the Rev. Charles Clayton, as examining chaplain. Mr. Clayton was at that time Fellow of Caius, and the foremost representative in Cambridge of the party of the Rev. C. Simeon. Never was there a man of more unflinching honesty and consistent attachment to the principles he professed; but, steadfast as was his allegiance to the tenets of a particular party, his evident holiness and earnestness of purpose compelled the respect of those who most disliked what they thought the narrowness of his theological position. Of the many hundred priests and deacons who were examined by him for Holy Orders, in the diocese of Ripon, there are few who have not a grateful remembrance of his personal kindness, and none can entertain a doubt that his task was fulfilled under a deep sense of prayerful responsibility.

But this appointment was not followed by any effort to harass or repel clergy of opposite views. It is conceivable that some young men from Oxford may have shrunk from encountering Canon Clayton's searching inquiries into their knowledge of the Articles on " original sin," and "justification by faith;" but those who came to Ripon found there was no attempt to narrow the comprehensiveness of the English Church, and earnest men of all sorts rejoiced to learn that the chief weight was given to knowledge of Holy Scripture, and signs of aptitude for real ministerial work.

Some of my father's Evangelical friends seemed to expect that he would find it difficult to work in harmony with the Vicar of Leeds; for it was notorious that Dr. Hook, with all his respect for the office of a Bishop, had achieved a position in Leeds which might have made him quite independent of episcopal control.

Shortly after his appointment to Ripon, my father was invited to preside in Leeds at the annual meeting of the Bible Society. He had given his consent to do so before he was aware of the strong dislike which the vicar felt to the methods of the society. Dr. Hook went so far as to claim that, since all Leeds was his parish, the Bishop could not fairly hold a meeting in the town for any object which had not his support.

My father was firm, mindful, no doubt, of his own deference to episcopal authority illustrated by the correspondence with Bishop Hamilton quoted above, and kept his promise to the society.

I mention this incident to show that the cordial relations which existed afterwards between himself and Dr. Hook were not purchased by the surrender of principle on either side.

In his journal Dr. Hook notes, on the appointment of Dr. Bickersteth to the bishopric of Ripon—

This is the first time that I have been placed under a Bishop younger than myself. He is almost young enough to be my son. It is difficult, therefore, at first to produce *filial* feelings towards him ; but they will come.

In a letter to Sir W. P. Wood, dated April 8, 1858, Dr. Hook says—

Easter Tuesday was a busy day. The Bishop laid the foundation stone of the Grammar School, with a beautiful service and an admirable address. We then gave the boys a dinner, to the high table of which subscribers were admitted. I was, of course, in the chair. Barry spoke admirably, and, of me personally, with such affection, that if I had not been in the chair I should have cried ; but I gulped down my maudlin with a glass of wine. Then we went to church, where the Bishop gave us a beautiful sermon, one of those sermons which remain upon my mind. He offered to go in his robes to open the schools, and to say grace for the children. He spoke of me as " his valued friend the vicar," which made my heart, as darling Jim would say, go pit-a-pat.

And in September in the same year, writing to a friend on the Queen's visit to Leeds to open the new Town Hall, there is a further allusion to my father :—

Amidst it all I lacked my old enthusiasm, and suffered somewhat from rheumatism. I must own to a little mortification at first, at being entirely superseded on my own dunghill. The Bishop said the prayer and spoke at the banquet. But this nasty feeling soon gave way when I found him doing everything so much better than I could have done it myself.

I have before me a number of letters from Dr. Hook, which make it evident how he and my father were at one in the effort to weld together the whole diocese in brotherly love ; and of these I quote one to show how much my father was assisted by his thoughtful consideration.

The Vicarage, Leeds, August 20, 1858.

My Lord,—I see by the papers that you have fixed the 27th of September for the Visitation in Leeds ; but as we have not received a formal notice, I write to say that this will be in the midst of the meeting of the British Association.   The Association meets on the 22nd, and will last till the 29th.

I do not know whether this will occasion any great inconvenience, but the town will be full, and the excursion trains will be going ; and I think it worth while to mention the circumstance, as it may be possible so to arrange matters as to have the Visitation a few days later.   At all events, I am sure that you will not think me officious in writing.

I should wish also to receive your directions as to the service.   I have hitherto had a plain service at the Archdeacon's Visitation, under the notion that some of the clergy might object to chanting ; but at the Bishop's Visitation I have directed our choir to attend.   It is a subject upon which I am perfectly indifferent.   Plain service and cathedral service are the same to me.   I delight in both. I mention this lest your Lordship, with your usual kindness, should take my supposed wishes into consideration. If you will consider what is best to be done, and then give your orders, I shall be ready to obey, and to take care that all things be done " decently and in order."

I am, my Lord,

Your Lordship's obliged and dutiful servant,

W. F. HOOK.

The Lord Bishop of Ripon.

That other High Churchmen soon learned to appreciate their Bishop is shown in the following letter from Canon Venables.   Writing to the *Guardian*, in May, 1884, he narrated a conversation between himself and Dr. Barry, then head master of Leeds Grammar School, and now Metropolitan of Sydney, in the course of which the latter said—

We cannot be sufficiently thankful for him.   The only complaint we have to make of him is, that he works so hard that there is a danger of our too soon losing the blessing of such a Bishop.

My father always remembered with pleasure having been able to number among his clergy, though only for two years, the great Vicar of Leeds. And he preserved with affectionate interest Dr. Hook's farewell letter to him on his appointment to the deanery of Chichester.

The Rectory, Eydon, Daventry, February 25, 1859.

"My Lord,—I can assure you that none among the many letters of congratulation which have flowed in upon me, has given me more sincere satisfaction than that which I have received from your Lordship.

I lament leaving your diocese and "dear old smoky Leeds," as my children call it. But my position had become anomalous by late Acts of Parliament, especially by that of Lord Blandford ; and the heavy responsibilities which rested upon me with respect to the chapelries and unendowed churches, together with other difficulties, induced me, after a day's consideration, to consider the offer of a deanery as a Providential call to an old man, from an active to a contemplative life.

I have become so much of a Yorkshireman that I feel that one suffers loss by a removal to any other county.

I have come here on a visit to my daughter, because I could not stand the *kind* of congratulations I received from my Leeds friends. I have to preach at Oxford on Sunday, and shall then return home.

I shall ever feel grateful for the kindness and consideration I have received from your Lordship. And when I have ceased to be one of your clergy, I hope you and Mrs. Bickersteth will permit Mrs. Hook and myself to be numbered among your friends.

I am, my Lord,
Your dutiful and obliged servant,
W. F. HOOK.

The Lord Bishop of Ripon.

CHAPTER VII.

The chief duty of a bishop—Incessant preaching—Outdoor services—
"Gig Bishops "—Sympathy with sufferers from the Oaks Colliery
disaster—A Sunday at Barnsley—Watchfulness and energy—
Confirmations—Tact in winning over Dissenters to the Church—
Letter from Sir E. Baines.

" PRÆDICATIO evangelii est præcipuum munus episco-
porum." This is the motto which is placed in the first
page of the Bible which was the constant companion
of Bishop Bickersteth in his journeys throughout the
diocese. The quotation is taken from the decrees
of the Council of Trent,[1] and my father cordially
accepted it as a true definition of the chief function
of a bishop. It has been often said that he was
eminently a preaching prelate. In his parish work
he had laboured incessantly to win souls for God
by preaching Christ. He was, before all things,
an "evangelist;" and in his eyes the chief attraction of the office of a bishop was, that it gave wider
opportunities of preaching the everlasting Gospel of
the Prince of Peace. He desired to preach in every
parish of his diocese. By his study table hung

[1] Sess. V. De Reformatione, Cap. II.

a list of all the churches, and one by one those were marked off in which he had had an opportunity of preaching. He was ready for all occasions. As he said at a public luncheon in Bradford, in 1877—

There were so many claims on a bishop, that it was impossible for him to meet them all. Certainly some of the clergy were ingenious in finding out reasons why they thought the Bishop ought to attend their parish and preach. He had been asked to preach a charity sermon for the purpose of draining a churchyard ; and again, he had been desired to preach for the purpose of raising a harmonium. These objects were certainly, in one sense, insignificant ; but it had very rarely occurred that he had not complied with the demands, as he believed that one of the greatest functions of a bishop was to preach the Word.

It mattered little to the Bishop why they asked him to preach, for he felt that God called him to deliver His message. Wherever he was he spoke as the messenger of God, and as one who was charged with the care of the souls of men.

It was the fashion in the early days of the Oxford Movement to disparage the value of preaching. It was said that people thought too much of preaching and too little of worship. And there is a sense in which this is certainly true ; but earnest men have recognised that preaching the Gospel is the necessary preliminary to any worship worthy of the name. This was certainly the method of men like Dr. Hook, whose work at Leeds was not accomplished without incessant preaching. Often he would preach, especially in Lent, day after day ; for he knew that if men were to use the Sacraments aright, and value the other Services of the Church, they must be quickened by the power of the Word.

By example and precept my father was never tired of inculcating the same truth. Thus, in his first Charge, he writes—

With regard to the ministry of the Word. It is almost impossible to over-estimate the importance of preaching. It is the distinguishing ordinance of the Gospel dispensation; the instrumentality whereby God is ordinarily pleased to convert souls, and to save them that believe. Need I say that with regard to the subject-matter of preaching, the one theme is Christ?—Christ in the dignity of His Person, and the all-sufficiency of His Work; Christ, as Head over all things to His Church—Prophet, Priest, and King; the only Mediator, Advocate, Redeemer, Theme of all prophecy, and Anti-type of all type; Christ, as crucified for our sins, according to the Scriptures, and risen again for our justification; Christ, as ever living to intercede for those who believe in His Name; Christ, as ordained of God to be the Judge of quick and dead; Christ, as the sinner's substitute, who of God is made unto every believer wisdom, and righteousness, and sanctification, and redemption; the Author and Finisher of our faith, the Giver of all grace, and the Fountain of all blessing. This is our one theme, " We preach not ourselves, but Christ Jesus the Lord." " Whom we preach, warning every man, and teaching every man in all wisdom; that we may present every man perfect in Christ Jesus."

Such being the subject-matter of our preaching, great is the importance of the manner in which the message is delivered. Public attention is keenly alive at the present day to the defects of the pulpit. Men demand a great deal, and eagerly cavil at whatever comes short of the standard which they erect. What we especially seem to want, with regard to the manner of our public ministrations, is *reality, earnestness, affection,* and *unction.*

We want *reality.* Possibly the reproach is not altogether undeserved, that much of the preaching of the present day is devoid of apparent reality. The preacher uses a set of phrases which, however familiar to theological students, are little understood by common men. Thus there grows up the feeling that the preacher has not thrown himself into the case of the hearer ; that there is a want of sympathy between the messenger and those to whom the message is brought. A high standard of spiritual excellence is uplifted and recommended ; but sufficient care is not exercised to point out the means whereby, in dependence on Divine grace, this standard may be reached.

Possibly, if we used greater plainness of speech, and endeavoured to point out the connection between vital religion and all the diversified cares, pleasures, trials, or pursuits of daily life, there would be the appearance of greater reality, and therefore a vast accession of power and effectiveness in the delivery of our Master's message.

So, again, with regard to *earnestness.* If the preacher be not thoroughly in earnest himself, it will be hard to make his hearers so. If he really is in earnest, he will make it appear that he is so. I do not mean that this is to be done by vehemence of manner or of gesture. There is a gravity and solemnity which ought never to be absent from our pulpit ministrations. But when a man feels strongly, the strength of feeling will display itself in an earnestness of tone, of look, of utterance, which none can mistake. And what can justify a man in being thoroughly in earnest, if not the feeling that he stands up as an ambassador for Christ, to plead with his fellow-men for the salvation of their immortal souls, and that of those souls he must give account at the bar of Christ ?

Again, there must be *affection* and *unction.* We need affection like that which filled the Apostle Paul, and gushed forth in such expressions as these : " My heart's desire and prayer for Israel is, that they might be saved ; " " My little children, of whom I travail in birth again until Christ be formed in you ; " " Many walk of whom I have told you often,

and now tell you even weeping, that they are the enemies of
the cross of Christ." And, in addition to this, we need that
unction which shall make it plain that the truth we preach
is "with the Holy Ghost sent down from Heaven;" that
it is not a mere theory, but a living reality, and that what
we have heard, what we have seen with our eyes, what we
have looked upon, and our hands have handled, of the
Word of Life,—that we declare unto men.

For twenty years my father was able to go on
preaching incessantly, and in days of health and
strength often preached to overflowing congregations three times a day.

The author of " Our Bishops and Deans " pub-
lishes a letter from a friend, who describes a Sunday
which he spent in company with the Bishop :—

When staying with a manufacturer, an old friend of
mine near Barnsley, I had an example of the Bishop's
labours. He was a guest with the manufacturer, and that
Sunday preached three times, each time extempore, with
great power and feeling, and wonderful simplicity. The
Bishop was quite forgotten in the earnest preacher. He
preached that day in three different churches, which were
all filled with attentive congregations. The intelligent
artisans of the manufacturing districts, I believe, know how
to appreciate the devotion, simplicity, and natural eloquence
of their good Bishop. His presence in the pulpit is noble
and impressive, and his manner dignified, and yet at the
same time humble. As I accompanied the Bishop that
Sunday from church to church, I could not help rejoicing
in the immense amount of good his preaching must effect
throughout his diocese, in the course of successive years.
And I understood this was a sample of his ordinary Sundays. There are few of our bishops who are serving their
generation more faithfully and self-denyingly and suc-
cessfully.

Nor was my father's preaching confined to stated sermons to ordinary congregations, and Confirmation addresses. He was never happier than when taking part in mission services, or addressing large bodies of men supposed to be outside the pale of the Church. In days when the idea of episcopal dignity was much stiffer than it is now, my father caused some surprise to old-fashioned people by delivering an address to the crowd which assembled to witness the consecration of a cemetery.

To him the episcopal acts of consecration with legal formalities were incomplete without something to express the overflowing desire of a heart that yearned over the people committed to his care. He would take such an opportunity to speak in language of the utmost plainness to those who gathered as mere sightseers, of the great realities of death and judgment, which lay behind the unhappy divisions of Christian people, and which concerned churchmen and Dissenters alike.

The writer well remembers listening to such an address at the consecration of a cemetery. He stood beside a Dissenter who listened at first with critical interest, and then with rapt attention ; and when the Bishop's words were done, he heard him say, " If Church parsons were all like 'yon,' there would be no dissent."

Nor was it only in the manufacturing districts that the Bishop won the hearts of the people. The venerable Archdeacon Boyd, whose bright example has done so much for the Church in the West Riding during the last fifty years, was among the first to recognise the simple earnestness of his new Diocesan.

In those days churchmen generally, led by "S. G. O.," in the *Times*, were asking for what they called "Gig Bishops." The days when it was thought natural for a bishop to drive about in a coach and four were passing away; and as my father made his first appearance at Arncliffe in the humble vehicle which had brought him across the moors from Pateley, Mr. Boyd rejoiced in the fulfilment of his ideal.

It often happened in the Yorkshire dales that all those who came over the hills to hear the Bishop could not find places in the church ; and then, when prayers were over, he would gladly preach from a tombstone to those who were gathered outside.

The Bishop was so strongly possessed with the parochial instinct, that he was never happier than when he could arrange to spend a whole Sunday with some earnest clergyman. On those occasions he would visit the schools, speak to the teachers, address the children, and enter into all the parochial machinery with eager interest; and it was no empty phrase he often repeated in his Charges, that he longed to share in the labours of the clergy.

The Rev. Clement Cobb, sometime his chaplain, gives a graphic account of my father's conduct on the occasion of a terrible disaster—the explosion of the Oaks Colliery at Barnsley, on December 12, 1866 :—

"I had charge," he writes, "of one of the parishes in Barnsley ; and the explosions having happened on the Wednesday and Thursday previously, I received a letter from the Bishop on Saturday, to say that as he was sure we should want much help, and as he had no engagement for the Sunday, he would come and assist us.

" When he arrived we drove up to the colliery, and saw the sad sight of a crowd of new-made widows standing at the pay-offices, to draw the last wages of their husbands.

" We went into the room where was weeping the widow of the steward, and the Bishop knelt down and commended her and the wailing crowd outside to the Father of mercies.

" The lips and faces quivered with emotion at his genial and outspoken sympathy. A black rain was steadily pouring on our dismal streets and courts where these poor men had lived. We went into the house of one widow whose husband and sons were lost. She said, 'All my house is lost down that pit.' He knelt down on the stone floor to ask for her comfort. In another cottage, a woman rocking on her bed in grief told us she had lost all her five sons in the explosion. ' Ach !' she said, ' but they were good lads, and they were good sons.' The Bishop told her of Aaron, about whom it is written, that when he lost both his sons in one day he held his peace.

" At my house in the evening some of the influential gentlemen of the place came to meet the Bishop, who readily gave us his sage and business-like advice about our efforts to raise a sustentation fund for the widows and orphans, in which we succeeded to the extent of £60,000. On Sunday he preached solemn and touching sermons in each of our three churches, and accompanied me to the cemetery where I think about seventy bodies which had been got out after the explosion were to be interred, in the presence of multitudes of sympathisers. Five coffins and five parties of mourners were received in the chapel at one time. The Bishop put on a surplice and took his turn with his clergy, each undertaking one set of five at a time for service, first in the chapel, and secondly at the graves. So in work he made himself one of the clergy, and in heart one of the people."

In later years I remember an unhappy scandal, when a clergyman made the terrible mistake of refusing to bury a parishioner until an exorbitant fee was paid.   My father heard of the case, and was hardly prevented, though weak and ill at the time, from undertaking a journey of some hours to perform the last offices in person for the unfortunate people, who were the victims of the clergyman's misguided folly.   He told me that in his earlier days he would certainly have gone, but contented himself very reluctantly with telegraphing to the nearest clergyman to set the matter right.

It was this sort of watchfulness over details, and readiness to undertake any work in person, which made his administration seem so vigorous and successful.

His constant activity soon made him familiar with almost every parish in the diocese, and large as ` the area was, it was hardly possible for anything to occur in its remotest corner which escaped his observation.   A gentleman whose official duties called him to all parts of the diocese wrote to my mother a letter of sympathy, in which he said—

I desire to bear very ample testimony to the real love— there is no other word—with which the Bishop was every- where regarded.   So far as I know, I do not remember a parsonage where his portrait did not hang, often twice or thrice ; and in the best parlour of the glebe houses it was seldom absent.   Churchwardens in out of the way villages, and on those hills and in those dales the Bishop so much admired, have told me curious anecdotes of his wonderful recollection of minute details which happened years and years ago, and the reproofs administered to them for neg- lected recommendations.

For the purpose of his Visitations my father collected statistics with extraordinary care.   Great piles of MS. testify to the laborious industry with which he tabulated the answers to his inquiries. People were sometimes surprised that he insisted on doing with his own hand work which might have been easily done by others ; but he felt the time was well spent, for it served to impress upon his mind the circumstances of every parish in the diocese.

His first Charge was delivered in 1858 ; and by that time, after a residence at Ripon of less than two years, he had made himself acquainted with the details of diocesan work in a way that completely astonished those who heard it.

With reference to this Charge, the Rev. W. N. Molesworth wrote to the *Guardian* on May 1, 1884. He says—

Shortly after the appointment of Dr. Bickersteth to the See of Ripon, I met Dr. Hook ; and, after our first greetings, I said, " Well, how do you like your new Bishop ? " rather expecting an unfavourable answer ; but the reply was a warm eulogy of the newly-appointed Prelate, concluding with the words, " There is not another bishop on the Bench who could have written such a Charge as he has lately delivered to the clergy of his diocese."

The first Charge, like all the rest, does not challenge comparison with the utterances of bishops who are essentially theological students. He was rather fitted, alike by previous training and natural inclination, to suggest to the clergy methods of practical work.

He had to complain in the first Charge that there were still a considerable number of churches where the Holy Communion was celebrated less frequently than once a month. He says—

I

It is most desirable that in every parish church the Lord's Supper should be celebrated at least once in the course of every month. I cannot regard it as a sufficient reason for infrequent Communions that the number of those who frequent the ordinance is small. A scanty attendance, when it occurs habitually, may be due to ignorance or misapprehension. Surely this should supply a motive for multiplying, in place of diminishing, the opportunities for the exercise of so plain a duty. The proportion of communicants to the regular congregation in any given church will generally afford an index of the extent to which vital religion prevails. How, then, can it be otherwise than a source of painful anxiety to a minister who is watching for souls, as "one that must give an account," when the average number of communicants falls habitually below what he might reasonably expect?

In each succeeding Charge he is able to notice a steady improvement, alike in the number of communicants and in the frequency of Celebrations.

In those days early Celebrations were a novelty, at least in the North, but my father was able to quote from his own experience as to their great value.

He went on to speak of the great importance of Confirmation, and expressed his readiness to increase the number of centres. The clergy soon took advantage of his readiness to do so, and thus in the course of his episcopate the annual number of Confirmations rose from nineteen to sixty-three.

In Confirmation my father took a real delight. Often he would take two or three Confirmations a day, for weeks together, so as to meet the wishes of the clergy, who naturally like to have their candidates confirmed in Lent, in readiness for the great Festival of Easter.

There was a wonderful freshness about the addresses. To the candidates he spoke of the solemn responsibility of the step they were taking, and never failed to remind them of the privilege they would henceforth enjoy of becoming regular communicants.

It was no part of my father's Evangelical creed to disparage the value of the Sacraments; and if his language sometimes fell short of what High Churchmen desired in defining the nature of the Mystery, they never had cause to complain that he did not give the Holy Communion a prominent place. He constantly urged upon the clergy the duty of keeping together those who had been confirmed, and pressed them all to keep a *speculum gregis*, or list of communicants.

A clergyman told the writer how once, when the Bishop was present at a gathering of so-called Evangelical clergy, he pointedly asked them why it was that Mr. ——, a well-known High Churchman, was so much more successful than themselves in keeping together his communicants. It was terrible to my father to feel that any who gloried in the name of Evangelicals, should be behindhand in the exercise of pastoral care.

Other clergymen gratefully remember how the Bishop would ask them, before the Confirmation, whether there was any special subject they wished him to mention, and how he always strove to give emphasis to the teaching the candidates had already received. Sometimes when the candidates in country districts were listless and inattentive, he would pause to ask them questions; but it was very seldom that he failed to secure the deepest attention before he proceeded to administer the Apostolic Rite. Usually my father repeated the words several times as he passed along the communion rails, but he was always glad to fall in with the wishes of the incumbent; and on more than one occasion he consented to sit down and confirm the candidates two and two.

In some places it was not easy to secure a fitting degree of reverence. Sometimes the church would be crowded with mere sightseers, who had no notion of the solemnity of the service. My father would speak a few earnest words; and even if the old-fashioned galleries were full of Dissenters, or persons quite ignorant of Church order, the Bishop's manner soon reduced them to attention.

Confirmations in Yorkshire are very different from those in the South. In not a few parishes a large proportion of those confirmed in recent years have been adult converts from Dissent; and in many cases those who come to be confirmed do so in spite of considerable opposition from their companions in the mills.

In one large parish where the Bishop was confirming, it came to his knowledge that a local Dissenting minister had circulated tracts dissuading the people from Confirmation, and pouring contempt upon the ordinance of the Church. A large congregation assembled when the Bishop arrived, and he took with him into the pulpit a copy of the tract which had gained considerable notoriety.

Answering its objections *seriatim*, he first gave a lucid history of the Rite, showing how literally the Church followed the practice of the Apostles ; and then spoke of the wickedness of trying to hinder those who were coming forward publicly to profess their allegiance to their Saviour.

The tables were completely turned, and no more was heard, in that parish at least, of public opposition to an ordinance which was capable of such Scriptural defence.

My father had the gift of winning the sympathy of those who valued Evangelical truth, even if they had an imperfect view of Apostolic order ; and I venture to think that his special tone of Evangelical churchmanship was designed in the Providence of God to conciliate those who would have resented a more aggressive assertion of some doctrines of the Church.

His episcopate was a time of transition. If it was true that when Dr. Hook came to Leeds, Methodism was the established religion, it is admitted to-day, by some of those best able to judge, that while Dissent is losing ground, the religious earnestness of the people is finding once more its centre in the Church. Those churchmen have been most successful in welcoming back people once estranged, who have recognised most cordially all that was good in the old-fashioned belief. The writer well knows the value of definite dogmatic teaching ; and perhaps the time has come for speaking out still more emphatically on the spiritual constitution of the Body of Christ ; but he is convinced that the wise moderation of Bishop Bickersteth was as opportune as it was successful. The pious folk learned to trust him, and so were led to see that the Church was able to preach to them, in all its fulness and simplicity, the Gospel they loved so well.

My father greatly valued the friendship and esteem of members of the Nonconformist body. He liked to dwell rather on truths they shared in common than on points of difference, however important he considered them to be. I venture to publish a letter which shows the terms of affectionate regard which he enjoyed with one whose name stands very high in Yorkshire for Christian principle :—

St. Ann's Hill, Burley, Leeds, December 8, 1880.

My dear Lord Bishop,—Your name to my memorial, and your cordial congratulations on the honour I am to receive from her Majesty, are of the highest value in my estimation. For, much as I respect the friendship of others, it is the sympathy of the true Christian that makes my heart glow, and assures me that I am in the right way. From the days of my conversion I have felt my faith strengthened into assurance by my consciousness of the love I bear to the followers and ministers of Christ. Therefore I hailed the very sight of your letter, being sure that it would contain words of Christian wisdom and sympathy ; and so I found it. Accept, my dear Lord Bishop, my warmest thanks for your goodness in sparing some of your precious time to cheer and help an old fellow-pilgrim. Your esteem is highly valuable to me, but your " speech of Zion " is much more so.

How certain I am to be right and safe, if I can view earthly honour as our Lord would have viewed it ! And how should I be put on my guard, if I should feel puffed up or drawn down to backsliding. May your valuable life be long spared, as a teacher and example of the doctrine and spirit of our Blessed Lord! And then may we meet amidst the unfading joys before the Throne.

I am, my dear Lord Bishop,

Yours most truly,

EDWARD BAINES.

The Lord Bishop of Ripon, D.D.

In this chapter I have tried to convey some impression of the way in which my father infused warmth and earnestness into the diocese by his incessant preaching, and the contagious example of a life wholly devoted to his Master's service. His own life was the best commentary on the burning words with which he concluded his Charge in 1876, when, after twenty years of incessant work, he was still full of energy and fire :—

For a season we depart, some of us, probably, never to meet again at a similar Visitation. We go to resume our wonted duties in that part of the vineyard in which Christ has appointed us severally to labour. May we go with an increased sense of the magnitude and responsibility of our work, with fixed resolve to apply ourselves with redoubled energy to the fulfilment of the task which God has given us to perform. For myself, suffer me to say, I long to be more and more your fellow-helper, by prayer, by counsel, and by sharing, so far as it may be permitted to me, in all your efforts for the glory of God and the salvation of souls. Ours is a glorious embassy ; to be the torch-bearers of light to a dark world ; the messengers of pardon to the guilty, peace to the troubled conscience, salvation to a world lying in ruins. The work is, indeed, one of incomparable difficulty ; but we are not left alone in its execution. Our sufficiency is of God. His promise ensures the requisite strength for the performance of His command. The presence of the Redeemer is never wanting to His faithful ministers. "Lo, I am with you alway," is the unchanging promise given to His faithful ministers. The same grace which made Apostles valiant for the Faith, even when confronted by the opposing forces of Jewish unbelief and Gentile superstition, so that they counted not their lives dear to them, if only they might finish their course with joy : the same Divine aid which upheld the noble army of Martyrs, and sustained Confessors amid the tortures of the flame, is freely offered to each one amongst ourselves. Let us be diligent while the time lasts. It needs no prophetic insight to perceive tokens of a coming consummation. In the stir and upheaving of nations and systems ; in the development of anti-Christian heresy ; in the march of infidelity ; in the visible pressing into the kingdom, of God's elect, we may almost hear the distant sound of the chariot-wheels of the Son of Man returning in glory to judge the world. Yet a little while, and the long-delayed, long-expected Advent will come. The Chief Shepherd will appear, and we, His ministers, if we have been faithful to the trust confided to our keeping, shall share His triumph and inherit the promise, " They that be wise shall shine as the firmament, and they that turn many to righteousness as the stars for ever and ever."

CHAPTER VIII.

Home life at Ripon—Depth and tenderness of domestic affection—
Letters to his wife—The Palace and the garden—The village of
North Leys—Spiritual care of the villagers—Early rising and
methodical habits—Sundays at the Palace—A custom of the
Clapham sect—Letters to his children—Tender solicitude for their
spiritual welfare—Advice on school and college life—On ordina-
tion and the choice of a curacy—Happy relations with the
cathedral and city—Dr. McNeile—Letter from Dean Fremantle
—Singular happiness of his home life—The first break in 1872—
Death of Ernest—Letter from his tutor—Recollections of Rev. C.
Cobb.

In many ways the most difficult part of my task is
to give some account of my father's life at Ripon.
One shrinks from speaking too much of those sacred
memories, which, dear as they are to the home circle,
have little connection with his public life. And yet
I think people understand a man's life and work
better when they get some idea of what he was as
a husband, a father, and a friend. It often happens
that the publication of a biography by a near relative
throws a different complexion upon a public life, and
one learns to know and love a man the better when
one sees him at his ease.

The life of Charles Kingsley, written by his

wife, is a case in point. Even his books, which are
so expressive of the real thoughts of a true man, do
not teach us half so much as the record of his ordinary life and talk, and the outpouring of his heart
in letters which were never meant for the public
eye. And there is another book which many who
read this sketch will remember, "The Life of
Catherine and Craufurd Tait." The Archbishop
was right when he decided that the record of those
saintly lives would help a wider circle even than
that of those who were privileged to know them.
The charm of that book, which all its readers gratefully acknowledge, is that it shows how the deepest
Christian principle may underlie the simple duties of
social and domestic life.

I am encouraged to say something of my father's
private life by the letters and words of friends, who
say how much they owe to the charm of his personal
intercourse.

No man ever loved his wife, his children, and
his home with more passionate devotion. Those
who knew the dignified reserve and absorption in
his public work, are hardly prepared for the tenderness which comes out in letters to his wife and
children in the intervals of public business. Most of
them are far too sacred for any eye but theirs for
whom they were intended; but a scrap like this,
written at the Bounty Board, reveals what he was
as husband and father :—

Thank you for your very precious letter of this morning.
I am so thankful for all you say about the darling children,
and especially R. and F. You cannot imagine how I long
to see them sometimes. I can scarcely bear to look at

little children for the longing desire I have to see my own.

It was a great disappointment during the first year or two of his episcopate that he was detained in London all through the spring and summer by the duties of Chaplain to the House of Lords, which then, as now, devolved on the junior bishop.

On May 15, 1857, he writes from the House—

I must send you a line from my new sphere of action ! I have just been reading prayers for the first time. I took my seat last evening, and this morning, 10.30, have commenced my duties. The Bishop of London has asked me to dine with him on Monday, the Lord Chancellor for Wednesday, the Archbishop for Thursday, so that I shall have as much dining out during next week as is good, if not rather more. I met nearly all the bishops yesterday. They were all very friendly and kind.

Soon afterwards he writes—

I am rejoicing to think I shall be with you this day week ; but I am quite dreading the future, for I find there is the greatest difficulty in getting the duty taken. The House of Lords is quite uncertain as to the time it meets, and I am obliged to be always in the way.

The Palace at Ripon was built in the time of Bishop Longley, and it was a source of unfailing interest to him and to his successor to watch the trees he had planted gradually growing up around the Palace, and surrounding the house with a belt of leafy verdure. The garden was attractive ; the roses on the terrace were the admiration of the neighbourhood. The laurel walks ; the shady path through the wood ; the mound upon the lawn ; the old chestnuts that flanked the west parlour, as it was called before the Holden Library was built ; the apple tree, which went on bearing though its roots were mostly above ground, and the tree prone upon its face,—were landmarks as dear to the Bishop as to his children.   No country squire with ample leisure was more particular than my father in keeping everything in perfect order.   A broken railing, or a gate off its hinges, was soon detected in some ramble with his children ; and the gardeners knew that the Bishop's oversight of his temporal possessions was as vigilant as the watch which he kept upon his flock.[1]

About half a mile from the Palace northwards is the little village of North Leys, containing two farmhouses and a dozen or more cottages.   My father, following the example of Bishop Longley, took this as a semi-parochial charge, and constantly visited the sick and the poor.   He used to tell with great satisfaction the story of his greeting from a poor woman in the village.   On his first visit to the Palace, accompanied only by his eldest boy, he repaired to the village to make the acquaintance of his poorer neighbours.   He was greeted in the first cottage at the door of which he knocked by a poor woman, who first indulged herself with a good look over her visitor, and then said with thorough Yorkshire bluntness, " Well, thou beest our new Bishop, I suppose !   Thou bearest a pretty good character.   I hope thou deservest it ! "   If the villagers of North Leys were polled after a pretty long

---

[1] My father sought to recommend the Dilapidation Act to the clergy by his own example. He invited the Diocesan Surveyor to inspect the Palace and the premises, that the expenditure in painting and repairs might be done under his direction, and that the Bishop might hold the five years' certificate.

experience, they might be trusted to own that the Bishop had proved himself a good friend to them.

In St. Giles's my father had been deeply interested in the question of providing better dwellings for the poor, and at North Leys he found that there was in this respect much room for improvement. He was never satisfied until he had induced the Ecclesiastical Commissioners to pull down the insanitary tenements, of which there were too many specimens in the village, and to build in their place a row of substantial cottages. He considered all the plans, and insisted on an adequate supply of light, water, and sleeping accommodation, with as much care as though he had nothing else to do. He invited the villagers to attend the chapel services on Sunday afternoon, and in his busiest days found time to visit his little flock. There are frequent entries in his diary such as these, taken from different years :—

Aug. 30.—Rose at 6. Mr. F. and Mr. Wise called. Very busy writing. Held a Confirmation in Ripon Minster at 2 ; a large number confirmed. Called on Geldart's boy and Mrs. Hardy in the village afterwards. Wrote some of my Charge in the evening.

July 14.—My groom attacked with illness ; in great danger. May the Lord be merciful to him for Jesus Christ's sake.

March 5.—Rose at 5.45. Busy with correspondence all the morning. Walked with B. to the village in the afternoon. Snow deep on the ground. Called on Mrs. H. ; prayed with her.

Jan. 2.—Called on Mrs. A., who is seriously ill ; administered the Holy Communion to her.

April 30.—In the afternoon, with B., called on all the poor people in the hamlet.

The Church lands surrounding the Palace were all made over to the Ecclesiastical Commissioners, so my father had not the obligations of a landlord; but he cultivated friendly relations with the farmers, who all felt that in any dealings with the Commissioners the Bishop would be sure to stand their friend.

In his children's sports my father took the keenest interest, and it gave him real pleasure to hear of a good day's shooting or a large capture of the perch in Queen Mary's Dubs. His own chief recreation was riding, and he was known as an excellent horseman. When the shocking news of Bishop Wilberforce's death from the fall of his horse reached Ripon, it was remembered by those who had seen the Bishop and my father ride together, that the former had not so safe a seat as his Northern brother. My father thoroughly enjoyed a good gallop across country with his children, and he also had much pleasure in quieter rides, when he was accompanied in early days by Dean Erskine, or in later years by one of the canons of the Minster. A list of forty rides all upon grass was compiled by his desire, and many of them went by the name of one of the family, or were called after passing incidents, trivial enough in themselves, but linked with happy associations. His children remember how, in later years, my father would often draw rein in some silent wooded lane, and repeat passages of a sermon which was revolving in his mind, to be preached on the next Sunday in some busy manufacturing town.

The life at Ripon was orderly and punctual. For the greater part of his time there my father used to

rise at six, and the early morning hours were spent in
devotional reading, prayer, and meditation. He read
prayers in the chapel at nine o'clock for the household and outdoor servants, and after breakfast set
himself to the task of answering a great pile of
letters. He never cared for the services of a regular
secretary or chaplain, but succeeded in getting
through all his writing in person by his singularly
orderly and methodical habits. He answered every
letter by return of post with his own hand, till quite
recent years, when he availed himself of his daughter's
help. At the same time, however, he owed an
immense debt of gratitude to his Ripon secretary,
Mr. Samuel Wise, whose ripe judgment and unfailing courtesy were valued as much by the clergy as
the Bishop, though the latter had fuller opportunities
of knowing his inestimable private worth.

Mr. Wise was the first to welcome my father to
Ripon, and the Bishop wrote not long before his
death of the "thoughtful kindness in which, for four
and twenty years, he had never known him wanting."

The mornings were spent in writing and interviews with clergy, lasting till two or three o'clock ;
and then would come a ride or drive. The later
afternoon and evening were spent usually in more
general reading. My father was exceedingly fond of
good English prose ; he generally had in course of
reading some such authors as Macaulay, Alison, or Sir
Walter Scott ; and he also looked forward with eager
interest for the arrival of new books, and especially
the *Quarterly* and *Edinburgh Reviews.* His own
library was a good one, for he spent on books the
proceeds of his literary work in London ; and it

was a real pleasure and interest when Mr. Holden of Liverpool left to him and to the See a library of some six thousand volumes. With the books was bequeathed a sum of money, part of which was utilised in building a room at the Palace for their reception; and the remainder was invested for the maintenance and increase of the library. Up to the time of my father's death, however, there was little opportunity for purchasing new books, as a good deal of the income was swallowed up in binding, and other preparation for eventually lending the books to clergy and students of divinity.

After dinner my father sometimes found pleasant relaxation in a game of draughts or chess; in the latter he was more than usually proficient. The writer remembers that when he was receiving his first lessons in the game, and was absorbed by its strange fascination, the Bishop suggested that it was unsuitable for Saturday nights, such was the strong feeling he had of the need of preparation for the due observance of the Sunday.

It is impossible for any one to forget what the Sundays were at Ripon on the comparatively rare occasions when my father was at home. He always attended the cathedral in the morning; and in the afternoon there was service in the Palace chapel, crammed with a congregation, which comprised not only his family, servants, and villagers from North Leys, but also included the students from the Training College and visitors from Ripon. On these occasions my father used to preach in a way that was quite distinct from his ordinary style, but singularly impressive and persuasive.

After dinner on Sundays there was a custom, handed down from Acton and Sapcote traditions, and continued long after the elder children at Ripon had left the parental roof, on occasions when they returned for a Sunday at home. Every one, including any guests who might be present, was asked in turn to repeat a hymn, beginning with the youngest and ending with the Bishop himself. By this means my father took care that, from their earliest days, the minds of his children should be stored with a rich treasury of all that was best in English hymnody. Keble's "Christian Year," Mrs. Alexander's " Hymns for Little Children," Kemble's and Mercer's collections, Lord Selborne's " Songs of Praise," Hymns Ancient and Modern, and the Hymnal Companion to the Book of Common Prayer, were all brought into constant requisition ; but of the hymns which my father used to repeat himself, none were oftener on his lips than Toplady's matchless " Rock of Ages," " O God, our help in ages past," a short hymn of which his own father was the author, beginning, " Heaven is our promised, purchased home," and (especially in later years) " Jesu, Thou Joy of loving hearts." The same custom of repeating hymns after dinner on Sunday prevailed in the house of my father's lifelong friend, Mr. Henry Thornton, of Battersea Rise, at Clapham ; and, probably, it was one of the habits of the good old Clapham sect, not the least part of whose tenets was their reverence for the day of rest. I do not think my father ever forced religious conversation, but it was easy to see that he was not content if Sunday talk was not befitting the day. For many years whenever he

K

was at home, he preached once a month in Ripon, at Trinity Church.   He also, from time to time, though at rarer intervals, occupied the pulpit in St. John's Chapel, Bondgate, or in the chapel attached to the ancient almshouses, on the opposite side of the Cathedral city.

The letters to his boys at school are interesting, because they sometimes give glimpses of his work, and always reveal a heart overflowing with tenderness and solicitude for his children's spiritual welfare. Thus he writes to a son just gone to Eton :—

The Palace, Ripon, January 28.

The day must not pass without a line to you, although this is my twenty-fifth letter, and I am still far from the end of what I ought to do ; and I am expecting all the rural deans !   But it would be strange indeed if my pen could not express what my heart is full of—tender love to my precious boy, and earnest prayers that he may be constantly kept under the care and protection of our Heavenly Father.   May God bless you !   Next Saturday ! and (D.V.) we shall meet.   All are well ; the weather delightful.   I have had two pleasant rides with Trot.

Ever your own loving
Πατηρ.

P.S.—I send an autograph for the boy who wants it.

All the letters to his children, even when they are written to amuse, and speak of their shooting or other sports, turn into a prayer, showing that the uppermost thought in his mind was his children's growth in grace.

Sometimes the letters speak of his work. Writing from near Mirfield, in playful allusion to the not infrequent criticism of those who derided

Lord Palmerston's bishops, he says (September 28, 1861)—

Would my son like to know what the lazy, indolent, do-nothing Palmerstonian Bishop of Ripon has been doing during the last few days, and has to do before he returns home ?

Saturday, September 21.—Ordination at Ripon and sermon.

Sunday, September 22.—Two sermons at Harrogate, morning and evening.

Tuesday, September 24.—Consecration of church and churchyard at Dunsforth and two sermons.

Wednesday, September 25. — Sermon at Milnsbridge, near Huddersfield, at 11 ; and consecration of cemetery at Sowerby Bridge, at 4.

Thursday, September 26.—Confirmation in Halifax parish church, at 10.30 ; 441 candidates. Confirmation in Brighouse, at 3 ; 94 candidates. Sermon in Brighouse, at 7.30.

Friday, September 27.—Confirmation in Batley, at 11 ; 66 candidates. Confirmation in Dewsbury, at 3 ; 279 candidates.

In futuro !—

Hodie, September 28.—Confirmation in Mirfield, at 10.30. Consecration of churchyard, at 12.15. Confirmation in Birstal, at 3.

Sunday, September 29.—Sermon in Earls Heaton, at 10.30. Sermon in Ossett, at 3. Sermon in Earls Heaton, at 6.30.

Monday, September 30.—Consecration of cemetery in Hanging Heaton, at 10.30. Consecration at Cleckheaton, at 1. Go home.

I wonder what Palmerston can have been about to appoint such lazy drones. They ought to be made to work. Don't you think so ! Farewell, my own precious boy. God bless you.

Ever your own loving

Πατηρ.

This letter may be illustrated by quotations from his sermon register. He kept a book showing the number of sermons preached in each year, no mention being made of Confirmation Charges or informal addresses.

The list rises from 96 in 1857, to 149 in 1875; and even in the year 1880 he preached no less than 80 times.[1]

Here is another letter, written to a son who had to choose between business and the University :—

My dearest ——,—The great anxiety which I feel respecting your future prospects at this crisis leads me to put down my wishes in writing, and I hope you will carefully read this note before my letter goes to —— and let me have your answer to-morrow. You have a momentous choice to make, and you should seriously weigh the consequences involved in it. You know my willingness to send you to the University, but you must look steadily at what this involves, and count the cost of it. Experience has taught me the necessity of laying down some fixed rules with regard to University life. The University is a scene of terrific temptation, especially to the idle and to any who go thither without a fixed purpose, by God's grace, to resist temptation and to secure the intellectual advantages which the University affords. You must clearly understand that the only condition upon which I send you to Oxford is, that you promise to practise industry and economy, with a view to obtain a good degree, with no more expense than is necessary to your position. I wish you to promise me that while you are at college you will give not less, *as a*

[1] The following occurs in a letter to one of my brothers who was abroad in 1872 : "My father is as busy as ever ; he was away all last week confirming at Leeds, Halifax, and elsewhere, and to-day he has gone to confirm at the Grammar School at Richmond. Between Monday and Saturday in last week he confirmed 2,800 children, and preached fifteen times! I think he is none the worse for it, in spite of the weather, which has been miserably cold."

rule, than from seven to eight hours daily to reading, including lectures ; that you will keep morning chapel and abstain from going to parties which would draw you into idleness and expense. In saying this, it is not my meaning to find any fault whatever with you ; but I think these rules are necessary for your success, and for my own peace and satisfaction in sending you to college. If you will only adhere to them, you have sufficient ability to ensure your passing through the University with honour and credit, and you will be a source of joy and comfort to us all. . . .

Ever your loving
FATHER.

The letters to his children give ample evidence of his unfailing generosity. And in this place it should be noted, that throughout the period of their education my father made a point not only of corresponding regularly with his sons, but also of paying them frequent visits whenever work in London or elsewhere brought him within reach of them. Probably no public man who led an equally busy life ever contrived so many opportunities of personal intercourse with his sons during their terms of residence at school or college. His personal self-denial was extreme, and he cheerfully dispensed with holidays and trips abroad to secure for his sons the inestimable blessing of University education. To all his children alike my father represented that the work of a clergyman was the highest and happiest calling on earth, but he never pressed his personal wishes in the least, and in the case of those who did not feel something of an inward call, he never uttered a word of reproach.

The writer possesses many letters written to himself on his approaching ordination, and on the

choice of a curacy, from which the following extracts
are taken :—

I wish you many happy returns of your birthday anniversary, and pray that every blessing may rest upon you
now and always.   It is likely to be a most important
year upon which you will enter to-morrow.   I trust it will
witness your entering upon the work of the ministry—the
noblest calling which any one on earth can embark in,
and, if only entered upon with right motives, the very
happiest.   No words can describe all I fear and desire in
your behalf in connection with the great work ; and I trust
that He Who has guided you so far will graciously bless
and prosper you in all that lies before you.

In another letter when the Rev. G. W. Kennion,
now Bishop of Adelaide, had been kind enough to
offer his son a curacy at All Saints, Bradford, my
father wrote—

It weighs very much with me that Mr. Kennion's offer
has come unsought and unsolicited, and may fairly be
considered as a Providential offer.   All my own steps in
the ministry have come in the same way, and this fact has
been an inexpressible comfort to me.   Almost the only
place for which I became a candidate I did not get.   I do
not attribute much importance to your having a longer
stay than till next Lent at the clergy school.   You will
have been there fully six months next Lent, and you are
not to expect to go from thence with an education fully
complete.   Your whole ministerial life will be an education,
and you will learn more in a few months of practical ministerial work than you would learn in years of college life in
Leeds.   I would not wish to say anything against a parish
church curacy in Leeds, but I think you would learn more
and have more experience in preaching in Mr. Kennion's
parish.   You will see, therefore, which way my inclination
bends.   I pray God to guide you and to bless you in the

momentous decision which you have now to make. All my sympathies and your mother's sympathies are with you, and our prayers. May God guide and bless you.

Your loving father,

R. RIPON.

With the home life at Ripon is naturally connected the memory of much happy intercourse with friends and neighbours, and the citizens of the little borough, for which my father had a real affection. He was always ready to take part in local matters : the grammar school, the local charities, schemes for improvement of the city, had always a claim on his interested attention ; and he took it as a special compliment to himself when one of his sons who had entered the corporation achieved the dignity of mayor. With the cathedral clergy and with six successive deans, he maintained most cordial relations.

It was a source of real happiness to my father when Lord Beaconsfield gave the deanery of Ripon to the venerable Hugh McNeile. My father had stood beside him in Liverpool, and on the platform of Exeter Hall, and used to tell us of his extraordinary power as an orator, and his influence as a champion of Evangelical truth. Dean McNeile was already in failing health when he came to Ripon, but there were times when the old fire of his eloquence broke out, and his dramatic power held spell-bound the cathedral congregation.

My father felt how much a younger generation lost, who never knew him at his best; but for himself it was a source of keen enjoyment to have the opportunity of hearing him preach, and to talk over subjects on which they shared intense convictions.

There were those who thought that Dean McNeile was an unlikely man to superintend the restoration of the Minster; and yet it was in his time that not only was the restoration of the material fabric brought to a successful consummation, but also the long-neglected double daily service was restored, and a precentor appointed—the Rev. S. Joy—under whose guidance the choir was brought to a state of efficiency and a point of reverence and order which left little to be desired.

Perhaps it is not too much to say that my father's hearty interest in and advocacy of these reforms were the means of removing the scruples of a Dean, whose natural bent was not in the direction of merely ecclesiastical improvement.

Certainly the Bishop took a keen delight in the cathedral service, and whenever it was possible he walked in from the Palace, a distance of nearly two miles, to be present at the daily evening prayers.

The venerable Canon Worsley, who, though many years his senior, survived my father, wrote to say how much the Chapter was indebted in old days to the Bishop's ready co-operation and tact. And the following letter from the present Dean will be of interest to many :—

The Deanery, May 10, 1886.

Dear Miss Bickersteth,—You have asked me to send you some reminiscences of my friendship with your dear father. I will endeavour to put together a few thoughts which may add to the many expressions of affection for him you have no doubt received. My acquaintance with the Bishop dates back a good many years, and has always worn the same complexion of respect and love. I had not been thrown much with him in private or social life until I came to Ripon ; but from my intimacy with his uncle, Edward Bickersteth of Watton, and with other members of his family, I have always felt that I knew him, as I knew them ; and this enabled me to form the high estimate of his character which I have always had. I was brought into nearer acquaintance with him publicly upon his appointment to St. Giles's, when, through the late Bishop Villiers and Alexander Dallas, I came to know more of his parochial and missionary work ; and from that day to the day of his death have followed with admiration the steady, faithful, and courageous consistency of his conduct, which has been so great a help to myself and to many others in these days of change and of controversy. I do not hesitate to say that when the appointment to the deanery was offered to me, the prospect of being under the shadow of your father and being brought into association with him in diocesan work, was one of the principal inducements to my acceptance of this office ; and I shall not forget the solemn and loving manner in which he welcomed me to Ripon, and after prayer instituted me to the deanery. It would be difficult for me to refer to any particular events during the last ten years. I must speak generally of my official and social intercourse. In them I was always struck with his prompt decision and business-like way of dealing with the subjects which were brought before him. As chairman of a committee, or as president of a conference or congress, he specially excelled. There was a profound reality in his decision arising, as it always appeared to me, from the depth of his sense of responsibility. With some this might appear to assume an air of coldness and reserve ; but his conception of duty was of a high order, and he seemed to have known what St. Paul says, 2 Cor. ii. 17 : " As of sincerity, but as of God, in the sight of God speak we in Christ."

In the part I have taken to erect a fitting tribute to his memory, by placing a grand west window in the Cathedral in the place of one upon which he never looked without a

sigh, I have received many letters full of the most affectionate regard from all parts of the diocese ; and I trust that
the example he has left us of what a bishop can be in all
godliness, consistency, and zeal, may never be lost in the
annals of the Church of England and the clergy of this
diocese.

I am yours affectionately,

W. R. FREMANTLE.

When my father came to Ripon his family consisted of four sons and one daughter, and in the
following year the youngest son was born.   Up to
1872 there was little to mar the singular happiness of his home life ; but in that year came a heavy
trial, in the sudden death, in the nineteenth year of
his age, of the fourth son, Edward Ernest.   This
event, the first shadow of death upon our home,
may justify a slight digression, for Ernest was one
who cannot easily be forgotten by many besides the
members of his own family.   His childhood was
full of promise, and his ways were wonderfully
winning.   As a boy, his uncommon beauty had
attracted the notice of Mr. Sant, who met him when·
staying with his parents at Battersea Rise, the home
of their kind friends and constant hosts, Mr. and
Mrs. Henry Thornton.   The artist, whose pictures
of children are so justly prized, begged to be allowed
to paint Ernest's picture, which was exhibited in the
Academy in 1865.   His face was the index of no
ordinary mind.   After his first term at Eton his
tutor wrote as follows :—

My Lord,—I do not think there can be many pleasures
in the life of a tutor equal to that of writing an account of
a boy who has done well and met with deserved success.

I do not much care to tell you of the honours which Ernest
has gained, and which he has probably told you himself.
I think his perseverance and evident interest in his work
are points more worth dwelling on than the success which
happens to have rewarded them. . . . He has a scholar-
like and accurate mind, and is fond of acquiring knowledge.
He has also a keenness in competition which I think he
will not allow to mislead him. I am glad to see also that
he takes a vivid interest in things exterior to his school-
work, and has a thoroughly healthy tone of mind. The
way in which he has been prepared reflects great credit on
the school he was at before he came to Eton.[1] With regard
to other matters, he has a reverence for sacred things, and
a love of what is good, which gives a public and an ever-
increasing value to a clever boy's influence. You will see
from what I have written that I have a very warm affection for the boy. His simplicity, and his desire to please
me and to do his duty, have quite won my heart ; but I do
not think I have been partial in what I have said. The
fact is, it is very hard to over-estimate the reasons which
one has for taking pleasure in a good boy. The good that
may be done, the value of example, and the pleasure of
feeling that one's work is appreciated, are considerations
which make it a real pleasure to have to do with such boys.
I have one other boy near him in school who is rather like
him. To see these two working, and the mutual influence
of what they did, has been a study of the greatest interest.

With regard to his Trials, I was surprised at his taking
so high a place, for in some of the papers of which I saw
the marks, I thought he had done less well than I should
have expected ; *e.g.* in the Greek Testament and divinity
paper. But I saw none of the composition, in which he is
very accurate.

Believe me, my Lord,

Yours very faithfully,

ARTHUR JAMES.

[1] My father placed all his sons in turn, under the care of the Rev. R. S.
Tabor, at Cheam.

The promise of his first term was sustained. He passed through Eton with credit, and entered King's at Cambridge, in January, 1872. In the long vacation of that year he went abroad with an Eton master and an old schoolfellow. One summer evening in July there came a letter to say that he had caught a chill on the top of Strasbourg Cathedral, and was lying seriously ill at Baden Baden. Not many hours afterwards a telegram summoned my father to come at once, but it was too late. He died with no relatives at hand, and his father only arrived in time for one last look at his beloved child before he was laid to rest in the beautiful hillside cemetery far away from home.[1]

This blow, all the more crushing because my father had good hope that Ernest would be the first of his sons to take Holy Orders, was borne by the Bishop with a Christian fortitude remarkable to those who knew the intensity of his paternal affection. For years afterwards he was as strong and vigorous for public work as ever; and though the home at Ripon was never the same again, amid the disappointment of the brightest earthly hopes, he looked forward to the reunion with loved ones in the Eternal Home in meek submission to the Will of God. Many letters of friends, which have been gratefully preserved, show that others outside his family recognised that the death of Ernest was no ordinary bereavement. A schoolfellow and college friend wrote of him—

[1] A white marble cross, erected by my father, marks his grave. His parents also founded in his memory a small lending library in connection with the British chaplaincy at Baden Baden. It is known as the Bickersteth Memorial Library, and there is reason to believe that it is much appreciated by the English community.

Your letter only came this morning. You must know the grief it is to me, for I think you knew more than any one how much I loved him. The happy days at Helsdon I remember as if they were yesterday. He was the most lovable person I ever knew ; so bright and yet so very tender to others. His friendship for the last five years has made those years the happiest of my life, and as such I shall remember them, with his figure standing out most prominently in the memory. I think you are right in saying that he would not have been altogether a happy man. I often talked with him about his anxieties as to a profession, and often thought that he would be always rest-less in his eager aspirations. He confided to me, at Cambridge, a plan of his for doing good to the poor—going among them as one of them—which seemed to strike his imagination as possible, and which touched his tender heart. Almost my first thought was of you, whether you were with him, and I am glad to know you were. He will have many mourners besides his own family, for there was no one who attached his friends to him as he did, and there is no one I could less easily resign. I cannot say half of what I feel, for it is too soon yet to realise that the boy I loved best in the world I shall see never again ; it seems so hard to lose him after such a short five years. I re-member now bitterly that I never saw him to say good-bye before he started ; little omissions are magnified now by grief. But there will always remain the great thankful-ness for having known him and loved him. It was very good of you to think of writing to me, a part of the great kindness with which you have always looked upon my love for him.

The writer, whose name will be learned with interest, is the Hon. and Rev. Arthur Lyttelton, Master of Selwyn, and examining chaplain to the present Bishop of Ripon. Another letter from a relative runs as follows—

We met an Eton master who spoke so highly of your dear boy Ernest, as one of "rare excellence." "A character you seldom meet with," he said ; "too good to be long for this earth."

But perhaps the most touching tribute of all to Ernest's memory was that which appeared a few weeks after his death in the magazine conducted by his former schoolfellows. The following extract is taken from the first number of the *Eton College Chronicle* for the next ensuing half-year, and those who read the pathetic and unaffected words of grief will probably agree that no apology is needed for their reproduction in these pages.

In Memoriam.

The worthy son of a noble father is dead. Edward Ernest Bickersteth has gone "where the wicked cease from troubling, and the weary are at rest." He died at Baden, of fever, July 30, 1872.

Many who read this will have known him : some as a passing school acquaintance, others as a valued friend ; besides those in whom his whole life was bound up by the ties of the warmest affection, and who will ever connect with his dear name the happy and unfading memories of their boyish days. All these, from first to last, must and will lament the untimely end of him who is as deeply and poignantly regretted in his death as he was beloved and cherished in his life.

Thus will the memory of our dead schoolfellow remain with us, hallowed and unforgotten among the many Etonians who have so lately died, who are "ever going, thick and fast, like falling leaves."

The picture of the Bishop's home, which it has been the object of this chapter, however slightly, to pourtray, can best be supplemented by a further

quotation from Mr. Cobb, who was so intimate a
guest at the Palace, and, as one of his chaplains,
in such frequent attendance on my father in his
travels through the diocese, that his reminiscences
have a special value. He writes—

My little sketch would not be complete if I did not say
a word about my observations on his domestic and personal
character. It was a marvel to me to witness the combination of domestic tenderness with public energy—thoughtful love for his own with abounding labours abroad. I
suppose such a combination is a sign of real greatness. I
can picture him to myself riding in the lovely lanes about
Ripon, with a whole troop of pony-mounted children, all
radiant with health and joy. With surprise and admiration, knowing his enormous correspondence, I heard him
say to one of his boys just returning to school, "Now,
——, if you will write to me once a week, I promise to do
the same to you;" and I saw him, just as the intense
strain of an Ordination was over, himself closing and directing a school hamper for one of his sons.

The dark shadow of a terrible loss passed over the
home, and if his grief for his own bereavement could not
be concealed, his tender care to shelter others from every
circumstance which might reopen healing wounds was
still more conspicuous. Often he would say, "It is not
work, but worry, which kills a man." And when, in addition to his enormous burden of public work, domestic trials
became mingled with that soothing peace of home which
most of all recruits the man who labours to weariness
abroad, it was impossible not to see that native energies
were strained almost beyond power. But the good Bishop
lived in a power and strength beyond his own, and I well
remember his saying to me, as we were driving about to
the scenes of his labours in the magnificent country of the
West Riding, "The thoughts which are ever floating
about my mind and at present bear me up, when power to

bear seems to be almost overborne, are those of the
beautiful hymn—

> " Abide with me ; fast falls the eventide ;
>   The darkness deepens ; Lord, with me abide ;
>   When other helpers fail, and comforts flee,
>   Help of the helpless, O abide with me."

His warm affection and geniality as a friend, his brightness and self-forgetting courtesy as a host, the patience,
carefulness, and sagacity of his counsels, will never be forgotten by the writer of these lines, and seem like a bright
dream gone for ever and too soon.

> " And the stately ships go on
>   To their haven under the hill ;
>   But O for the touch of a vanish'd hand,
>   And the sound of a voice that is still !
>
> " Break, break, break,
>   At the foot of thy crags, O Sea !
>   But the tender grace of a day that is dead
>   Will never come back to me."

Never on *earth ;* but those who were privileged to know
and to love our dear Bishop here, and who belong to the
same Master he so faithfully served, will have the fountains
of pleasure in association with him gush forth once more,
when they see the many gems which will shine in the
crown he will lay at that Master's Feet. I think the first
sermon I ever heard him preach was from the text, "The
Lord God is a sun and shield : the Lord will give grace
and glory : no good thing will He withhold from them that
walk uprightly. O Lord of Hosts, blessed is the man that
trusteth in Thee." That blessedness he is realising as "he
rests from his labours."

CHAPTER IX.

Church building and restoration—Movement in the great towns—
Splendid liberality of Yorkshire churchmen—Letter to a non-resident incumbent—Jealous regard for the interest of the Church and
tenderness in censuring defaulting clergy—Letters from friends of
one to whom the Bishop specially ministered, and from Bishop
Kennion of Adelaide.

THE last fifty years have shown a marvellous development of activity in the erection of new churches
and the restoration of others which had long suffered
from ruin and neglect. To give some idea of the
work accomplished during my father's episcopate, I
quote the figures compiled by the Rev. Canon
Kempe, the indefatigable editor of the Ripon Diocesan Calendar. He writes—

In 1836, when the See of Ripon was constituted, the
population of the diocese was 870,000; in 1856, when Bishop
Bickersteth succeeded Bishop Longley, 1,120,000 ; and in
1881 had increased to nearly 1,600,000. During the episcopate of Bishop Longley 137 churches were consecrated
in the diocese, of which 113 were new parish churches, 18
were churches rebuilt or enlarged, and six were chapels of
ease, built for the most part in more or less remote hamlets

L

of large parishes. During the episcopate of Bishop Bickersteth 158 churches were consecrated, of which 92 were new
parish churches, 47 were churches rebuilt or enlarged, and
19 were chapels of ease. In 1836 the number of incumbents was 418, and of curates 146; and in 1883 the number
of incumbents had risen to 500, and of curates to 266. In
1857, the first year of Bishop Bickersteth's episcopate, the
number of Confirmation centres was 19, and the number of
persons confirmed was 3753; in 1883 the Confirmation
centres were 63, and the number confirmed 10,781 ; so that
whilst the population increased by some 50 per cent., the
number of persons confirmed increased by nearly 200 per
cent.

The following Table, extracted from the Bishop's
Charges for 1867, 1870, 1873, 1876, and 1879, shows
the sums raised and expended in the diocese for
Church purposes during the fifteen years, 1864 to
1878 inclusive, (1) For the increase of church accommodation, (2) For the restoration of churches,
(3) For the erection or enlargement of schools, (4)
For the building of parsonage houses, and (5) For
the augmentation of endowments, irrespective of all
contributions to societies, diocesan or general :—

	1864-6.	1867–9.	1870–2.	1873–5.	1876–8.	Total.
	£	£	£	£	£	£
1	112,498	112,514	63,227	98,773	137,400	524,412
2	87,468	88,678	106,042	113,380	87,892	483,460
3	41,021	59,197	119,081	99,576	47,415	366,290
4	40,098	36,767	39,569	41,986	14,512	172,932
5	27,780	33,059	16,147	40,958	30,024	147,968
Total	308,865	330,215	344,066	394,673	317,243	1,695,062

The work of church building was promoted not
only by the Diocesan Society to which allusion has
already been made, but by the local societies formed

by the public spirit of the wealthy manufacturers in the large West Riding towns.

Twice did the churchmen of Leeds meet together to hear an address from the Bishop and the Vicar on the spiritual destitution of the town, and twice they pledged themselves to the erection of at least ten new churches. Like results have been achieved in Bradford, Huddersfield, Dewsbury; and the local pride has been turned to good account when men have vied with one another in works to promote the glory of God and the good of their poorer neighbours.

In the country districts, if there has been less need for the erection of new churches, the age has been especially one of restoration. In the course of Confirmation tours the Bishop never missed an opportunity of calling attention to churches which were unfit for their purpose, and squires and parsons alike were stimulated by his pointed rebukes.

My father used to tell with some satisfaction the story of a church in the Archdeaconry of Richmond which sorely needed restoration. There was no resident squire; the newly-appointed incumbent was young and inexperienced, and much as he desired to see his church restored he knew not how to begin. The Bishop volunteered his services. He asked the clergyman to call the farmers together, and himself met them in the schoolroom. He talked to them in that homely way in which he knew how to go straight to Yorkshire hearts, commenced a subscription list with a substantial donation from himself, and there and then obtained from the farmers present the promise of a sum which enabled them to commence the work at once.

Nor was the Bishop's idea of a restoration easily satisfied. The writer remembers that he went with his father many years ago, when the Bishop was to preach at the reopening services of a church which had been, as the promoters thought, thoroughly restored. When the village was reached it turned out that nothing had been done except the merest necessary repairs, and the churchwardens had sought to cover all deficiencies by a plentiful use of white-wash. Doubtless they expected a sermon which would eulogise their efforts and praise a magnificent restoration; but the Bishop from the pulpit called attention to the unsightly pews and structural defects which still remained, and urged them not to rest content until they had made their church far more worthy of the worship of Almighty God.

On the other hand, when the work showed signs of generous sacrifice and loving zeal, the Bishop did not withhold words of hearty approbation which are gratefully remembered. Thus in the course of a sermon at Netherthong he said—

Now, my brethren, you would be disappointed if I did not say a word with regard to the occasion which has brought us together to-day. I do sincerely congratu-late you upon what you have done for the restoration of this church. I cannot look upon the change which has been effected in this sacred edifice without feeling that it reflects the greatest possible credit upon all who have been concerned in carrying out the work, whether by contribut-ing the necessary funds, or by managing the details which have resulted in our having a church now so thoroughly fit for a place of public worship, in which you may meet to-gether to pray, and to praise our God and Father in Heaven. We rejoice in all such works of restoration, not because we can admire what is architecturally comely and beautiful, but because there is a very close connection—depend upon this—between a well-ordered church and that spirit of reverence which is an essential part of true religion. Go into one of your churches—happily they are rarely to be found now-a-days—one where, in the first place, the whole building is blocked up with unsightly pews, telling of a spirit of exclusiveness and selfishness, which is the last spirit which ought ever to be found within the walls of a building devoted to the worship of God. Go into a building where the walls are green and mouldy, where there is no appearance of comfort, but every appearance of neglect or decay, and what feeling of reverence is likely to be produced in such a building as that? Will not all of you say that such a building indicates a neglect and contempt of what ought to be found in a place of which we may speak as a palace for the Lord, and not for man? And when, on the other hand, we come into such a building as this, which you have cleansed and adorned and beautified, we cannot but feel as we enter the building, that this is indeed the house of God, a place where everything tends to lift up the mind from earthly to heavenly things, and to make us realise the truth that this is none other than the gate of heaven. I sincerely trust that this restored church will be what many a restored church has proved in other places—instrumental to a spiritual revival among the population. God grant that this church may be a nursery for many, many souls who shall be nourished and developed in the truth as it is in Jesus, and prepared for that heavenly temple above not made with hands.

Amongst the works of restoration, first and foremost stands that of the venerable Minster church of Ripon. The writer remembers his first experience of going to church was sitting in one of the old green baize boxes which disfigured the fair proportions of the cathedral choir. The whole structure

betokened terrible neglect, and the arrangements
were as unsuited for the due performance of public
worship as those of the most neglected parish church.
The responsibility for the cathedral fabric and the
credit of its restoration rest, of course, with the
dean and chapter; but my father looked upon it
as a diocesan work, and greatly aided in the collection of funds.   In 1867 he wrote in his Charge—

I must at this time allude to the efforts that have been
made for the restoration of the ancient cathedral of Ripon.
More than five years have elapsed since active measures
were adopted with this end in view.   The cathedral was at
that time in many parts in a state of perilous dilapidation.
Had not steps been then taken for its preservation, it is
more than probable that some portion of it must have
actually fallen.   Aided by public subscriptions, which have
amounted to £18,287, a donation from the dean and chapter
in their corporate and private capacity, and a grant of
£10,000 from the Ecclesiastical Commissioners, applicable
only to repairs essential for the safety of the fabric, the
Restoration Committee have been enabled to effect the
necessary repairs; but the restoration is still far from complete; and from a Report recently issued by the Committee,
it appears that the funds are exhausted, and a sum of £7000
is still required.

Now, the cathedral is the mother church of the diocese;
nor is it fitting that the cathedral should be inferior to any
other church in the diocese in its external appearance, or
in its proper adaptation to the solemnities of Divine worship.
The time has arrived at which a vigorous effort should be
made to raise the sum which is required to complete what
has thus far been well and prosperously accomplished.

As the result of a pastoral letter which the Bishop
put forth, accompanied in many cases by private,
personal appeals, the money was raised, and the

restoration was completed in January, 1867, at a total cost of £40,000. Amongst the parish churches restored two stand out prominently—Wakefield, soon to be a cathedral; and Halifax, no less fit for such a purpose.

Nor was this widespread zeal for church building and restoration merely utilitarian. In the neighbourhood of Ripon, by the princely munificence of Lord Ripon, who provided the whole cost before his lamented secession from our communion, and Lady Mary Vyner, two memorial churches were built at Studley and Skelton, which are replete with the most lavish adornment, and represent an outlay of not less than £60,000. But, in the manufacturing districts, churches have been erected as noble gifts to God and the poor, which minister not to the enjoyment of those who are the favoured denizens of nature's fairest fields, but form the one bright spot on which the eye can rest of those whose daily toil confines them to the unlovely surroundings of a busy, smoke-begrimed town. Such is the exquisite fabric erected by Colonel Akroyd at Haley Hill; and the noble church of All Saints, Bradford. Here Mr. F. S. Powell built a stately church, with schools and a parsonage house. His large-hearted charity has been rewarded by seeing that within twenty years the parish has become a model. Between 700 and 800 communicants frequent the church; nearly 2000 scholars and teachers assemble in the schools; and not only the church itself, but two flourishing mission churches are filled with large congregations of the working class. It is one instance out of many where the new-born zeal for church building has proved an incalculable benefit to the people. Nor are the Leeds churches devoid of beauty. St. Bartholomew's Armley, and All Souls (the Hook Memorial), to mention two out of many, are very different from the old chapels of ease which were once thought sufficient. Happily they remind us more of the days when men gave God of their best, and did not count the cost when they sought to do honour to His Holy Name.

In all this work my father bore a share, not only by his wise counsel and unostentatious liberality, but chiefly by the example of sacrifice in the ready surrender of time, health, and strength for God. This was cordially recognised by clergy and laity alike, and it would be easy to quote scores of tributes like this taken at random from an article in the local press reviewing his Charge of 1873 :—

The Charge bears unconscious testimony to the inestimable services which the Right Rev. Prelate has rendered to the Church in his own district; for the activity and vitality of which it gives evidence are unquestionably due, in a large measure, to the example of zeal set by the Bishop himself.—*Yorkshire Post*, May 3, 1873.

But the building and restoration of churches are valuable chiefly as the expression of the revival of true religion, of which they are only the sign ; and my father's labours were directed far more to the inward and spiritual than the outward and visible structure.

His Charges are still read, not so much for the statistics which he could arrange with remarkable skill, nor for the weighty expression of his views on questions of current controversy, but because they breathe throughout a spirit of fervent piety, and have not lost their power to stimulate and quicken.

When he came to Ripon, in spite of the untiring efforts of Bishop Longley the standard of spiritual life amongst the clergy was by no means high. It is not so much that there were cases of moral failure and open scandal as that there was a low standard of clerical duty.

In later years my father was fond of contrasting the present with the past. Thus, in the course of a speech at Huddersfield, he says—

If our Church survived that long period of deadness, coldness, and want of energy, and want of vitality, surely, now that she is in such a state of fervent activity in every part of the country, we may take courage, and feel that God will not desert her.

Let us look at the present state of things. I confidently hazard the opinion that in no past period of our Church's history since the Reformation has there been — I will not say more—so much of that activity, energy, piety, and devotion to their work on the part of the clergy, speaking of them as a body, as you have at the present day. Why, I can recollect in the early period of my history a clergyman was thought very active indeed if he preached two sermons on the Sunday. I remember when I first came to this diocese twenty years ago, I went to stay with a gentleman, who showed towards me that hospitality which I have experienced in such large measure from the laity in every part of the diocese for so long a period. When he heard that I intended to preach three sermons on the Sunday, I really think that for the moment he thought I had left my senses behind. He could not believe it. He asked me if I thought it possible to do so. I said I did. You would be amused if I were to tell you all the kind and thoughtful provision he made for my reception when Sunday came. He would not let me have a single meal with the family, because I was not to talk. He would have me left alone. He seems to have thought I ought to go to bed between each sermon. He was so careful of me that I really believe he feared that I could not survive the exertion. Thank God, I have survived many a day of the kind since. The standard of activity amongst the clergy has risen almost incalculably, not only in the discharge of their public duty, but in their parochial work. I remember a clergyman who thought it was a very peculiar kind of proceeding indeed, not at all becoming a clergyman, to go out amongst the poor parishioners, visiting them from house to house. Now we all hold that it is a very apostolic thing for a clergyman, and what St. Paul would have had them do; and we consider it a very great neglect on the part of clergymen who fail in the visitation of their flock. I have heard the same clergyman say that times have so much altered that he had begun occasionally to lift the latch of his poor parishioners' doors and visit them, and he thought it a great achievement.

My father helped to bring about this change, not only by example and public exhortation, but by not shrinking from the far more difficult task of personally appealing to those who needed his fatherly admonition.

Here is an example of the delicate courtesy with which such appeals were made :—

4, Gloucester Square, Hyde Park, July 7, 1858.

Reverend and dear Sir,—I have received an application this week from a gentleman who states that you are willing to give him a title to a curacy, provided I can accept him as a candidate for Deacon's Orders. I have written to appoint him an interview, and in the meanwhile I write to make a communication to you with regard to the two parishes of N. and M., which I wished to have made earlier, but have refrained from doing so, in the hope that I might hear from you first on the subject. You will, I am sure, pardon me for writing with great frankness, and attribute my doing so to no other motive but a sincere desire for the spiritual welfare of the parishes with which you are ministerially connected. First, I must express my regret that these important parishes should be held by you in connection with your very important and responsible duties at ——. My own experience, both of cathedral duties and of parochial ministration, enables me to say that the duties which devolve on you in virtue of your office in ——, are amply sufficient to engage the sole energies of a clergyman, even had he no other duties to attend to. But this is a matter of long standing, and however much I may regret for the sake of the Church that it should be so, any change in that respect must, of course, emanate from yourself; nor should I allude to it, but for the sake of writing with perfect frankness.

Assuming, however, that there can be no change in this respect, I have felt for some time past the necessity for a change with regard to the provision for the two chapelries of N. and M. I do not think it possible for one curate to perform the duties of those two parishes.

N. and M. are five miles distant from one another. N. has a resident population of 700 people, and, if I am credibly informed, an increasing population. L. (another hamlet) is more than a mile from the church, and a mile from the school. The population at L. is, I am informed, in a most deplorable state. Immorality prevails, and there is great alienation from the Church. Then, in addition to this, you are aware there is a Roman Catholic chapel, school, and priest's house in M. The Dissenters are active ; they have a chapel and school there. All these circumstances point to the absolute necessity of a resident clergyman, who can give his whole energies to the work of the ministry in M., unless the Church of England is wholly to yield up her proper standing.

At present M. has only alternate services on each Lord's Day. There ought decidedly to be two full services, and a sermon at each on every Sabbath. It will require years of patient and laborious effort to recover the ground which the Church ought now to be occupying in M. I have formed this opinion partly upon my own knowledge of the facts of the case, partly from representations which have been made to me by persons in the neighbourhood, who take an interest in N., and partly as the result of conversation which I had some time since with Mr. —— ; and the result is, that I do not feel that it would be my duty to sanction a similar arrangement in future to that which has been hitherto the case ; *i.e.*, I consider N. needs an active and efficient curate, on whom no other duty is to devolve but the care of N. and L. ; and this will, of course, involve a separate arrangement for M. I feel a confident persuasion of your desire to do what is best for the interests of the Church, and I hope, upon consideration, you will agree with me that the present circumstances of N. are such as to make it essential to have a separate curate for M., so long as N. has a non-resident incumbent.

I am, reverend and dear Sir,

Very faithfully yours,

R. RIPON.

This letter not only shows the tact with which the Bishop pressed upon his clergy a higher sense of ministerial responsibility, but it shows how accurately he considered the needs of what might be thought an insignificant country parish.

Though the Bishop never sought to enforce obedience by an appeal to the law, yet there were instances in the course of his long episcopate, in which clergy who had been guilty of moral lapse, and obliged to leave their parishes, submitted to his judgment. In such cases he knew how to combine a jealous regard for the interests of the Church with the tenderest sympathy for the accused, if he was really penitent. I have before me a long correspondence relating to a clergyman of great excellence in many ways, who had been overtaken in a grievous fault. I choose two letters out of many, in which his family and himself expressed their gratitude for the Bishop's fatherly attitude towards him :—

My Lord,—The account I have received of your kind and affectionate visit to my beloved brother has filled me with gratitude. It is about the only thing which could give us all comfort. For, first, it shows your forgiveness of the past, and that my brother retains an affection which he so dearly prized. Secondly, and more especially, because it opens a ministry to him which, above all others, is what I should have wished. You know, perhaps, his early and long love of God, and devotion to His service. You know how many souls he has helped to bring into the fold. You can hardly know the deep tenderness of his affections, and in some sense the simplicity of his nature. But your Lordship also knows that he has fallen in various ways. I will only add that, should you be able to repeat your visit, and to give us any assurance of your sense of his penitence and grounds for acceptance with God through Christ, it will be a great and unspeakable comfort.

I am, my Lord,
Yours with deep respect,
———.

The clergyman himself wrote as follows :—

My dear Lord,—I left the Palace yesterday, thinking I should meet you on the way towards Ripon. I longed much to have one more word with you ; but simply to tell you how deeply grateful I felt for all your conduct to me yesterday, and for your truly fatherly love shown towards me. I thank you for every word you said, and I only entreat that, whenever you wish it or think it right, you will always speak openly to me; and I believe, under God, it will be received with a most grateful and attentive ear and mind. It was a great pleasure to me to be back again in a place which I have ever associated with some of my happiest thoughts of —— and its work; and I left the Palace full of comfort and gratitude.

I remain with the deepest respect,
Yours ever affectionately grateful,

——.

It would be easy to illustrate far more fully my father's relations with the clergy, but I will only add a letter addressed to the writer by one to whom he is bound by ties of the closest gratitude and affection :—

Bishop's Court, Adelaide, South Australia.

My dear Cyril,—You have asked me to place on paper some recollections of your dear father. His kindness to me when I was a boy I can never forget. This he showed, not only in thoughtfulness for my amusement when I went to stay with him—riding with me to places of interest, and talking cheerily and brightly about great duties and great work—but doing these things in a manner most attractive to a boy. He was a capital rider, and mounted me well; and he always looked so bright, and had so many jokes and stories, that it was no wonder that, as a boy, I learnt thoroughly to admire him. And there were closer ties that bound me to him. When I was at Eton—I suppose it would be in 1860 or 1861—my sister was to be confirmed at Harrogate. We naturally had a wish to be confirmed together. I had not been prepared for Confirmation at Eton, and when I came home for the holidays there was little or no time in which I could be prepared. Your dear father heard of this, and sent for me to come and stay at the Palace, and there most gently and affectionately talked of deep spiritual truths to me, and so won me that I cannot say how much I owe to him. When my dear father

died he drove over from Ripon to see my mother, and
nothing could exceed the tenderness with which he spoke
to her and prayed with us. After this I did not see much
of him until, in 1876, I was appointed to a benefice in his
diocese ; and when he instituted me, gave me his blessing,
and prayed with me, he seemed to be a real Father in God
to his newly-instituted priest. Whenever he afterwards
came to confirm at All Saints, he always inquired most
earnestly into the state of the parish and the kind of
work that was being done, and made a point of asking
me, before he gave his Charge to the candidates, whether
there was anything particular that I desired to have said
to them.

Our people there had a great admiration for him :
business men, in particular, listened with the greatest
interest to all his utterances, because, as they said, "everything he said was so clearly put that they could carry it
away with them." The high estimation in which they
held him was, no doubt, partly due to the fact that he was
an excellent man of business, so clear-headed a chairman,
and so punctual in keeping all his engagements.

Perhaps even you, my dear Cyril, hardly know how
deeply your father was overcome by joy when it was
decided that you were to be ordained. When it was
arranged for your coming as my curate to Bradford, he invited me to visit him at Ripon, that he might talk over the
matter with me. I remember well with what thankfulness
he was speaking of Dr. Gott's work in Leeds, and especially
of the Clergy School, where you were at that time. He
paced up and down the garden with tears filling his eyes
as he spoke, with deep reverence and thankfulness, about
his youngest son becoming a clergyman of the Church.

It was natural when I was offered the bishopric of
Adelaide that I should go at once to my Diocesan. Few
men could have had a kinder friend to whom to go. He
entered warmly into all my anxieties about leaving my
parish, and gave me most cheering and useful advice about
my future work.

Although, generally speaking, he was impressively grave and serious in his manner, the Bishop was sometimes full of humour. One of the last stories he told me, he told with infinite amusement. One of his ordination candidates had shown a lamentable ignorance of Holy Scripture in his papers. In his interview with the Bishop he was asked whether he read his Bible every day. "Certainly, my Lord, every day." "Have you any plan upon which you read your Bible, Mr. —— ?" "Certainly, my Lord." "Do you follow the Church's Calendar, and the lessons provided for every day?" "Oh no, my Lord." "Have you a plan of your own, then?" "Certainly, my Lord." "What is your plan?" "Oh, it's just a plan of my own. I always read what I think is likely to bear on the events of the day." "Well, to-day, for instance; what did you read?" "Oh, my Lord, knowing I was going to see your Lordship to-day, I just read all the *comforting* passages I could."

I leave it to others to describe the admirable way in which he conducted, as chairman, the business of the Diocesan Conference, or of any public meetings in which he was concerned. Notably this was the case at the Leeds Church Congress in 1872, and it ought never to be forgotten that it was to him we owe the introduction of the recitation of the Creed at the commencement of each annual meeting of the Congress. Two further points are worth noting. First, the promptitude with which he invariably replied to any letter addressed to him by any of his clergy; and, secondly, the fact that in spite of the widely divergent opinions of some of the clergy of his very large diocese, no single prosecution on account of ritual ever took place during his episcopate.

Speaking for myself—and I think that I should represent the feelings of many others—we realised that we had in our bishop one whose quiet, steady judgment seemed a strength on which we could always fall back, and who, while he was ready to support us in any work which we attempted, always left us plenty of room in which to do it without interference.

I have not alluded to the extraordinary growth of the Church in his diocese during his episcopate, simply because I expect that others better qualified will give full information upon this point.

Yours affectionately,
G. W. ADELAIDE.

Testimony like this shows that the material and spiritual progress of the diocese went side by side; or, in other words, that the Bishop, whose skilful organisation led to so large an increase in church building and restoration, sought to be to his clergy a true Father in God, winning their love and admiration no less than their deference to his authority.

M

CHAPTER X.

THERE was no part of his work in which my father
took a deeper interest than that of selecting candidates for Holy Orders. As compared with the efforts
made now in many dioceses to conduct the ordinations with due solemnity, the plans adopted at Ripon
thirty years ago seem simple ; but no bishop laboured
more earnestly to impress upon his candidates a
devotional spirit.

Some months before the ordination, my father
insisted upon a personal preliminary interview ; and
in this way he was able to prevent many candidates
from appearing at the examination who would certainly have failed. He usually asked them to con-
strue a few verses of the Greek Testament, and
inquired into their theological reading ; but in every
case he asked candidates to define their views on
certain fundamental doctrines.

He had especially prepared a volume, in which

candidates' names were entered ; and, as an illustration of his careful accuracy, it may be interesting to see the form.

Each page contains the following :—

1. Candidate's name. 2. Address. 3. Age. 4. College. 5. Parentage. 6. Preliminary education. 7. References. 8. Title. 9. Application (whether one had previously been made to another bishop). 10. Motive. 11. Sunday school ? 12. Parish work.

13. *Reading.*—Bible, Greek Testament, Church History, Articles, Prayer-book, Pastoral Theology.

14. *Fundamental Doctrines.*—Human Depravity, Atonement, Justification, Sanctification.

15. *Remarks.*

As, in every case, an answer was required to each of these queries, it is evident that the Bishop could easily form an impression of the capacity of the candidate, as well as of his motives and character. The terms in which a man would answer my father's question as to his motive in seeking Holy Orders, were sufficient to give a good idea of his character ; and in not a few cases the Bishop was able to suggest the higher and deeper motive, when a young man had been first led to devote himself to the ministry in deference to a parent's wish, or some other reason far short of the highest.

It was sometimes supposed that the examination at Ripon was less searching than that in other dioceses ; and certainly it was not possible to maintain so high a standard as in those nearer the Metropolis, which naturally attract the abler University men. And yet the examination conducted by Mr. Clayton and his brother chaplains generally

proved disastrous to some of those who presented
themselves, while many more were rejected by the
Bishop himself at his preliminary interviews.

The writer remembers that the Bishop once told
him that he believed that he had applications from
Dissenting ministers seeking Orders in the Church,
on an average once a fortnight. This is a startling
fact, as showing how gladly many Nonconformists
would enter the ministry of the Church. Of these
candidates many were disqualified by age, many
by deficiency of education, and others were apparently only anxious to share the social position
of the Established clergy, and had no sense of the
spiritual superiority of the Church.

There were, however, many Nonconformists
ordained by my father, who brought into the Church
intellectual and spiritual qualifications of the highest
order.

My father had a great desire to raise the
standard of intellectual attainments in his candidates
for Holy Orders ; and it was to him a matter of
great regret that so many University men choose
the Southern Dioceses rather than the hard work of
our Northern manufacturing towns. The following
letter was addressed to his brother, the Dean of
Lichfield, and contains a fuller statement of his
views than is usually found in his hurried and con-
cise correspondence :—

The Palace, Ripon, November 21, 1878.

My dearest Edward,—I only returned home this morning, otherwise I would have answered your letter by return
of post. I have not any hard and fast rule respecting candidates from Lichfield, or any other Theological College, but

my aim is, as far as possible, to secure University men for ordination, in preference to those who have only been trained at a Theological College. The proportion of candidates for ordination who have graduated has considerably increased in this diocese of late, and I wish to encourage University men to come forward. This has made me decline some who have applied from Theological Colleges, whom otherwise I might have accepted. Again, the standard of attainment which secures the usual certificate of Lichfield is, so far as I can judge, not high. The Mr. A., whom I ordained last September, did most feebly in the Examination. He knows nothing of Greek, and it was mainly due to your recommendation of him that the examiners agreed to treat his case as exceptional. But if this were to occur frequently, it would involve considerable inconvenience to the examiners, and an appearance of injustice to other candidates. Besides, I was recently informed, upon what seemed good authority, that Bishop Maclagan now requires a higher standard than has been usual hitherto in candidates for ordination from the Lichfield Theological College. One result of this is that for a time, till a new class of students has been admitted, there will be a flight of Lichfield students to other dioceses for ordination, because of their inability to meet the requirements of the Bishop of Lichfield. This has suggested a little extra caution in accepting Lichfield students just at present.

I am afraid you may think this reply vague and unsatisfactory, but I think you will sympathise in my desire to obtain candidates who have a degree, and to make the admission of candidates from Theological Colleges who are non-graduates, the exception. Of course all this relates to intellectual training ; but I would infinitely prefer a man from a Theological College of high spiritual qualifications, though of inferior mental culture, to a man of the highest intellectual attainment, with a low standard of piety, whatever his academic distinction.

I need hardly add that I shall always be most grateful for any private and confidential communication from you in respect of any candidates for whom you think an exception ought to be made.

Ever your affectionate brother,

R. RIPON.

This letter refers, of course, only to those Theological Colleges which attempt to supply the sole intellectual, as well as theological, training for the ministry.

My father felt the great value of institutions which were intended to supplement, by a special theological and devotional training, the advantages of an University education.

He watched with the keenest interest and the heartiest approbation the Clergy School at Leeds, which, founded by Dr. Gott, the Dean of Worcester, is justly regarded as the model of a clerical seminary, which combines theological reading and spiritual training with opportunities for gaining insight into the varied machinery of a large and well-worked parish.

The Leeds Clergy School is only for graduates of Oxford and Cambridge, and the credit of its foundation belongs exclusively to the Dean of Worcester. It was solely owing to his munificence and his fatherly oversight that it attained an unique position, cordially recognised by the whole English Church. It has not yet become strictly a diocesan institution; but my father from the first watched its progress with the deepest interest. He was frequently a lecturer within its walls; he was glad to offer his counsel whenever it was sought, and used his office as Visitor, not to direct or control, but to stamp with his approval an Institution of whose value he was deeply sensible. He frankly recognised that it helped to raise the standard of clerical efficiency in the diocese, and expressed to its founder and the lecturers his heartfelt thanks for the training which they supplied.

Since the above was written, the writer has seen the eloquent sermon preached by Canon Temple, on the occasion of the Clergy School Commemoration Festival, on June 8, 1886; and he is glad to have his account confirmed by the high authority of one who knew its history from the first :—

Exactly ten years have elapsed, or will have done so when St. James's Day comes round, since I had the privilege of standing in the parish church pulpit and preaching, not the anniversary sermon (for anniversaries had not then begun to arrive), but the first festival sermon in connection with the Leeds Clergy School. That duty I had been asked, on short notice, to discharge. It had been undertaken in the first instance by one who very highly honoured this then infant Institution, who laboured personally to serve it, who showed the value he set on its work by sending his own son to reap benefit therefrom— the late Lord Bishop of Ripon. He had been taken ill, and was unable to do what he had promised ; and I well remember the letter of fatherly, kindly appreciation, in which he afterwards expressed thanks for, and approval of the effort unworthily made by another to supply his place. Pardon this personal reminiscence. It is made solely on account of its reference to the departed. For, indeed, it was a point of first consequence in the struggling babyhood of the Clergy School, that it threw itself boldly on the sympathies of its Bishop, that he responded frankly and warmly to its action in so doing ; and while refusing pointedly, as I believe he did refuse, all responsibility for, or interference with its independent management, he yet gave it that warm-hearted countenance and support, without which it could never have become what, in fact, it has become, or have enjoyed the success which has, in fact, by God's gracious blessing, crowned the earnest and watchful efforts of its founder.

My father felt very strongly that no young man should undertake the awful responsibilities of the ministry without a thorough previous training; and he constantly urged candidates not to present themselves for Holy Orders until they had gained some practical experience by taking cottage lectures, or at least by teaching in Sunday schools.

And he used to enforce the same views on clerical education in his Charges. Thus, in 1876, he writes—

I am aware of the great difficulty which is experienced in finding, in sufficient number, really efficient curates, especially if the range of choice is limited to University men. The difficulty may fully be accounted for without supposing that there is any falling off in the number of young men who wish to enter the ministry of our Church. The explanation is found in the constantly increasing number of new churches; the far more general employment of curates by incumbents; the higher standard of piety and efficiency which incumbents seek for in those whom they select; and the large demands of the Colonial Church for English clergymen. At the same time I would urge the importance of selecting candidates for ordination as far as possible from amongst those who have graduated at one of the Universities.

I am far from wishing to speak in any tone of disparagement of Theological Colleges. In the existing state of the Church they are simply a necessity; a sufficient number of candidates to meet the demand for curates cannot be obtained from the Universities. Many of these

Theological Colleges are doing their work most efficiently. In some instances I have found candidates from these institutions excel even University men in the examination previous to ordination. If considered merely as supplementary to the University, affording a more specific training in theology than could be obtained at the University, their value can hardly be overstated ; and yet I think it would be a serious evil should it ever come to pass that a majority of candidates for Holy Orders should be drafted from Theological Colleges, without having received any University training. There are advantages combined with education at the University which cannot be secured at any Theological College. The teaching in the latter is directed to a special end. A large proportion of the students have been imperfectly educated, to begin with, and they resort to the Theological College with the view of qualifying themselves in the cheapest and most expeditious manner to pass the ordination examination. The students are all destined for the ministry. This, which might be deemed in some respects an advantage, is not without a serious drawback. No man, it has been said, is a good theologian who is nothing but a theologian. The education of a Theological College is necessarily a class education. This is the last thing to be desired for the clergy of our Church. If they are really to influence society, if they are to mould or direct the current of thought on questions of vital importance in the affairs of ordinary life, not less than in matters of religion, there should be a breadth and depth in their education which the contracted sphere of a Theological College does not permit. They should mingle freely, during the period of their intellectual training, with students for other callings in life, if they are to escape the narrowness of view which generally characterises persons who associate exclusively with one class. It is surely a part of our high vocation, as ministers of Christ's Church, to exercise a wholesome influence on all orders of men and all classes of mind. Now, the system of a Theological College, if relied upon as the only preparation for the ministry, is, to say the least, not favourable to this.

Upon the whole, then, assuming the existence of personal piety, which is the first and highest qualification, for the want of which no degree of intellectual ability or attainment is any counterpoise, you are more likely to find the elements which combine to make an efficient clergyman in one who has received an University education than in one who has merely passed the prescribed course in a theological college. Having this conviction, I strongly recommend that in the selection of candidates for ordination, every effort should be used to procure them from graduates of one of our Universities."

The Rev. Clement Cobb, from whose recollections more than one quotation has been already made, writes of the ordinations at Ripon :—

Most solemn and heart-stirring were the ordination seasons. Before he began work the Bishop called his chaplains to earnest prayer for the presence and help of the great Head of the Church. While we set the papers, and conducted the written examination, he was in a separate room, and had each candidate for a private interview. This was in addition to a preliminary interview, on which he always insisted before accepting any man as a candidate. I was never present at any of these interviews, but I believe there was always *viva voce* examination in the Greek Testament, a careful and suggestive sifting of the motives which were leading a man to seek the ministry, and in the case of deacons, an examination into their work and self-culture during the diaconate. The examination at Ripon had the character of not being severe ; but while the experience of rejecting men was the most painful, it was a satisfaction to my mind, as proving the reality of the test, at least to some measure, that I hardly ever assisted at an examination that one or more men were not rejected.

Our examinations were usually spread over four days

and on three of these, after the work was over, all were
gathered together to hear an address from one who truly
stood before them as a Father in Christ. The addresses
were most solemn, most heart-searching, most moving.
The Bishop would clearly set forth the qualifications and
credentials which were necessary and desirable to constitute
the outward call to the ministry. Then he would pass, in
clear and careful discrimination, to the indispensable inward
call—the "moving by the Holy Ghost" about to be publicly
professed, the personal reception of those truths which they
were about to teach, so that they became a very constituent
part of our moral and spiritual nature.

Nor were the men thus with prayer and pains, carefulness and earnestness, examination and exhortation, admitted
to Holy Orders afterwards forgotten. The Bishop always
had his eye on good men to be placed in charge of parishes
in his diocese as they fell vacant. It is not too much to
affirm, that not only parishes were blessed with a happy
revolution by many of these appointments, but that the
whole tone and character of Church life in some of the
great towns of the West Riding was rectified and revived.
To be sure, there was one great difficulty, which the
Bishop's desires and cares could not overcome ; and that
was, that many of the so-called livings to which he had to
present were starvings, and he could not get good men
to take them. Hence he thought that an arrangement for
the augmentation of poor livings should be prior in its
claims even to one for the augmentation of curates' stipends.

In my last interview with him, when by the sea, in
health broken down prematurely by his over-abounding
labours, he referred to the early days of his episcopate, and
went over with pleasure the names and locations of those
whom he had ordained. "Ah! I have always felt the
greatest interest in So-and-so ; he was one of the very first
whom I ordained."

One plan he adopted with excellent results, viz. to
hold his ordinations not always at Ripon, where people
were accustomed to them, but in various populous centres

in his diocese, *e.g.* Leeds, Huddersfield, Bradford, Richmond, etc. The large old parish churches were crowded with interested worshippers, who thus, generally for the first time, learned the solemn responsibilities to which ministers of the Church pledge themselves. The laity of the place chosen had the option put before them of receiving the candidates for ordination as their guests during the examination. This was done with more than readiness, and the Bishop courteously went round to call on the hosts and offer his thanks in person. Thus he wove bonds of union in the Church, and he told me with amusement that he found one great advantage resulting from this kindly hospitality was the profound impression established of the searching character of the ordination examination. The hosts with one consent had been moved to sympathy by the keen anxieties of " their gentlemen."

In later years, when health and strength were failing, my father sought the aid of others to give devotional addresses during the week of examination, but in earlier days he used to give all the addresses himself, and frequently preached in person on the ordination day.

It is difficult to convey to those who never heard them the subtle charm and the intense force of words which came from his very heart ; but not a few of his clergy will never forget the impression of their Bishop's character which they gained on the eve of ordination.

One gentleman, a stranger to the writer and no longer in the diocese, has kindly sent a little note which he terms—

ORDINATION REMINISCENCES : A PERSONAL TESTIMONY.

I shall never forget my ordination in 1857. On many accounts it was a season to be thankfully remembered.

From my boyhood I had read with much interest, and I hope profit, the writings of the revered Edward Bicker-steth of Watton ; and when I decided to enter the ministry, I determined to seek ordination at the hands of his epi-scopal relative. After some correspondence I obtained an interview with the Bishop in London, who examined me carefully as to my object in seeking Holy Orders, my religious experience, attainments, etc., and finally com-mended me in prayer to God in a way that won my heart. He was kind enough to mention my name to several incumbents in the diocese, so that I soon received four different offers of a title to a curacy. Choosing one of these, I duly presented myself at Ripon with a number of other candidates. During the examination the Bishop addressed us every day in the Palace Chapel, and nothing, I am persuaded, could surpass the earnestness and pointed character of his appeals. They were most solemn, eloquent, impressive, and led, I know, to great searchings of hearts on the part of his hearers. Even at this distant day I seem to see his fine handsome countenance glowing with emotion, and to hear his voice pleading with intense fervour the cause of our own and of our future congregations' immortal souls. Alas! for the Church he loved and served so well, that that voice of powerful entreaty should have been put to silence in the grave. On the succeeding Sunday morning it was arranged that we should walk to the cathedral in our gowns, two and two. The gentleman appointed to accompany me was a stranger. I had scarcely noticed him previously. But we soon got into conversa-tion, and I could not help referring to the Bishop's ad-dresses, and saying what cause we had for thankfulness that Providence had directed our steps to that place. " I especially have reason to say so," said my companion ; and on my looking for an explanation he remarked, " I was ordained deacon some time ago by the Bishop of ——. The whole proceeding was cold, formal, lifeless. It made no impression upon me whatever. But immediately on my coming here I was effectively aroused. For the first time my eyes were opened to see the responsibilities I had incurred. As the examination went on I became very uneasy, perceiving myself to be utterly unfit for the work I had undertaken. I felt I must speak to the Bishop and lay my case before him. Obtaining the desired interview, his lordship," continued my informant, with faltering accents, "received me most kindly, listened to me, questioned, counselled me, and then, kneeling down at my side, prayed for me in words and with a sympathising fervour I can never forget, that the event might be a turning-point in my ministerial life; that I might hereafter be endued with 'power from on high,' and made the means of winning many sinners to the Saviour. And now," added my friend, "I shall, please God, return to my parish to work as I have never worked hitherto, with a new motive and a higher aim, trusting my labours in the future may be owned and blessed." By this time we had reached the cathedral doors, and were soon in our seats. The service we all, I think, felt to be refreshing. The Bishop's sermon was from the text, "I will go in the strength of the Lord God: I will make mention of Thy righteousness only." He urged us to take this verse for our motto in our ministry, to prosecute our work in the Lord's strength, and to preach His righteousness alone to our respective flocks. Never, I imagine, will the discourse be forgotten by those who heard it. Then came to us, the candidates, the great event of the day. But I shall not attempt to describe the solemn and impressive manner of that laying on of hands. It need not be told how the remainder of the day was spent, partly at the Palace, nor how the Bishop watched over us subsequently with unabated interest and kindness; but I cannot close this hasty sketch without remarking—Oh that all ordination services were of the same character; oh that we had more such prelates!

CHAPTER XI.

IN a former chapter mention has been made of the great reluctance with which my father was absent from his diocese when detained by duty in the House of Lords, and he never attempted to take any considerable share in the business of that assembly. And yet on the one or two occasions when he spoke, he showed that he possessed more than ordinary power.

Early in the year 1858 he was asked by the Archbishop of York (Musgrave) to speak in answer to the late Lord Redesdale, who had entered into a controversy on the subject of the Northern Convocation. On July 19, the Archbishop wrote as follows :—

Bishopthorpe.

My dear Lord,—A thousand thanks for your valuable and very efficient help on Friday last. From a near relative, who was in the House at my desire, I heard that you were well and most attentively heard by those who were present, and Lord Redesdale had clearly little to say in answer. You made all the use that was necessary of the papers with which I troubled you. The weight of your own business and correspondence I can well guess at, and I was quite sorry to have to add to your labours.

＊　　＊　　＊　　＊　　＊

From time to time my father spoke in the House on a subject with regard to which he took a line quite distinct from most of his Episcopal brethren ; this was the question of marriage with a deceased wife's sister, upon which the substance of his views may best be gathered from the following *resumé* of a speech which he delivered in the House of Lords in the session of 1870 :—

He asked for the indulgence of their Lordships while he stated the grounds on which he should support the Bill ; and he asked for it the more earnestly, because it was his misfortune to differ from the large majority of his Right Rev. Brethren, and also from many others, whose opinions he greatly respected, and to whose judgment, if it were possible for him to do so, he would gladly bow.

The first question which presented itself to his mind in connection with the particular class of marriages which the Bill proposed to legalise was, "What is the voice of Scripture with regard to these marriages?" If that voice had clearly and definitely spoken, and if the Word of God had prohibited these marriages, no human enactment could possibly make them lawful. Indeed, the mere attempt to do so would be wholly unjustifiable. After a most patient investigation of the subject, he was entirely unable to arrive at the conclusion expressed by his Right Rev. Brother (Ely) who had just addressed the House, that Scripture prohibited these marriages. On the contrary, he believed that tacitly, and by implication, the Law of God permitted them. He would not attempt to follow his Right Rev. Brother into the intricacies of that verbal criticism which he had made of different texts of Scripture, but he wished to quote the testimony of some theologians who were admitted to be very able and learned, whose attention had been specially directed to this particular question, and whose opinions entirely coincided with his own as to the lawfulness, according to Scripture, of these marriages. He then cited in turn the opinions of the Bishop of St. David's (Dr. Thirlwall), the Rev. Dr. McCaul, and Dr. Tregelles.

If he stood alone in his opinion that the Word of God was not opposed to such marriages, he should be ready to suspect the soundness of his judgment ; but when he found that his opinion was confirmed by some of the ablest and most diligent students and interpreters of the Scriptures, he felt strengthened in the conviction that the restriction on such marriages as this Bill proposed to legalise was not founded upon any authority of Scripture. If, then, Scripture did not support the existing law, was it wise or right to make, by human enactment, that a sin which the Word of God does not declare to be a sin ?

Of course, if the Scriptural argument against such marriages were abandoned, those who objected to them were, as every one acknowledged, thrown at once upon social considerations. Now it seemed strange to assume that the various social evils which had been referred to would certainly arise in this country if these marriages were legalised, although in countries where these marriages had always been permitted by law no such evils were found to exist. He believed this was almost the only country in the world in which a marriage with a deceased wife's sister was illegal ; and he had not heard that any of the social evils which existed in countries where such unions were lawful could be directly traced to the state of the law. Bishop M'Ilvaine stated that in America, although these marriages were celebrated without disapprobation, he was not con-

N

scious of any evil having arisen from them. But it was said that the sanctity and purity of domestic life would be imperilled if this Bill were allowed to pass. He confessed, however, that he had a far higher opinion of the sanctity and purity of domestic life in this country than to believe that it rested on so weak a foundation as a restriction which was not sanctioned by the Word of God.

He believed the sanctity and purity of domestic life would remain unaffected if this Bill became law, as he sincerely trusted it would. All the arguments employed with respect to the social aspect of the question were directed against certain imaginary evils, which it was assumed would arise if the law were altered; there had been no allusion whatever to the great social evils which existed at the present time, and which might be directly traced to the operation of the law. Was it no evil that we should have a law which was found in practice utterly impossible to maintain, and which was broken and violated continually? Was it no evil that there should exist among a large class of the population a sense of wrong and oppression, because it was felt that the law of the land hindered them from doing that which by the law of God they were permitted to do? Lastly, was it no evil that the existing state of the law was in many instances directly provocative of crime?

He wished to adduce some testimony on this point. His Right Rev. Brother who last addressed the House stated that he had been stationed in many different parishes with large populations, but that he had seen no evils resulting from the operation of the law as it now stood. The Right Rev. Prelate's experience had been singularly fortunate. He had himself had the care of parishes with large populations, and he had seen very great evils result from the operation of the law. He would not, however, quote his own authority, but would take the testimony of one who was revered by a very large number of Christians in this country, and who, to the regret of his friends, had been recently removed from among them—Dr. Dale, Dean of

Rochester, who for a long period of his life had charge of very large parishes. . . .

He would also cite the testimony of another divine, whose name was never mentioned without honour—he alluded to Dr. Hook, Dean of Chichester, who had, perhaps, had a larger experience than any living man in the charge of large parishes. Also he would quote, to the same effect, the Dean of Carlisle, Dr. Close, and the testimony of the Dean of Lichfield, better known as Canon Champneys.

Such were the opinions of eminently practical and Christian men who had had wide experience in dealing with large parishes. The Bill would affect a class of cases involving very great hardships which ought to be removed by the legislature. After the passing of the Act of 1835, commonly called Lord Lyndhurst's Act, there was a very general impression—whether a right one or not 'he would not say—that persons who wished to contract such marriages as were under discussion might legally do so in a foreign country where such marriages were lawful. It was believed that marriages so celebrated were lawful according to the law of this land. In very many instances persons had acted in this belief; they had gone abroad and had complied with all the conditions which they supposed necessary to make their marriage valid ; and it was not until a decision to the contrary was recently given (*Brook v. Brook*) by one of the superior courts of law that for the first time they learned that they had acted under a mistake, and that their marriage could not be recognised by the law of this country. Such persons had to endure a great hardship in no legal remedy being provided to render valid marriages which had been so contracted. This Bill would have that effect, and for that, among other reasons, he most earnestly hoped it would pass into law. Believing, as he did, that the restrictions which were sought to be removed were not founded upon any authority of Scripture ; that, on the contrary, the Word of God tacitly sanctioned such marriages ; that the existing restrictions imposed a grievous burden on men's consciences, and that they were in many cases provocative of crime ; and believing that the alteration of the law would be a great relief to many who justly deserved to receive it, although it was with the deepest regret that he found himself at variance with the opinions of so many for whom he had a profound respect, he must vote in favour of the Bill.

It was characteristic of my father that he never swerved from an opinion once deliberately formed ; and he continued to vote on the same side, even when he had no longer the powerful support of men like Bishop Thirlwall ; while other prelates, who felt less strongly on the matter, shrank from opposing their brethren on the Bench and the great bulk of clerical opinion.

At the request of some, by whom the impression which it made is still remembered, I insert here the speech which my father delivered on the second reading of the Irish Church Disestablishment Bill. As an example of his style the speech is none the less valuable because it was delivered in aid of a lost cause, and those who remember the circumstances of the debate and read it with attention, will understand why some good judges thought that my father's speech compared not unfavourably with the brilliant oration delivered on the same occasion by Bishop Magee.

He said—

It is with the utmost diffidence that I venture to take any part in this debate. Nothing but a sense of duty would induce me to trespass, even for a few moments, on your Lordships' attention. But this is a question on which I cannot give a silent vote. With the details of the measure under consideration I will not attempt to grapple ; partly because I look upon this as being the proper stage to discuss its principle, and partly because I deem it right frankly to confess that, in my judgment, that principle is so bad, that I despair of rendering the Bill a good one by any manipulation of its details.

A variety of arguments have been urged in the course of this debate against the measure, in all of which I fully concur.

Its principle is the disestablishment and disendowment of the Church in Ireland.

Now the primary objection which I entertain to it is, that it involves the assumption that it is no part of the duty of a Christian State to connect itself with the maintenance of Christian truth. Should this Bill become law, the State, so far as Ireland is concerned, will have disconnected itself altogether from religion. It will have virtually declared that all creeds are equally true, or equally false, that it will recognise none, and have a preference for none. This conclusion I deprecate in the interests of the Church, but still more in the interests of the State itself. I believe there is a national as well as an individual responsibility. Nations as well as individuals are morally accountable, and we cannot ignore this responsibility without challenging the disfavour of God. If we believe that all power is from God, and that the powers which be are ordained of God, then I cannot see how it can be right for those in possession of power to ignore their responsibility to Him from Whom it is derived. And how, I would ask, is a State to exercise this responsibility except by connecting itself with some ecclesiastical organisation ?

Now I, for one, altogether deny that the question on which that organisation should depend is the question of the majority of the people. There are higher questions than that at issue. The question of truth ought, I contend, to be paramount to every other consideration. I believe it to be the duty of a Christian State in determining the ecclesiastical organisation with which it is to connect itself, to look mainly and chiefly to the question of religious truth. This principle is recognised by the British Constitution. The Church is an integral portion of the State. It is inseparably connected with it. You cannot impair the position of the one without injuring that of the other. You cannot destroy the Church without pulling down the Constitution of which it forms a part. Notwithstanding, I may add, all that has been said on the subject, I confess I entertain the opinion that the principle of this Bill is inconsistent with the Act of Union.

It must, of course, be admitted that it is competent to Parliament to repeal and alter laws which itself has made. This is the case with reference to all ordinary Acts of Parliament, but it seems to me that the case is altogether different when we are dealing with the Act which has been passed for an express purpose to ratify a treaty entered into between two independent nations. I, for one, believe that it is a breach of national faith and honour to ignore the conditions of a treaty thus solemnly entered into—conditions without which that treaty would never have been accomplished.

I concur, moreover, in the opinion that this measure is calculated to have an indirect effect in shaking the security of property. I admit that there is a difference between private and corporate property ; but to ignore the undisputed possession of three hundred years is, in my opinion, to unsettle the security for all property ; and this Bill I think calculated to inflict a blow on the security of property of every kind. Upon that point I would quote the testimony of the late Mr. Anthony Richard Blake, a Roman Catholic layman, given on oath before a Parliamentary Committee. He said :—

"The Protestant Church is rooted in the Constitution ; it is established by the fundamental laws of the realm ; it is rendered, as far as the most solemn acts of the Legislature can render any institution, fundamental and perpetual ; it is so declared by the Act of Union between Great Britain and Ireland. I think it could not now be disturbed without danger to the general securities we possess for liberty, property, and order, without danger to all the blessings we derive from being under a lawful Government and a free Constitution. Feeling thus, the very conscience which dictates to me a determined adherence to the Roman Catholic religion would dictate to me a determined resistance to any attempt to subvert the Protestant Establishment, or to wrest from the Church the possessions which the law has given it."

I entertain another objection to this Bill, founded on what I conceive to be the probable effect of its passing into law. It has been called a great measure, and I think, notwithstanding what fell from my Right Rev. Brother the other night, who called it a little Bill, that it is a great measure. The noble Earl who moved the second reading, told us that it had engaged the most anxious labour and thought of the Government in its preparation. The noble Lord who moved its rejection, spoke of its striking at the roots of the Constitution. By others it has been termed, and I think rightly, a revolutionary Bill ; but, be that as it may, few, I presume, will deny that it is a measure of great importance. If that be so, I cannot help feeling that we are entitled to ask for some evidence to show that it will accomplish the end which its authors propose to themselves—an end which we all desire to see attained—the welfare and prosperity of the sister country. Is this Bill, then, likely to promote the pacification of Ireland, or to confer important benefits on that country? My own conviction is, that if passed into law, it will not have a feather's weight in producing contentment and peace in Ireland. And in support of this view, I would ask, in what manner has it already been received by the Irish people ? Has the notice of it been welcomed as an olive branch of peace, or has it not rather been received as an apple of discord ? Has not the discontent by which that unhappy country has so long been distracted been rather increased than otherwise, since the measure has been brought under the consideration of Parliament ? Are your Lordships not aware that the great grievance of Ireland, as proclaimed by the Roman Catholics of that country, is, not the existence of the Established Church, but the position of the land question ; and that Irish Roman Catholics affirm, they will never be satisfied until that question is settled ?

I entertain another objection to this Bill, founded upon the inopportune period at which it seems to me to have been introduced.

Among the many arguments employed in favour of this measure there is one that is frequently used—that the Established Church in Ireland has not discharged its missionary obligations ; that it has failed to perform the duties that devolve upon it with regard to the whole population of Ireland. I must say here that the clergy of the Established Church in Ireland have, as it appears to me, been very unfairly dealt with. If they confine their ministrations to the Protestant parishioners of their respective parishes, they are told that the Church has failed in discharging its missionary obligations ; and if, on the other hand, they display any zeal in endeavouring to gain converts from among the Roman Catholics, they are immediately denounced as firebrands. And yet it must be within the cognisance of all your Lordships that there has been a most remarkable revival of fervour and zeal among the clergy of late years, showing itself in increased efforts for the conversion of the Roman Catholic population, and that these efforts have been attended by the most remarkable success. Having visited those portions of Ireland where these missionary efforts have been most vigorously and actively carried forward, I can testify, from personal observation, to the importance and genuineness of the work which is being accomplished.

But we are not merely dependent for proof of the success upon Protestant testimony. The *Nation*, the organ of the intensely Irish party in the country, says of Ireland :—

"There can no longer be any question that the systematised proselytism has met with an immense success in Connaught and Kerry.

"It is true that the altars of the Catholic Church have

been deserted by thousands, born and baptized in the ancient faith of Ireland. Travellers who have recently visited the counties of Galway and Mayo report that 'the agents of that foul and abominable traffic'" (the term they apply to the work of our Church) "are every day opening new schools of perversion, and are founding new churches for the accommodation of their purchased congregations. Witnesses more trustworthy than Sir Francis Head, Catholic Irishmen who grieve to behold the spread and success of the apostacy, tell us that the west of Ireland is deserting the ancient fold ; and that a class of Protestants, more bigoted and anti-Irish, if possible, than the followers of the old Establishment, is grown up from the recreant peasantry and their children."

We have, then, incontrovertible evidence of the fact that the Church in general is making exertions hitherto unexampled in modern times for the purpose of winning Roman Catholics to the fold of the Established Church ; and yet we are told, as an argument in support of this measure, that the Irish Church has failed to discharge its missionary obligations.

But this measure is recommended to us on the plea of justice and religious equality. There is one consideration with respect to this plea of justice which has occurred forcibly to my mind in the course of this debate. Justice is a high and sacred principle. Now, if there is injustice in the existence of the Established Church in Ireland at the present moment, there must have been injustice in its establishment at the time of the Union, and there must have been injustice in its continuance from the time of the Union down to the present moment. If this be so, how is it that the plea of justice has never been mooted before ? It is not that Ireland has been neglected in the deliberations of British statesmen. It is not that Ireland has not had its full share in the consideration of Parliament. Statesmen the most sagacious, keen-sighted, and far-seeing have, from time to time, considered the interests of Ireland. Ireland has given rise to questions which have, I believe, on more than one occasion decided the fate of Governments; it has occupied the anxious and solicitous attention of numbers of those who have been called to the helm of the Constitution. Are we to suppose that they have not been far-sighted enough to see the injustice, if it existed; or are we to admit—a supposition which is still more untenable—that if they did perceive the injustice, they were unwilling to interfere to redress the grievance? But I take the testimony of a Roman Catholic on this point, and, according to his testimony, I think it is conclusive that, in the opinion of some enlightened Roman Catholics, there is, in reality, no such injustice. Dr. Slevin, a Roman Catholic professor at Maynooth, in his evidence before the Commissioners of Education in 1826, said—

"I consider that the present possessors of Church property in Ireland, of whatever description they may be, have a just title to it. They have been *bonâ fide* possessors of it for all the time required by any law for prescription; even according to the pretensions of the Church of Rome, which require one hundred years."

Another plea is that of religious equality. I would not on any consideration utter a harsh or unkind word with respect to my Roman Catholic fellow-subjects. I am not conscious of entertaining an unkind feeling towards them, or of having, at any time, uttered against them an uncharitable word. I believe toleration is a great principle, and that to exercise toleration is the duty of a Christian State as well as of a Christian Church; but equality, as between Roman Catholics and Protestants, you cannot possibly have. It is not in the essence of Roman Catholicism; it is not in the essence of Protestantism. Between the two there is an impassable gulf. We Protestants hold that Roman Catholics entertain fundamental errors, and the Church of Rome hurls her anathemas against Protestants for repudiating that which she maintains to be fundamental truth. The effect of this measure will be to produce, not religious equality, but Romish ascendency. I believe no other result will follow this measure, than to give to Rome

the ascendency in Ireland ; and, therefore, the very evil of
which the noble Earl complains, would exist, even if this
Bill were passed into law.

I will not touch upon another question—the verdict of
the country with regard to this measure—beyond saying
that I concur with those who have said that they are
not satisfied that the verdict of the country has been
pronounced upon this particular Bill. I will go even further
than this. It is my honest conviction that there is a
change coming about in the feelings of the country at
large with respect to this Bill ; and although a taunt was
thrown out the other evening with regard to what were
called the tumultuous assemblages which have been convened with regard to this measure, I cannot help saying
that in that part of the country with which I am officially
connected, and especially in the great towns of the West
Riding of Yorkshire, I have satisfactory evidence that there
has been a change in the feeling with regard to this measure
—a change expressed not in noise or tumult, but in calm,
clear, and unwavering utterances of dissatisfaction and disappointment ; and it is my conviction, that if your Lordships reject this Bill on the second reading, and it be
submitted to the country for further investigation and consideration, the verdict of the country will ultimately confirm
and approve the decision of your Lordships.

I listened with the greatest attention to the speech of
the noble Earl who addressed the House at the opening
of the debate on Tuesday evening (Earl Grey), when he
endeavoured to show that it was our duty to accept the
second reading of the Bill, and then try and improve it in
Committee. If it were merely a question of political expediency, if no moral considerations were involved, I might
feel disposed to accept that advice ; but, believing, as I do,
that it involves moral considerations of the highest importance, I cannot prefer to accept expediency as my guide,
rather than what is morally right ; believing, as I in my
conscience do, that this Bill is not called for by any claim
for justice to Ireland ; believing that it will not confer any

lasting benefit upon that distracted and unhappy portion of the United Kingdom ; believing that it will prove a blow to Protestantism, and a triumph to Romanism ; believing that it will exasperate Protestants, without conciliating Romanists ; believing, further, that it will necessarily be the precursor to other measures still more disastrous to the Church and the Constitution ; believing that the adoption of this measure would amount to a national sin, and that what is morally wrong can never be politically right,—I must enter my protest against the second reading of this Bill.

During his shorter visits to London, when my father was alone, he stayed at the National Club, in Whitehall Gardens ; and at other times he was the guest of Mr. and Mrs. Isaac Braithwaite, who had been amongst his chief friends and supporters at St. Giles's. Occasionally he was obliged to stay in town, sorely against his will, for a longer period, and then he usually occupied a house in South Kensington. In London his Sundays were fully occupied. Once he wrote home to say, " I wish I had a sermon every night, for I feel so idle when I am away from the diocese." And no wonder that he liked to preach, when he was cheered with abundant proof of the way in which people hungered for the Word of God. He wrote on March 23, 1858 :—

Last night, after remaining in the House till near seven, I went to preach in Spitalfields. I think you would have been greatly struck with the scene. It is a very large church. It is where I was once lecturer for a short time, when I first came to Clapham. It was *crowded* with the poor Spitalfields weavers from end to end. Galleries and aisles all full, and many standing. Patteson read the Litany, and then I preached for fifty minutes. They were amazingly attentive, and listened with great eagerness to the end.

When all was over I yielded to Patteson's entreaty, and went into the rectory, which was close by. Presently some one came and told us that the crowd was waiting at the church door, and would not go away till I was gone. He sent one of his curates with a message that I should be in his house for half an hour, and it was no good their waiting. However, they said they did not care ; they would wait. And when, at last, I came out, they were in great numbers filling up the street, and standing all round the cab. So I just called out once or twice, " God bless you all, my good people ! " and they then cried out, " God bless you, sir ; God bless you ! Thank you ; and won't you come again ? " It was very touching, and one cannot help hoping there may be some fruit seen from it in Eternity. The Bishop of London has asked me to preach for him in April. I said, " By-all means ; only, please don't send me to Deptford." " Oh," he said, " but that is where they want to have you again." So one hopes my stay in London may have been, through God's grace and mercy, of some blessing to some.

On questions of general politics my father was in the main a Liberal. His genuine sympathy with freedom and progress, and hearty advocacy of all schemes calculated to advance the interest of the working classes, leave no doubt as to the spirit in which he was ready to approach the perplexing social problems of the day ; but when confronted by those who advocated a more Radical pro- gramme, he would frequently describe himself as a " Palmerstonian," in playful allusion to the Minister to whose recommendation (under Divine Provi- dence) he owed his bishopric. He possessed the friendship and respect of political leaders on both sides ; and Mr. Gladstone and Lord Beacons- field alike placed considerable reliance on his judg- ment. Confidential inquiries as to the fitness of

particular men for important posts are not available
to illustrate this without trenching upon boundaries
of discretion which ought not to be overstepped;
but there is no reason why it should not be known
that in one weighty instance, and that a case of no
little difficulty, Mr. Gladstone in after-years expressed
his satisfaction that the Bishop's advice should have
turned the scale in the direction of a particular
appointment. The nomination in question had in
some quarters been warmly opposed, and in others
its announcement was received with a certain amount
of disfavour; but it has since been reckoned by
universal consent amongst the substantial benefits
which Mr. Gladstone has conferred upon the Church.

Less reserve is necessary in making public the
following letter from Lord Beaconsfield, which will
be interesting to many people, not only because it
shows what that eminent statesman thought of my
father's judgment, but also because it shows that
Lord Beaconsfield himself deserves credit for a deep
sense of responsibility in his ecclesiastical appointments, and for a personal interest in theological
questions, which he has not generally received.

My father wrote to inform him of the sudden
death of Dr. Goode, and received the following
reply :—

[*Confidential.*]

Hughenden Manor, August 15, 1868.

My dear Lord,—Your letter of the 13th instant gave
me a great shock. You will fully comprehend this, when
I tell you, in confidence, that being forced to consider
within the last few days, unhappily, the probability of a
vacancy on the Bench which you yourself adorn, I contemplated advising the Queen to nominate the Dean of Ripon

to the See, which would in that event have been at Her Majesty's disposal. It is therefore unnecessary for me to assure your Lordship that you need be under no apprehension, that in the appointment of his successor, I shall not be influenced by the representations which you have made to me. I am myself bound up with no party in the Church. I frankly admit that my bias, years ago, was to High Church principles, which I held not only to be consistent with the principles of the Reformation, but their best safeguard and security. The secession of Dr. Newman, however, and his friends very much affected me in this respect, and I have ever laboured since to induce moderate men of both parties to act together against the combined efforts of disguised Jesuits and avowed infidels. I should feel very much obliged to your Lordship if, in confidence, you would indicate to me any men who, not only from their Protestant principles, but their becoming learning, knowledge of mankind, and administrative power, would be fitting in your opinion for the Prelacy. No one is more impressed than myself with the present critical state of affairs, both for the Church and the Nation. It cannot be exaggerated. But whatever may happen, I wish to have the consolation, that in a responsible position I have, under Divine Providence, done my utmost to maintain the true interests of the Church of England.

I have the honour to remain, my dear Lord,

Yours faithfully,

B. DISRAELI.

Another expression of Lord Beaconsfield's views on ecclesiastical questions occurs in the following letter, written by Bishop Baring to my father :—

Auckland Castle, Bishop Auckland, December 9, 1878.

My dear Bishop,—You will have heard of my intended resignation of my See. To my great surprise, not only did Lord Beaconsfield write in reply a most kind and complimentary letter, but added at its close, "Ecclesiastical appointments in these days of difficulty and trial are those which cost me the greatest anxiety. I should feel obliged to you if, in strict confidence, you would give me some names of those whom I might consider for your See."

I have sent him but two names, and have placed yours very decidedly first. There will be doubtless other influences at work, but I think it possible that without letting any one know the contents of this letter, you might know some friend of Lord Beaconsfield who would confirm my recommendation.

Yours very truly,
C. DUNELM.

Those who knew my father need not be told that he did not act on the Bishop's suggestion. Never in his life did he ask for preferment for himself;[1] and he wrote to Bishop Baring, grateful for his kind thought, but saying that he left all such matters in the Hand of God, and would certainly make no effort in his own behalf.

Lord Beaconsfield was happily guided to the choice of Dr. Lightfoot, and my father's friends cannot regret that he was not summoned to undertake a new charge at a time when his working days were drawing to a close, and when it needed the strength and vigour of a younger man to divide the great Border diocese, and to create the See of Newcastle.

It is in this chapter that I have tried to show something of my father's public work outside the diocese. When in London, he was constant in his attendance at the Bounty Board; and on the Eccle-

---

[1] The occasion mentioned in my father's letter, quoted on p. 134, can hardly be called an exception. The allusion in that letter is to my father's unsuccessful candidature for a London preachership, to which no one could be appointed who had not allowed his name to be brought before the electors.

siastical Commission his business talents were the admiration of his brethren on the Bench. One of them, Dr. Thorold, of Rochester, who followed my father at St. Giles's, wrote an obituary notice for *Church Bells*, in which he says—

As a speaker and debater he was cogent, vigorous, and sometimes impassioned. His striking presence, singularly beautiful countenance, and melodious voice, winged his words. One adjective exactly characterises his administration—*habilis*. He was one of the ablest men that ever sat on the Bench; and the writer of this notice well remembers once sitting with him at a Trust meeting, and observing how the Junior Optime, by his quickness of resource, decision of character, and prompt acumen, distanced in his faculty of business a double first class man at his side, as completely as a greyhound would run past a cob. He saw instantly the kernel of a question, went at it, and, when it was possible, settled it.

My father usually spent the months of May and June in London, ever ready to preach for charitable objects; and no bishop figured more often at the meetings of the great societies in Exeter Hall.

The old-fashioned prejudice against the appearance of bishops at such meetings has long passed away, and the Evangelical clergy no longer monopolise the month of May with meetings of an exclusively party character. If the Evangelical bishops led the way, the great body of their brethren now take their place as platform speakers; but none have exercised a more powerful influence over the public of Exeter Hall than he who gained their veneration as Rector of St. Giles's, and made the name of the Bishop of Ripon a household word throughout the Evangelical world.

O

CHAPTER XII.

IT has been often noticed that during the whole of
my father's long episcopate, the diocese was quite
free from any of those vexatious prosecutions for
ritualistic practices which excited elsewhere so much
ill feeling, and are now generally condemned. And
yet the diocese of Ripon contains representatives of
all parties within the Church, and there were times
when it needed much patience and forbearance to
prevent the combustible elements from bursting into
flame.

People who knew how strong my father's personal convictions were, and how heartily he disliked
whatever he thought was disloyalty to the principles
of the Reformation, wondered at this result. The
limits of this book would be unduly extended were a
detailed account to be given of the different questions

which came before him ; but it is only right to show what were my father's opinions on some of those matters which still perplex the Church, and how he dealt with various cases of complaint.

In the autumn of 1860 was published the once celebrated volume entitled " Essays and Reviews." In one book were bound up some articles to which, in themselves, little exception could be taken, with others which were perceived to strike at the foundation of the Faith; and the publication, as a whole, gave rise to the gravest apprehension. My father joined with the other bishops in uttering a solemn protest against the book, but expressly declined to be a party to the prosecution of the authors. In answer to a clergyman in the diocese, who forwarded a petition on the subject, my father wrote—

My dear Sir,—I beg to acknowledge the receipt of your letter of the 16th instant, which has reached me by this morning's post.

I do not believe there is a single clergyman in this diocese who can have any doubt as to the opinion which I entertain respecting the volume entitled " Essays and Reviews." I have never attempted to conceal the abhorrence with which I regard the spirit of irreverence and unbelief with which the truth of God's Word is handled in that pernicious book.

At the same time, and with special reference to the line of conduct which you suggest at the present crisis, you must allow me to say that it is in my judgment a point of practical wisdom to refrain from a course of active opposition, in the face of an absolute certainty that such opposition will be of no avail whatever to avert the result at which it is aimed.

Our best resource, under existing circumstances, is earnest prayer that God may be pleased to overrule for good the many trials with which the Church is at this time afflicted.

> Believe me,
> Very faithfully yours,
> R. RIPON.

In the Charge of 1861, after alluding to the proposed revision of the Book of Common Prayer, which was then desired by those who were anxious to be rid of the Athanasian Creed, etc.—a proposal which he emphatically condemned—my father went on to say—

Important, however, as the foregoing topics are, they are trifling in comparison of the perils by which we are threatened from a different quarter. I refer to the dissemination, on the part of eminently learned and distinguished members of our Church, of opinions which go to unsettle all the grand fundamentals of the Christian Faith, which scoff at the idea of a direct inspiration from God, exalt the human intellect to the position of sitting in judgment on revealed truth, discard the doctrine of the Atonement, discredit the truth of prophecy, and disparage the evidence of miracle.

It is, indeed, cause for humiliation and reproach that opinions such as these should have emanated from members of our own Church, upon several of whom the solemn vows of ordination rest to dispense faithfully the Word of God, and to administer the Holy Sacraments. We have surely fallen on perilous times when ordained ministers, who have professed to subscribe willingly and *ex animo* our Thirty-nine Articles, and all things contained in them, can reconcile it to their sworn allegiance to the Church at whose altars they minister, to propagate opinions to which avowed infidels turn in confirmation of their sceptical theories. I fully agree in what has been so ably and truly said of the book to which these remarks mainly refer, by one whose judgment is entitled to great consideration :—" I say, without the shadow of a doubt, that the book does tend and minister to infidelity, and to nothing else. It tends neither to real soundness and clearness of thought, nor yet to real truth, nor yet to a high standard of action ; it will not add one to the Kingdom of God ; it will not convince a single gainsayer of any one Christian truth ; it will not win over to Christ a single enemy ; it will not confirm a single waverer ; it will not satisfy a single doubt, or solve a single difficulty ; it will but suggest doubts where they have been hitherto unthought of, and confirm them where they already exist." [1]

It is not my intention here to detain you by any refutation of these pernicious writings, still less to indulge in any harsh expressions concerning their unhappy authors ; but I should be unfaithful to my office were I not to deliver a warning against them. You will find it common to all the writings to which I have referred to call in question the authority of the Bible as the inspired Word of God, to overlook the fundamental doctrine of the corruption of human nature, and to invalidate the doctrine of the Atonement of our Blessed Lord and Saviour. Be it your constant endeavour, my Reverend Brethren, to set these doctrines plainly forth, and the rather because of the assault which has been directed against them. Uphold the doctrine of the Inspiration ; show in what sense you regard the Bible to be an inspired record ; not because you take it to be the production of men of brilliant genius, but because you believe it to have been written by men who spake as they were moved by the Holy Ghost. The distinction between the Inspiration of Scripture and that of any other production of human intellect is not a difference of degree, it is a difference of kind. In the imagery of Homer, or the rapturous flights of Milton, I recognise the play of marvellous intellect ; but this is as remote as possible from the Inspiration of the Bible. In the one case the production is human ; in the other, Divine. In the one

[1] " Supremacy of Scripture : an Examination, etc., in a Letter to the Rev. Dr. Temple." By William Edward Jelf, D.D.

case, I may criticise, censure, or approve. In the other, I hear the Voice of the ever-living Jehovah, which it must be at my peril to disregard. You cannot be too careful to point out that while it comes legitimately within the province of reason to collect and to weigh the evidences upon which the truth of Inspiration depends, having once established the point that the Bible is Divinely inspired, our only attitude with regard to its statements must ever afterwards be that of reverential submission.

Dwell likewise upon the doctrine of human corruption. Let there be no reservation on this point. Scripture is plain : be our expositions of Scripture plain also. Man is by nature alienated from God, afar off, an enemy in his mind by wicked works—the heart deceitful above all things, and desperately wicked—the carnal mind at enmity against God, the understanding darkened, the will perverted, and the moral powers enfeebled. "The natural man receiveth not the things of the Spirit of God, for they are foolishness unto him, neither can he know them, because they are spiritually discerned." The reception of such Scriptural statements as these will leave no plea for the arrogant assumption of "a verifying faculty" in man qualifying him to sit in judgment upon the truth of Revelation.

In the Charge of 1864, after dealing as usual with diocesan details, my father went on to trace, in a passage of much force, the subtle connection between two apparently opposite tendencies which he equally condemned :—

Within the memory of most of those whom I am now addressing, two opposite schools of theology have displayed within the bosom of our Church the greatest activity. They are still striving for ascendency. The distinguishing feature of the one is the exaltation of authority ; the distinguishing feature of the other is the exaltation of intellect. By the one class of theologians, implicit, almost unquestioning obedience is claimed on behalf of the Church, on the ground of her Divine original ; her Ministry derived by an unbroken series of links from the Apostles themselves ; her right of administering the Sacraments, her traditions, her guardianship of Holy Writ ; her office both to keep and to expound the mysteries of Divine truth. By the other class of theologians, this claim on the ground of exclusive authority is, to a great extent, if not altogether, set aside. Truth is to be tested by the powers of human reason. Revelation itself must submit to the same searching process of investigation as that by which the facts of profane history or of science are weighed and determined. Conscience is elevated to a position of pre-eminence over the revealed Word of God, and a claim is set up on the part of man himself to the possession of a verifying faculty, by the exercise of which he may determine what is to be accepted and what rejected, even in the volume of Revelation itself.

How far it may be the case that secret affinities exist between these two apparently antagonistic schools of theology is a question by no means devoid of interest. It might not be difficult to show that the natural consequence of claiming more than is due on the side of authority is to provoke resistance to every species of control. Unnatural restraint almost inevitably leads to unbridled licence. It is therefore more than possible that, with all their palpable divergencies, the two schools of theology to which I have referred have this relation to each other. The extravagant claim on the footing of authority which has been set up by the one has prepared the way for the extravagant exaltation of reason, as independent of authority, by the other.

But in each case the real root of the evil is to be found in the want of due reverence for the supreme authority of Scripture as a Divine revelation. In each case, singularly enough, the practical result is the same as regards the dishonour which is done to the Word of God. The disciples of the one school maintain that we are indebted

to the Church for the possession of the Scriptures, and
that, independent of her teaching, we are not at liberty to
interpret their meaning. The disciples of the other school
maintain that, owing to the extraordinary advance of
historical, geographical, or scientific research, the progress
of human intellect, and the freer range of thought, the
time has arrived when the facts and even the doctrines of
the Bible must be submitted to methods of trial and
investigation similar to those which are applied to verify
the conclusions of the historian or philosopher. Thus, in
either case, the fundamental truth of the supreme authority
of Revelation is practically obscured or denied, and we
are in peril of being drifted into superstition on the one
hand, or swallowed up in the vortex of infidelity on the
other.

In 1867 my father writes :—

When I addressed you at my last Visitation, the
necessity was laid upon me to warn you against the
dangers to which we were exposed from the attempt to
shake our confidence in the veracity of God's Word. To-
day, it is my no less solemn duty to lift up a voice of
warning against a tide of error, which threatens to destroy
the heritage of truth, which our forefathers recovered by
the battle of the Reformation. . . . If I use great plainness
of speech, it is, nevertheless, my desire to fulfil the Apostolic
injunction, Ἀληθεύοντες δε ἐν ἀγαπῇ.

It is always painful to have to speak in terms of censure
of any of our brethren ; but the interests of truth are
paramount to every other consideration ; nor should it be
forgotten that personal piety and zeal do not afford a
criterion by which to determine that a man is sound in the
Faith. Amongst the disseminators of error have often been
found men of a blameless life, of untiring energy, and of
intense religious feeling. Whilst, then, we admit the zeal
and devotedness which characterises many of those who
have taken a prominent part in controversies which now

agitate the Church, we cannot allow their personal excellence to blind our eyes to the pernicious character of the agitation with which they have become identified.

Foremost amongst these matters of controversy to which I allude is the so-called question of Ritualism. We all admit that ritual is an essential feature of public worship. It was prescribed under the ancient dispensation by God Himself; and although the Jewish ritual together with the whole ceremonial system, of which it was a part, has been abolished, yet it must be clear to any one who reflects on the subject, that an established religion can scarcely exist without an appointed ritual. Far be it from me, then, to disparage the importance of a due regard to rites and ceremonies, which, although they have been devised by man, are still reserved, according to the statement in our Book of Common Prayer, "as well for a decent order in the Church, (for the which they were at first devised) as because they pertain to edification, whereunto all things done in the Church (as the Apostle teacheth) ought to be referred."

Within the last few years, however, we have witnessed a movement in favour of ritualistic observances which has taken the country by surprise, led to much controversy, and aroused both the indignation and alarm of many of the best friends of the Church. Whether or not this movement is only the natural development of principles which have for many years past been industriously propagated by an active party within the Church, it is beyond dispute that it involves a strange innovation upon the established usage of the past three hundred years. The promoters of it claim to have discovered that the legal vestments to be worn by the officiating minister in the Celebration of the Holy Communion are such as, to say the least, have been in disuse if not altogether unknown to the Church from the time of the Reformation. Not only this ; changes have been introduced in the internal arrangement of churches, and in the mode of conducting Divine Service, which convey to all ordinary observers the appearance of a close and studied assimilation of the ritual of our Church to that of the Church of Rome. The costly and elaborate decoration of the Communion-table ; the blaze of candles in broad daylight when the Holy Communion is celebrated ; the practice of mixing water with the wine in the Lord's Supper ; the elevation of the Elements in the act of Consecration, and the various postures assumed by the officiating minister,—are amongst the innovations, the introduction of which in some churches have shocked the minds of many who love and reverence the Church of England as a pure and reformed branch of Christ's Holy Catholic Church, and are not willing to see her simple ritual exchanged for the imposing ceremonial of the Church of Rome. As regards some of these innovations there is confessedly a degree of ambiguity in the law. It may or may not be true that the adoption of these obsolete vestments is legally permissible. Opposite opinions on this point have been given by lawyers of great eminence and learning. At the same time, I think it should occur to those who are eager to introduce innovations of this kind that it must tend to the entire subversion of due order and discipline if individual clergymen, acting on their own judgment, may exercise the liberty to disturb the uniformity which the custom of three centuries has established. Such persons might do well to consider the forcible words in our Book of Common Prayer, " Although the keeping or omitting of a Ceremony, in itself considered, is but a small thing ; yet the wilful and contemptuous transgression and breaking of a common order and discipline is no small offence before God. *Let all things be done among you*, saith St. Paul, *in a seemly and due order :* The appointment of the which order pertaineth not to private men ; therefore no man ought to take in hand, nor presume to appoint or alter any publick or common order in Christ's Church, except he be lawfully called and authorized thereunto."

Now, the adoption of these novel vestments has received almost every kind of censure short of a direct judicial condemnation. It stands condemned by the custom of three hundred years; by the almost unanimous voice of the rulers of the Church; by the Convocations of both Provinces; and, lastly, a Royal Commission, appointed to make inquiry concerning this and other matters, has reported, "that it is expedient to restrain in the public services of the United Church of England and Ireland, all variations in respect of vesture from that which has long been the established usage of the said United Church." It remains to be seen how far this Report from a Commission so constituted as to afford the most ample opportunity to the Ritualists for the full exposition of their opinions, will have any weight with those of whom it is no breach of charity to say they have manifested hitherto very little disposition to defer to advice or counsel from those in authority.

But it is transparent to every one that the real importance of this Ritualistic movement is not to be measured by what only meets the eye. The colour and shape of a vestment may be in itself utterly insignificant. But if the vestment be made a symbol of a particular set of doctrines or opinions, then it is no longer a trivial matter. It is this which renders the whole question now under consideration one of such serious moment. There can no longer be any doubt that the revived Ritualism of the present day is meant to be the exponent of certain doctrines which its advocates are eager to restore to the Church of England. We are not left to infer this merely from manuals of devotion, hymns, and a host of other publications which have streamed from the press under the sanction of names which are identified with the movement, but with singular openness and candour the fact has been again and again avowed. Thus, "Ritual," we are told, "is the expression of doctrine and a witness to the Sacramental system of the Catholic religion."[1] Again, "The whole purpose of this great revival," it is affirmed, "has been to eliminate the dreary Protestantism of the Hanoverian period and restore the glory of Catholic worship. The churches are restored after the mediæval pattern, and our Ritual must accord

[1] " Directorium Anglicanum."

with the Catholic standard." [1]   And in language still more
bold and explicit, another organ of the Ritualistic party
writes thus :—" There is no attempt to disguise the fact
that the Eucharistic Vestments are adopted as significant
of the Sacrifice of the Mass, and the *Church Times* justly
regards them in this light." [2]   Nothing could be further
from my wish than to misrepresent in the smallest particular the character of this movement.   I am willing to hope
and believe that many have been drawn in by the current
who are little aware of its dangerous direction ; but I doubt
if any one can attentively examine the subject and deny
that the questions at issue in this whole Ritualistic revival
are questions of doctrine, and not of mere dress or ceremonial.

Nor can there be any real difficulty in determining
what these questions are.   One point is self-evident : that
in some way or other they all centre in the Holy Communion. " The fact," as it has been justly observed, " which
presents itself most obviously on the face of the whole
matter is the change which has been made in the administration of the Lord's Supper ; the Communion Service of
the Prayer-book is set, as it were, in the frame of the
Roman Catholic ceremonial, with all the accompaniments
of the high and chanted Mass—vestments, lights, incense,
posture, and gestures of the officiating clergy.   It is inter-
polated with corresponding hymns, and supplemented by
private prayers translated from the Roman Missal." [3]   It
is abundantly clear that the doctrines which it is the design
of this Ritualistic movement to assert, relate to the nature
of our Lord's Presence in the Holy Communion and to the
sacrificial aspect of this sacred ordinance.

It therefore becomes of the utmost importance to
ascertain how far the plain and obvious teaching of the
Church of England is in favour of or against the doctrine
of the " Real Presence," and of the sacrificial nature of the

---

[1] " The Church and the World."
[2] Leader in the *Church Times*, June 1, 1867.
[3] Charge, by the Bishop of St. David's, 1866.

Lord's Supper, as these doctrines are maintained by the advocates of modern Ritualism. In the present controversy all turns upon this point. It is the bounden duty of the clergy to examine how far the doctrines in question can or cannot be maintained consistently with the loyalty we owe to the Church of England.

Now, the ultimate standard of appeal in all matters of faith is, according to our Sixth Article, " Holy Scripture." " Whatsoever is not read therein, nor may be proved thereby, is not to be required of any man, that it should be believed as an Article of the Faith, or be thought requisite or necessary to salvation." At the same time the standard of doctrine, which our Church holds and teaches, is to be found in the Thirty-nine Articles and in the Book of Common Prayer. It is assumed that both the Articles and the Liturgy are agreeable to God's Word. The clergy are bound by the standard which they exhibit. They are not at liberty to teach otherwise. I have yet to learn how a clergyman can with a clear conscience retain office in the Church of England unless he fully holds and maintains the doctrine which is plainly taught in the Liturgy and the Articles of the Church. Hence the inquiry, which is forced upon us by the present aspect of the Ritualist question, is simply this : What is the teaching of the Church of England as contained in the Articles and in the Book of Common Prayer concerning the nature of our Lord's Presence in the Holy Communion ? Does that teaching support or contradict the views of those who maintain the Real Presence in the Sacramental Elements and the sacrificial nature of the Holy Eucharist ?

Now, it is not unimportant to remark that the term " Real Presence " does not once occur in the Prayer-book. There is a sense, no doubt, in which our Church maintains that Christ is really present with His faithful disciples in the Holy Communion. It is a most precious truth, and full of comfort to every true Christian, that our Blessed Lord, seated though He is at the right hand of the Majesty in the heavens, is present in that sacred ordinance, through the operation of the Holy Ghost in the heart of every faithful communicant. And the teaching of our Church is most explicit against the notion that the Sacraments are merely bare signs, and in no sense means of grace, for the Twenty-fifth Article affirms, "The Sacraments ordained of Christ be not only badges or tokens of Christian men's profession, but rather they be certain sure witnesses, and effectual signs of grace, and God's good will towards us, by the which He doth work invisibly in us, and doth not only quicken but also strengthen and confirm our Faith in Him."

But this is an essentially different doctrine from that which affirms that Christ is present in or with the Sacramental Elements themselves by virtue of the act of Consecration, and more particularly if this view of the matter is pushed to its necessary consequence, that every communicant who partakes of the Sacramental Elements is a partaker of the Body and Blood of Christ. For this latter doctrine of the "Real Presence," whatever support it may be supposed to obtain in the writings of the Fathers, I can find no support in the Articles or the Liturgy; but, on the contrary, I do find in those formularies statements which are clearly inconsistent with the maintenance of it.

Thus in the first exhortation appointed to be read at the time of the celebration of the Holy Communion, we have this hypothetical form of expression, "For as the benefit is great, IF with a true penitent heart and lively faith we receive that holy Sacrament; for THEN we spiritually eat the Flesh of Christ, and drink His Blood." According to this language the reception of the Body and Blood of Christ is evidently contingent on the possession of repentance and faith, and it is a *spiritual* participation to which reference is made. Surely this is inconsistent with the idea of a "Real Presence" in or with the Elements themselves.

Again: in the prayer of Consecration we have this petition, "Grant that we receiving these Thy creatures of bread and wine, according to thy Son our Saviour Jesus Christ's holy institution, in remembrance of His Death and

Passion, *may be* partakers of His most Blessed Body and Blood." No words could more distinctly imply the possibility of partaking of the Consecrated Elements without necessarily partaking of the Body and Blood of Christ ; yet how could this be the case if by virtue of the act of Consecration Christ becomes present in or with the Sacramental Elements ?

The form of words which the minister is directed to use in delivering the Consecrated Elements is also very significant: " The Body of our Lord Jesus Christ, which was given for thee, preserve thy body and soul unto everlasting life. Take and eat this in remembrance that Christ died for thee, and feed on Him in thy heart by faith with thanksgiving." The first clause directs our thoughts to the Body which was given, to the Sacrifice which was presented once for all on Calvary. The second clause directs our thoughts to the Sacramental sign, and bids us take and eat this *in remembrance* that Christ died. Memory relates not to what is present, but to what is absent ; the bread is to be eaten in *remembrance*, and we are bidden to feed on Christ, not with the mouth, but in the heart, by faith with thanksgiving.

Again : what can be more explicit than the statement which occurs in the rubric at the end of the service for the Holy Communion ? "The Sacramental Bread and Wine remain still in their very natural substances, and therefore may not be adored ; (for that were Idolatry, to be abhorred of all faithful Christians ;) and the natural Body and Blood of our Saviour Christ are in Heaven, and NOT HERE ; it being against the truth of Christ's natural Body to be at one time in more places than one." It is wholly irreconcilable with this plain statement to maintain that the Body of Christ is so present in the Sacramental Elements, that It may be eaten by the mouth of the communicant.

On the other hand, our Church distinctly holds that there may be a reception of the Body and Blood of Christ without any participation whatever of the Sacramental Elements ; for in the rubric at the end of the office for the

Communion of the Sick, the words are as follow: "But if a man, either by reason of extremity of sickness, or for want of warning in due time to the Curate, or for lack of company to receive with him, or by any other just impediment, do not receive the Sacrament of Christ's Body and Blood, the Curate shall instruct him, that if he truly repent him of his sins, and stedfastly believe that Jesus Christ hath suffered death upon the Cross for him, and shed His Blood for his redemption, earnestly remembering the benefits he hath thereby, and giving Him hearty thanks therefore, he doth eat and drink the Body and Blood of our Saviour Christ profitably to his soul's health, although he do not receive the Sacrament with his mouth."

The doctrine of the "Real Presence" in the Sacramental Elements is inconsistent with the definition of a Sacrament as given in the Catechism. A Sacrament is there defined to be "an outward and visible sign of an inward and spiritual grace given unto us, ordained by Christ Himself, as a means whereby we receive the same, and a pledge to assure us thereof." Now the word "Sacrament," as applied to the elements in the Lord's Supper, can only refer to the Consecrated Elements. The bread and wine are clearly not Sacramental till after Consecration. According, then, to the definition given in the Catechism these Consecrated Elements are "an outward and visible sign." If, however, the Body and Blood of Christ are in or with the Elements on the Holy Table, the sign ceases to be a sign through being changed into the thing signified, and thus the nature of the Sacrament is overthrown.

The Catechism again distinctly teaches that it is the faithful by whom the Body and Blood of Christ are verily and indeed taken and received, *not* according to the words there employed, "in the Sacramental Elements," but "in the Lord's Supper."

From the Liturgy and the Catechism I turn to the Articles. The Twenty-eighth Article states, "The Body of Christ is given, taken, and eaten, in the Supper, only after an heavenly and spiritual manner. And the means

whereby the Body of Christ is received and eaten in the
Supper is faith." Again: the Twenty-ninth Article states,
" The wicked, and such as be void of a lively faith, although
they do carnally and visibly press with their teeth (as Saint
Augustine saith) the Sacrament of the Body and Blood of
Christ, yet in no wise are they partakers of Christ: but
rather, to their condemnation, do eat and drink the sign or
Sacrament of so great a thing." If language has any meaning, surely these Articles plainly declare that it is by faith
only, and spiritually, we can feed on Christ in the Eucharist,
and that the wicked are not partakers in any sense of Christ
in the Lord's Supper, even though they do eat and drink
the Sacramental Elements.

If we turn to the Homilies, we find statements to the
same effect. In the first part of the " Homily of the worthy
receiving and reverent esteeming of the Sacrament of the
Body and Blood of Christ," the following passage occurs :—
" It is well known that the meat we seek for in this Supper
is spiritual food, the nourishment of our soul ; a heavenly
refection and not earthly ; an invisible meat and not bodily ;
a ghostly substance and not carnal ; so that to think without faith we may enjoy the eating and drinking thereof, or
that that is the fruition thereof, is but to dream a gross
carnal feeding, basely objecting, and binding ourselves to
the elements and creatures ; whereas, by the Council of
Nicene, we ought to lift up our minds by faith, and, leaving
these inferior and earthly things, there seek it where the
Sun of Righteousness ever shineth. Take then this lesson,
O thou that art desirous of this table, of Emissenus, a
godly father, that when thou goest up to the reverend
Communion to be satisfied with spiritual meats, thou look
up with faith to the Holy Body and Blood of thy God, thou
marvel with reverence, thou touch It with the mind, thou
receive It with the hand of thy heart, and thou take It fully
with thy inward man."

These passages, when taken in their plain and obvious
meaning, are inconsistent with the belief of the " Real
Presence" in the Sacramental Elements ; and I am con-

P

firmed in this conclusion when I call to mind what many
of our greatest Divines have written on this subject. At
the period of the Reformation, it is well known that the
great controversy with the Church of Rome centred in
the Sacrament of the Lord's Supper. Many in the noble
army of martyrs, who loved not their lives unto death,
died rather than admit the doctrine that the Elements are
changed in the Lord's Supper, by the act of Consecration,
into the Body and Blood of Christ. I admit, of course, the
distinction between the Romish doctrine of Transubstanti-
ation and the doctrine of the "Real Presence," as maintained by some who still remain in communion with the
Church of England. At the same time I must say that
the terms in which this latter doctrine is avowed are such
as to render it extremely difficult for ordinary minds to
detect wherein it differs from the former. Arguments
against the one apply with equal force against the other.
The same terms in which the Reformers of the sixteenth
century contended against the Romish error might be
applied against the doctrine of the "Real Presence" as
asserted by some at the present day. Thus, Bishop Ridley
maintained that the Body of Christ is "communicated and
given, not to the bread and wine, but to them which
worthily do receive the Sacrament;" and when Archbishop
Cranmer was asked, "When Christ said, 'Eat ye,' whether
meant He by the mouth or by faith?" his reply was, "He
meant that we should receive the Body by faith, the Bread
by the mouth."

Take, again, the testimony of Richard Hooker :—" The
Real Presence of Christ's most Blessed Body and Blood is
not, therefore, to be sought for in the Sacrament, but in
the worthy receiver of the Sacrament. And with this the
very order of our Saviour's words agreeth. First, 'Take,
and eat;' then, 'This is my Body which was broken for
you.' First, 'Drink ye all of this;' then followeth, 'This
is my Blood of the New Testament, which is shed for many
for the remission of sins.' I see not which way it should
be gathered from the words of Christ when and where the

bread is His Body or the cup His Blood, but only in the very heart and soul of him which receiveth them."

Bishop Jeremy Taylor writes :—" By ' spiritually ' they (*i.e.*, the Romanists) mean present after the manner of a spirit ; by spiritually we mean 'present to our spirits only ;' *i.e.*, so as Christ is not present to any other sense but that of faith, or spiritual susception ; but their way makes His Body to be present no way but that which is impossible and implies a contradiction ; a body not after the manner of a body, a body like a spirit ; a body without a body ; and a sacrifice of body and blood without blood, *corpus incorporeum, cruor incruentus.* They say that Christ's Body is truly present there as it was upon the Cross, but not after the manner of all or any body, but after that manner of being as an Angel is in a place ; that's their ' spiritually ;' but we, by the ' real spiritual presence ' of Christ, do understand Christ to be present as the Spirit of God is present in the hearts of the faithful, by blessing and grace, and THIS IS ALL WHICH WE MEAN BESIDES THE TROPICAL AND FIGURATIVE PRESENCE."

To my own mind the conclusion is evident, whether you examine the Book of Common Prayer or testimony such as that which I have quoted from the writings of men who, by the depth of their learning, and the fervour of their piety, shed lustre on the age in which they lived, and on the Church to which they belonged, that if we are to understand by the Doctrine of the Real Presence that Christ is in any sense bodily present, by virtue of the act of Consecration, in or with the Sacramental Elements, this is a doctrine which is not maintained in the Articles or the formularies of the Church of England, nor can it be held consistently with those standards of belief.

The Bishops are often rebuked for trying to enforce the law in the case of those who err by excess, while they leave without rebuke those who err by defect; and it is sometimes said that they do not themselves show an example of obedience.

My father was anxious to leave no room for such a charge. The celebrated Purchas Judgment called attention to the Twenty-fourth Canon, which runs as follows :—

In all Cathedral and Collegiate Churches the Holy Communion shall be administered upon principal feast-days, sometimes by the Bishop if he be present, and some-times by the Dean, and at sometime by a Canon or Pre-bendary, the Principal Minister using a decent Cope, and being assisted with the Gospeller and Epistler agreeably according to the Advertisements published Anno 7 Eliz.

My father felt it his duty to obey this judgment in his Cathedral, and secured the concurrence of Dean McNeile. The writer well remembers the first Christmas Day when the Bishop and Dean both appeared in the Minster, arrayed in purple copes. The Bishop was the Celebrant, and the Dean was the preacher. The latter prefaced his sermon with words to this effect :—

Good people, you will be surprised to see your Bishop and myself arrayed in these unwonted vestments, but we have been reminded that it is our duty to wear them, and we wish to set an example of obedience to the law.

The people of Ripon were not likely to accuse either Bishop or Dean of a newborn love of eccle-siastical millinery, but his ready compliance with the law as then interpreted certainly strengthened my father's hands in appealing to the clergy to accept the decision of the court. My father continued to wear the cope on all great festivals, when he took part in the Celebration of the Holy Communion at Ripon ;

and I believe three or four other bishops, including the late Dr. Jackson, of London, adopted the same use. It will be remembered that Bishop Fraser, when challenged to do the same, endeavoured to show that the cope was represented by the "chimere" which forms a part of the usual episcopal robes. This is a question for experts in ritual on which the writer is not prepared to express an opinion ; but the Bishop's attitude in the matter showed a readiness to sacrifice personal feeling and a deference to authority which is worth recording, for it was thoroughly characteristic.

In several cases, when "aggrieved parishioners" complained to the Bishop of changes in the accustomed order of service, he was very successful in acting as mediator between the clergyman and his people. He asked them to show a spirit of mutual forbearance, and often the clergy showed their gratitude for his fatherly admonitions by yielding to his request. My father very much preferred to settle these and other disputes by a personal interview. Of these interviews of course no record remains, but the following letter, written to a clergyman in the diocese, who has since died, illustrates the way in which he treated cases of the sort. It is only fair to say that the particular instance was one in which the clergyman had introduced some of those eccentricities of Ritualism which go far beyond what is now practised even in so-called advanced churches. The church was attractive to sightseers collected from a distance, while the parishioners were alienated and ordinary parochial work was at a standstill :—

The Palace, Ripon, January 19, 1876.

My dear Sir,—I am sorry to find from your own account that the statement which I forwarded to you is correct. I had hoped that you would have followed the advice which I gave you a few months since, not to introduce any novelties into the mode of conducting public worship in your church, without consulting me.

I should be the last to desire to abridge any liberty which the law allows to the clergy, but I think, upon calm reflection, you will see that it is surely not right for individual clergymen to make changes of this kind in dress and in the mode of celebrating public worship, without any regard to the general usage of the Church, or to the judgment of their own diocesan.

It may be to some extent for the present an open question how far the vestments which you have adopted are legal or otherwise. It is certainly not clear that a bishop has power to forbid their use. The same might be said of a variety of other points which the law has not particularised. But it is an ungenerous use to make of the liberty which the Church allows to her members, to adopt a practice which is clearly foreign to the spirit of our Church system, even though its observance may not be expressly forbidden. I cannot entirely regard these innovations of dress as merely circumstantial and non-essential. In the eye of the Church at large they are almost inseparably associated with tendencies to Romish error and superstition, and I do not believe it to be possible for you or any other clergyman who makes such innovations to acquit himself in the judgment of the Church at large of an attempt to assimilate our own forms of worship to those which our Reformers repudiated. But even if these matters were altogether non-essential, should not this constitute a strong reason for being guided by the authority to which, both at your ordination and upon subsequent occasions, you have promised to yield obedience? In the present uncertainty of the law, I have no power to prohibit (so

far as I am at present advised) your wearing the unusual
vestments, but I feel it my duty to tell you frankly that
the wearing of them by any clergyman in my diocese is
contrary to my wish, and can only be done in defiance of
any authority which I might exercise to prevent it.

I am, dear sir,

Very faithfully yours,

R. RIPON.

The Rev. ——.

With my father's well-known views on the
matter, it is not surprising that he supported the
Public Worship Regulation Act of 1874, for which
Archbishop Tait and Lord Beaconsfield were mainly
responsible; but he was quite unprepared for the
unfortunate results of that Act, which led to the
imprisonment of hard-working clergymen who refused to recognise its authority. He was utterly
opposed to proceeding to such violent extremes,
and saw clearly enough that anything which looked
like religious persecution could only strengthen the
cause of those who were attacked.

In quite recent years, when High Churchmen
were indignant at the continued imprisonment of
the Rev. S. F. Green, a meeting was held in Leeds,
at which an appeal was made to moderate men to
join the ranks of the English Church Union as a
protest against further prosecutions. The Vicar of
Leeds, Dr. Gott, whose large-hearted charity has
done so much to soften the bitterness of party strife,
reminded the meeting that they had the best possible
guarantee for the peace of the diocese of Ripon,
at least, in the rule of a wise and tolerant bishop.

In closing a chapter in which I have quoted so

largely from his Charges, it may be well to notice my
father's practice with regard to his Triennial Visitations.   At first he followed the prevailing custom of
delivering the written Charge at the various centres.
Finding, however, that its freshness was lost, when
those whom he met had already perused the substance of it in the columns of the press, he adopted
the plan of delivering the Charge once for all at
Ripon or Leeds.   He then utilised the time left
at his disposal by speaking of matters more especially interesting to the separate localities.   One
of his chaplains, the Rev. Canon Pulleine, writes :—

I remember at a Visitation at Skipton with what sympathy he described the difficulties and trials of the country
clergy, calling forth the openly expressed gratitude of
more than one for his helpful words.   One was struck by
his great knowledge of the details of his diocese.   He
knew the character of his clergy and the circumstances of
their parishes.

In this chapter I have been obliged to tread on
delicate ground.   In justice to my father's memory,
I could not set aside the emphatic expression of his
views on subjects about which his clergy were not
all agreed ; but I gladly close with a quotation from
his Charge in 1873, which was welcome to men of all
shades of opinion who could appreciate the burning
words of one who longed to kindle the strongest
sense of ministerial responsibility :—

My Reverend Brethren, by the tremendous responsibilities of your sacred office, that office to which you consecrated all your powers at the solemn period of ordination ;
by the eternal issues of glory or of shame which are
suspended upon its exercise ; by the priceless blessings

which you may be instrumental to convey to others, and
by the recompense you may yourselves inherit; by that
"greater condemnation," which is the doom of the faithless
Shepherd, suffer me to entreat of you to aim more and
more at the great end of your ministry, even the salvation
of souls. Every other object is insignificant in comparison
with this. Short of this result the main purpose of your
ministry is not accomplished. The *ministerial* reward will
not be gained. Let not this Visitation pass by, without a
fresh resolve, that, by God's grace, we will be more than
ever devoted to our sacred calling. The influence of a
deeper spiritual life in our own souls would make itself felt
throughout the diocese; we should be more earnest for the
salvation of others; we should be more united amongst
ourselves. In drawing nearer to Christ, the true Centre of
unity, the Fountain of all life and blessing, we should be
insensibly drawn nearer to one another, and realise more
of that blessed and holy fellowship, which binds together
in one the members of the mystical Body of which He is
the living Head. In proportion as we contemplate more
steadfastly the great purpose of our ministry, and fix our
attention more earnestly on the swiftly-approaching day
when each of us will be called to give in his account of
talents, responsibilities, opportunities, of souls committed
to our care, we shall enter into the mind of the Apostle,
when he exclaimed, "This one thing I do, forgetting those
things which are behind, and reaching forth unto those
things which are before, I press toward the mark for the
prize of the high calling of God in Christ Jesus." May
God of His infinite mercy pour down upon us more
abundantly the gifts and the grace of His Holy Spirit.
May He increase amongst us true religion—may He
nourish us with all goodness, and of His great mercy keep
us in the same through Jesus Christ our Lord. Amen.

CHAPTER XIII.

DIOCESAN WORK: EDUCATION.

Diocesan work—Education—The Training College—Progress of ele-
mentary education in the diocese before 1870—Great increase of
Church schools—Diocesan inspection in religious knowledge—
The Bishop deeply thankful for Mr. Forster's Bill—Analysis of the
Act—He warmly advocates the increased efficiency of Church
schools and the importance of religious teaching—Speech at
Huddersfield, in 1879.

SIDE by side with the work of church building and
restoration went forward that of religious education ;
and in connection with the latter it is right to mention the erection of the Training College for mistresses at Ripon.

This was an institution in which my father took
the warmest interest. Up to the year 1860 there
had been a department for females in connection
with the Training College at York, but the institution
was not in a good condition, and it was thought
advisable that the two departments for male and
female students should be kept distinct.

My father gave the College a hearty welcome to
the diocese, and amongst his earliest public appeals
for funds, was that which he made for the erection
of the commodious building at Ripon.

The Principal, Canon Badcock, writes :—

It was mainly through his influence and exertions that the Diocesan Training College was established at Ripon. On February 1, 1860, he presided over a public meeting, and forcibly recommended the scheme for the building of the College, of which he laid the foundation stone on December 4 of the same year.

From that time, and to the end of his life, his interest in the Institution never flagged. He made a point of being present at the meetings of the committee of management. I well remember how frequently he used to come to the College and to address the students on the duties and responsibilities of their future work. Often he was accompanied by friends who were visiting at the Palace, and evidently it gave him pleasure to explain to them the working and arrangements of the Institution. Sometimes he sat down to the harmonium and practised the pupils in singing hymns (in preparation for the Chapel service on Sunday afternoons).

He was conversant with all details of the work, and annually, until he was prevented by illness, he even took the trouble to come to the College to audit the accounts. It was an immense encouragement to the governesses and officers of the Institution to know that the eye of their good Bishop was always upon them ; and after the students had left the College they still felt that his influence and interest extended to them. He often mentioned that he had in the course of his travels among the towns and villages of Yorkshire, met with schoolmistresses who had been trained at the College, and he was pleased when he found them faithfully carrying out the work for which they had been educated.

It was to my father a most important part of his episcopal work to exercise a direct control over the institution, and especially to have the opportunity of preaching to the students afforded by their attendance at the service in the Palace. It has already been mentioned that when he was able to spend a Sunday at Ripon, my father always attended the cathedral in the morning, but preached at the afternoon service in his private chapel. The little building was on these occasions filled to overflowing with a somewhat miscellaneous congregation; but the chief interest to my father was the presence of the Training College students, to whom he spoke very earnestly of the immense responsibility of the work to which they were called.

He never failed to remind them that, next to that of the clergyman, theirs was the highest calling on earth, for all education worthy of the name was pregnant with results that only eternity can reveal.

As no attempt is being made to give a strictly chronological account of my father's work at Ripon, it may be well to bring together here his views on the education question expressed at various periods of his episcopate. To many persons of a younger generation, and from the tenour of not a few political speeches, the impression is given that the Education Act of 1870 found the country and the Church in a state of complete apathy on this important question. That this was not the case, at least in the diocese of Ripon, is manifest from the way in which the subject constantly recurs in my father's earlier Charges. The Church was certainly grappling with the problem; and though no one can say that the efforts to provide elementary education were adequate, yet each Triennial Charge speaks of continuous progress. Thus in 1858 there were 57,180 day scholars attending Church schools, and in 1864 the number had risen to no less than 74,412.

In 1867 the Bishop records :—

Your returns on the all-important subject of education show that 407 parishes in the diocese are supplied with elementary day schools in connection with the Church. The number of registered scholars, including boys, girls, and infants, is 78,434. This exhibits an increase of 4022 scholars compared with the numbers in 1864. . . .

I regret to find that there are twenty-three separate parishes in which there is not any elementary school over which the clergyman exercises control or supervision. A large proportion of these are, however, newly constituted parishes, where sufficient time has not yet been afforded to establish schools. In other cases the defect is explained by the circumstance that it is found convenient to let one school building serve for two small contiguous parishes. At the same time, the ecclesiastical organisation of a parish is incomplete without a school, in addition to the church and parsonage. There is no function of our sacred office of higher importance than to make due provision for the education of the poor ; and I would strongly recommend every clergyman who is in charge of a parish not to rest content without a good elementary school for the benefit of his poorer parishioners.

That only twenty-three parishes out of 407 were unprovided with schools three years before the passing of the Act of 1870, is a sufficient answer to the charge that the Church had altogether neglected elementary education.

In the same year my father commenced a system of diocesan inspection to promote the efficiency of Church schools. He writes :—

My attention has been directed to the benefit which might be derived from the adoption of a system of diocesan, in addition to Government inspection. The system has been tried and found to work well in other dioceses. The additional stimulus supplied to the teacher, the advantage gained by the scholars through being subjected more frequently to examination, the fuller information to be obtained as to the actual state of education in the diocese, are amongst the reasons by which the recommendation to appoint diocesan inspectors of schools has been urged. To these it may be added that many schools, not being under Government inspection, never undergo any examination ; while in other schools, which are subject to the visits of Her Majesty's inspector, there is some reason to fear that, owing to the operation of the Revised Code in making the Government grant depend mainly upon proficiency in secular subjects, the religious element does not receive all the attention which it ought. In such cases, the visit of a diocesan inspector, one of whose chief duties would be to examine the scholars with respect to their knowledge of Scripture facts and doctrines, would supply a remedy for this evil. Influenced by these considerations, and aided by the advice of the arch-deacons and rural deans of the diocese, I have resolved to provide for the diocesan inspection of elementary schools. There are no funds out of which to provide for the proper remuneration for an inspector for the whole diocese, whose time should be exclusively given to this work. Under these circumstances, the plan which I have thought best to adopt is to appoint a separate inspector to each rural deanery. In several cases the rural dean has kindly undertaken to. inspect the schools in his deanery ; but where, from the pressure of other duties, the rural dean is unable to discharge the office, it will be filled by one of the incumbents in the deanery. Already fourteen rural deaneries are provided with a diocesan inspector, and appointments will speedily be made in the remaining deaneries, which are as yet unsupplied. I wish it to be clearly understood that this inspection is not intended to interfere in the smallest degree with the legitimate authority of the incumbent within the limits of his own parish. It must rest entirely with each incumbent to avail himself or not of the services of the diocesan inspector. No school will be examined without the sanction of the clergyman to whose parish or district it belongs. I am thankful to find that a large number of schools have been already examined. A strong opinion has been expressed by several of the clergy in favour of the plan, and in only one or two cases hitherto has the visit of the diocesan inspector been declined.

This is interesting as showing how the way was prepared for the appointment of a special diocesan officer, aided by volunteers, when the complete separation of religious and secular inspection was rendered necessary.

Firmly as my father maintained his strong conviction that education, to be worthy of the name, must be essentially religious, he welcomed in no grudging spirit the great Act of 1870.

For Mr. Forster personally he entertained a very high regard, and he was convinced that the author of the Act intended by it no injury to religious education.

On this, as on many kindred subjects, my father's liberal sympathy and generous appreciation of religious effort outside the Church disposed him to interpret to the clergy in the most favourable light acts of the Legislature in which some of them were apt to read only hostility to the Church.

He writes in his Charge of 1870 :—

A more important problem than how to secure a both sufficient and suitable elementary education for the country at large could scarcely at any time occupy the attention of Parliament ; and without pronouncing an unqualified approval of the mode in which this problem has been solved, it does appear to me that, taking into consideration all the practical difficulties with which the subject is confessedly beset, *we have reason to be deeply thankful for the Elementary*

Education Act which received the Royal assent in August last.
On the question as to the best mode in which the influence
of the Government should be exercised for the promotion
of elementary education, there were three rival plans proposed for adoption. On the one hand there were those
who advocated a system of purely secular instruction.
Their theory is that the teaching of religion should be
banished from the school, and relegated to the homes of
the scholars. The advocates of this system will not allow
that it is a main part of education to impart moral as well
as intellectual culture, and they appear strangely to overlook the consideration, that to withhold religious instruction
in elementary schools would necessarily be in a large proportion of cases to abandon the scholars to utter destitution
of all religious teaching. Those who are practically
acquainted with the class from which the scholars in
elementary schools are for the most part drawn, must be
well aware of the extreme improbability which there is
that the majority of the pupils, if denied the advantage
of religious instruction in school, would receive such instruction either by precept or example elsewhere.

There were others, again, who, although alive to the
importance of making religion the basis of education, even
if with no higher end in view than to produce loyal and
good citizens for this world, advocated an elimination of all
distinctive doctrine from the religious instruction given
in school; they were in favour of a system of religious
teaching which should be perfectly colourless, which should
not exhibit a shade of dogma, in order that it might
disturb no prejudice and awaken no controversy.

It is difficult to understand how any persons who really
believe that there are such matters as fundamental truths,
—truths which are necessary to be believed for the soul's
salvation, can give their adherence to such a system as this.
The remaining alternative seemed to be to invigorate and
extend the system to which the name of *denominational*
has been given, and in connection with which the country
has already derived large and beneficial educational results.

The advocates of the purely secular theory of education have made no secret of their dislike of this system. Whatever may have been the origin of that dislike, whether it was due to the inherent nature of the system, or whether it arose on account of the preponderating influence which, under its operation, the Church has acquired in the education of the country, the fact is beyond dispute that the zeal of the Education League was energetically directed against the denominational system, with a view to its entire demolition.

Happily, however, the feeling of the country, both in and out of Parliament, has been unmistakably manifested in favour of religious, as opposed to merely secular education. The belief was firmly rooted in the public mind, that to offer nothing better than mere secular instruction to those who need education at our hands, would be to act the part of unnatural guardians, and give to the hungry a stone in place of bread.

At the same time, the more the matter was discussed, the more evident it became that it would be equally wasteful and unwise to abandon a system which has existed for many years ; with which the country has grown familiar ; which has shared to a considerable degree the public confidence ; on whose maintenance large sums have been expended, and under the operation of which the education of the country has advanced with great and surprising rapidity. True, the system was not perfect ; it had its defects ; the whole country was by no means adequately provided with the machinery for education ; masses of the population might be found whom no efforts either of the Church or of Nonconformists to impart elementary education had hitherto reached ; and it might be said without risk of exaggeration, that thousands of children were growing up in ignorance, whom the existing system, unless it were modified or supplemented, never could reach.

And yet for all this, could it be fair to overlook the fact that by the aid of this denominational system, in the comparatively short space of thirty years, the number of scholars

Q

in elementary Church schools has risen from 1 in 36·7 of the population to 1 in 13, and that out of 14,709 parishes in England, 13,016 have schools of their own ; that 1355, although not possessing schools, are supplied with education in adjoining parishes, while only 338 remain which have neither schools of their own, nor the means of instruction within a moderate distance? These results—and I am speaking only of Church schools—indicate a degree of power and vitality in the system to which they may in a great measure be attributed, which entitle it to a better fate than the process of "painless extinction" to which the Education League would have gladly consigned it.

Parliament has pronounced that this system shall not be recklessly abandoned. An Act has been passed, from the operation of which we may reasonably expect that in a few years the country will be adequately supplied with the requisite machinery for a complete system of National Education. The attempt to destroy the denominational system has signally failed, and the efforts which the Church has put forth in the cause of education have been fairly recognised.

At the same time some changes have been introduced, by which existing schools will be affected, of a nature which none can regard as trivial, and many must view with deep regret. Amongst these changes the most prominent are the following. Hitherto the managers of Church schools have been at liberty to enforce, as a condition of admission to the day school under their charge, the attendance of the scholars at the Sunday school and the services of the Church. This liberty is at an end for the future, in all schools which are under Government inspection. Again, while no restraint is placed upon the kind of instruction in religion which may be given in existing elementary schools receiving Government grants, such instruction must in future be given only at the commencement, or at the close, or at both the commencement and the close, of the school hours. Moreover, any parent is to be at liberty to withdraw his child from such religious instruction without forfeiting any of the other benefits of the school. Again, it is to be no part of the duty of Her Majesty's inspector to make any inquiry as to the religious instruction given in the school; nor is the annual grant which the school may receive from the State to be in any respect regulated with reference to the religious instruction which the scholars receive.

With these important exceptions, existing schools which are doing their work efficiently will be left undisturbed. They will be aided more liberally than heretofore by the State; but this is a boon which would be more welcome if it were not clogged with the condition,—that the annual grant shall not in any one year exceed the income of the school for that year, which is derived from voluntary contributions, school fees, and from any sources other than the Parliamentary grant. There is reason to fear that by the operation of this clause efficient schools in poor and populous districts, where help is most needed, will obtain the smallest share of Government assistance; while schools in wealthy parishes, where subscriptions are most easily procured, and where State aid is less required, will benefit most largely.

So much for existing schools. But the Act regulates for the establishment of schools in places where the provision for elementary education is inadequate or unsuitable. An inquiry will be first made as to the provision which exists; should that provision be pronounced inadequate, and should no prospect appear that within a limited period the deficiency will be supplied by voluntary effort, then schools will be established, and placed under the management of a school board, the cost of their establishment being defrayed by a rate to be levied under the authority of the Act. In schools thus established—I quote the words of the Act—"No religious catechism or religious formulary which is distinctive of any particular denomination shall be taught." In certain specified cases the school board will have the power to make the education entirely free of charge to the parent, thereby, of course, throwing an additional burden on the rate ; a discretionary power is also given to the school board in certain cases to make the attendance of children at rate-supported schools compulsory.

Such are the main provisions of the Elementary Education Act so far as this diocese is likely to be affected by it. Some important questions arise for consideration in connection with the changes which the Act will introduce. Foremost among them is the probable effect of the measure with regard to religious instruction. The introduction of the principle of a conscience clause need not of itself excite any alarm ; in most large elementary schools the principle has been tacitly recognised for many years past. I do not anticipate that the enforcement of this principle by Act of Parliament will occasion any great change. Instances seldom occur in which parents having on the one hand shown confidence in an elementary school by seeking admission for their children, betray on the other hand a want of confidence by stipulating that they shall not share with the other scholars in the religious instruction. Such exceptional cases will not in all probability be more numerous in consequence of the passing of the Elementary Education Act. But should it be otherwise, it will be well to bear in mind that the liberty which a clergyman may justly claim to have every doctrine of God's Word taught in his parish school is left unfettered ; and it is in reality the liberty of the parent to exercise a control over the religious education of his child for which provision is now for the first time made by Act of Parliament. But what we have real cause to apprehend is this. The religious instruction given in an elementary school which receives Government aid is not, as I have explained, in future to come in any shape within the inquiry of Her Majesty's inspector. His report will contain no allusion to the religious teaching or condition of the school. His estimate of the character or capabilities of the teacher will be formed without any reference to skill or fidelity in communicating religious knowledge. The grant from Government upon which the support of the school and the credit of the teacher may so materially depend, will not be regulated in the smallest degree by the proficiency of the pupils in Scriptural knowledge. Not a fraction of the aid given by the State will depend upon the condition of the school with respect to religion. Will not this fact operate on the mind of the teacher? Will he be proof against the temptation to slight the subject which the Government inspector ignores, and expend his teaching energies on those branches of learning which have a palpable influence in procuring a favourable report, and, in consequence, a liberal grant?

To guard against this result will demand the utmost care and vigilance. You will agree with me, my Reverend Brethren, that at all cost the religious instruction and the religious tone of our elementary schools must be maintained. As one practical mode of securing this result, I think it essential that we should have thorough and effective diocesan inspection of all Church schools. I am not insensible to the advantages which have accrued from the system of diocesan inspection which we already possess. My grateful acknowledgments are due to those who, at my request, have filled the office of diocesan inspectors. They have freely given their time and labour to the discharge of this office, and by the zeal and tact with which they have performed its duties they have entitled themselves to the thanks which I now tender in my own behalf, and in behalf of the managers of the schools which they have inspected. But the altered circumstances in which we are now placed seem to render a different arrangement necessary in future. If the religious teaching is to be upheld in thorough efficiency, it is all but indispensable that we should have a paid diocesan inspector, whose main duty shall be to examine the schools placed under his supervision with respect to their religious knowledge, and whose whole time shall be devoted to the duties of his office.

The only practical difficulty is the financial one. Whence are the funds to be derived for the salary of such an inspector? Now, if the managers of our Church schools are alive to the importance of upholding the religious standard, and if they are convinced of the danger which exists of this standard being lowered unless some effective means are adopted for diocesan inspection, is it too much to hope that a fund may be created by a contribution from each Church school, and that out of such a fund, supplemented by a grant from the Diocesan Board of Education, the means may be provided for securing the services of a competent inspector, and also for affording some pecuniary inducement to the teachers of elementary schools not to relax their endeavours to impart religious instruction to their scholars ?

Another consideration arising out of the changes to which I have referred is also of pressing importance. Inquiry will be instituted without delay into the existing amount of school accommodation. Where a deficiency is proved to exist, and where there appears to be no prospect of its removal by voluntary effort, a school board will be elected, and a school established in which neither the Church Catechism nor any other distinctive religious formulary may be taught. It is the plain duty of Churchmen to anticipate this inquiry, and by prompt effort to aim at founding Church schools wherever the necessity is found to exist.

Your replies to my Visitation queries afford some data for guidance in this matter. It appears from these returns that there are thirty-five benefices which have no Church school connected with them. In four of these subscriptions have been already obtained which will ensure the erection of schools in the course of a few months ; nine are newly-constituted districts where there has not been sufficient time since the consecration of the church to provide schools ; in a small proportion of the remaining cases sufficient school accommodation is met with at a moderate distance ; but as regards the rest, there can hardly be a doubt that the result of the inquiry which is already in progress will be that the school accommodation will be pronounced inadequate, and unless due provison is made, within a reasonable interval by voluntary effort, the alternative will be schools provided by rate, and placed under the direction of a school board.

It appears from the returns now before me that the numbers upon the register in elementary Church schools in the diocese are 41,732 boys, 30,838 girls, 22,258 infants. The Sunday schools have 83,009 scholars, and there are 8131 scholars in attendance at night schools for adults.

The Bishop promoted religious education not only in these Charges to the clergy, but also by appealing to the religious instincts of the main body of the people. He had the utmost confidence in the right instincts of the people if they had the truth placed before them. Thus he gladly availed himself of an opportunity, which was offered to him in Huddersfield, of addressing a mass meeting of working men held in the Armoury in 1879.

I quote from his speech on that occasion, as it seems a good illustration of his capacity for making great truths clear to a popular audience.

The Bishop was warmly received, and said the meeting had been called for the twofold purpose of advocating the cause of religious education set in contrast with a system of secular education ; and to offer an opportunity for stating the claims to public support of the National Society for the Education of the Poor in the Principles of the Established Church. He wished, then, first of all to consider whether they really understood the full force and meaning of the word "education." He was inclined to think there were many persons who talked about education, who scarcely realised the exact meaning of the word "education" itself. Education was not comprehended in what was commonly spoken of as teaching the three R's, still less in cramming the mind with facts, whether of history, literature, or science. Education he took to be the calling forth, or the development, of the faculties with which God had endowed them, with a view to their employment for the good of others, as well as for the glory of God, which was the highest object at which any human being could aim. If that were a correct definition of the term "education" he came to consider the fact that man was a compound being; that every human being was so constituted as to consist of a natural part subject to death and dissolution, of a mental part, by which he was distinguished from animals that could not reason, and of a spiritual part, which was destined to survive the wreck and ruin of matter, and to live throughout eternity. If man was thus constituted, and if education rightly meant the calling forth, or the development, of faculties with which he was endowed, then he maintained that education which really deserved the name ought to touch each of these three parts of man's being; and education which did not touch each of those parts he pronounced to be essentially defective. With regard to man's physical constitution, education to be valuable ought to teach the laws of health, and develop all those physical powers which so much contribute to their enjoyment, and to their ability to discharge the various functions of life. As to their intellectual being, education to be valuable ought to teach the laws of thought, to supply the mind with facts, whether of history or of science, and to cultivate all those powers by which man might be able adequately to discharge the various duties which devolved upon him as a reasoning, intelligent being.

Secular education exclusively was both defective and mischievous: defective, because it did not touch the higher part of man's being, the moral and spiritual part; mischievous, because while secular education endowed the student with enormous power, it omitted altogether the communication of the only principle by which that power might be used to advantage. The power which knowledge gave might be used for good or for evil, and he maintained that it would only be used for good in proportion as it was under the control of right principle. Directly they came to speak of right principle as the governing power, they must have religious teaching to educate man's moral being. What was the highest knowledge which a man could acquire as a spiritual being? Was it not a knowledge of God? Were they not told that this was eternal life—" To know Thee the only true God, and Jesus Christ, Whom Thou hast sent"? And was it not a fact that moral power, or the education, which they sought to give with a view to man's moral being, must take into account the relation in which they stood towards God, and the relation in which God had been pleased to place Himself towards men? Well, then, if they were to have moral teaching, he came to this further point, that they must have Bible teaching, the teaching of revealed religion. He thought that must be evident to those who would consider the fact for a moment. There were two ways in which God had been pleased to reveal Himself. He was revealed in His works; He was revealed in His Word. The book of Revelation admitted that God was revealed in His works, for they were told, " The heavens declare the glory of God, and the firmanent sheweth His handiwork." It was impossible to gaze abroad on the works of God unfolded to them in the visible creation without deriving many a lesson with regard to the power, the wisdom, the faithfulness, the constancy of Jehovah. He maintained, on the one hand, that the revelation of God in His works was in a measure defective ; and he maintained, on the other hand, that by reason of sin man had lost the power which, as an unfallen being, he possessed of reading and discerning the lessons which the works of God were intended to teach. Now, if there were any truth in these observations, then they were driven to the conclusion that if man was to know that which was most essential for him to know with respect to God and his prospects, they must have Bible teaching. . . . He was very far from speaking against secular education. He would have secular education carried to its very furthest point, in order to qualify a man for the right discharge of the duties appertaining to his particular vocation in life,

be what it might.   But he maintained this: if they neglected to sow the seeds of religious principle in what he
might almost venture to assert the virgin soil of youth,
they neglected an opportunity which they would never
regain.   That soil might become prolific only of weeds,
which might otherwise be prolific in the fruits of Divine
grace.   Therefore it would be wrong on the part of those
who undertook the education of children to neglect their
religious education.   Suppose it were the highest object of
education (which he did not at all admit) to cultivate the
intellectual powers to the utmost, he would still denounce
the unwisdom of excluding religious teaching.   He would
tell them why.   The laws of mind in some respect were
similar to the laws of matter.   They knew in respect to
material things that the muscle which was unused dwindled
and decayed, that if they wanted to develop the muscular
system they must call the muscles into play—must make
them familiar with exercise so as to develop their power
and strength.   Now, if they wanted to invigorate the powers
of the mind, they must bring those powers into contact
with subjects which demanded thought and careful study.
The mind had the property of gradually contracting itself
to the limit of the matter with which alone it was familiar-
ised ; and if the mind was in contact only with things which
were trivial, small, and minute, the powers of the mind
gradually dwindled and decayed; whereas, on the other
hand, in proportion as the intellectual powers were summoned to grapple with what was large and difficult did
they develop and strengthen.   Where in all the range of
science, or philosophy, or of secular knowledge were there
any truths to compare with the truths of revelation in
respect of the grasp of thought which they required in
order to reach their full understanding ?   Try and measure
eternity.   Try and measure the attributes of God, His
omnipresence, omniscience, omnipotence, and they would
find that as the powers of the mind were called to grapple
with such truths as these, they would grow in power and
force, just as the muscle was developed by being used to
overcome what was difficult.

The Bishop went on to advocate the principles of the National Society ; but while he urged Churchmen to maintain their denominational schools, he was no less anxious to urge the general public to see that that religious education was supplied in the Board Schools, which the illustrious author of the Act of 1870 so earnestly desired.

The Education Acts have done so much for the people, and the future is so full of vast possibilities for good, that the writer trusts this weighty speech may be read with attention by many who, whether in Church or Board Schools, can direct the education of the young.

CHAPTER XIV.

RETREATS, MISSIONS, CHURCH CONGRESS, AND DIOCESAN CONFERENCE.

Retreats and Missions—Letter from Dr. Gott—My father conducts the
first Episcopal Retreat for Clergy—Bishop Kennion's notes of his
address—Advocates Mission work and takes an active part in
Missions in Bradford, Huddersfield, Leeds, etc. — The Leeds
Mission in 1875—Letters from Canon Temple on the Church
Congress at Leeds, and on the Diocesan Conference—Bishop
Forbes of Brechin—Letter from the Rev. H. D. Cust Nunn on
the rural deans' conferences.

ALLUSION has been already made to my father's
connection with the first of the four distinguished
men who, during his episcopate, held the Vicarage
of Leeds. Another of them, when he heard that
a sketch of my father's life was contemplated, expressed his warm interest and the wish to write
a letter to the biographer, giving his recollections
of my father's work in Leeds ; but Bishop Woodford's lamented death has deprived the reader of what
would have lent a special interest to this book. The
Dean of Worcester has very kindly filled the gap,
and has written the following letter, in which he
brings out the part my father took in two very
important branches of directly spiritual work. He
says :—

My dear Cyril,—I wish I could help you worthily in the life you are writing for us, for your book is a true chapter of English life, telling of a ripening Church, and a Bishop's constant presence, touch, and blessing on a teeming part of England, which seems to many of us a typical diocese of the nineteenth century.

The only difficulty I have is the simple fact that the Bishop was permeating all things and places so habitually, that there were no comings and goings in a way that would make scenes and events ; there were few incidents, for his life was a single incident in the growth of the Church in the North. This was specially the case in Leeds, in and out of which he was passing two or three times every week, for it was the road to many of the chief towns of the diocese, and the scene of most of his diocesan meetings.

Yet some things stand out in the front of my memory, for to your father we owe the first authorised Retreat for Clergy, to which he summoned us during the summer of 1876. Many clergy had held aloof from any devotional time of this kind, until it was conducted by their Father in God, by one who had authority to speak to the conscience, and appeal to the spirit of a clergyman ; and it was, perhaps, the last addition which he made to the spiritual organisation of the diocese.

When I first wrote to ask him for work in Yorkshire, he put my purpose through a long and hard trial, lest it should be the child of secondary motives. When Yarmouth was offered me, and I laid the matter before him, he asked me three questions. (1) Did my doctor allow me to undertake a parish of that size? (2) Was I needlessly leaving the work at Bramley to which God had called me? (3) Had I raised a finger to get myself the offer of this church?

In one of those walks or rides in which he used to draw us out, and put his own experiences and higher aims into us, I asked him how he had managed to be the parish priest in society when he was a vicar in London. He described the ways by which he gradually led his people to wish him to have family prayers at the close of their parties, and the habit that grew among his own parishioners of referring to him some intellectual difficulty of the Bible, or the application of some chapters to modern life and London society, until this became a common practice when he spent the evening socially in his own parish.

And he always honoured the priesthood of his clergy. In the first parish I held in his diocese, one of my wardens complained to him that I had introduced a hymn-book containing expressions that he considered very High Church ; he thought he should find a willing ear in Dr. Bickersteth, but he found something better, for the Bishop bade him look out all the hymns in the book that would help him to Christ, and to put the best construction upon those of which he complained.

These are among the blessed memories that recall the Father in God ; not only the ordainer of his clergy, but our director and counsellor, who stood by us, and helped us to rise to the height and ripeness of our ministry. Other memories are not wanting ; let me go to the opposite end of a bishop's life, his touch on the outside world, "the people," (especially as they rise to the crown of their wave in the men that work in our great factories).

We were planning a great Mission for the whole town of Leeds, and the question arose, What part shall we ask the Bishop to undertake ? if he preached at any one church, it would be unfair to the others ; and if he scattered himself among the churches, preaching once to each of the leading congregations, it would interfere with the plan of the regular missioners. He consented, therefore, to address the chief mills of the town. The manufacturers willingly opened their works, and made excellent arrangements for gathering their people round the Bishop.

The men came in orderly crowds, and gave us a lesson in the art of listening. Yet it cost them much. In many mills the masters gave them half an hour or an hour out of working time, at a cost in some cases of £100. In others the masters gave twenty minutes, and the men out of their dinner or tea-time gave as much more. In this way the

Bishop addressed all the larger mills and workshops of the town, three and often four a day, for ten days. The vicar of the parish and two or three younger clergy generally accompanied him, to learn their lesson, or to follow up the work afterwards. It was certainly the most difficult, and often the most valuable part of the Mission. It brought the Church to the masses ; the men said it brought it home to them.

The people saw the use of a bishop, and grew to know him personally. It showed that religion was distinctly in its place in working days and scenes, a thought that seemed new to many. Deeper results mostly work out of sight, yet the men told us that their Bishop's presence in their mills brought numbers of them to Church.

Nor did his contribution to our Mission stop here ; it began before this, and ended afterwards. To his hand we owed the Pastoral that authorised and founded our work ; he preached to the clergy and churchworkers before the Mission commenced ; his words summed up the whole at the conclusion of the ten days, and his hands confirmed double the usual number of candidates two months after the missioners had left us.

The youngest lay helper felt himself a fellow-labourer with his Bishop, and the new communicant recognised his part in sealing the influences that had moulded him.

I have only touched two points of his work among us, its innermost and its outermost point ; yet these may fairly serve as samples of the life and ministry that has passed but not passed away from the heart of the Diocese he ruled for a great quarter of a century.

Yours ever affectionately,
JOHN GOTT.

In his Charge of 1876, insisting as usual on the absolute necessity of personal holiness in the clergy, my father suggests the observance of a Retreat or time of special meditation for deepening the spiritual life. He writes :—

First, and above all things else, let me implore you to aim at raising the standard of personal holiness amongst yourselves. This is the secret of all ministerial influence and success. Come any trial to the Church rather than the lack of a pious clergy! The severest calamity which could possibly befall a Church would not be the want of worldly resources, nor the disruption of the ties which unite her with the State, nor the want of learning in her ministers (although this would be a fearful disaster), nor the want of gifts, but the *want of personal holiness in those who minister at her Altars.* Apart from this, human wisdom, ability, or eloquence, are of little or no avail. Covet earnestly, if you will, the best gifts; but still there is "a more excellent way." Grace is more than gifts. As the standard of our own spiritual life is raised, we shall be stronger and stronger for the work which lies before us.

To this end need I observe how necessary it is to secure time for prayer, meditation, and the study of God's Word? We live in a busy and restless age. Amidst the ceaseless activities of a public ministerial life, there is often a strong temptation to abbreviate the time which ought to be devoted to private communion with God. We have each need to keep in mind the exhortation to which we hearkened at that solemn period of our lives when we were called to the priesthood, which bade us "continually pray to God the Father, by the Mediation of our only Saviour Jesus Christ, for the heavenly assistance of the Holy Ghost; that, by daily reading and weighing of the Scriptures, ye may wax riper and stronger in your Ministry."

Amongst the means which may tend to the deepening of spiritual life, I believe that seasons of retirement for prayer and meditation and mutual exhortation out of God's Word would be found eminently useful. We have the warrant for this in the example set by our Blessed Master. To His chosen Apostles, the daily companions of His ministerial life, He said, "Come ye yourselves apart unto a desert place, and rest awhile." If they needed such a season of rest and meditation, although living daily within the hallowing influence of personal intercourse with Jesus, how much more must we, His ministers, need it, whose lot is cast in the midst of temptations, and who find it often hard to realise the Presence of Him Whom, having not seen, we love. Such seasons for special retirement have been found precious in the experience of the many who have enjoyed them ; times of spiritual refreshment which have left a special blessing behind. I am not without hope of being able in the course of the present year to arrange a season for private devotion and meditation upon God's Word for such of the clergy as may desire to avail themselves of it.

I am indebted to Dr. Kennion, the Bishop of Adelaide, for the following notes of an address given by my father at the Retreat for Clergy, held at the Training College, Ripon, in August of the same year, 1876 :—

HEB. xii. 14.

Peace and holiness our object.

Our hearts must be grateful for the office we hold.

Yet dangers from office :—

1. Professionalism in spiritual things.
2. Critical (only) study of Holy Scripture.
3. Errors we meet with.
4. Our very successes retard growth in grace.
5. Want of intercourse with one another.
6. Misconception of each other's views.

It is a solemnising thought that we meet here to *help* one another.

Weighty responsibility on each of us.

Our subject :—

Sanctification, its necessity.

    ,, ,, means.

    ,, ,, source.

R

Necessity of Holiness.

1. Perception of spiritual truth depends upon degree of Holiness.
   " If any man will *do* His Will, he shall *know*."
   Surely essential to Ministry.

2. To make us meet for inheritance of Saints in light.
   Holy Ghost will not dwell where impurity reigns.

3. Holiness very atmosphere of Heaven.
   Pure in heart shall see God.
   Holiness always implies separation, dedication, or consecration.
   Christian consecrated by vows of Holy Baptism.
   Holiness involves purity of *thought, word, act*.
   In Heaven but *one* mind, one impulse.
   Where all these are consecrated to God's service there you have a foretaste of true Sanctification.

Source, Holy Ghost.

What worth without the Holy Spirit?
His province is to *quicken*.
Resort to prayer.
Seconded by effort.

(Here the notes break off.)

Each of these points was clearly and lovingly enlarged upon.

To the best of my recollection the Bishop spoke on the " means " of Sanctification, though, with the exception of the two last phrases recorded, the notes do not allude to what he said.

This was, I believe, the first Diocesan Retreat conducted by a bishop in person for the benefit of his clergy; and the part my father took in it disarmed the opposition of those who supposed that there was something un-English and anti-Protestant in such a movement.

The following letter to the clergy was sent out in 1880, and perhaps, considering the growing interest in devotional meetings of the sort, it may be interesting to see what the proposed arrangements were.

"Again I say unto you, That if two of you shall agree on earth as touching anything that they shall ask, it shall be done for them of My Father Which is in heaven. For where two or three are gathered together in My name, there am I in the midst of them" (Matt. xviii. 19, 20).

"We will give ourselves continually to prayer, and to the ministry of the Word" (Acts vi. 4).

The Palace, Ripon, May 3, 1880.

In compliance with an earnest wish which has been expressed to me by some of the clergy, I am making arrangements to hold a Retreat, or private meeting of Clergy for prayer and meditation, with a view to the deepening of their spiritual life, at the Female Training College,[1] Ripon, in August next, from the 9th to the 12th.

At the suggestion of several of my Reverend Brethren, who feel a warm interest in this proposed gathering, I have consented to take the principal part in the conduct of the religious exercises. The great aim to which our thoughts and prayers should be directed is the glory of God in the increase of our own personal piety ; the promotion of a higher standard of devotedness in the service of our Lord and Saviour Jesus Christ; the growth of brotherly union between all, who, whilst differing, it may be, in minor matters, recognise the solemn responsibilities of the Sacred Ministry, and the indispensable need of personal holiness for the effective discharge, under God's blessing, of the work of winning souls.

The General Arrangements will be as follows :—

The clergy will assemble at the Female Training College, Ripon, on Monday, August 9th. Sufficient bedroom accommodation will be provided in that Institution for those who shall have previously signified their intention to

[1] This large and commodious building was available for the purpose owing to the absence of the students for their usual summer holidays.

attend.   The time of the gathering will extend from Monday evening, the 9th, to Thursday morning, the 12th of August.   All meals will be in common in the College Hall, and the expense to each will be limited as nearly as possible to fifteen shillings.

PROPOSED ORDER OF PROCEEDINGS.

Monday, August 9.

5 p.m.—Clergy arrive at the Training College and select their rooms.

6 p.m.—Tea in the Dining Hall.

7 p.m.—Service in Magdalene Chapel, with Address.

8 p.m.—Silent Prayer and Meditation.

9 p.m.—Supper.

9.30 p.m.—Prayer.

10 p.m.—Retire for the night.

Tuesday, August 10.

8 a.m.—Holy Communion in the Magdalene Chapel.

9 a.m.—Breakfast.

10 a.m.—Morning Prayer in the Magdalene Chapel.

10.30 a.m.—Address, followed by Silent Prayer and Meditation.

1 p.m.—Dinner.

1.45–3 p.m.—Free time.

3 p.m.—Address.

4.15 p.m.—Service in the Magdalene Chapel.

5.30 p.m.—Tea.

6–7 p.m.—Free time.

7 p.m.—Service in the Magdalene Chapel, with Address.

8 p.m.—Silent Prayer and Meditation.

9 p.m.—Supper.

9.30 p.m.—Prayer.

10 p.m.—Retire for the night.

Wednesday, August 11.

8 a.m.—Holy Communion in the Magdalene Chapel.

9 a.m.—Breakfast.

10 a.m.—Morning Prayer in the Magdalene Chapel.

10.30 a.m.—Address, followed by Private Prayer and Meditation.

1 p.m.—Dinner.

1.45–3 p.m.—Free time.

3 p.m.—Address.

4.15 p.m.—Service in the Magdalene Chapel.

5.30 p.m.—Tea.

6–7 p.m.—Free time.

7 p.m.—Service in Magdalene Chapel, with Address.

8 p.m.—Silent Prayer and Meditation.

9 p.m.—Supper.

9.30 p.m.—Prayer.

10 p.m.—Retire for the night.

Thursday, August 12.

8 a.m.—Holy Communion in the Magdalene Chapel.

9 a.m.—Breakfast.

10 a.m.—Morning Prayer in the Magdalene Chapel.

10.30 a.m.—Address.

11 a.m.—Disperse.

Each clergyman to whom this paper is sent is particularly requested to let me have a line within the next ten days, to say whether or not he intends to be present; if no answer is received by that time it will be assumed that he does not mean to come. I have only further to entreat the prayers of my Reverend Brethren that a blessing from God may rest on this proposed gathering—that it may tend to God's glory, to our own growth in grace, and the good of His Church.

It is expected that those who signify their intention to be present, will let nothing short of absolute necessity prevent them from coming.

R. RIPON.

To the Reverend ——.

In the other branch of spiritual work to which Dr. Gott refers, my father took the warmest interest. In the Charge of 1876, he writes of Missions :—

My next counsel is this. Do all in your power to cultivate the as yet unreclaimed portion of the field committed to your care. It may be you have an eager and crowded congregation. You cannot be too earnest or prayerful in dispensing the Word of Life to those who thus wait on your ministry. But bear in mind the wandering, and as yet unfolded sheep. Do all in your power to gather them in. Be instant in season, and out of season ; testify publicly, and from house to house, as did the Apostle. Adapt your ministrations to meet their special need. Multiply services in their behalf. Preach, if necessary, and if strength will allow, in the open air ; establish Mission-rooms, and Missions for them, till you render it impossible for any member of your flock to say with truth, " No man careth for my soul." You may say all this involves expenditure. So it does ; but I believe the necessary means will be provided for the clergyman who is evidently fully bent on making full proof of his ministry. Missions such as those which have been held in so many places, and with such wonderful results, are invaluable not only for breaking up fallow ground, but also for quickening spiritual growth in those who are already followers of Christ. I have seen results over which angels in heaven rejoice, follow from such Missions. It is not all passing excitement ; I believe some permanent blessing invariably attends a carefully prepared and rightly conducted Mission. Let me say one word by way of caution, and it is this : Under God the success of a Mission such as I am recommending depends upon the previous preparation. Months of preparatory work are not too much, if you would ensure a lasting blessing. I have not known an instance in which such preparation was made, and the simple message of the Gospel has been the key-note of the Mission, where a visible blessing has not followed.

The Bishop took an active personal part in special Missions in Bradford and Huddersfield, and in the great Leeds Mission of 1875.

In a very interesting account of the Leeds Mission, which was drawn up by the committee, and published by Messrs. Jackson, is to be found a fuller account of my father's special work to which Dr. Gott alludes.

There had been long and thorough preparation, and almost all the clergy in the town took part in the movement. Three or four months before the Mission my father met the clergy in the parish church for a day of special preparation.

At 11 a.m. there was a Celebration of the Holy Communion, and the Bishop preached from 2 Chron. xxix. 36: "And Hezekiah rejoiced, and all the people, that God had prepared the people." The preacher, after expressing his gladness that a Mission was to take place, and his pleasure at being invited to address his reverend brethren on a subject of such importance and interest, said—

"I will speak to you with regard to—(1) The objects of the Mission; (2) The means to be employed to secure its success ; and (3) The results which we may reasonably anticipate from the Mission.

"1. The minister's work is partly pastoral, partly missionary : pastoral as regards his congregation ; missionary to those outside who seldom or never come to the House of God, and who are careless as to their eternal interests. One great object of the Mission is to bring the Gospel message to every home and every heart. Another object of the Mission is to leave the beaten track, and by a special effort to endeavour to arouse the members of our congregations who are but Christians in name, to rebuke their lethargy, to raise them to a higher spiritual level.

"2. There can be no success to the Mission unless God the Holy Ghost gives spiritual life. In dependence on His promised aid we must—

"(1) Recognise the magnitude of the work to be done. A combined attack is to be made on the empire of Satan.

"(2) Examine well the state of our own hearts. We who are Christian ministers need greater zeal, humility, love ; more of the Mind of Christ.

"(3) Not only amongst the clergy, but amongst the people at large there must be preparation for the Mission. Sunday school teachers, district visitors, tract distributors, Church workers, should pray for its success, speak of it to others ; and when January comes take part in it.

"(4) In the Mission, and in preparation for it, Christ and Christ alone must be exalted. Let there be no divisions, no party feeling, no aim lower than this—to exalt the Redeemer, and to bring souls to Christ.

"3. If God gives success, as I trust He will, we may anticipate—

"(1) A higher standard of spirituality amongst ourselves.

"(2) Greater union.

"(3) The conversion of souls.

"(4) Larger congregations and growth in zeal and holiness.

"(5) An increase in the number of persons who openly profess Christian discipleship by presenting themselves for Confirmation.

"(6) An increase in the number of Communicants.

"These are great results. They have accompanied and followed special Missions in other towns, and I trust they will do so in Leeds."

When the Mission began in January, the Bishop went to Leeds for ten days, and his time was fully occupied. The addresses to which Dr. Gott alludes were delivered day after day in the various factories. Once the pulpit was an enormous Armstrong gun, from which the Bishop addressed a workshop densely crowded with foundry men fresh from their work. He thoroughly enjoyed these services, and always looked back upon them with the deepest thankfulness.

At the parish church the chief missioner was Dr. Wilkinson, now Bishop of Truro; and my father greatly valued the opportunity of making the acquaintance of one for whom he conceived a sincere love and admiration.

He wrote at the time, speaking of Dr. Wilkinson's sermons :—

I have never seen the parish church so full as it was last night. There were certainly more than 3000 present ; and I have never listened to a more thoroughly clear, simple, and loving statement of the Gospel. It was indeed a glorious sermon, and must do good. The people were riveted the whole time. After the sermon came a hymn, and then an after-address. The service began at 7.30, and was not over till nearly 10. I have just had a visit, in the morning-room which the Gotts have kindly given up to me, from Mr. Wilkinson. There is certainly a wonderful charm about him. He came to ask my advice on some points connected with the Mission, and to ask me to pray with him. . . .

I am quite well, thank God, and not at all tired. Some of them seem amused at my strength, and tell me I must be a very strong man.

As the value of Missions becomes more widely known and felt, there may be improvement in the method of conducting them ; but there can hardly ever again be such a Mission as the one in Leeds, in 1875, for its novelty and the power of the missioners engaged, combined to make a profound impression on the town.

The shops were shut throughout the week at an early hour, and the busy manufacturing community seemed stirred to its very depths.

In addition to the addresses in workshops and

sermons to special classes in various district churches, the Bishop usually presided at the prayer meeting which was held daily in the Church Institute from 2.15 to 3.

The report of the Mission having given a brief account of its origin and history goes on to say—

It only remains to ask—What has been the result? There were long and anxious preparations for it; thought and care and toil were expended; prayers were offered in family circles, in churches, in schoolrooms, in sick chambers, in private and in public—not only in Leeds, but in distant places. It was known that during the Mission Week petitions were publicly offered to God in at least sixty churches in different parts of the world; in Cornwall and other English counties, in Scotland, in Ireland, in France, in India. Missioners came from busy towns and quiet country parishes; Church workers of every rank toiled and prayed; crowded meetings and crowded churches were seen on every hand; men who for years had never been within the doors of a House of God, and who at first seemed utterly at a loss what to do when there, or how to follow the service, were found night after night listening to the Gospel Message. It has been computed that during the Mission about 40,000 persons were at one and the same time listening to the Word of God.

What is the produce of the vast machinery set in motion? With so much sowing of the good seed, is there any fruit?

To begin with, so manifestly had the Divine Presence and Blessing been felt during the Mission Week, that the clergy, unknown to each other, announced that in their various churches, a special Service of Thanksgiving would be held. And there was a universal feeling amongst the missioners, parochial clergy, and Church workers, that there should be, for themselves specially, a United Service of Praise to God for His goodness to them, and for prospering their work.

This last took place on Monday morning, February 1, in the parish church. It consisted of the Administration of the Holy Communion, and sermon by the Bishop of Ripon, from Rev. i. 5, 6: "Unto Him that loved us, and washed us from our sins in His own blood, and hath made us kings and priests unto God and His Father; to Him be glory and dominion for ever and ever. Amen."

The Bishop said: "We meet together in this sacred place to offer up our united praises and thanksgiving to God, for the blessing which He has been pleased to pour down upon the Mission. I believe very few of us fully anticipated so copious a shower of blessing as that which has been received. God has abundantly answered our prayers: He has been better to us than our fears. Far be it from me to use the language of exaggeration, but I think on reviewing what has taken place during the last week, I am not mistaken in saying that this large and important community has been deeply stirred. There has been a remarkable unanimity amongst the clergy with respect to this great work. With very few exceptions, the whole body of the clergy of Leeds have thrown themselves into it; and I learn, with the deepest satisfaction, that through all the preparatory work that has been going on for months with respect to it, there has not been one jarring note of discord; all has been harmony; all have been of one mind.

" The Mission has been remarkably characterised by the absence of every kind of excess and of undue excitement. There has been a very kind and generous feeling expressed on behalf of the Mission by all classes of the community. Even those who do not belong to our own Church have, nevertheless, wished God-speed to the effort; and, if I am rightly informed, in the chapels of some of our Nonconforming brethren, prayers have been offered that God would pour down His abundant grace upon this great effort to win souls to Christ. Most of the principal firms in Leeds have kindly thrown open their places of work, to allow the preaching of the Gospel to the hands whom they employ.

Those opportunities were freely accepted by the men for whose benefit they were intended. Our churches have been crowded with eager and attentive listeners. Many have come inquiring about their soul's salvation. Many have been anxious who were never anxious before about their spiritual state ; and can we for a moment doubt that many, through God's grace, have been brought to Jesus, and have found joy and peace in believing, and that a fresh anthem of praise has resounded through the courts of Heaven, over many a returning sinner brought to God, instrumentally through this Mission ? . . . . On the review of the Mission, the first feeling which ought to be uppermost in our minds is one of profound humility. All the success of a Mission like this is of God, and not of man. It is not man's eloquence, nor man's imagination, nor any gifts which God may have granted to any to possess ; but if there is any success, as we doubt not there has been, " Not unto us, O Lord, not unto us, but unto Thy Name give the praise." The next feeling we ought to cherish is one of greater personal devotedness to our Blessed Lord and Master. Every one who takes any part in Missions ought to look for an increase of spiritual grace in his own soul. We should also, on reviewing the Mission, cherish a feeling of greater earnestness than ever in seeking the salvation of souls around us. Let us bind ourselves on this, the day of our thanksgiving, that we will, with redoubled energy, devote ourselves to the work of trying to bring poor wandering sinners to the feet of Christ."

The service closed most appropriately with singing the *Te Deum.*

The Bishop had the best means of judging of the success of the Mission, for he found a very great increase in the number of Confirmation candidates, especially in the case of adults, who were brought into the Church chiefly through the special efforts which were then put forth.

When the time came round for another Mission in Leeds, in 1883, my father was no longer able to take a personal share in the work, but he wrote the following Pastoral, and prayerfully watched its progress :—

On behalf of this Mission, the Bishop of the diocese earnestly invites the co-operation, and bespeaks the cordial sympathy of all classes. The object at which we aim is to uproot the seeds of vice and immorality, to check the growth of infidelity, to advance the cause of pure and undefiled religion, and to raise the standard of vital godliness in the heart and life of professing Christians. In the midst of this vast and overwhelming population, notwithstanding its many churches, chapels, schools, teachers of religion, and multiplied agencies for the spread of living Christianity, we are surrounded by tens of thousands who are living without God in the world, without care for their eternal welfare, ignorant of Christ and His blessed Gospel, with no thought for their souls, for Heaven or for Hell, for God or for the Judgment to come. · Is it not a duty to endeavour to rouse such persons to a sense of their peril, and to prevail with them to ask the question, " What must I do to be saved ? " They are not reached by the ordinary means of grace ;—the Sabbath bell in vain calls them to the house of prayer ; all its many opportunites for religious instruction are for them provided in vain. May we not hope to reach them by special efforts on their behalf ? Such efforts have been tried and proved effectual. They were tried in this town some eight years ago, with results which astonished many, and put to shame the unbelief of thousands who doubted the effect which may be expected to accompany such an attempt, made in reliance on the living power of God the Holy Ghost. The clergy of this town, charged with the duty of watching for souls, have determined, after much thought and prayer, to repeat the effort. We will undertake it in dependence on Divine strength, and in reliance on Divine direction.   To convert, or to save the soul, is not in the power of man ; but the power of God is made effectual in connection with the use of appointed means.   Earnest, believing prayer, the ministry of the Word, heart-stirring appeals to the conscience, the faithful delivery of the messages of the Gospel, telling of the love of Jesus, of His ability and willingness to save to the uttermost all who come unto God by Him,—these are the means which have not lost their efficacy ; under their faithful use strong hearts have been broken, souls dead in trespasses and sins have been quickened by the power of Divine grace, drunkards have been reformed, unchaste lives have been purified, evil habits have been renounced, peace and purity, holiness and happiness, have shed their moral fragrance, where all was formerly strife and misery and sin.   I ask you to unite in this special effort, from which we confidently anticipate many spiritual blessings.   Among them, not the least will be a growth of spiritual life, zeal, and fervour among the professing disciples of Christ. . . . . To your fervent prayers I commend this Mission, and may it please Almighty God to grant that, in answer to our supplications and united efforts, there may be poured down copious showers of blessing.

Passing from the subject of Retreats and Missions to another important event in my father's episcopate, I am greatly indebted to the kindness of Canon Temple, who has written an account of his work, as President of the Church Congress held at Leeds in 1872, and also of the formation of the Diocesan Conference, which was summoned to meet for the first time in 1878.

Canon Temple writes :—

Leeds Church Congress, 1872.

In the minute book of the Nottingham Church Congress, which now lies before me, is found the following statement :—

"At a meeting of the Executive Committee, held after the Congress Morning Session, on October 14, 1871, the Bishop Suffragan in the chair, Archdeacon Emery read a letter, signed by Dr. Woodford, of Leeds, and others, inviting the Congress to hold its next meeting in that town.

"Archdeacon Trollope moved, Rev. G. Venables seconded, and it was resolved,—'That the next meeting take place at Leeds.'"

This is the first indication given of an event which was fraught with important consequences to the Church in the diocese of Ripon, namely, the meeting of that Church Congress in which Bishop Bickersteth played so important a part, first as its chief promoter, and afterwards as its president. In November, 1871, the first meetings were held to prepare for the coming work. In spite of some little difficulties raised at these early meetings, a spirit of harmony and energetic co-operation very quickly became the distinguishing mark of all that was done. That this was so, every one felt was due in large measure to the tact and courtesy of the Bishop, and perhaps not less than this to the firm resolution which he evinced at an early stage of the proceedings, as one of the General Committee phrased it, "to drive the coach himself."

The difficult and laborious work of presiding, so far as one man could do it, over the deliberations of the Congress as a whole, was accomplished by Bishop Bickersteth at once with distinguished ability and with transparent fairness. These qualities were exhibited repeatedly in the course of the discussions, and very notably during one rather painful scene, at which strong words were used by some members of the Congress, while the President seemed to be confronted at the moment by a brother prelate of the very highest mark in the Church, and of standing considerably senior to his own.

The ideal which the Bishop set before himself of the proper functions of a Church Congress, was well sketched in his inaugural address. "We do not meet," he said, "as a Church Congress to discuss the grand fundamentals of the everlasting Gospel. There are no fresh discoveries to be made in what is to be received as fundamental truth : we have neither to report nor to investigate any new developments of the Faith which was once delivered to the Saints. . . . These organic doctrines of Christianity lie beyond the province of debate by this assembly. But there is an ever-widening field for discussion upon matters of supreme importance to the efficiency of the Church, and the adaptation of her machinery to the shifting requirements of the age in which we live. A state of great activity is a marked feature of the Church at the present day. The torpor of a past age has given place to an awakened energy and zeal, which, if rightly directed, may lead to the most beneficial results. We are learning by degrees the need of greater elasticity and freedom in our Church system.   I suppose that most men now recognise the necessity,—if the National Church is to retain, or, speaking more correctly, if she is to recover her influence over large masses of our fellow-countrymen,—that she should be emancipated to some extent from those rigid and unyielding bands of uniformity, which have too often tended rather to impede than to further the Church's progress.

" In such a period of reawakened activity, conference is of inestimable value.   A hundred problems are sure to arise, as indeed they have arisen, for the wise solution of which nothing is more to be desired than the calm deliberation of thoughtful minds, and the contributions of experience which may be imparted by those who have tried, each in his own sphere and in his own method, to work out the problems which the circumstances of the Church and the age force on our notice.   Problems, for example, such as these :—how to win back the multitudes who, from whatever cause, have become estranged from our Communion, or, what is far worse, estranged from Christianity itself ; how to adapt the ministrations of the Church so as to reach the largest number, and to convey the fullest measure of spiritual blessing ; how to utilise to the utmost the services of the lay members of the Church, without trenching upon the province which is peculiar to an Ordained Ministry; how to counteract the tendencies of the age, whether towards scepticism in one direction, or towards superstition in another; how, without the smallest surrender of essential truth, to cultivate brotherly union between all who profess to be followers of the same Divine Saviour; how to preserve the distinction between fundamental truth, which we must die rather than compromise, and that which, though equally true, is not equally important, and about which we may safely agree to differ till the prayer of our Divine Lord is accomplished, 'that they all may be one; as Thou, Father, art in Me, and I in Thee, that they also may be one in Us: that the world may believe that Thou hast sent Me.'"

The Bishop then proceeded to give, as the Committee had requested him to do, a most interesting account of Church work in the Diocese of Ripon since its reconstitution in the year 1836. The substance of this part of his address has already been quoted from the Bishop's tribute to his predecessor in his first Charge. He went on to say—

"The expansion of the Church, and the hold which it has upon the affection of the people, may fairly be tested in a diocese like this by the erection of new churches, by the number of candidates who offer themselves for Confirmation, and by the voluntary contributions in aid of Church purposes.

"Applying, then, these three tests to the question of Church progress in the diocese, the following are the conclusions arrived at :—

"In the five years which preceded the formation of the See of Ripon in 1836, the number of churches consecrated within the limits of the present diocese was exactly four. In the five years which immediately followed the constitution of the See in 1836, the number of churches consecrated was thirty-three. In the five years ending with the present, the number of churches consecrated is forty-two.

"I have not any lists of the candidates who were con-

S

firmèd during the episcopate of Bishop Longley. But the number of those who were confirmed in the five years, from 1856 to 1861, was 19,086; and the number confirmed in the five years terminating with the present is 29,776.

" I have no means of ascertaining how much was raised in the diocese for Church purposes at an earlier date ; but I have exact returns for the three years ending with 1866, and the three years ending with 1869.

" In the first of these triennial periods the diocese raised for Church purposes £308,565 ; in the second triennial period it raised £330,215 ; making a total in six years of £638,780, which may be regarded as the free-will offering of new members in furtherance of the work of the Church within this diocese. These figures do not include the contributions which have been given in aid of the Church extension beyond the limits of the diocese.

" These are facts from which I augur hopefully for the progress of the Church, not here only, but throughout the length and breadth of the land. They are not solitary facts ; other dioceses might, I doubt not, furnish a parallel. But these facts speak for themselves ; they tell of a depth of attachment to the National Church, of an amount of zeal and liberality which must spring from a deep conviction that the National Church is a national blessing ; that, notwithstanding all her faults and all her shortcomings, she is a witness for God and for truth in the land ; a bulwark of the throne and the constitution ; a tree planted in our midst, whose leaves are for the healing of the nation. . . ."

After pleading once more for a spirit of charity and mutual forbearance, the Bishop concluded by making the following suggestion, which was adopted with enthusiasm at the time, and has been a characteristic feature of each subsequent Congress :—

" One word more. We commenced our proceedings by an act of worship—of prayer and praise. I think it is meet that a Church Congress should also commence its proceedings with an act of faith, by showing to the whole world that we cling fast to apostolic truth. I therefore invite this vast assembly to rise as one man, and recite with me the Apostles' Creed."

With the exception of his inaugural address, and such little interpositions as every chairman of a great meeting has to exercise in preserving order, the President only made three speeches : one at the Working Men's Meeting, and others, very short ones, at the meeting on Friday morning, about the Deepening of Spiritual Life, and at the final meeting. The first of these three meetings is somewhat more than historical. All readers of the "Life of Bishop Wilberforce" are familiar with the exceedingly graphic letter written by that able prelate from the Congress Hall to the Rev. Hugh Pearson, in which he criticises fearlessly some, and applauds with discrimination others of the utterances which fell from the lips of those around him. I venture to quote the concluding passages of that famous letter: "Now old Woodford speaks ; he has been rapturously received and is speaking excellently well. Of the old Church. The Church of England, not an aristocratic Church (*very* fine : in his best mode). An analysis of the real religious state of the town, lightly but very effectively done. Why do respectable working men not worship? 'Talk it out, sift it, weigh it, twist it, and then come and tell us what we can do to take stones out of your path and make the way easier to you : and do what you can to bring others with you. You can do what we cannot. You can pass thresholds we cannot cross,' etc. He has ended excellently, in great applause. Bishop of Ripon before closing, wishes to say a word. Universal interest in the Congress, shared by Nonconformists, including our chief civil magistrate : the Mayor (applause). (He gave us turtle soup to day). He watches for the welfare of the good old Church of England, and he *may* speak to-night, and so he rises (stupendous applause), speaks sensibly and well. The clock strikes ten, and we break up in search of horizontality."

The Leeds Church Congress far exceeded in the number of its members all similar gatherings which had taken place up ,to that date. And though the numbers have been larger at some later assemblies, it may be doubted whether, on the whole, any other of these meetings has exercised a more permanent influence for good, either on the particular place in which it has been held, or on the Church at large.

If this be so, all who like the present writer witnessed the great effort from beginning to end, will recognise that, second only to God's gracious guidance, the result was due to the courtesy, dignity, firmness, and ability of the President. They will gladly echo the words of Canon Bernard : " We are of one mind about the presidency, because we have all felt the impartiality and decision which has kept all things in perfect Christian peace, when from the nature of the subjects discussed, and the variety of opinions represented by those who have attended the Congress, we might have expected a very different result. We have all felt, and we now acknowledge, the courtesy, the judgment, the composure of voice and manner which have seemed to diffuse their own influence over the minds of this vast assembly."

It is true that some of these expressions may seem now a little in excess of what the case demands, but it must be remembered that the present orderly and forbearing attitude of the Church Congress has been a matter of growth, and that the full expression of feeling and of thought which is so easily tolerated now presented in earlier days a front of difficulty which only a really strong President was properly qualified to face.

Amongst the many happy recollections of the Congress was the friendship which my father formed with the saintly Bishop Forbes. One who was present wrote—

I walked with the Bishop out of the hall where the

Bishop of Brechin read his deeply searching paper, "On the Deepening of the Spiritual Life," and I remember him saying with deep emotion, how much he had gained from the paper, and how "his heart yearned to know more of the reader."

That the feeling was reciprocal, was shown by the dedication which the Bishop of Brechin prefixed to his paper in its final form—

TO THE RIGHT REVEREND

ROBERT,

BY DIVINE PERMISSION, BISHOP OF RIPON,

IN WHOSE PRESENCE THE GERM OF

THIS LITTLE TREATISE

WAS READ, AT THE LEEDS CHURCH CONGRESS,

OVER WHICH HE PRESIDED

WITH GRACE, DIGNITY, AND JUSTICE,

THIS IS

INSCRIBED.

Canon Temple has been good enough to add to his most interesting account of the Church Congress a sketch of the causes which led to the formation of the Ripon Diocesan Conference, and the part which my father took in its early organisation. The Bishop was so much more a man of action than of mere speech, that he was inclined to hold back until he saw that the Conference was really desired by clergy and laity alike, and would be likely to prove of real advantage in the practical working of diocesan institutions. Canon Temple was one of those whose judgment influenced my father in the matter, so it is interesting to hear from him how the movement grew :—

Ripon Diocesan Conference, 1878.

The quickening of Church life, so far as that is syno-nymous with spiritual life in the heart of each separate Christian, may be regarded as God's special gift to this nation at the close of the last, and the beginning of the present century.   The Saviour, of course, in every part of Christendom has always had His chosen ones, whose lives of battle with the enemy, and rest in the Lord, have been a perpetual witness to Himself in the face of an unbelieving world.   But it is not too much to say that the great Evangelical Movement, which may be considered to date from the days of Wesley, was a marvellous expansion of life such as had known but a sickly and stunted existence since the days of the Restoration of Charles the Second. In like manner, God's gift to our own day has been a quickening of the Church's corporate life.   And this has brought in its train a certain Catholic feeling and a yearning for communion, alike of Christian with Christian and of Church with Church, which could not be repressed, and which refused to satisfy itself with the conviction that individual salvation was the Christian's sole or noblest aim. If the Master had founded a Church, had called that Church His Body, had furnished it with limbs and an organic constitution, it could not be safe for Christians to ignore such a fact in their approaches to the Most High. Such conduct was not only a waste of power, it was a sapping of the springs of life.   And so within the Church of England, at any rate, there sprang up a desire that Churchmen should know their own minds and the minds of their brethren, and that the united body should be able to speak with some approach to the confidence of those who dared of old to say, "It seemed good to the Holy Ghost and to us." This has shown itself in the constitution, or reconstitution, of Church Assemblies, some formal, some informal, and notably in the revival of Convocation ; in the invention of that very molluscous, but most useful assembly, the Church Congress ; and, as a sort of combination of these, more popular but less regular than Convocation, more regular but less popular than the Congress, in the gathering of the Diocesan Conference. The first of these last-named assemblies had been held in the diocese of Ely, wherein also the Church Congress had first seen the light. It was impossible that a mind like that of Bishop Bickersteth could miss reading the signs of the times with reference to this subject ; and so early as the year 1870, at his Visitation held in Leeds, he had convoked, without formal election, but by personal invitation from himself, a sort of Conference, which discussed various important subjects, especially Foreign Missions and National Education, with considerable freedom, and not, it is hoped, without edification. This Conference sat on two days, viz. the tenth and eleventh of October. The writer does not remember that it passed any formal resolutions. The proceeding was altogether tentative, and it seems to have been an experiment founded on a discussion held in the Palace at the meeting of rural deans in 1868. The subject ripened in the Bishop's mind, and in 1876 he threw the question out openly before the clergy at each Visitation call, " Is it desirable or not to hold a Diocesan Conference ? " An answer in the affirmative was all but unanimous. With the help of his archdeacons and rural deans, the Bishop sketched the form of a provisional constituency. Certain persons became members *ex officio*, a few were allowed to be nominated by the Bishop, and the above-named provisional constituency elected the remainder. The Conference so constituted met for the first time in Leeds on the tenth of October, 1878 ; and its first business, after the President's preliminary address, was to take into consideration its own constitution. In the inaugural address the Bishop explained very lucidly and distinctly the *raison d'être* of the Conference, and gave an historical account of how it came to be assembled. He well pointed out that though, unlike the Church Congress, it could formulate decisions and frame resolutions, it yet was not a synod, and could not legislate in any sense whatever. It could embody the collective opinion of a diocese, but it could do no more. Yet, doing so much and no more, it might be the spring of a great deal of practical work. Separate parishes would be likely to act upon its suggestions. Church Defence might almost take a new departure from its support. Unworthy prejudice might vanish before it, as mist before the sunshine. It might excellently well handle such subjects as Diocesan Organisation and Diocesan Finance. It might prove the possibility of Churchmen meeting together to discuss the highest interests of the Church ; and might demonstrate that differences of opinion upon some points did not render men unfit to consult together with profit and edification upon all.

Under the direction of its President, the Conference had sufficient wisdom to avoid spending too much time on its own formation and order of proceeding, when it was of the first importance to show that it knew how to proceed. Accordingly, it very quickly began a spirited debate on the subject of Diocesan Organisation and Finance, including Diocesan Societies. This led to the formation of a Lay Committee, and the drawing up of a Report which it is hoped may yet some day bear fruit, such as has been borne by similar action in other dioceses.

Among the various subjects discussed at the Conference, that one on which, at the present time, our readers will most desire to have the late Bishop's opinion is undoubtedly the division of the diocese, and the formation of a new See within its area. His remarks were as follows :—

"The question before the Conference was not one directly how to raise funds in order to set on foot the new bishopric ; but the object of the resolution was simply to express general approbation of the Act which, though permissive, empowered the constitution of a new bishopric for Yorkshire, provided the funds for so doing were raised. When the great meeting to which reference had been made was convened, the simple fact that a Diocesan Conference had pronounced an opinion in favour of the formation of the new bishopric would be of great advantage, and would stimulate the generosity of churchmen. The measure was one in which he felt the deepest interest. He could not but have mingled feelings with regard to it : and when he looked to that large belt of the diocese which it was proposed to sever from the existing diocese, and when he recalled the many happy hours he had spent in that part of the diocese, and the many friendships he had formed there, which he trusted would never be severed : and when he recalled the happy intercourse he had had with his brethren, the clergy, and how he had rejoiced in seeing their work,—he could tell them if he gave way to selfish feelings only, he should deprecate the formation of the new bishopric. But, in a matter of this kind, which affected the interests of the whole Church, all private feeling must give way. He wished to bury private feeling in the matter, and to consult only that which might promote the glory of God and the good of the Church : and he believed the time had come when the creation of a new diocese in Yorkshire would be for the glory of God and for the advantage of the Church. Since the diocese of Ripon was constituted, forty years ago, one new church had been consecrated and made the centre of a new district once every two months. That work was not at a standstill. Last year he consecrated nine new churches ; and before the close of the present year he expected the number would be eight ; so that there was no diminution of zeal on the part of the Church of England to meet the spiritual wants of the diocese.

" It must, therefore, be patent to every one that such an increase in the number of new churches in the diocese must very considerably multiply the labours of the Church. The question then arose, could a bishop adequately discharge those labours if the number of new parishes was utterly beyond his power efficiently to superintend ? Upon considerations like these—and he would not detain them by referring to other facts leading to the same conclusion— the time had arrived for the subdivision of the diocese.

He did not originate the scheme ; he should not have thought it his duty to have come forward to propose such subdivision.   But when he found some most earnest churchmen in the diocese, and some of his warmest friends, coming forward to propose the scheme, he could not but say that they had his hearty good will, and that he would give them every assistance in his power. He would say further, that he did not contemplate the carrying out of the scheme as likely palpably to effect any diminution of his work. He did not wish to lead an idle life. He might almost adopt the words of Dr. Hook on leaving Leeds, on going to what some considered a position of repose. Dr. Hook said, ' I don't mean to go to Chichester to be idle ; if I don't find work there, I will make it.' A large portion of the West Riding, with its large towns, and its incessant temptations to work, might be taken away from him ; but he could find work in other parts of the diocese, and God helping him, he might find enough to do, and perhaps more than he was able to accomplish in other districts, which, with their scantier populations, might have had some reason to complain that they had not been visited so often as they might have been by the Bishop of the diocese."

The Bishop always spoke with earnestness about the satisfaction he derived from that his first real Diocesan Conference ; and he proved his earnestness in the matter by repeating the experiment thus made in the following years.

Here may be added a letter from one who thought that some allusion should be made in this memoir to the annual conferences of archdeacons and rural deans.   These meetings were far more than an occasion of extending hospitality to a number of the clergy, though the opportunity of pleasant social intercourse at the Palace is gratefully remembered. The Rev. H. D. Cust Nunn writes :—

There was, to my mind, no occasion on which the Bishop's great powers of method, of gathering into focus, and of presidential acumen, displayed themselves more thoroughly. I have before me some agenda papers, which were sent out to each member of this Conference some three weeks before the day of meeting, and to show how wide of range were the subjects for discussion, I should like to quote one or two.

August 22, 1877.

1. The Diocesan Conference.
2. The present aspect of the Burials Question.
3. The Ornaments Rubric.
4. Parochial Associations in aid of Foreign Missions.
5. Elementary Education ; should the Clergy serve on School Attendance Committees? Arrangements for Diocesan Inspection.

August 11, 1881.

1. The mode of electing clerical representatives for the Diocesan Conference.
2. The Revised Version of the New Testament.
3. The working of the Ecclesiastical Dilapidations Act.
4. How may the Riding Charities for the relief of the Clergy become more effectual ?

One of the chief arguments advanced for making the office of rural dean of an elective character, is the supposed well-nigh servile dependency that characterises the present system of nomination by the bishop. I have often thought as I looked upon the circle of my brethren, as they sat around the library at the Palace, how thoroughly misleading is such a view. For here were representatives of all parties, and, what is more, men who, of whatever party they were, were known to be some of the most independent spirits in the diocese ; and these the selection of the Bishop. And, as in the choice of men for the office, so, too, in the act of consultation with his officers, I can testify how far Bishop Bickersteth ever was from seeking to unduly influence their own individual views. I have often taken part in discussions at the Palace on such questions as "the advisableness of frequent Celebrations of the Holy Communion," when views have been freely expressed, most probably not in accord with his; when not a word of rebuke has fallen from his lips. Moreover, the same spirit of liberality has been extended to the youngest men as to the elders. Indeed, I think it was rather a feature of Bishop Bickersteth's character—not always to be found in leaders—to credit young men with their due and proper share of sense and power. I have said enough to show, what indeed is generally acknowledged, that, as a President, he excelled in keeping men to the subject of discussion, in guiding their thoughts with tact, and in gathering up to a point the bearing of the whole.

CHAPTER XV.

TWENTY years of incessant work began to leave their
mark upon a constitution naturally very strong and
vigorous. A more careful expenditure of time and
strength might have added many years to the
Bishop's life, but the value of a life must be measured by another standard than that of time. It
was the rarest thing during the greater part of his
episcopate for my father to take a holiday. In the
years 1869 and 1873 he went abroad for a few
weeks, and found the most intense enjoyment and
refreshment in mountain scenery; but generally his
only recreation was variety of work.

The diversified character of the Ripon diocese
was not without advantage, for a Confirmation tour
in the northern dales was a refreshing change from
arduous work in the West Riding. In alternate
years Confirmations took him into the outlying

districts of Arncliffe, Hawes, and Sedburgh, or the even more remote centres of Stanwick, Barningham, Romaldkirk, and Bowes. The latter round was usually accomplished in a way which gave him a very delightful holiday. Leaving home in his own carriage, accompanied by my mother and one or two children, he would post through the dales; and the pleasure of these Confirmation tours was greatly enhanced by the hospitality of many kind friends among the laity. On many successive tours he was the guest of Mr. Michell, of Forcett Park, the Duchess Eleanor of Northumberland, Mr. Hutton, of Marske, the late Lord Zetland, Mr. Morritt, of Rokeby, and many others who furthered his progress from place to place, and did all in their power to make his work agreeable and easy. These friends in the North did for him what was done by many others of the laity in the manufacturing districts. It is impossible to enumerate all those whose houses were open to him when work called him to their neighbourhood; but the hospitality he most frequently enjoyed was that of Mr. Rawson, of Mill House, and Colonel Akroyd, at Halifax, the late Mr. John Rand, at Bradford, and Mr. Bickerton Turner, at the Bank of England in Leeds. These visits were always connected with some public duty; but Sir Charles Lowther, at Swillington and Wilton Castle, and Miss Rawson, of Nydd, were amongst the number of those who tried to detain him for a few days of rest and quiet in the intervals of exhausting work.

The late Mr. Mark Milbank used to entertain him at his shooting-box at Barningham, from whence he could reach the out-of-the-way districts on the borders of the Tees ; and from Bowes, where he was often the guest of the late Dr. Headlam, who was for a long time Chancellor of the diocese, he would ramble over the hills, and point out to his children the redoubtable mansion of Dotheboys Hall, where there still flourished the lineal descendants of the eminent pedagogue who was the original of the great Mr. Squeers.

My father greatly enjoyed the hearty greetings with which the dalesmen received him, and when staying in a country parish he would often accompany the clergyman to visit sick or bedridden parishioners, who remembered the Bishop's sermons in former years, or desired to be reminded of their Confirmation by receiving again his blessing.

Whenever he was thrown in the way of working men, whether they were farmers in the dales, or porters on the railway, or labourers on the country roads, my father sought opportunity to speak to them of spiritual things.

His admirable tact enabled him to do this in a way which made a deep impression, for none could mistake the reality of the interest which he took in the highest welfare of all alike who came within his reach. Navvies, and other working-men, have often surprised people by their grateful recollection of the Bishop's words, and of the direct, personal way in which he spoke to them of giving their hearts to God.

There was no more familiar figure on the railway between Leeds and Ripon than the Bishop, who was passing to and fro often three or four times a week. His movements were all arranged by himself, and the Confirmation tours were planned not without an accurate study of Bradshaw, which ensured an unfailing punctuality. On one occasion, rather than miss an important engagement, he reached his destination in a somewhat remarkable way. The congregation knew that there had been a mistake about the trains, and expected that for once the Bishop would fail to appear. The churchwardens, however, refused to postpone the service, certain that he would come somehow; and surely enough the Bishop arrived, having travelled on the engine of a goods train.

Once, and once only in all his travelling, my father met with a railway accident. He was a passenger from Leeds by the 5.30 p.m. express on January 25, 1872. Some three miles from Harrogate, on the dangerous curve leading to the Crimple Viaduct, the train was going at excessive speed, and an accident occurred, in which the Bishop and a number of other passengers escaped death or severe personal injuries in a manner that may be regarded as little less than miraculous. There was something wrong with the facing points where the loop for Harrogate leaves the old main line. The engine, tender, and three or four carriages passed safely over the points; then there was a severe shock, and the carriages composing the latter half of the train were driven upon the wrong line of rails. The coupling chains snapped, the engine swerved and ran into the embankment, half burying itself in the soil. Several carriages, including the one in which my father travelled, were completely overturned. He was precipitated into the arms of a fellow-passenger, and escaped entirely unhurt. He climbed through the window of the broken carriage, and after seeing that there was no one seriously injured he walked on to Harrogate.

Alarming rumours soon spread that the accident had been of a very serious character, and it was feared that the Bishop was hurt. For the next few days he was overwhelmed with letters of kind congratulation and inquiry, and these he carefully preserved as a memorial of an escape for which he was deeply thankful to the protecting Providence of God. Incidents of this kind from time to time gave people the opportunity of showing the love and veneration with which they regarded their Bishop.[1]

The first prolonged interruption to his work took place in the spring of 1877, when he was laid aside by illness for a month in London. On his recovery, by the advice of Sir James Paget he went abroad, accompanied by his daughter, to spend several weeks with his friend, Mr. (now Sir Francis) Cook, whose family had been amongst my father's warmest supporters in early days at Clapham, at his beautiful Villa of Monserrate, near Cintra, in Portugal.

The life at Cintra was so novel an experience, and he saw there so much that was interesting, that a few extracts from his letters home are well worth preserving.

They sailed from Southampton on Monday, the 9th of April, and after a rather rough voyage across the Bay of Biscay reached Lisbon on Friday morning, the 13th. The next day they joined Mr. and

---

[1] By my father's desire, mention was made of his escape in the General Thanksgiving at the Cathedral on the following Sunday.

T

Mrs. Cook in Lisbon, and proceeded to Cintra, a drive of about sixteen miles. Of this journey my father writes :—

The road from Lisbon to Cintra is not pretty till you get within sight of the Cintra mountains. But it is strange to see the hedges for the most part formed of aloes, and occasionally with geraniums growing quite wild. We halted three times on the journey to give the horses bread and wine ! and arrived at Monserrate (which is about two miles beyond Cintra) at seven. Darling F. did not seem fatigued ; but we were quite ready for dinner at 7.45. The servants here had only got the letter announcing our coming at three in the afternoon ; they displayed wonderful energy in getting all ready in so short a time.

The scenery is exquisite. It is a combination of majestic rocks, hills, forests, most beautiful flowers, and a view of the sea in the distance. The Cooks are as kind as it is possible to be. . . . This morning (Sunday) at eleven we had a service in the drawing-room. There is no English service or clergyman at Cintra, so that we are entirely shut out from all public means of grace. But God can supply the want when, in His Providence, we are deprived of them. We are eagerly looking out for letters from you. . . . You shall hear from us constantly, but I am afraid the letters will be five or six days in reaching you.

In another letter to my mother the following day, April 16, he writes an account of the house itself in which he spent the six weeks' holiday :—

Our rooms are in a tower which we ascend by stone steps. There is no fireplace in the whole house. The drawing-room felt cold yesterday till they warmed it with a charcoal brazier. I give you a sketch of the shape of my room. . . . The views from the windows are extremely pretty : from one window I look on the king's palace, which is on a lofty hill about two miles off ; from another, on the sea in the distance; and from the third, on to the garden. It would be hardly possible to give you any idea of the house or grounds. The house is somewhat in the style of the Alhambra, with long corridors and lofty domes. Every room abounds with curiosities or relics of antiquity. Mr. Cook seems to have ransacked the world to enrich the house with objects of interest. The whole length of the principal corridor has columns of coloured marble on each side. The gallery, at nearly the top of one of the domes, is panelled with marbles which were taken from the palace of the King of Delhi. In the grounds you find nearly every kind of tree which grows in tropical climates, and azaleas, rhododendrons, roses, geraniums, fuchsias, are in full flower and wild profusion. There are quantities of aloes, myrtles, arbutus trees, and palms. The cork tree seems the commonest. Then there are beautiful pine trees of every description. How you would enjoy the flowers!

To the same :—

There is a large library here, but the great majority of the books are in Spanish and Portuguese, and therefore of little use to any one in the house. I have, however, found some English books amongst them. I have read nearly the whole of Milton aloud to F. while she was sketching. I am reading Southey's "Letters on Spain and Portugal;" they are written in an amusing style. F. and I have also read some of Gibbon's "Lives of Eminent Women;" and I am reading over again "Chalmers on the Romans," which I admire and value more and more. . . .

Another letter gives a graphic account of a pleasant expedition :—

It is my turn to write to you to-day; and first I must tell you about our proceedings yesterday. . . . About half an hour after breakfast Mrs. Cook, F., Miss G., Mr. M., and I set off in an open carriage for Cascailles, a little sea-bathing town about nine miles off. The place is pronounced

"Cask-kies." The weather was magnificent, bright and genial without any oppressive heat. We arrived there about 12.30. The road is excellent, and in many parts of it there were hedges on both sides of aloes and geraniums, growing wild, and in full flower. As soon as we reached the town we went to the sea-shore, and chose a place amongst the rocks for our picnic luncheon. It is a wild, rocky shore; we were seated on rocks some thirty feet above the sea. They had all been covered in the early morning by the high tide. The Atlantic rolls in with grand effect; and as wave after wave broke against the rocks the spray rose up to a great height, and sometimes nearly reached where we were sitting. Having finished our picnic, F. and Miss G. chose a place for sketching, and were occupied for an hour and a half in taking a view of the rocks, the lighthouse, and sea. This is very near where we spent the night of April 12, tossing about and waiting for the morning, to cross the Bar and come up the Tagus to Lisbon. . . . We returned about six o'clock, and found our letters, for which we send you a thousand thanks. . . . To-day we have had another excursion, although a much shorter one. After breakfast we drove to Cintra, and took our station in front of a house on an eminence, to see a Roman Catholic procession. It appears that there is an image of the Virgin which is made to take a circuit of twenty parishes, and is brought into each of them in turn with grand demonstrations. It remains in the principal church a whole year, and then is conveyed to another parish for a similar period. This image was brought to Cintra about this time last year, and to-day it has been conveyed to another parish. The procession consisted of a number of carriages drawn by mules, some representatives of the Government on horseback, and a band of music in a curious chariot drawn by six mules. Then a small coach, gilt, with glass sides, not unlike a miniature of the Lord Mayor's coach, with a wax doll inside, dressed in blue silk, with a shawl over it, which represents the Virgin Mary. There was a cart in the procession full of sky-rockets.

Every now and then the procession made a halt, and one of the boys on horseback shouted at the top of his voice a notice of all the blessings which the Virgin bestows wherever she comes. Then they let off a number of the rockets ; the band plays, and the guns in Cintra fire. It is almost incredible that any persons of sense and intelligence can believe in, or practise such superstition.

My father took a great interest in the Missions to Roman Catholics which were directed by Mr. Pope, the British Chaplain at Lisbon. He visited several of the schools, talking to the teachers, and examining the children ; and both at the time and afterwards watched with deep sympathy the effort to introduce a purer form of faith, where the worst superstitions of Romanism were terribly rife.

During the time he was at Monserrate my father conducted services in the house every Sunday, which were attended by English residents at Cintra ; and on the way home he preached in Lisbon.

My father rapidly regained strength during his stay in Portugal, and in answer to a letter from my mother urging him to prolong his holiday, he wrote :—

It is meant, I know, very kindly when people say I ought not to return to work for months to come. But they little know what self-restraint it costs me to stay away at all now that, through God's mercy, I am quite well. . . .

He reached home by midsummer, 1877. During this year the Spring Confirmations were taken by Bishop Ryan, who had succeeded Dr. Burnett as Vicar of Bradford in 1870, and gave my father much invaluable help.

The Bishop was now strong and vigorous, and quite up to his work, and the summer and autumn of this year were fully occupied. No less than ten new churches were consecrated, and restorations were completed at Cawthorne, Pickhill, Pudsey, Netherthong, Rokeby, Silsden, and Meanwood.

Hitherto no allusion has been made to a part of his work which my father felt was a source of greater anxiety than satisfaction ; I mean the distribution of patronage. As in the case of other recently consti-tuted dioceses, the number of livings in the Bishop's gift was small, and of these some of the most im-portant were outside the diocese. He sought to exchange some of the latter with the Crown, so as to obtain the advowson of important parishes within his own jurisdiction. In applying to Lord Palmerston with reference to these exchanges, he wrote :—

> My only desire in seeking this exchange of patronage is to enable me to reward the deserving clergy of my own diocese, without sending them out of it ; and I have care-fully endeavoured to make such a proposal as would secure as nearly as possible an equivalent on either side of the exchange, reference being had to the total result.

He was successful in making a few of these exchanges, Wakefield being amongst the number which he secured ; but Lord John Russell refused the assent of the Crown to the exchange of Halifax for Stanhope, on the ground that the former carried with it so much patronage and influence as to be almost a bishopric in itself. Thus my father had twice in his lifetime to appoint to Stanhope, which is the only very valuable living in the patronage of the Bishop of Ripon. Once he had the pleasure of bestowing it upon the Rev. Charles Clayton, whose work as examining chaplain well deserved substantial recognition, and at his lamented death upon the Right Rev. Bishop Ryan.

No public patron can escape criticism, and my father was conscious sometimes of making mistakes which caused him the deepest regret; but the clergy generally recognised that he was scrupulously just, and the claim of hard work was never forgotten, even when it was accompanied by views differing from his own.

The following was written by a clergyman in the diocese after my father's death :—

I cannot refrain from writing you a few lines to express my deep sympathy with yourself and your family in the sudden calamity which has befallen you. It was only about a week ago that I had a most kind letter from your father, and I shall ever have great reason to remember his kindness to me. I believe I am the last man whom he presented to a living, and I need scarcely tell you how deeply I appreciated this mark of his favour; and all the more because he must have known me to be one not holding precisely his own views. I take this as an instance of his general fair dealing with his clergy. He will ever be remembered as a hard-working bishop who strove to do his duty; and no man can do more. Forgive me for writing thus freely, but I felt very anxious that you and your family should be assured of my true sympathy, and of my earnest prayers that you may be comforted from above in this your time of need.

There are many letters which show what anxious inquiry was made about the fitness of possible candidates for a post; and the Bishop's judgment was so much trusted by lay patrons in the diocese, that indirectly his influence in appointments was much greater than would appear from the number of livings actually in his gift.

In the exercise of his patronage my father showed a thoughtful consideration for the wants of his clergy, as well as for the people to whom they were sent.   The following incident is so remarkable as to be worth recording.   An exemplary clergyman, with a small living and a large family, wrote to the Bishop to say that he found himself obliged to resign his living and seek work abroad, where he would be better able to provide for his children.   His letter was crossed by one from the Bishop offering him an important living, where he could do work for which he was exceptionally qualified, and which would set him free from pecuniary anxiety.   It was curious that the Bishop had anticipated the letter, and that the clergyman in question could feel that his wants were supplied before he had himself made them known to his Bishop.

In the appointment of rural deans and hono- rary canons of the Cathedral, the Bishop cordially recognised all parties in the Church, and gave great satisfaction to High Churchmen in the diocese by the appointment as archdeacon of one who had lost his seat in Convocation by what was thought an unworthy display of party spirit.

It was a source of great sorrow to my father that so many livings in the diocese of Ripon were miserably poor, and he fostered a great variety of local schemes for the increase of endowment.   In this direction there has been, on the whole, a steady advance ; but there were often cases, known only to the Bishop, where the clergy were struggling against terrible poverty.

In some cases his delicate tact and generous sympathy suggested means of relieving their need, but these acts of charity were literally done by stealth.

It is only since my father's death that a clergyman told his family of an act of generosity which the Bishop had never mentioned to any one.

The clergyman in question had been suffering from much anxiety, owing to serious and prolonged illness in his family. He and his wife had made it a matter of earnest prayer that God would provide the means of obtaining the change so essential to the health of their children. They received a letter from the Bishop, saying that he had heard of their trouble, and begged them to accept a present of £50, only adding that they must let no one know whence it came.

On the same subject, I have before me a letter from another clergyman. He writes :—

My Lord,—I am greatly obliged to you for your very kind letter, and for your very handsome gift to the poor ——s. I hope, however, your Lordship will not think that in writing to you, I had any intention whatever, or any thought of asking you for such assistance as you have so very kindly given. I know too well how numerous are the calls made upon you, and I could not venture to add to them. In writing to your Lordship, I was thinking only of the diocesan societies. I sent your cheque to Mr. —— yesterday. They will indeed be all most grateful to you, and feel your kindness and sympathy very deeply, as I do.

With many grateful thanks,

I am, my Lord, etc.

These were acts of private benevolence; but after 1867 my father had also the happiness of administering a charity, founded by the liberality of Mrs. Danby Vernon Harcourt, of Swinton. She made over to the Bishop and archdeacons a capital sum, yielding about £200 per annum, for the relief of necessitous clergymen, their widows and orphan children, in the diocese of Ripon.

In late years my father took a prominent part in the work of the Church of England Temperance Society. He had always, of course, been the advocate of temperance, but he had not joined the movement heartily until the double platform introduced by Canon Ellison smoothed the way for those who were not prepared to insist on total abstinence for all.

My father tried at various times to become a total abstainer, but was called to order by his doctors.

Twice in the course of one autumn he spoke on the subject in Leeds: once addressing a large meeting, under the auspices of the local branch, at the Victoria Hall; and once at the meeting when the diocesan branch was inaugurated, on December 17, 1878. Whenever the Bishop threw himself into a movement of the kind, his office of president was no sinecure, for he brought to bear his wide experience in the formation of rules and constitutions which would generally be left to persons of greater leisure.

A notable instance of this was found in his relations with the Navvy Mission Society. A member of the committee wrote:—

One of the objects of usefulness in which Bishop Bickersteth took a warm and kindly interest was the Navvy

Mission Society; indeed, he was one of its earliest promoters. A chain of large waterworks were being constructed in his diocese, on the moors between Harrogate and Bolton Abbey, and a large number of navvies congregated there. Another large reservoir was at the same time being constructed for Halifax, at a spot called Blackamore Foot. At first, as usual, what was no man's business became no man's work ; but the Rev. C. S. Green, at Blackamore Foot, and the Rev. L. M. Evans, at Lindley Wood, one of the Leeds reservoirs, had their hearts stirred by seeing such masses of fine, hard-working men left spiritually uncared for ; and, without any knowledge of each other, or any assistance from others, began and carried on at their own cost, at the sacrifice in both cases of their health, a mission work which lasted for years amongst the navvies who had collected in the neighbourhood of their respective parishes.

When the men left, and sheets of water filled the valleys lately occupied by huts, shants, stables, engine-houses, schools, and temporary churches, their efforts ended as similar ones had done in former years at other places. But the Rev. L. M. Evans could not be satisfied that such should be the case. He had seen what by the blessing of God could be accomplished at one spot. He had seen the lives of many men entirely changed, and the general character of a large settlement completely altered ; but he knew that there were scores of similar public works where nothing at all was done, save providing a drinking shant for the navvies ; and he made inquiries at all the places he could hear of, which confirmed to the full the worst accounts he had gathered from the men. At seventy-two places only Sunday service was held ; at four, Sunday schools ; at three, night schools ; and at four, only day schools. Mr. Evans brought the matter forward by an appeal to the public to provide means whereby Navvy missionaries, chaplains, services, schools, reading-rooms, savings-banks, and other means for the spiritual and temporal benefit of an hitherto outcast and neglected class, might be provided. Bishop Bickersteth heartily approved of the proposal; and when it pleased God to crown Mr. Evans' appeal with success, and sufficient funds had been collected to warrant the formation of the new society, the Bishop became an annual subscriber, and chairman of the committee. This committee met at the Deanery, Ripon, where Dean Fremantle, Dr. Gott (then Vicar of Leeds), Canon Jackson, and the Rev. J. H. Goodier, who were its earliest helpers, still manage its now extensive operations. The earliest days of the Navvy Mission were its most trying ones. The opposition and dislike it encountered were enormous : every one looked on it either with suspicion, or as chimerical. Clergy, contractors, engineers, from some preconceived notion, or one motive or another, disliked it. The general Christian public regarded another society as a (probably useless) burden. The navvies themselves were the first to shake off their suspicions and to welcome its operations.

The difficulties of carrying on the work, even when it was fairly started, were very great. The right men for missionaries are most difficult to find ; and never, even now, is a Mission carried on without innumerable difficulties springing up, which have to be met and overcome constantly in the course of its existence. Each station is a cause of anxiety to the committee, and nothing but the conviction of the amount of good which has been done, and of the ample blessing God gives to their efforts, has enabled them to continue at their post. Much wisdom, as well as charity, much judgment, much organising power, were needed, especially at the first ; and all these qualities Bishop Bickersteth possessed in a pre-eminent degree. Until his health completely gave way, he was never absent from a committee meeting at Ripon. No difficulty arose, however complicated, but, with wonderful acumen, he at once saw what ought to be done, and pointed out quietly and firmly the line which must be taken. And his judgment always proved correct. It gave him much pleasure to see the Navvy Mission grow in favour and influence. He took the chair at one of the first drawing-room meetings held for it (at the Earl of Aberdeen's house) in London, and frequently afterwards, both at public meetings in London and in his own diocese. He did this, too, amidst the pressure of over-burdening labour, always so cheerfully and so willingly, it doubled the sense of the kindness. To one of the committee, who, on several occasions, was obliged to consult him between the times of the meetings on various difficult matters which needed settling then and there, and could not wait, he said, in reply to some expressions of regret at being so troublesome, " Come to me whenever you wish; I am always glad to help the Navvy Mission."

Even when he became too ill to take any longer his accustomed place at the committee, he would ask earnestly after the welfare of the society, and was delighted to freely license the Mission-rooms (where it was asked for) for the Celebration of the Holy Communion. He wrote himself one of the earliest numbers of the Quarterly Letters to navvies, and asked the editor to send him a copy each quarter ; and this was done up to the end of his life. Only those who had the honour of working under Bishop Bickersteth can tell how terribly he is missed. The Dean of Ripon and Canon Jackson still, thank God, are with us, but the Bishop's place, its first president, is vacant ; but, doubtless he knows, and rejoices in knowing, that the feeble effort he assisted to promote, has taken root in the hearts of the navvies all over England ; that clergy and contractors have become its kind friends and helpers ; that in the nine years which have passed since he presided at its formation, the whole of a great neglected class has been raised by its efforts ; and, best of all, that through its work many many souls have been called out of darkness into the glorious liberty of the sons of God.

CHAPTER XVI.

CLOSING YEARS. THE END.

Death of Craufurd Tait—Pan-Anglican Synod—Sermon before the Synod and the Church Congress at Sheffield—Visitation in 1879—Growing weakness—Hard work in 1880—Winters at Bournemouth—Arrangements for the appointment of a suffragan—Kind help of Bishops Ryan and Hellmuth—Weakness, but regular attention to letters, and fervent intercession for the diocese—Return from Bournemouth in March, 1884—Great hopes of recovery, and the sudden end on Easter Tuesday—The funeral, and extracts from letters.

THE year 1878 was an eventful one ; and, in addition to the growing pressure of diocesan work, there were family anxieties, culminating in a bereavement which was to my father hardly less trying than the loss of his son Ernest, in 1872. There had sprung up a warm friendship between my father and Archbishop Tait, which would have been cemented by a marriage to which both alike were looking forward with the most joyous hope.

The Archbishop himself has told in language so touching the story of the illness and death of Craufurd Tait, that there is no need for another to dwell on the bright hopes which were shattered by his untimely death.

My father had spent a fortnight at Addington in May, and was summoned to Stonehouse, the Archbishop's house in Thanet, just in time to see

Craufurd pass away. He remained some time in the house of mourning, for the Archbishop seemed to lean on the sympathy and friendship of one who so fully shared his grief.

That summer he paid as usual a visit to his friends, Mr. and Mrs. Henry Thornton of Battersea Rise, and was present during the great Pan-Anglican Synod which met at Lambeth in June. At the same time he sat to Mr. Watts for the portrait which was presented by the clergy and laity of the diocese, and now hangs in the hall at the Palace. The portrait displays much of the painter's genius, but it is too faithful a witness to the fact that this summer was a time of anxiety and overstrain, which left behind that look of weariness from which the Bishop never again was free.

Ten years before, my father had been doubtful about the wisdom of holding a Pan-Anglican Synod at all; but this year he threw himself heartily into the scheme, not only because he desired to support the Archbishop under the heavy strain of the public work which followed so closely on his private sorrow, but because he valued the opportunity of counsel with many of the Right Reverend Fathers, whom he had never met before.

He preached before the great body of the bishops and an enormous concourse of people at St. Paul's, on behalf of the S.P.G., in July. In the same year he preached the sermon at the Sheffield Church Congress, and took for his subject the work of the Holy Spirit. Of this sermon I quote the concluding paragraph :—

Men and brethren, may He not be grieved, may He not be resisted and provoked by ourselves? He is the

Spirit of Truth. Every wilful leaning to error, every departure from the plain teaching of His inspired Word, must be grieving to Him. He is the Spirit of Holiness. Every deviation from purity in life or doctrine must be offensive in His sight. He is the Spirit of Unity and Concord. Every breach of mutual charity, all needless strife and division, whatsoever is foreign to brotherly kindness amongst professing disciples of Christ, is a provocation to the Spirit. We have need to pray earnestly for a large outpouring of His gracious influence. Who can estimate the effect on the Church and on the world, were there to come in these last days such a Baptism of the Holy Ghost? The parched desert would become a fruitful field; the wilderness would blossom as the rose. The Church would rise with renewed energy to her lofty vocation, and go forth on the work of evangelisation fair as the moon, clear as the sun, and terrible as an army with banners. Such an outpouring of the Holy Ghost would bind all hearts together as one man, and kindle in the Church a zeal like that which inflamed Apostles of old. This would cause to cease unseemly contention about matters in themselves indifferent; this would make us follow the things which make for peace, and things wherewith one may edify another. The strength of the Church, the strength of each member of Christ's mystical Body, lies in the felt Presence of the Lord God the Spirit. May He vouchsafe His special Presence in the midst of our gatherings this week; may He grant us the spirit of charity and mutual forbearance; may He guide us into all truth; may He impart the wisdom which is from above, which is first pure, then peaceable, gentle, and easy to be entreated, full of mercy and good fruits, without partiality and without hypocrisy! Then shall this Congress be for the glory of God and the edification of His Church; and those who have gathered here from many distant homes, to be cheered and refreshed by mutual converse, will depart with firmer resolution than ever, by the Grace of God, to continue in the Faith and to persevere in well-doing, with this promise to sustain and to animate—"The Spirit of Truth will guide you into all truth, He will show you things to come."

The writer of a leading article in the *Guardian* of October 2, 1878, said—

Whilst these lines are being worked off the Church Congress of 1878 has assembled at Sheffield. . . . Dr. Bickersteth is now considerably the oldest and most experienced of the bishops of the Northern Province, and the selection of him as preacher on this occasion—one of no small ecclesiastical importance to that densely-peopled and ever-growing district—was natural and right. He has never swerved from those views with which his name is identified, and which, in their measure, led to his promotion under Lord Palmerston's Ministry in 1857 ; whilst yet he has, on many occasions, manifested a just and conciliatory spirit towards those who belonged to other parties in the Church, and has administered the ecclesiastical concerns of a strong-willed and very numerous population with diligence and success.

In the same month my father preached two sermons at Liverpool on behalf of the Seamen's Orphanage. At the second of these, in St. Andrew's Church, a noteworthy incident occurred. After an earnest appeal for the Charity there was found in the offertory a massive gold chain, in addition to a collection of £62 in money. A week later came the first Diocesan Conference, of which Canon Temple has given a sufficient account.

In 1879 the Bishop held his last Visitation, and all through that and the following year there was no abatement of energy in his work. He still accepted invitations to preach, one after another, in unselfish disregard of the fact that his strength was unequal

U

to the strain.   In the autumn of 1880, for instance, he had some public engagements every day for many weeks.   He said to his daughter with great satisfaction one morning, " Mr. Oxley has asked me to preach at the Harvest Festival at Grewelthorpe (a little village six miles from Ripon), and that fills up my last free day for the next month ! "

At the close of this month of incessant work came the two days of Diocesan Conference ; and a serious breakdown the following week proved how much too heavy the long-continued pressure had been.   It was about this time, October, 1880, that unmistakable signs appeared that his constitution was undermined, and the doctors said that his life of active usefulness could only be prolonged by much greater care and abstention from unnecessary engagements.   He was urged to discontinue the practice which he had so long maintained of early rising, and to avail himself as much as was practicable of the help of others.

In the following spring he spent six weeks at Bournemouth, where Mr. Spencer Stanhope kindly placed at his disposal his very comfortable house, among the pine woods on the East Cliff.

Bishop Ryan was at this time the incumbent of St. Peter's, and my father enjoyed opportunities of intercourse with him and many other old friends, amongst whom were Bishop Perry, Dean Close, Canon Carus, the Bishop of Cashel, and Lord Cairns.

The rest and change had a good effect, and he came back quite capable of moderate work.   But the work of the undivided diocese of Ripon can never be regarded as moderate, and as yet there seemed no hope of its subdivision. My father was, however, able to secure help in his episcopal work by presenting Bishop Ryan to the living of Middleham.

During the time of his residence at Bradford Bishop Ryan had rendered to my father invaluable assistance, as Archdeacon of Craven, and in many branches of diocesan work; but there he had been burdened with the charge of an immense parish, in which he maintained a large staff of curates, and greatly promoted church building in the town.

Middleham was a less exacting post, and thence Bishop Ryan was able to undertake a good deal of episcopal work during the years 1880–1883.

In these years my father had to learn a difficult lesson. It was hard for him to refuse work, and the nature of his illness left him at times much depressed. On January 1, 1882, there is written in his diary the following prayer :—

To Thy mercy and loving-kindness I humbly commend myself, O Heavenly Father, and all near and dear to me, for the coming year. Whatever lies before us, may we each be kept by Thy mighty power through Faith unto salvation ; may we be washed from sin through the precious Blood of Jesus ; may we be clothed with His righteousness, endued with Thy Holy Spirit ; and may we so fight the good fight of Faith, and lay hold on Eternal life, that we may at length attain to the bliss of the life Everlasting, through Jesus Christ our Lord. Amen.

Perhaps there was a foreboding of coming trouble, which found utterance in words of such touching resignation ; for two or three days later an attack of serious illness laid him aside.

His first public work this year was the ordination in March, to which he looked forward with special interest, as his youngest son was to be made a deacon. The Bishop took no part in the examination, except to give a very solemn address to the candidates on the Saturday afternoon; but he was able to go through the Ordination Service in the Palace Chapel without fatigue.

This ordination was to my father a time of deep thankfulness, as the fulfilment of what had long been his earnest prayer. His other sons were also settled in life, and he lived to see three of them married, and to christen three little grandchildren belonging to his second son, who was resident in Ripon. In days of weakness and depression he took the greatest delight in having these children around him.

During all this and the following year my father's health was treacherous and uncertain. At times he felt so well that he looked forward to getting back into regular work; and as he was only sixty-five at the time, there was nothing in his years to forbid the hope. The doctors all noticed his extraordinary recuperative power, and encouraged him to believe that his weakness would pass away under the influence of rest and careful nursing. Sir William Jenner and Sir Andrew Clark, no less than his usual medical attendants, strongly dissuaded him from resignation. However, in 1883, he felt that he must make further provision for the needs of the diocese.

The scheme for subdivision was not prospering at the time, partly because of the local jealousy of towns which competed for the honour of giving its name to the new See, and partly because the manufacturers of the West Riding were suffering from a prolonged period of unprecedented depression. My father felt the scheme would hardly take effect in his own lifetime, but he was determined to make other arrangements for the due oversight of the diocese.

From Bishop Ryan he received the most constant and ungrudging help ; but while he was himself laid aside my father did not care to impose upon one, however willing, so much of the burden of episcopal work. He therefore resolved to petition the Crown for the appointment of a suffragan, and his application was received with sympathetic kindness by Mr. Gladstone, who had himself gone for rest to Cannes.

Under the Act of Henry VIII. c. 14, is a list of places which were to give their titles to suffragan bishops as occasion required, and amongst them the nearest available was Hull. Hull is in the diocese of York, but the Archbishop kindly wrote as follows:—

Bishopthorpe, York, March 7, 1883.

My dear Bishop,—I most truly hope that the appointment of a suffragan in Bishop Hellmuth may be blest to the restoration of your health. The anomaly of his being Bishop of " Hull " is not greater than is the case of London being helped by " Bedford."

The great point is that you should be able to have complete rest, and should be able to study your health. By a long day's work, and a good one, you have gained the right (as men speak) to an evening's repose.

Ever with much regard,
Yours,
W. EBOR.

It is best to give an account of the appointment of Bishop Hellmuth in my father's own words, and so I quote the following letter :—

The Palace, Ripon, March 21, 1883.

My Rev. and Dear Brethren,—For many months past it has pleased God to afflict me with illness, which has disabled me from the discharge of my public duties as Bishop of this large diocese. So far as the business could be transacted in private or by correspondence, I trust that my absence has not been materially felt ; and through the kind assistance of my Right Rev. Brother, Bishop Ryan, the public duties of my office have been effectively and ably discharged, without interruption. To him, in common with yourselves, and all to whom he has ministered in spiritual things, I am under a debt of deep obligation. By the arrangements which I have made with him, he will still continue to render me the benefit of his valued assistance.

But the time has arrived when the diocese may reasonably expect that some more definite arrangement should be made for the performance of the duties of the Episcopate.

I have prayerfully and anxiously considered whether I ought not to resign. With a view to guide me to the right decision, I have sought the advice of many of my brethren the clergy, and of eminent medical authorities. All the opinions, however, which I have received, both from the clergy, and from Sir William Jenner and Dr. Andrew Clark, are strongly opposed to the idea of resignation, so long as a probability remains, which the latter tell me is still the case, that a period of rest may by God's blessing, be the means of enabling me to resume my accustomed work. Yielding to their earnest advice, I have petitioned the Crown to grant me a suffragan bishop. Her Majesty has most graciously acceded to my request, and arrangements are now in progress by which I trust that in a short time the Right Rev. Dr. Hellmuth, at present Bishop of Huron, will become suffragan for this diocese, under the title of Bishop of Hull. He is now in America, for the purpose of resigning his Canadian See, and expects to return in the course of the summer, to help me in the work of this diocese.

I sincerely commend him to your sympathy and prayers. To some of you he is already known, and I am persuaded. the more fully you become acquainted with him, the more you will learn to appreciate his many claims, of piety, talent, and zeal, to your confidence and affectionate regard. It is my earnest prayer, in which I ask you to unite with me, that these arrangements may, by God's blessing, tend to the spread of true religion, to the efficiency of His Church in this diocese, and that, if it be His Will, I may be once more permitted to resume the work in which I have found so much happiness for nearly thirty years past.

For all the unwearied kindness you have shown me during the many years I have laboured amongst you, for your zealous co-operation with me in every good work, and for your patient forbearance under the trial of protracted illness, I heartily thank you, and pray God to requite you. May He grant you the privilege of witnessing the success of all your endeavours to advance the welfare of the Church, of which you are ministers ; and may He finally bring us all to share in the blessedness of His Eternal Kingdom, for Jesus Christ's sake.

Believe me, my Reverend and Dear Brethren,
Yours most faithfully and sincerely,
R. RIPON.

To the Venerable the Archdeacons, the Rev. the Rural Deans, and the Clergy of the Diocese of Ripon.

It turned out eventually that the Act did not allow one who was already a bishop to take the title of suffragan ; but in other ways the arrangement held good, and my father had the happiness of feeling that he had secured for the diocese two efficient coadjutor bishops.

Bishop Hellmuth undertook the work of the southern part of the diocese, while Bishop Ryan acted chiefly for the Archdeaconry of Richmond.

My father received much encouragement by hearing from many different sources that Bishop Hellmuth, as well as Bishop Ryan, was most kindly received by clergy and laity alike; and the number of Confirmations, which continued to increase, showed that there was no lack of energy and life in the diocese.

And yet, to my father, personally, it was a sore trial to be laid aside. He loved his work, and he had left little leisure to form for himself secondary interests which would have relieved the monotony of an inactive life.

The venerable Canon Jackson, who had been for a long time one of his closest personal friends amongst the clergy, told the writer of a touching interview he had with the Bishop in 1883.

My father was, just then, considered too ill to receive visitors; but, hearing that Canon Jackson was in the house, he wished him to come to his study. In a few words that came from his very heart, my father spoke of the heavy trial it was that he could no longer preach Christ, and with some penitential expressions that greatly touched his guest, he asked him to kneel and pray. He was comforted by the suggestion that the effort which it cost him not to speak for Christ was proof of his own acceptance with God.

It was not the least part of my father's trial that for many months his strength was unequal to the full Sunday services in church. Sometimes he would go to the afternoon service in the cathedral, and he greatly enjoyed the solemn addresses which Mr. Aitken gave on week-day mornings during a Mission held at Holy Trinity Church in Ripon. Usually, however, he had to be content with the services in his own chapel, or with reading the morning and evening prayers with his wife and daughter quietly in his study.

. To be cut off from public worship was a keener trial to him than to others, for he had the most intense enjoyment in all public means of grace. During the last year, when he was quite unable to go to church, he used frequently to receive the Holy Communion from the hands of his youngest son, who was ordained priest in March, 1883.

The Bishop took the warmest interest in the work at All Saints', Bradford, his son's first curacy : he liked him to come home as often as possible, accompanied sometimes by one of his brother curates, or other clerical friends. On these occasions he would ask for a full account of their parish work, and shared in all the joys and trials of a young clergyman's experience.

Of the last year there is little to tell. His life was very quiet. He was able to attend to all business which could be transacted in his own home ; to answer letters, chiefly by his daughter's hand ; and, on any question submitted to him, his judgment was as clear as ever. Sometimes he was able to do more, and sometimes less ; and when fairly well, he greatly liked to have the clergy, one or two at a time, to stay for a night or so, if there was any point on which they desired his counsel and sympathy.

Perhaps outsiders foresaw the end more clearly than those who watched from day to day, but it was never clear to those who loved him most that they must give up all hope of his being restored to further active work.

There was, not unnaturally, a little impatience amongst some of the clergy at the prolonged absence of the Bishop from public work; but a few hasty letters in the local press only served to draw out the loyal sympathy, not only of the clergy as a whole, but of the laity of the diocese, and amongst them not least that of working men, who were pained that any should breathe a word against one they loved so well. Letters of kind inquiry and affectionate sympathy kept pouring in from public bodies and individuals alike.

The writer of a notice in the *Guardian*, signed " J. G." (a signature known to be that of the Dean of Worcester), in speaking of the last years said :—

To work for Christ was to live in Christ with him, and even to the end he could only lay down his service and his life together. Some blamed him for this, but he felt that he had wedded his diocese, his life and his love were hers, and divorce was wrong. . . . The Bishop was living to make intercession for his people; the manifold system of spiritual work continued its great toil with machinery no slower and with fruits no fewer. The whole statistics of the diocese unite in their witness to this true undercurrent of work. He still administered the diocese, though it was through the ministry of other hands. And even in his weakest days his own labours were not wanting—*e.g.*, hearing of a working man of Leeds, who had to emigrate a few days before his Confirmation, he bade his vicar send him straight to the Palace at Ripon, where he confirmed him privately in his own chapel, and entertained him as his guest. The writer heard from that man on his outward voyage, and at least one Australian took into the gold-fields a very true love of his Father in God in the home Church.

At last he rests ; and the peace of God, which he so often gave to others, has enfolded himself and his life-long toil.

My father spent the winter of 1883–4 at Bournemouth, and returned to Ripon in March. Almost the last words in his diary record the deep thankfulness with which once more he reached his home. He now seemed very much better, and when he saw Bishop Hellmuth on the 2nd of April, he made arrangements with the consent of his doctors to take his Trinity Ordination himself ; but, alas! there was not to be, as he hoped, a renewal of active work. The recuperative power was at last exhausted, and the voice which had stirred Yorkshire hearts so deeply was to be heard no more.

Holy Week and Easter passed, but the Bishop could not go to church. On the Monday he seemed unusually well. He answered his letters, arranged for the institution of some clergymen a few days later, drove out in the afternoon, and in the evening he read aloud to his family and conducted prayers for the household. He was looking forward to Easter Tuesday, as the day on which he would receive his Easter Communion from his son, fresh from the work of Holy Week in Bradford ; but his longing for union with the Risen Saviour was to be satisfied more fully than he foresaw. Early that morning, April 15th, he was seized with another sudden attack of illness, and never spoke again. All the

morning he lay unconscious, and, happily, free from
pain.   The son, who had come home cheered with a
better account, was only able to be with him for an
hour, and then breathe the Commendatory Prayer
as, at 1.30, the Bishop passed away.

The blow at last was terribly sudden and unexpected by his family and the public, but he himself
probably felt that the end would come as it did.

Certainly he was not unprepared.   For years he
had lived as all of us would like to live if we knew
that the passing day would be our last.   In his
constant recollection of the Presence of God, in his
ardent desire to depart and be with Christ, he was
only waiting till the call should come, "Well done,
good and faithful servant : enter thou into the joy of
Thy Lord."

Of a father's personal religious life, a son has no
right to speak ; but none who knew him could fail to
see that he lived, to use an expression often on his
lips, when speaking to others about spiritual things,
very near to God.

The orderly arrangement of books and papers,
the thoughtful care with which directions were left,
was like that of a traveller who was packing up for
a journey into a far country, and yet thought more
of those he left behind than of what might befall
himself.

This was the habit of a life, and my father used
often to thank God that he had lived long enough
to see his children settled, and to make due provision
for those whom he left behind.   And if it seemed
hard that he should pass away at sixty-seven, while
other men are strong beyond the threescore years

and ten, it was clear that he had done a long life's work. And the best rest when life's work is over, is not the calm decay of a long old age, but the rest of the blessed dead in the Paradise of God.

There, in the Presence of Jesus, with the spirits of just men made perfect, "till the morning breaks, and the shadows flee away," rests one, who, if less stained with sin than others, yet offered as his only plea, and claimed as his only righteousness, the spotless robe of Christ.

Those who lost most by his death, have cause to say most fervently, "We also bless Thy Holy Name for Thy servant departed this life in Thy faith and fear ; beseeching Thee to give us grace so to follow his good example, that with him we may be partakers of Thy heavenly Kingdom."

* * * * *

The words surrounding the grave are as follows :—

𝔖𝔞𝔠𝔯𝔢𝔡 𝔱𝔬 𝔱𝔥𝔢 𝔐𝔢𝔪𝔬𝔯𝔶 of

ROBERT BICKERSTETH, D.D.,

BISHOP OF RIPON.

BORN AUGUST 24, 1816.

CONSECRATED JANUARY 18, 1857.

ENTERED INTO REST ON EASTER TUESDAY, APRIL 15, 1884.

The texts upon the cross are :—

" Be thou faithful unto death, and I will give thee a Crown of Life."

"They that be wise shall shine as the brightness of the firmament; and they that turn many to righteousness as the stars for ever and ever."

BE THOU
FAITHFUL UNTO DEATH AND
I WILL GIVE THEE A CROWN
OF LIFE

GRAVE AT RIPON.

On Saturday, April 19, the Bishop was laid to rest beneath the shadow of the Minster Church. There is no need to speak of the heartfelt sympathy and profound regret with which the city of Ripon, and the diocese at large, followed to the grave their beloved Diocesan. Churchmen and Dissenters alike strove to show every mark of respect to his memory; and though, in accordance with his known desire, the arrangements for the last service were of studied simplicity, the multitude of mourners showed a spontaneous tribute of reverential love. Canon Pulleine wrote in his parish magazine a touching notice which supplies all that need be said, and is here reproduced :—

In the morning the Bishop's family and household received the Holy Communion in the Palace Chapel, at the hands of Bishop Ryan and Canons Badcock and Pulleine. The coffin had been brought into the chapel the evening before, and was covered with wreaths, crosses, and palm branches, which had been sent by private friends and, in some cases, by parishes and institutions with which he had been specially connected. Among the latter were offerings from Ripon Cathedral, Leeds and Bradford Parish Churches, All Saints' Bradford, and St. Mark's Low Moor, the first church consecrated by the Bishop after his own consecration.

As the sun shone softly in upon the quiet congregation of mourners, the peace of the dead was bestowed upon the living, and we felt that we were still worshipping with him whose spirit had passed into Paradise, and we realised our faith in the Communion of Saints, which has brought such infinite comfort to mourners in all ages.

A few hours later, at the Cathedral, a large multitude had gathered, and in the centre of the nave two hundred clergy formed a passage, along which was to be carried the body of their chief.

The service was simple, solemn, and stately as was meet, the subdued music comforting and inspiring. The "Dead March" was followed by the three opening sentences, which so beautifully represent the voice of the Saviour, the voice of the dead, and the voice of the mourner. The softly chanted psalms, the well-known hymns, "O God, our help in ages past," and "Lead, kindly Light," were all in sad harmony with our feelings. Then we went forth to the grave, in a quiet nook beneath the Cathedral wall, and laid him there at rest.

" Brother, thou art gone before us."

The sympathy of unnumbered friends was lavished on the widow and the children who had lost so much, and to quote all the treasured letters which have special interest for them would be an endless task ; but there are some which will interest a wider circle.

Bishop Fraser of Manchester, Bishop Jackson of London, and Bishop Woodford of Ely, are now resting with my father in the Paradise of God. Each of them has left behind a record of strenuous work and devoted service, and there lie before me the letters in which they speak of my father's death.

London House, St. James's Square, S.W., April 21, 1884.

My dear Mrs. Bickersteth,—Now the last sad parting is over I cannot refrain from telling you how truly I have sympathised with you and yours in your sudden and heavy sorrow. . . . I was much disappointed when I called a few weeks ago in Cromwell Road, and found that you had all already left London. I regret it still more now. May God in His mercy grant us a meeting hereafter in the Church beyond the grave. I have always regarded Bishop Bickersteth as a model of unsparing hard work—too unsparing, perhaps, for his physical powers ; but his heart was in his diocese, and he obeyed, without stint, his heart's impulse. He might have been spared to work longer if he had worked less strenuously.

To him the weakening of his strength must have been peculiarly trying ; and there is comfort in the belief that this sudden summons was the Master's call of the wearied labourer to his rest and reward. But the loss to you and yours must be great indeed. May God be near you all with His felt presence and comfort, is the prayer of

Yours truly,
J. LONDIN.

Bishop's Court, Manchester, April 16, 1884.

My dear Mrs. Bickersteth,—My dear wife and I both wish to offer you our respectful sympathy on the death of the Bishop, your husband. . . . He had a special claim upon my affection, because he was one of my Consecrators, and his was one of the hands placed on my head when I was sent forth to the same work which he so long and faithfully fulfilled. For himself, he has exchanged a life which, I fear, for some time has been a life of suffering, for one of which we are told " there shall be no more pain " there, and which will bring him nearer to the Master Whom he has served.

The respect in which he was ever held will be not the least of the many comforts that you and his family will feel as often as they dwell upon his memory. I can never forget his much-valued personal kindness towards myself.

I am, with my wife's kind remembrances also,

Yours very sincerely,
J. MANCHESTER.

Bishop Woodford, who had a special connection with the diocese, as a former Vicar of Leeds, would have preached at Ripon on the Sunday following

X

my father's death, had it been possible to postpone some diocesan engagements.

He wrote as follows :—

Ely House, 37, Dover Street, W., Sunday morning.

My dear Mr. Bickersteth, — I only received your telegram late last evening, on my return to London from a series of Confirmations in Huntingdonshire—too late to send an answer until to-day. . . . And now, may I say how deeply, how *very* deeply I mourned with you for your father ? I conceived a true affection for him whilst I was at Leeds, and never in my whole clerical life have I been so happy under the authority of any one, as I felt under his large-hearted and kindly rule. I shall always have a sincere reverence for him as a Bishop, and affectionately cherish his memory as a friend.

Will you give my best remembrances to your mother and the other members of your family ? . . .

Believe me,
Ever yours most truly,
J. R. ELY.

The following address to my mother was prepared by the archdeacons, and signed by every clergyman in the diocese :—

The Archdeacons, Rural Deans, and Clergy of the Archdeaconries of Craven and Richmond, desire to present to Mrs. Bickersteth and Family the expression of their sincere sympathy, in the heavy affliction with which it has pleased the Almighty to visit them. They earnestly pray that the abundance of Heavenly consolation may be extended to them in this their time of sorrow ; and trust that the remembrance of the late Bishop's Christian character and his many excellent qualities, may shed the balm of its happy and soothing influence over them.

To form any proper estimate of our late Bishop's work in the Diocese, we must carry our minds back for over a quarter of a century, when his Lordship commenced that system of Episcopal administration, which he for many years maintained with untiring zeal, so valuable to the Church at large, but most laborious and trying to himself. These continued efforts were fully recognised at the time, and ought never to be forgotten. We therefore wish to testify our deep sense of our late Bishop's worth, of the value of his work, and our estimation of him as a Christian chief Pastor, by presenting to his bereaved Widow and Family this assurance of our heartfelt. sympathy, and prayers for their comfort at the throne of Grace.

(Signed) ⸺

To Mrs. Bickersteth, the Palace, Ripon.

A well-known layman wrote as follows :—

. . . My warm regard for the good and able Bishop, now lost to this diocese, began many years ago. It was not long after his consecration that, at my father's house at Dewsbury, he joined me in more than one long country walk when stopping with us ; and by his gentle and elevated wisdom did much to purify and elevate the thoughts of one, like myself, just entering into life. And ever since that time, whenever we met, he so kindly remembered me, and entered into my thoughts and prospects so pleasantly and cordially.

It is hard for us all, as we grow older, to feel ourselves stripped of our leaders and wise elders, and pushed alone to the front. And if I feel this in the present instance, how terrible must be the blank in the dear home to your mother and sister, and how you must all feel the chief stay and centre of your lives has been removed. May the bright and noble example of him who has now gone before, comfort and support you all in this trial. . . .

The last letter is from one who should not be nameless, for the name of Canon Jackson is inseparably linked with Ripon diocesan history, since the days when he served, under Dr. Hook, as senior Curate of the Leeds Parish Church.

Leeds, May 1, 1884.

My dear Mrs. Bickersteth,—The sight of your writing has affected me more than anything since I stood by the grave, at the corner of the Minster.

Then it was difficult, and almost more than could be borne, to believe *he* was lying there ; he, so wonderfully the ideal of calm strength and innate vigour ; he, so fully the impersonation of directing and controlling authority, of a strength and ready wisdom on which all around him could so fully and confidently rely ; he, so indeed one, who, it seemed, ought not to die ! Yet, there he was ; and the wrench to one who had known him, and known his value from his first coming into the diocese, was great indeed.

But now to see your writing—as *his widow ;* you, who were so bound to him, and bound up with him ; whose life was one full sacrifice and offering for him—for his comfort, for his safety, for his success ! I laid down the letter, and memory brought back you and him standing in the drawing-room, one of the last times I was at the Palace ; he so pale and languid, you so worn and anxious—the intensity of feeling on both sides bringing one's self into sympathy with it. The exclamation rose to my lips, "How can she live without him !" And yet, my dear friend, you will live, and live as he would wish you to live. You will still live *with* him, and even for him—live to be again with him, and, until then, to serve all those interests which were alike dear to him and to you.

For myself, I only wonder that I should survive him— I so feeble for years back—he then so likely to live to pro- tracted age. . . . You will have peace, for you know where and how to obtain it ; and there will be quiet, calm even- tide, and softened beams of light, and the feeling of his dear presence, and of your most true and ever-enduring union with each other, in the fulness of His love, which we humbly, but confidently, believe our beloved Bishop now enjoys.

        With my Christian love,

          I am, my dear friend, yours truly,

                    ED. JACKSON.

INDEX

www.ingramcontent.com/pod-product-compliance
Lightning Source LLC
Chambersburg PA
CBHW020933030726
47496CB00005B/1171